The Cotswolds Christmas Café

The Cotswolds Christmas Café

Lizzie Lee

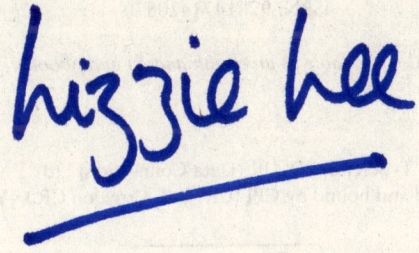

First published in the UK in 2025 by

An imprint of Bonnier Books UK
5th Floor, HYLO, 105 Bunhill Row,
London, EC1Y 8LZ

Copyright ©Lizzie Lee, 2025

All rights reserved.
No part of this publication may be reproduced, stored or transmitted in any form or by any means, electronic, mechanical, photocopying or otherwise, without the prior written permission of the publisher.

The right of Lizzie Lee to be identified as Author of this work has been asserted by them in accordance with the Copyright, Designs and Patents Act, 1988.

This is a work of fiction. Names, places, events and incidents are either the products of the author's imagination or used fictitiously. Any resemblance to actual persons, living or dead, or actual events is purely coincidental.

A CIP catalogue record for this book is available from the British Library.

ISBN: 9781471420870

Also available as an ebook and an audiobook

Typeset by IDSUK (Data Connection) Ltd
Printed and bound by CPI (UK) Ltd, Croydon CR0 4YY

The authorised representative in the EEA is Bonnier Books
UK (Ireland) Limited.
Registered office address: Block B, The Crescent Building,
Northwood, Santry, Dublin 9,
D09 C6X8, Ireland
compliance@bonnierbooks.ie
www.bonnierbooks.co.uk

For Zoë and Ed

Chapter One

Marnie pulled off the motorway at last, grimacing as she swallowed the dregs of the now-cold coffee she'd picked up at the services an hour earlier. She sighed. It wasn't as late as it felt, but it was already dark and they'd had an early start.

Mid-November wasn't an ideal time to be moving house, as Lauren had not hesitated to tell her. 'Why can't you at least wait till the holidays?' she'd asked. 'Now I'll have to start a new school right in the middle of term.'

Marnie had tried to sound calm. And cheerful. 'The house is sold, we have to move now, we don't have a choice.' She managed to stop herself adding, *your dad wouldn't wait to put it on the market, he wanted the money straight away*. Not that there was much of that, they weren't even close to paying the mortgage off, but at least it had given her a small safety net for their new start. But she refused to bad-mouth Lauren's father to her. However tempting it was. 'Anyway, it'll be fun in the country,' she said. 'We could get you that puppy you always wanted.'

Lauren had glowered from under her fringe. 'Mum, I'm not seven. When I wanted a puppy you wouldn't let me have one because we lived in a city and we were too busy. Now I want to live in a city and be busy, you drag me to the Village of the Nearly-Dead and offer me a pet I don't want any more.'

That was a bit harsh, but she chose not to respond. There were families in the village too, not just old people, or at least Marnie thought so. It was almost a decade since she'd been back. But she could see that this perhaps wasn't the company her thirteen-year-old daughter was looking for.

She drove on autopilot, wishing that it was still light and she could properly admire the rolling fields, hedges and trees they were passing. There was something calming about the sense of space, she had always found. She needed that right now. She hadn't planned to return to live in her mother's old cottage in the Cotswolds at the age of forty, leaving behind an ex-husband and bringing their daughter with her.

But that's what had happened, and Marnie had responded in the only way she knew; by organising every detail of their new life. They had somewhere to live, Lauren had a place at the local school and Marnie had bought the uniform and books she needed weeks ago. The van would be waiting with their furniture when they arrived, and Marnie had brought enough food to last several days. Everything was under control.

You're lucky, Marnie reminded herself. You have somewhere to go, for now, at least. You have friends waiting. And you have Lauren.

She glanced over to see Lauren's morose face lit up by the phone she stared into, and tried to ignore the doubt squirming in her stomach. The truth was, despite her best attempts to have everything under control, she had no idea what they were coming to. She hadn't lived in the village for years, and she had no regular job lined up, just some bits of freelance translating work that she hoped would be enough to tide them over for a few months. She would only be paying a family-rate rent to her mum for the cottage in return for sprucing it up a bit after years of apathetic tenants, but they still needed to live. And her mum had been typically vague about how long they were free to stay in the cottage; Marnie wouldn't put it past her to decide to sell it once all the work had been done.

The thought made her feel sick. She tried to focus on the calming silhouettes of trees against the night sky as they drove.

They finally reached the village. Even in the dark, Babblebrook was as pretty as a picture, the rows of cottages tucked back from the lane, windows lit up warmly behind floral curtains. Marnie slowed the car to a crawl, taking in the familiar sight. She released the breath she'd been holding – the doubts that had plagued her about starting again in a tiny village after the city life they'd been used to began to fade a little as she imagined their own cottage, filled with their furniture, a fire crackling in the grate and cosy lamps lighting the rooms. It would be a welcoming start to their new life.

Passing the little row of shops sitting in the glow of the street lamp – the post office, sweet shop and bakery – Marnie frowned. They were closed of course, so the dark windows didn't help, but the bakery owned by Auntie

Pat and Uncle Matt was looking particularly shabby, with peeling paint and a wonky letter or two on the sign above the door. It had always been their pride and joy. She couldn't think how it had become so neglected.

Pat and Matt weren't her real aunt and uncle, just the couple that lived in the cottage next door to Marnie, her brother David and their mum. The nearest thing to extended family their flighty mother had been willing to provide, and the greatest stability in her life growing up, at least for the periods when they were settled in Babblebrook. She felt a stab of guilt. She should have checked in more often. It had been years since she'd seen Pat and Matt, and though they'd kept in touch through phone calls and birthday cards, she had never arranged the visit she kept intending to make. Life had got in the way.

'Here we are,' she trilled, the note of enthusiasm in her voice ringing false even to herself. 'Home sweet home.'

Lauren sighed and slumped a little further down into her seat. For once, Marnie was too distracted to worry about her. Her frown deepened. Something was wrong.

She slowed to a stop outside the cottages, the ones on either side lit up and with smoke curling from the chimneys, their own squatting in the middle, dark and silent.

Where was the removals van?

*

Even the fire wasn't working. Pat and Matt had swept out the log burner and laid kindling and wood so that all Marnie had to do was set a match to it, but something must be blocking the chimney; the flames sulked and sputtered, sending smoke drifting through the gaps in the door and into the room. Lauren coughed and pulled a face.

'I'll get it fixed,' Marnie promised. 'We'll have it comfy in no time.'

Lauren said nothing, and even Marnie struggled to feel convinced. Glancing around at the room with its torn curtains and damp creeping from the corners, she had to blink away tears. This was not the snug country cottage she remembered. There wasn't a stick of furniture, other than the rusty old axe she'd spotted in the garden and had already warned Lauren to keep away from, and she had no idea what had happened to their own. She knew the cottage had been empty for a while, the last set of tenants leaving abruptly after some upset, according to her mum. But she hadn't expected it to be in this state.

This wasn't how it was supposed to go. She had organised it all, she'd had everything under control; by now they should be sitting on their own sofa drinking hot chocolate out of their favourite mugs. Marnie had planned everything, she had researched removals firms and booked in plenty of time. It should have been perfect. But her attempts to contact them when she'd finally managed to pick up a signal had been met with a recorded message saying they were closed. Even with her best efforts it had all gone wrong, and she hadn't given Lauren the happy start in their snug new cottage that she'd worked so hard to make happen. She'd let her down.

At least they'd had a warm welcome. Pat and Matt had been so happy to see them after all this time, bursting out of their front door as soon as they saw Marnie's car pull up. They'd listened as Marnie explained about the van and had taken Marnie and Lauren into their own cottage, warmed and fed them. They were greyer than Marnie remembered, and Pat used a walking stick. That was new. But they were as energetic as ever, Matt feeding them piles of sausages and creamy mash, Pat beetling round setting the table.

'Oh don't you worry about this old thing,' Pat had said, waving the stick that Marnie was eyeing. 'Temporary. Had a little accident.' She winked and glanced at Matt, grinning.

He rolled his eyes. 'I've told her she's too long in the tooth for that motorbike, but she won't listen.'

'You came off?' Marnie asked, tucking into her meal. Even Lauren seemed to have perked up now she was faced with a plate of delicious food.

Pat shook her head. 'Oh it was terrible, Marnie.'

'I bet it was! You should listen to—'

'I was so close to winning, and then it just slid out from under me.' Pat handed her the pepper.

'You're not still racing?'

Pat shrugged, her eyes glinting with mischief. 'Hardly ever. It was the classic bikes summer . . .'

'You try talking some sense into her,' Matt said, pecking Pat on the cheek. 'I've given up.'

Marnie didn't fancy her chances.

Pat and Matt were all for putting out a plea on the village WhatsApp for someone to house them, but Marnie had insisted they would manage on their own.

'Are you sure?' Pat had asked, grunting as they finished clearing the table and she settled herself onto the sofa. 'The Barretts have got at least one spare room, and they're very friendly.'

'You could have used ours, but it's full of bits of old motorbikes,' Matt said, looking pointedly at Pat and handing round a battered Roses tin full of homemade biscuits, the scent of butter and syrup rising from them. 'But there's them at the big house on the corner, Ivy Cottage, although it's not exactly . . .'

Pat snorted as she bit into a biscuit, crumbs flying from her mouth. 'Cottage, my rump, you could fit four of this place into it easily.' She brushed crumbs from her lap. 'Pardon my French.'

Marnie bit her cheek to stop herself laughing. They really hadn't changed at all. And she loved them for it. Still, she had no intention of spending the night with total strangers, however friendly or big their house, and from the look of abject horror on Lauren's face, she wasn't keen either.

'We'll be fine,' she said firmly, helping herself to another biscuit. 'These are lovely, by the way.'

Matt was smiling as though he'd been awarded a prize as he watched them all eating his biscuits. 'New recipe – just a little extra cinnamon makes all the difference.'

'Delicious,' Lauren said through a large mouthful, her words so distorted that she laughed suddenly, and half-chewed chunks flew out of her mouth.

Despite everything, Marnie's heart had lifted.

Now, in their own cottage, with her hair loose and wearing one of Pat's flannelette nighties as she sipped hot chocolate and squinted into the smoky fire, Lauren looked about eight. Marnie treasured the image, knowing better than to mention it. The last thing any teenager wanted was to look like a child.

She herself was in a borrowed pair of Matt's pyjamas, which she'd rolled up at the ankles but which sadly fitted perfectly around the waist. You'd think all this stress would at least have shaved a few pounds off. No such luck.

She drained her drink and began spreading blankets over the airbed Matt and Pat had lent them.

'Which side do you want?' she asked.

Lauren crawled in without answering, resting her head on the borrowed pillow and pulling the covers up to her chin. Her eyes were puffy and heavy. It had been a long day. She placed her hand under her cheek, just as she used to as a little girl, and once again Marnie felt that familiar twist of love.

'They're like people in a kid's book,' Lauren said sleepily.

'Who?'

'Pat and Matt. Even their names sound like book names. And they're all round with pink cheeks and those little round glasses. And they smell like warm bread.' Lauren closed her eyes.

Marnie laughed. She thought of Pat racing her motorbike too fast through the village, and Matt riding the wildest of horses without a shadow of fear. 'I'm not sure how they'd feel about that.'

'It's nice,' Lauren said through a yawn. 'They're nice.'

If Marnie hadn't been sitting already she would have fallen over. This was the highest praise anyone had earned from her daughter in months. It was, in fact, the most relaxed she'd seen her. She let herself dare to hope that this move might work out for them both after all.

Gently, she brushed Lauren's hair from her face and tucked the blanket tightly around her.

'Snug as a bug in a rug,' she whispered.

'You're weird,' Lauren murmured, without opening her eyes. 'Sound like you're ninety.'

*

Marnie jerked out of sleep, woken by a cacophony of banging and shouting. For a moment she couldn't remember where she was but, as she took in the dying fire and almost-deflated airbed, everything came flooding back.

The lump that was Lauren wriggled further under the blankets, covering her head. 'Make it go away,' she groaned.

Marnie staggered out of bed and attempted to do just that, yanking the front door open. The morning was cold and bright, and she was half-blinded by the sun, shading her eyes and blinking at the two figures on the step, who both talked at once.

'Morning, love, better late than never, eh?' the cheerful looking one said. 'Sorry about that, van broke down, would you credit it? Got the message did you?'

Marnie blinked and tried to ignore the other man, who was glowering and grumbling at her. 'Erm . . .'

The friendly one chuckled. 'Oh dear. Overslept?'

'Um . . .' Marnie tried to flatten her bed head and surreptitiously wipe off yesterday's mascara that was now no doubt smudged onto her face, finding herself somewhat distracted by the grumpy man's blue eyes and salt-and-pepper hair. Inexplicably annoyed with him, Marnie straightened up and addressed the other one.

'No,' she said. 'No message.'

He shrugged. 'We did text.'

'No signal,' she said.

The man's eyes widened as though she'd told him there was no running water. 'What, not even . . .?'

'It's called the *countryside*,' Grumpy said. 'Now when are you getting this moved? You're blocking me in and I need to go to work.'

Marnie was confused. She had assumed these were both delivery men, but now she realised that there was someone else unloading the van. Grumpy, she realised, had nothing to do with delivering her furniture. And he was less than happy about the disruption it was causing, by the sound of things.

The van driver sucked air through his teeth and shook his head. 'Be a while, mate, got to unload the lot and . . .'

Marnie crossed her arms over herself and hopped from foot to foot. She wished she was wearing something other than Matt's pyjamas. The air was cold, the floor was cold, and she did not look her best. Not that that mattered, she thought, glancing again at Grumpy.

'. . . go for a walk with Rosie, anyway,' he was saying. 'Then I need it moved. And do it quietly, loud noises make her nervous.'

The van driver doffed an invisible cap and rolled his eyes. 'Whatever you say, mate.'

Grumpy was already walking away, without so much as glancing at Marnie. She was sure she caught him muttering, 'I'm not your mate,' under his breath. And that, Marnie realised as she watched him march into the garden next door, was her introduction to their neighbour. Great.

Chapter Two

Lauren's bedroom was small, and Marnie's budget smaller, but she was determined to create a welcoming space for her daughter. Especially given that the cottage was generally so grotty. This was the one aspect of moving that Lauren had shown a modicum of enthusiasm for, as they'd pored over images on her phone and planned what to do.

Marnie had gently resisted Lauren's suggestion that the whole room should be painted black, thinking wistfully of the pink-and-white prettiness of the bedroom her daughter had left behind. Still, compromise was good, she thought as they finished up the paintwork; the one black wall in an otherwise white room.

Lauren stepped back and grinned. 'Looks great, doesn't it?'

Marnie carefully placed the roller back in the tray and nodded. 'It'll look even better once you've painted the stars on.'

'Yes, and with the fairy lights all along the top,' Lauren said. 'And the moon-shaped mirror here, maybe, above the bed. And some more lights on that.'

It wasn't what Marnie would have chosen. But it wasn't Marnie's room, and the smile on Lauren's face made her heart lift.

'Right,' she said. 'How about I buy you a Coke and some crisps in The Plough?'

Marnie stopped at the mirror on the way out to brush her dark curls and swipe a bit of mascara on; the long lashes that lined her brown eyes were the one feature she was proud of.

'What are you putting makeup on for?' Lauren scoffed. 'It's only Babblebrook.'

'No reason,' Marnie answered, thinking of the state she'd been in when their neighbour had knocked on the door. Not that she cared what that grump thought of her.

They passed him in his garden and, determined to have a fresh start with him, Marnie tried to catch his eye and smile. But when she saw what he was doing she came to a sudden halt, and Lauren bumped into her. He appeared to be stuffing a bar of soap into an old sock, frowning and muttering to himself.

They both stared, open mouthed, as he finally managed to wrestle the soap in and then reached up to tie the sock around one of the bare branches of the tree, the muscles of his forearms flexing as he stretched. Perhaps it was some strange pre-Christmas tradition. He caught them watching as he finished, scowling, and Marnie realised with a start that she was still staring at his toned arms and strong back. Blushing, she dragged her gaze away.

'What?' he snapped. 'You never seen a man protect his birds before?'

And with that, he turned and marched into the house.

'Almost as odd as you,' Lauren muttered as she followed Marnie out of the gate, absently swinging it behind her and ignoring it as it struck the latch without catching and stayed open.

Marnie murmured agreement. She was feeling a little flustered.

They crossed the road and walked across the green, Lauren stopping at the pond to throw her crusts from that morning's breakfast for the ducks.

'Hey, you big bully,' she grumbled at the drake that pushed all the hens out of the way to get to the food. Lauren threw the last few pieces so that they reached the other ducks first. 'Ha!' she said. 'See, I'm not letting you get away with that.'

She pointed to her eyes and then at the duck, grinning, and Marnie laughed, the image of her neighbour's powerful arms at last pushed from her mind. This was the daughter she knew and loved; playful, protective, fun. The carefree version of her from before all the arguments between her and Ian, and the eventual split. Catching a glimpse of her again made her heart soar. She breathed deep, savouring the scent of wet grass and pondweed; she remembered bringing David here to feed the ducks when he was little, smiling at the memory of her brother in shorts and wellies, crouching at the edge of the water.

Marnie felt her shoulders fall as she watched Lauren dash across the green to the Woods' field on the other side, where the beautiful soft-eyed cows gathered at the gate. She scratched one gently between its ears and laid her cheek on its face.

'Look, Mum,' she called. 'Come and see how cute they are.'

The cows blinked their big eyes and blew out straw-scented clouds of breath as they stood patiently, letting Lauren stroke their necks.

'They are lovely, aren't they,' Marnie said. 'Barbara, the farmer, let David feed a calf once when he was little, he loved it.'

Lauren gave the cows one last stroke and then tore herself away, turning to walk down the road past the primary school and rows of cottages. 'Maybe that's why he wanted to be a vet when he grew up.'

Marnie laughed. 'Perhaps it was.' It had never occurred to her, but now she thought about it, David had spent many happy hours at the Woods' farm whenever they were living in Babblebrook.

They walked past the little station at the end of the road, and turned the corner to The Plough, with its white walls, black-painted beams and light spilling invitingly through the latticed bay windows. The enticing smell of beer and fried food drifted out of the door as they walked in.

They sat next to the roaring fire, crunching through their snacks as Lauren looked around at the low beams and the horse brasses above the bar. She pulled a face and Marnie glanced apprehensively at Gillian the landlady. She had vague memories of her from childhood days in the village. She was a friendly woman but not one who suffered fools gladly. Or took kindly to criticism of her pride and joy, and Marnie knew that whatever verdict Lauren was about to make wasn't going to be flattering.

'Ugh,' Lauren said through a mouthful of crisps. 'This place is just perfect for the village.' It wasn't a compliment. 'Everything here is stuck in the olden-times. No wonder you like it so much.'

Gillian looked over at them and gave a tight smile. Marnie was sure she'd heard that. 'I like it,' she said, firmly.

Lauren frowned. 'What are you shouting it out like that for?'

'No reason,' Marnie said, glancing at Gillian. 'But – I thought you liked it here? There's Pat and Matt, and the cows . . .'

Lauren pulled a face. 'That's all for *kids*, though.' Her voice wobbled, and Marnie's stomach dropped. 'I miss my own friends. My own school, my own room. All the stuff we used to—' She stopped, blinking rapidly and slumping down in her chair, picking at a beer mat.

Marnie pushed her empty crisp packet away, feeling a little sick. She'd convinced herself that Lauren was happy with the move in the few days they'd been there. She'd thought that her fondness for Pat and Matt and her love of animals had helped her settle, but she saw now that she'd just blinded herself to the reality.

'Well,' she said, her voice falsely bright. 'Perhaps your friends could come for a visit? And you can FaceTime them as soon as—'

But Lauren was no longer listening. She was focused on the board on the wall that advertised The Plough's

Christmas Day meal; four courses plus a complimentary glass of mulled wine on arrival.

Marnie bit her lip as she watched Lauren. Every year she and her old school friends had gathered around Marnie's kitchen table to bake gifts for their teachers; one year rum truffles, another Santa hat cupcakes and last year, cornflake Christmas wreaths.

This year Lauren hadn't shown any of her usual enthusiasm for Christmas. She'd barely glanced at the decorations as Marnie had packed them up to bring with them, making none of her usual comments about the tackiness of the bright baubles that Marnie loved, or fussing as she always had in the past about wrapping the tasteful clear glass ones properly. Marnie had tried to tell herself it was all part of the normal process of growing up, but she feared there was more to it; Lauren must miss the prospect of a family Christmas together, and miss all the usual preparations with her friends too.

Marnie would've done anything to keep Lauren in her old school, but she had little choice about moving to Babblebrook. The cost of finding a place where they lived before was way beyond her means as a single parent. She'd thought village life would bring some comfort to Lauren, some healthy fresh air and calming countryside charm. Perhaps she'd been kidding herself.

*

Marnie sat at the kitchen table a few days later, trying to focus on the little bit of work that she had to do and not on the ancient food spatters that stubbornly remained on the walls, no matter how hard she scrubbed. The cottage still felt unwelcoming, marked by years of other people's dirt and neglect.

She'd had the chimney swept so at least they could light the log burner without the place filling with smoke now. Lauren seemed happy with her room, which was something, Marnie thought, picturing her daughter's miserable face as she'd left for school that morning.

She'd been there a week, but didn't seem any more settled. Every day when Lauren returned Marnie tried and failed to stop herself asking whether she'd made a friend or enjoyed her lessons. Lauren just shrugged and headed for her room. It was the one place that felt like home to her, and Marnie allowed herself a small amount of satisfaction that she'd achieved that, at least. But she was all too aware that her daughter was missing their old life, although whenever she tried to talk to her about it, Lauren changed the subject.

Making Lauren's room feel welcoming felt like Marnie's only success with the cottage. The rest of the place was damp and dejected, the paint faded, peeling and dirty, and she didn't know where to begin with getting on top of it. Missing her antique desk from the old house that had been too large to fit through the doors to the little cottage, she stared at the document she was supposed to be translating. There wasn't much of it, and no other work had come in that week. She couldn't afford to get someone in to decorate, and she couldn't do it alone, it was just too much work.

The night before, with one glass of wine too many inside her, she'd FaceTimed her friend Jo, a colleague from years back. She and Marnie had seen each other through marriage, babies, career changes and now divorce. Jo had known immediately that all wasn't well, though Marnie tried to put a brave face on everything. But she'd ended up admitting that she was worried about Lauren.

'She's just not herself,' she said. 'I know she's a teenager, but she was never this quiet, and she usually gets so excited for Christmas. Even in November.'

Jo had smiled reassuringly. 'Well she's dealing with a lot of change, she's bound to be wobbly, but you're a great mum and I'm sure you're looking after her.'

'I'm trying.' Marnie's voice shook. 'I know she must be missing Ian but she just won't talk about it at all and I don't know how to—'

'Give her time. It'll get easier,' Jo said calmly, and Marnie had nodded while trying not to cry. She had found herself longing for life as it had been, back when she'd trusted Ian and everything felt solid. When his wicked sense of humour would have her in fits of uncontrollable laughter, or when he joked around with Lauren, mimicking the actors on the TV programme she was watching until even her cool demeanour cracked and she would fall about laughing. When he would soothe all of Marnie's worries, taking her in his arms and assuring her that everything would be okay, no matter what, because they were in this together. Back when she and Jo used to go to the local bar and giggle over a bottle of wine, and she felt like she knew what life had in store for her, and it was good.

'It'll all work out, you'll see,' Jo continued. 'I think this could be good for you, Marnie. You know, a chance to start again, and maybe even think about yourself for once.'

Marnie had just taken a huge bite of homemade flapjack, and covered her mouth with hand. 'What do you mean?'

'Well, you know, you always put other people first. Lauren of course, and Ian, you were always so concerned about whether he was happy and supporting his music and all that but you never—'

Marnie's heartbeat quickened as she remembered Ian on stage, his hair flopping over his closed eyes as he sang with his band. They had never hit the big time, but Ian persevered nonetheless, and she admired that about him; his dreams of filling Wembley stadium had slipped away, and sometimes she had detected bitterness when he compared himself to more successful bands. But music was part of who he was, and gradually he'd come to accept that the smaller venues the band played was stardom enough. And he'd always been a star to her, no matter how small an audience he played to. She had never quite been able to believe that someone so charismatic had chosen her.

'Well, he is so talented.'

A flicker of derision flashed across Jo's face but it was gone before Marnie could question it. 'If you say so. But what I'm saying is, maybe it's your time now. Time to live for yourself, stop putting everyone else first for once.'

Marnie had no idea what that might involve; she had no passions or special talents like Ian, she thought as she took another bite of flapjack. Delicious, though she said so herself, her own recipe that included eggs for a nice, gooey centre and a sprinkling of salt that made them extra tasty. 'Putting yourself first is more my mum's style than mine,' she said. She didn't like being the centre of attention, happy to let others take the limelight. 'Right now I need to focus on Lauren.'

'No, but I mean . . . never mind,' Jo said. 'I'll come and visit. We'll open a bottle, it'll be like old times.'

She smiled and nodded and agreed that this was a good plan. But no plan was made, they were both so busy, and Marnie knew it wouldn't be happening any time soon.

She sighed and rose to fill the kettle. Her hands shook a little. She didn't even know exactly what she was doing the work on the house for, she'd totally failed to get any clear answer from her mum, and trying to arrange it all over FaceTime while she was travelling didn't help matters. Marnie had tried to pin her down on how long she was prepared to let them live there, but she'd rambled on about how she had no interest in living in Babblebrook herself but then also said she could rent the place out again at full price once Marnie had done it up. Any attempt to pin her down on a timeframe had been sidestepped.

The kettle boiled but Marnie didn't make the tea. She felt sick, thinking how uncertain the future was. She'd never felt so alone.

She was just debating calling it a day on her work day, when a sudden crash at the window had her shrieking, heart racing, and rushing outside to see what had happened.

A pigeon flapped around on the ground under the kitchen window, dazed but apparently otherwise unhurt, although it had left an unsightly smear on the glass.

'I don't know how you managed that,' Marnie said, as she watched it steady itself and fly away over the hedge. 'The windows aren't that clean, surely you could see the glass was there.'

The bird was gone, thankfully undamaged, and somehow the false fright had calmed Marnie's nerves a little. She stood looking over the hedge that her garden backed onto, watching the cows that stood there, nonchalantly chewing on the grass. Perhaps there were perks to country life after all; not everyone had such a view. David would be jealous; he and Greg had chosen a big house in Waterfield, near David's work, the train station and motorway, and overlooking the park. All perfectly comfortable and convenient, but not quite as close to nature as Babblebrook.

Marnie smiled, thinking of her brother who lived just a few miles away. And who she knew would do anything for one of her famous roast dinners.

She wasn't alone. She didn't need to keep struggling without support. And it occurred to her that perhaps there was something in what Jo had said; perhaps just this once she could ask someone to help her, instead of always being the one to help others. David was her little brother, and it had always been her role to take care of him, to make sure he was looked after when their mum was too busy to do it. But they were adults now. Perhaps if she needed help with the cottage, all she needed to do was ask.

*

They covered the carpets and furniture with sheets as they waited for everyone to arrive. Marnie had made a fresh batch of biscuits to keep the workers happy.

'I don't know why Gran can't do this herself,' Lauren grumbled as she half-heartedly pulled a sheet over the sofa.

'Well, that would be a bit tricky since she's in India. And anyway, she's letting us have this place at a bargain price, we need to earn our keep.'

Marnie smiled. Lauren didn't.

'Come on,' Marnie said as brightly as she could. 'Let's crack open the paint, we'll have this place spick and span in no time.'

Lauren rolled her eyes but as Marnie worked on the lid of the paint pot with a screwdriver she caught sight of the smile her daughter failed to hide.

'God, Mum,' she said, giggling. 'No one from this century talks like that.' She peered over Marnie's shoulder. 'And why did you choose such a boring colour? We could've done it red or blue or something.'

'Nothing wrong with a lovely bit of magnolia. You got to choose the colour for your own room, that's enough for now.'

'Half-choose,' Lauren said.

Someone knocked on the door and then walked straight in. 'Cavalry's arrived,' called a cheerful voice, and David and Greg appeared, weighed down with paintbrushes, rollers and masking tape. David shook his unruly dark curls, so similar to Marnie's, out of his eyes and grinned. He unbuttoned his muddy parka and unwound a beautiful hand-knitted striped scarf from his neck, dumping both on the back of a chair. Marnie thought of the rather straggled homemade scarves he'd sent her and Lauren for Christmas the year before and felt a little more hopeful for their gifts this year; his knitting skills had obviously improved. Greg, always so elegantly put together, shrugged out of his immaculate duffle coat, picked everything up, and hung them in the cupboard under the stairs.

Lauren squealed and ran to give them both a hug. David ruffled her hair, and Marnie marvelled that Lauren just grinned through such an indignity. Uncles could get away with much more than mothers, apparently.

'Wait, who's this tall thing and what happened to my little Laurie-pop?' David asked.

'You say that every time.'

'It's true though,' Greg said. 'You're so grown up!'

Lauren smiled.

He turned to Marnie. 'Where do you want us?'

David pecked him on the cheek, dumped the stuff he was carrying on the floor and made his way to the kitchen. 'Put the kettle on, shall I? Got any—Never mind, found them.'

Greg smiled and rolled his eyes as they all heard the pop of the lid coming off the biscuit tin. He kissed them both on the cheek. 'He's just made us a cooked breakfast. Fuel to get him through the day, he reckons.'

Marnie grinned. 'Well, he does love to cook.'

'Greg, come and see how boring the paint that Mum chose is, you've got taste, you tell her.'

Greg looked down at his stained t-shirt and torn jeans, so very different from his usual sophisticated look. 'Not very stylish today, in my painting clothes.' He laughed as Lauren waved a hand at the pots, an expression of disgust on her face. 'Well it's—Sometimes a plain background can bring out the . . .'

'It's boring. I told her we should've had red or something.'

'Well it's—yes, it's boring. Sorry, Marnie.' He shot her an apologetic look, but he was laughing.

Marnie handed him a roller. 'I don't care, you can be as rude as you like as long as you paint while you're doing it.'

They worked solidly until evening. Most of them did, at least, although David found plenty of reasons to put himself on tea duty, which seemed to mostly involve eating biscuits and going to talk to the cows over the hedge.

At one point in the afternoon, Marnie had followed him out, sneaking up behind him with a brush and then jumping out to splodge paint onto his nose. He yelled and pulled a screwed up tissue from his pocket, trying to scrub away the worst.

'Menace,' he said, laughing. 'What's got into you? You're supposed to be the sensible one.'

Marnie flushed. He was right, it wasn't like her. It was the kind of thing their mum would do. She couldn't help grinning, though, as she pictured his shocked expression. 'Can't be sensible all the time,' she said.

'You used to be,' he grumbled, turning back to the cows. 'But it's nice to see you a bit more relaxed, I suppose.'

She brandished the paintbrush in his face again and laughed as he lurched away. 'Come on, you lazy lump,' she said. 'We're all gasping for a cuppa.'

He grinned and carried on stroking the cows. 'All right, bossy.'

'Remember that time you fed the calf when you were a kid?'

He nodded. 'Babblebrook was always the best times back then, wasn't it?'

Marnie thought of those years of being dragged from town to town, trying to make friends at a new school only to leave again a few months later. Trying to make sure David was in the right uniform and did his homework while their mum went out with new-found friends or pored over an atlas dreaming of adventures. Babblebrook was the only place they returned to, and the only one that felt like home.

Their mum had inherited the cottage and had never shown much enthusiasm for it, bored by country life, but it had been a useful base between adventures. Marnie knew that her own need for order probably sprang from her chaotic childhood. She'd played the same part for Ian as she had when she was a child, drawn to his chaotic, charismatic energy that had felt so familiar. She was always the organiser, the steady one that could be relied on. The one in the background, never trying to share the limelight. Well, there was something to be said for being sensible; it might be boring, but she'd given Lauren a much more stable homelife than the one she'd had.

'I'm glad you're back, I hope you stick around for a while.' David finally turned away from the cows and threw an arm around her shoulder. 'Some more family time will be good. I know you've had a tough year, but Greg and I are here for you.'

It had been a tough year, the hardest Marnie had ever known, and his mention of it brought up all the memories that she'd been trying to bury—the furtive phone calls she'd caught Ian having, the suspiciously late nights he claimed he was rehearsing. The final confrontation, his furious denials and eventual tearful confession. The pain of realising that he really had betrayed her.

She shook herself, focusing instead on the calm chewing of the cows and David's solid presence as she swallowed the lump in her throat. One of the perks of moving back here was to have a chance to spend time with her little brother. It hadn't occurred to her that he might be the one looking after her.

'Come on,' he said. 'Quick, before that greedy daughter of yours eats all the biscuits.'

*

By the time the second coat was dry they were all yawning and splattered with blotches of magnolia. Marnie hugged David and Greg in the doorway.

'Thank you so much, honestly, we'd never have got this all done today without you.'

David zipped up his coat, picking at a flake of crusted dirt on the collar, and wrapped the scarf around his neck. 'That's what family are for.'

'I owe you. We'll arrange that dinner soon, I'll message—'

'Toodle-oo,' a voice called, interrupting her, and they all turned to see Pat and Matt walking down the path, both clutching bundles of cloth. 'The curtains are ready.'

David and Greg passed Pat and Matt in the doorway, laughing at their paint-splodged faces and kissing cheeks or clasping shoulders as they did so. And soon their second set of visitors/helpers that day were settled by the fire, admiring the freshly painted walls. Luckily Matt had brought a tin of his own biscuits around; Marnie's had mysteriously disappeared.

'Here,' Pat said, shaking out the bundle of cloth and holding it up. 'Look, see? All fine for you?'

She held out a pair of curtains she'd made for the living room window, a tartan pattern of deep red and beige.

'Oh they're perfect, thank you so much.' Marnie bent to kiss her and took the curtains, standing on a chair to hook them onto the rail. 'They look lovely, don't they?'

She turned and beamed at them all, and even Lauren looked impressed. 'At least the curtains have got some colour in,' she said.

Pat glanced around at the walls, pulling a face. 'Paint's a bit boring though, isn't it?'

Lauren nodded emphatically. Marnie tried not to roll her eyes, smiling.

'There's a little something extra here for you, too,' Matt said. He held out another set of curtains, pale with a delicate print of wild birds on.

Marnie looked from him to Pat, who was wearing an expression of glee. 'I don't—What's this?'

'Well, we wanted to—' Matt began, but Pat interrupted him.

'We knew you'd leave decorating your own room till last, and we wanted you to have something pretty for yourself so I made these. Be nice for you to be all settled in time for Christmas, not long now.' She looked worried, suddenly. 'Do you like them?'

Marnie thought of her room with its wooden bedframe and white cotton sheets. And the garish floral curtains that currently hung there.

'Oh, they're beautiful, and you know I love birds! Thank you so much. I don't deserve you.'

'Don't be silly,' Matt said.

'Well that's true.' Pat shrugged, grinning. 'But I'm sure you can make it up to us.'

'How about dinner one day?'

'Ooh, yes,' Pat said, clasping her hands. 'That'll do for a start, eh?' She winked at Lauren, and Lauren giggled.

Marnie looked around her living room, freshly painted and cosy with the new curtains, filled with the sound of her friends and her daughter chatting; in her old life she'd barely spoken to her neighbours and had been too far away from David to see him often. At last, this began to feel like it might be the right place to be.

Chapter Three

There was a lasagne, Lauren's favourite, ready to go into the oven. Cooking it had soothed Marnie's nerves, and she felt a little hopeful as she imagined Lauren tucking into it when she came home from school; perhaps she would have some story of making a new friend or feeling inspired in a lesson to tell now she'd been there for a few weeks. Marnie had wanted to make an apple crumble for pudding, but didn't have the ingredients, and so found herself standing in the sweet shop a few minutes before her daughter was due home, deciding what treats she might like. Anything to cheer her up a little.

She scanned the rows of glass jars filled with everything from aniseed balls to pear drops to chocolate jazzies. Her mouth began to water and she reminded herself that she was choosing for Lauren and not herself, glad that Anne Walker was busy serving another customer so she could take her time. She could still remember the excitement of Pat giving her and David fifty pence each to spend there when they were children, and the joy of the very serious decision of what to choose.

Marnie wiggled her fingers in front of the other customer's baby as he sat kicking in his buggy, and the woman turned to smile at her before continuing her conversation with Anne.

'Such a strange one,' Anne said, shaking her head as she weighed chocolate buttons into a pink striped paper bag. 'And I know what he's been through and everything but after all that at the Christmas—'

The customer sighed and took the bag from Anne as she began weighing out another. 'I do feel sorry for him though, but I wouldn't know how to begin a conversation with him to be honest. He was walking his dog down the street at school drop off this morning and he just stopped dead when he saw us all waiting outside the gates. I tried to catch his eye and smile but he just . . .'

Marnie tried to concentrate on whether Lauren would prefer a bag of Skittles or M&Ms, but she was finding herself a little distracted. She glanced at Anne just in time to see her purse her lips.

'No point even trying with that one. You know what a temper he's got.' She caught Marnie staring and smiled. 'Oh, and here's his neighbour, look—I bet you've not exactly had a warm welcome, have you?'

Marnie flushed, grabbing both the Skittles and M&Ms and trying to look as though she hadn't been eavesdropping. 'Oh I uh—Sorry, what?' She waved again at the baby as his mum handed him a chocolate button and smiled at Marnie on her way out.

Anne leaned over the counter, lowering her voice, although they were alone in the shop now. 'That neighbour of yours, Andrew.' She clicked her tongue and shook her head as she rang up Marnie's purchases. 'I'm not one to talk out of turn, but just to say, he's got a bit of a nasty streak. I mean, I know those young mums get all giggly around him, and I suppose you could say he's handsome, but I can't really see it myself . . .' At this point she drifted off, her eyes taking on a misty look, and Marnie once again found herself thinking of her neighbour reaching up to the tree in his garden and the way his shirt stretched across his taut back. Anne cleared her throat, and they both blinked. 'Anyway,' Anne said. 'I'd keep your distance if I were you, especially after what he did to the last ones.' She frowned and shook her head.

'The last ones . . .?'

'The tenants your mum had in the cottage before you. Why do you think it's been empty so long? They just upped and left without any notice, he threatened them, you see. Went round there, shouting the odds by all accounts and—Well, it wouldn't be the first time he's done that kind of thing, let's just say. Mark my words, dear. I'd keep away if I were you.'

'Oh.' Marnie thought of her neighbour, glowering at her with those blue eyes. It hadn't been a warm welcome, she must admit, but she hadn't seen anything that could be described as a nasty streak. Certainly nothing threatening. 'What did he do that's so . . . ?'

Just as Anne leaned her elbows on the counter and opened her mouth to fill Marnie in on all the gossip she was not one to talk about, the school bus swished past and Marnie, wanting to give Lauren her treats as soon as possible, tapped her card on the machine and left, calling a quick goodbye over her shoulder.

Glancing at the tidy garden next door as she walked up the path to her front door though, she couldn't imagine such terrible behaviour from a man who kept his flowerbeds so neat. But you never could tell about a person, she supposed.

*

That evening, as she sprinkled a few breadcrumbs in the front garden for the birds, shooing away a cheeky squirrel that scampered over and tried to steal them all, he walked past her hedge, obviously returning from walking his dog. Determined to keep an open mind, she smiled.

'Hello.'

He glanced at her, and though the frown didn't lift from his face, he nodded. Nothing too scary so far, she thought.

'Nice walk?'

He looked a little startled, but stopped and she thought for a moment that he was about to respond when a shockwave of sirens and screeching tyres came from the road that passed the village as an ambulance blasted past, shattering the peace of the quiet street. His dog began to tremble so violently that Marnie could see it from where she stood.

Andrew crouched down. 'Ah, girl,' he said softly, sighing and stroking her as she pawed the ground. 'You're okay. It's okay.' He ignored Marnie completely, totally focused on the dog. 'Even the backend of nowhere isn't quiet enough for you, is it? Any loud noise and you're a mess.'

Marnie looked at the little dog, trembling and cowering into Andrew's legs. 'Poor thing,' she said.

He didn't respond. Didn't acknowledge her presence at all. 'You were never like this when . . .' He scooped the dog up and she hid her face against his chest as he carried her up his path. 'Don't you worry,' he murmured into her fur. 'We'll get this sorted. We've got a plan, haven't we?'

He walked through the door without so much as glancing Marnie's way.

Chapter Four

Marnie pulled the oven door open, using a tea towel to bat away the cloud of roast-scented steam that billowed out. The chicken was crisping nicely, the potatoes were golden and beginning to turn crunchy round the edges, and the honey-roast carrots smelled delicious. She sighed with satisfaction, and set about making the gravy.

'How's the table looking?' she called to Lauren in the dining room.

'As good as I can get it.' There was something flat in Lauren's voice, a hollowness that sent Marnie's insides plummeting. She arrived in the kitchen, her face pale and pinched. 'The table's smaller than at home and I can't find the good cloth.'

Marnie stopped herself from reminding her that this was home, now. Instead she left the pan and went to squeeze her daughter's skinny shoulders.

'I'm sure it looks lovely. Thank you.'

Lauren shrugged. She looked miserable, and Marnie knew she was thinking about going to school the next day. It seemed that the children there were a close-knit group, keeping to the friendships they already had according to Lauren, and she missed her own friends. Marnie felt an answering stab of misery and guilt. She would do anything to protect her daughter from feeling this way, but she had no choice but to send her to this school.

The thud of the heavy metal door knocker brought a smile and a little brightness to Lauren's face. 'Auntie Pat and Uncle Matt!' she said, hurrying to let them in.

'Or Uncles David and Greg.'

It was actually all four of them huddled cheerfully on the doorstep, and Marnie immediately sent David and Greg to bring extra chairs from the kitchen so that they could all squeeze around the dining table Lauren had set.

Once again, she was grateful for the warm and stable presence Pat and Matt had brought into her life, her daughter now benefitting from it just as she and David had done as children. In the two weeks they'd been here, the only times she had seen Lauren properly smile was when they were with their neighbours. Now, as she heaved the chicken out of the oven, the babble of voices from the dining room reached her, and she could hear Lauren chiming in, sweetly chatting away.

There were oohs and aahs of appreciation as she piled the food and poured wine for the adults, lemonade for Lauren.

Pat clapped her hands together as she stared at the table heaving with food, her eyes bright and round. 'Oh my goodness, it looks like Christmas already!'

David gave a cheerful groan. 'Oh no, don't start—I know you're one of those that gets excited way too early, but at least let us reach December before the craziness sets in.'

Pat stuck out her tongue. 'Oh, you old Scrooge, you know you love it really.'

'Marnie, you really didn't need to do this,' Matt said, helping himself to butter-sautéed greens.

'I like cooking, it relaxes me.' She smiled at him, and he nodded. It was he that had taught her to cook, one long rainy summer when she was about eleven, and she, David and their mother were settled in the village for a few months. She and Matt had baked and fried and roasted, comfortable in their tasks. She'd loved cooking ever since. 'Just a small thank you,' she said. 'We'd have been lost without you these last couple of weeks. Wouldn't we, Lauren?'

Lauren nodded, mouth full of potato.

Matt chuckled. 'You'd certainly have been a bit stuck that first night, you'd have been sleeping in your clothes.'

'I don't think we'd have slept at all!'

'You know you could always have stayed with us,' David said, piling another couple of potatoes onto his teetering pile of food and rolling his eyes at Greg's plate of lean meat and greens.

'That removals firm was so useless,' Pat said, pouring more gravy. 'Gormless lot, leaving you stranded like that! But someone would have helped you out, everyone's very friendly in the village.'

'Or you could've stayed with us. You know, your family,' David said again, grinning.

'Waterfield's only a couple of miles away, but I know anything beyond the Babblebrook sign feels like the wild west to you lot,' Greg added, winking and earning a flick of Pat's napkin in his face.

Marnie reached across the table and squeezed each of their hands. 'I know, thank you. Believe me, we appreciate it.'

She suddenly found an image of her grumpy neighbour rising in her mind. She'd seen him a few times, driving his tattered truck and then coming back from walking his portly little dog the other day. Frowning, always. Anne Walker's warning was fresh in her memory.

'Not everyone's so friendly, though. What about that bloke next door, what's his problem? He was so rude when we first arrived, not much of a welcome, and he was behaving very oddly in his garden the other day, and he was rude then too, wasn't he, Lauren? I haven't seen him crack a smile yet, and Mrs Walker said he's got a mean streak.'

She looked around the table. Everyone seemed to be very focused on their food. 'I just feel sorry for his poor wife,' she continued, disregarding their lack of engagement and warming to her subject as she thought of her grumpy neighbour with the bright blue eyes. She took another sip of wine. 'I mean, imagine having to live with that! Poor woman. No wonder she's so nervous.' She shook her head.

Silence greeted her. Pat and Matt weren't even eating now, and she was sure she saw David and Greg glance at each other.

'What?' she asked.

Again, that look between them. 'Poor Andrew,' Matt began. 'He—You see . . .'

'His wife died,' Pat finished for him, her voice gentle. 'Few years back now. He's never got over it.'

Marnie flushed and placed her glass carefully down on the table. Lauren was looking at her with wide, accusing eyes. 'I—I didn't know.'

Matt shook his head. 'Devoted. Sad business.'

'But he—he said he was going for a walk with Rosie, I thought she must be . . .'

'The dog,' Pat said. 'Rosie's his dog, Marnie.'

Lauren shook her head. 'You idiot, Mum,' she said quietly.

'Well,' Marnie said, uncomfortable. 'I'm sorry about his wife of course, that's awful. Poor man.' She looked around at them all, greeted with nods and sympathetic looks, as they at last began eating again. 'And he does seem to love that dog.'

One of those that preferred animals to people, she thought. And he must have done something to make Anne speak about him like that. She felt sorry for him, of course. He was still annoying, though.

The evening passed easily after that, filled with good food and good company. And a little wine. After their guests had gone, Marnie having to physically wrestle them from the kitchen to stop them washing up, they sat by the wood burner. Lauren had tidied everything away and Marnie had washed the dishes.

'Thank you for your help tonight,' she said.

Lauren shrugged. 'I like them.' She stared into the flames, hunching over.

Marnie suppressed a sigh. Lauren had seemed almost her old self tonight, smiling and eating and answering Matt's questions about school in sentences of more than one syllable. She'd hoped it was a turning point, but she saw now it was just a brief respite.

'It will get better, you know,' she said softly, putting her arm around her daughter. 'You'll find some friends at your new school. And I know it's hard without Dad here, but things will—'

Lauren shrugged out of her embrace, licking the tears that began to trickle down her face as she stared into the fire. 'I don't want it to get better,' she said, her voice small and shaky. 'I just want to go back to how it was.'

Marnie swallowed her own tears. This was a worse heartbreak than anything Ian had put her through. 'I know, Squidge, and I wish I could do that for you. You're brilliant, and everyone will love you, I promise, and you can FaceTime Dad if you're . . .'

'God, Mum, don't call me that. I'm not a kid.' Lauren gave a loud, wet sniff and wiped her eyes.

All Marnie wanted to do was hug her daughter, hold her safe, as she had done when she was little. 'Sorry,' she said. 'I could—Do you want a hot chocolate?'

Lauren sighed. 'You can't cure everything with food, you know.' She stood up, barging past. 'I'm going to FaceTime Susie now.'

She ran up the stairs, feet banging on the wooden treads. 'And can you put some of that chilli in mine?' she called.

Marnie reached for the pan, smiling a little. She broke up a bar of good quality chilli chocolate, dropped it in and put the pan onto the lowest heat, watching it slowly melt, then added a little butter for the salt, and finally poured in cream. The result was a rich, sweet drink with a little heat from the chilli. Delicious.

Lauren was right, you couldn't cure everything with food. But it certainly helped.

Chapter Five

Sitting at the kitchen table with her laptop a few days later, Marnie stared blankly at the screen. She had work to do. Not much, just a short document to translate, and she was grateful to have it. Italian to English this time, though she was also fluent in French, Portuguese and Romanian.

In her old life she'd worked for a small publisher, translating academic texts. Not very exciting, and she had always dreamed of working as an interpreter, helping people in hospitals or police stations. But that involved a lot of travel and not much pay; one of them needed to have a regular job to pay the bills, and so she settled for the nine-to-five.

She needed to be around anyway, to help Ian organise gigs and negotiate the small fees the band were paid. She couldn't do that if she was travelling around the country for work. She liked supporting him, and she felt special, being involved this way; he'd smile at her, full of adoration, shaking his head and saying, 'What would I do without you?' And she would bask in his attention, his need for her, this star of a man who had chosen her. Every time he played other women gazed at him with longing, thronging around when he came off stage, and she always felt a thrill as he walked past them, kissing her passionately and throwing his arm around her as they made their way home.

The move had meant giving up her job, and so she was working freelance now. Another new challenge, involving drumming up business and doing the accounts, but she'd managed to find a few clients. Everyone was happy with her work, and she was sure business would improve.

This document would take her all of two hours once she got going, but she couldn't settle to it. Instead, she found her gaze straying out of the open door to where cows stood in the field, chewing on the hedge of her small back garden, and a sparrow hopped along the ground, searching for worms. She would buy a birdfeeder next time she was out; one of the reasons she loved country life was being able to spot these little creatures. She would always remember the time Matt showed her the red kites swooping over the fields when she was a little girl, instilling a love of birds in her that day that had never left her; she still had the book he'd given her that she had used to identify the birds she saw.

As a little girl Lauren had loved looking through that book with her, admiring the different colours of the birds and trying to say all their names. Marnie doubted she would show much interest now. She'd watched from behind a curtain that morning as Lauren had trailed out, the gate swinging open behind her as she slouched to the bus stop, standing apart from the other village children that waited there and staring at her phone. Marnie thought one of the girls who looked about Lauren's age had given her a shy smile, but Lauren was oblivious.

As she boarded the bus, Lauren had glanced over her shoulder at the house, and Marnie had ducked behind the curtain.

She remembered all too well the feeling of starting yet another school, of once again being the odd-one-out who knew no one. She and David had been through this time and again as children. It was lonely and exhausting, and Marnie had sworn she'd never put her own child through it. But here she was, watching her daughter trying to start all over again just as she was becoming a teenager. As if that wasn't hard enough in itself.

Marnie sighed and shoved her chair back from the table with a scrape. The air coming through the back door was crisp and chilly, but she left it open, hoping it would clear her head. Living in the grime of the city, she'd missed the freshness of the countryside, and she loved these cold, sunny days.

Absently, she reached for her mixing bowl, standing on tiptoes to reach it from the high shelf and cursing her shortness. She began to weigh out flour, sugar and butter. No margarine here, she couldn't resist the creamy taste of the real thing. She added chunks of dark chocolate and tiny slices of dried apricot, stirring until the mix was sticky and sweet, and she could dollop blobs of it onto a baking tray. She should be working, and trying to drum up more work, but the biscuits would only take a minute. They were Lauren's favourites, and it would be comforting for her when she came home from school.

Soon the kitchen was full of the smell of baking, and Marnie hummed as she washed up. Just as she'd run out of distraction activities and was reluctantly looking back at her laptop, something scuffled around her feet. Yelping, she jumped back, expecting to see a rat come in from the cold. Instead, she found a round, scruffy, waggy little dog. Rosie, the one from next door.

Marnie tried to feel irritated at the uninvited interruption, especially one that was related to Grumpy Andrew, but the dog blinked little brown eyes at her and wagged her tail so hard that her fat little bottom wriggled, and she couldn't resist. She crouched down, stroking the dog who immediately rolled over and laid out its round stomach for her to pat.

Marnie laughed. 'You are a soppy, creature aren't you? But you're lovely. Have you come to see me? Have you?'

'It's the smell,' a gruff voice said.

Marnie straightened up to find Grumpy Andrew in her doorway, a pair of headphones around his neck, frowning at her. 'I beg your pardon?' she asked. What smell? The kitchen might need a fresh coat of paint, but she'd cleaned it top to bottom when they moved in.

He bent down to pet the dog that was now standing at his feet, gazing at him adoringly. 'The baking,' he said. 'She likes the smell, that's why she came round.'

No wonder she was so fat. Still, she was sweet, and Marnie could see why he'd be tempted to give her one too many treats.

'Oh,' Marnie said. Then, remembering the biscuits were ready, 'Oh!' as she dashed to take them out of the oven. She reached them just before they burned.

'Well,' she said, pushing a chunk of hair out of her eyes. 'It doesn't matter. She's a sweet dog.'

He was staring at her, so intensely that she wiped her face. She must have got flour on her cheek when she was baking, she did that a lot. But her hand came away clean, and still she felt those eyes on her. What was his problem?

'I'm just about to take her for a walk,' he said, shifting his gaze to the floor and scowling.

'Oh.'

'It's a nice day.'

'Yes.' He was not the best conversationalist. There was an awkwardness to the way he spoke, a sharp edge, as though he resented the effort it took. She thought of Anne Walker's warning, and glanced towards her laptop meaningfully.

He didn't notice, but sighed and stared out of the window, the sunlight shining in his blue eyes and picking out silver flecks in the neat stubble that lined his strong jaw. There was something deeply melancholy in his expression, and Marnie wondered if he was thinking of his wife.

'I'll join you,' she said, the words out of her mouth before she'd thought them through. He turned to her with a startled expression. 'If you don't mind.' She smiled brightly and reached for her coat. 'I need to pop into the bakery anyway.'

He frowned. 'Oh, uh, I was going to listen to—But I suppose that would be . . .'

'Good.' She smiled determinedly as he stood staring at her. 'Let's go then.'

'Right, well. I suppose this is happening.' He clicked his fingers at the dog, who followed him enthusiastically, and trudged out of the door with a rather ungracious show of reluctance.

Marnie wondered whether she would regret this spur of the moment decision. But he was her neighbour, she couldn't change that, so she should make an attempt at friendliness, at least.

That's what she told herself, anyway, as she hurried after Andrew's slouching back.

*

Andrew turned out to be no easier company than she'd imagined, staring morosely over a hedge as he waited for his round little dog to do its business, and tutting as he shook out a bag to pick up the steaming results. Marnie took a step back, wondering if she wouldn't have been better to tackle that document after all.

Still, it was a beautiful day, the sky clear, sunlight falling onto glittering frost at their feet as they walked across the green. Over the hedge, mist lifted gently from the grass, drifting around the legs of the cows that stood there, slowly chewing and blinking big brown eyes. She clapped her mittened hands together and sighed, enjoying the pluming of her breath.

Lizzie Lee

'I love this time of year, don't you?' Marnie asked, trying to fill the silence that sat so awkwardly between them. She looked at him hopefully, but he just grunted in reply, staring at the ground as he trudged. 'Especially here in the country, it wasn't the same in the city, you could never really see the sky and you didn't see much in the way of frost really, with it all so built up, you know.' She took a breath. She was burbling nonsense at him, but the stoniness of his expression just seemed to make her want to talk more. 'And there's nowhere to walk, really, and I love walking, just getting the chance to take in the wildlife, I mean there is the park in the city but it's not the same . . . Well, I expect you know all about that, you've probably lived in cities too.'

She waited for him to confirm or deny this, but he simply shrugged, without even looking at her, and marched across the grass. As soon as they approached the pond the ducks raced towards them, quacking and flapping around Andrew. He grunted and let go of Rosie's lead to reach into his coat pocket. The little dog sat patiently at his feet. He threw handful after handful of what looked like pieces of perfectly fresh bread into the water, and the ducks squabbled as they raced after them. Marnie raised an eyebrow.

'What?' he asked, scowling a little as he retrieved the lead. 'They get hungry this time of year.'

Marnie merely nodded. She hadn't taken him for such a softie. A little bird bobbed along the edge of the pond, picking at the mud. She smiled as she turned to Andrew. 'Ah, look, *Motacilla cinerea*,' she said, and flushed as he frowned. 'I mean, a grey wagtail.'

He nodded, and his expression softened as he watched. 'Yeah, they nest by the brook sometimes.'

'Lovely.' They stood together for a moment, admiring the little creature.

Rosie let out a sudden, loud whine and flopped to lie on the ground, grunting. They both turned to her in surprise, laughing. Marnie caught Andrew's eye, and her stomach gave an unexpected flip at the sight of him like this, smile lighting up his face, frown momentarily disappeared.

'She's jealous she's not getting your attention for a minute!' Marnie said.

He bent down to stroke Rosie, who stood and nuzzled his hand. 'I'd be lost without her.'

Marnie opened her mouth to reply, a little taken aback by this unexpected openness, but Andrew set off again briskly, and she hurried to keep up. Buoyed by optimism after the brief moment of connection, she decided to make another attempt at conversation. 'Do you work from home, then?' she asked, as they walked back towards the village street.

'No.'

'Oh,' she said, confused. 'So you're . . .?'

'Day off.'

'I see.'

They walked on, down the road past rows of cottages, snuggled behind gardens and framed with roses or ivy. Smoke curled from chimneys, sending the scent of burning wood drifting through the air. Marnie didn't attempt more conversation. Despite the brief moment at the pond, Andrew had reverted to trudging with his head down, frowning at the ground; he was obviously the strong-and-silent type. Or, perhaps more accurately, the surly-and-silent type.

They rounded the corner to the row of shops and Marnie stopped to take in the sight. The post office and sweet shop were not much changed since her childhood, though freshly painted. The sweet shop window was adorned with bright bunting and a display of big swirly lollipops, baskets of glistening boiled sweets and shiny wrapped chocolates.

Her eyes strayed to the bakery. Every time she saw it, she was shocked by how dilapidated it had become, the paint on the door peeling and the 'k' of the 'Village Bakery' sign hanging at a dangerously haphazard angle. Pat and Matt would be in there now, behind those steamed windows, he busy baking in the back and she front of house, regaling customers with titbits of gossip.

'I spent so much of my childhood in there,' she said, to no one in particular.

Andrew's grunt of a reply sounded like it ended in a question mark, and that was all the encouragement Marnie needed to continue.

'Whenever we were living in the village, which wasn't that often but it was the most stable home of our childhood, every year or so we'd be here for a few months before we were dragged off to ... Anyway, I would always beg Lily, our mum, to let me spend evenings and weekends at the bakery. Not that she cared, just glad to get us out of her hair most of the time.'

Andrew glanced at her, his eyes filled with something that looked suspiciously like sympathy, and Marnie cleared her throat and smiled, embarrassed at the trace of bitterness that had crept into her story.

'Anyway. It was heaven, the *smell* of the bread baking and the doughnuts, and sometimes Matt would let me ice a biscuit or a bun and eat it, and everyone that came in would talk to me and ask about school or whatever. It was like a family, really.'

She stopped, embarrassed somehow that she'd let all of this pour out to a man she barely knew and didn't much like. He looked at her, giving a little nod, almost like he understood, while Rosie let out a loud sigh and flopped down at his feet.

Marnie waved a hand. 'Anyway. I'm boring you.'

He didn't disagree, and she felt absurdly affronted by his silence. Perhaps she'd been rambling on about herself too much though; she tried to think of something to ask him, but she knew so little about him and he wasn't exactly forthcoming when she'd tried to strike up conversations.

'Got anything nice planned for Christmas?' she asked, desperation making her voice strain to an unusually high pitch.

He stared at her as though she'd asked if she could roast his dog for Sunday dinner. 'It's not even December.'

Marnie gave up. There was no talking to this man. 'No. True. Never mind, then.'

'Well, time to head home, Rosie's had enough.'

Marnie glanced at the dog. She looked like she could do with a little more exercise, quite honestly, but Marnie held her tongue. 'Well, I'm going to go in and say hello, so . . .'

'Tell them I'll pop in later to—' He stopped, staring over her shoulder, as though frozen.

Marnie turned to see the woman she'd met in the sweet shop pushing her baby in his buggy. She smiled and waved, and the woman smiled back, nodding at her and then, a little hesitantly, at Andrew. She thought he would at least return the gesture, but instead he turned on his heel, stalking off in the opposite direction.

There was definitely something odd about that man.

Chapter Six

The soft ding of the bell as she walked into the shop was exactly as she remembered, but nothing else was quite the same. She noticed, as she did every time she came in, that the counter behind which the enticing rows of pastries, cakes and buns sat was a little shabby, the corners beginning to crumble, and there were a few cracks in the tiled floor.

The smell was just as good, though, and the food looked just as tempting. Marnie's mouth began to water as soon as she stepped in.

'Ooh,' Pat called, her face crumpling into a huge smile. 'Matt, come and see who it is.'

She struggled out of her chair and hobbled round from behind the counter, leaning on her stick and reaching out her free arm to hug Marnie.

'No need to get up,' Marnie said. 'This all looks delicious.'

Matt bustled through from the back, untying his apron and enveloping her in a hug. 'Ah, here she is! Our favourite customer.'

Their only customer, Marnie thought, glancing round the deserted shop.

'What would you like? Iced bun, as usual?'

He was already picking out a plump bun, thickly covered with glistening icing, and placing it into a paper bag for her. She hadn't eaten one for years, not since she was a girl, sitting in this very shop. He looked so pleased, like Father Christmas handing out a present to his favourite child.

'Thank you,' she said, taking the bag and immediately pulling out the bun and sinking her teeth in, savouring the sweet burst of icing and the soft swell of bread. Delicious. She opened her eyes to find both Pat and Matt smiling at her indulgently. As though she were still eleven, and not a forty-year-old single mother.

She cleared her throat, and began to speak while still chewing, covering her mouth with her hand. 'So, how's it all going here?'

A glance passed between them, but it was brief. Blink and you'd miss it.

'Fine,' Pat said firmly.

Matt looked down at his feet, kicking at an imaginary obstacle.

'Almost December,' Pat said. 'Soon we'll have people queueing up for Matt's mince pies and gingerbread biscuits and slices of Christmas cake.'

Her smile brooked no argument, so Marnie didn't venture one.

'My neighbour, that gru—that Andrew bloke said he'd pop in later.'

Pat nodded. 'Comes in most days, I don't know how one man can eat so much bread.'

Marnie glanced around at the empty shop. She didn't know why Andrew needed so much bread but she was glad someone was coming in regularly. Although one customer a day would hardly keep the bakery afloat. She remembered when people had been queueing out of the door for Matt's fresh bakes.

'He'll be out of luck today, though, there was a problem with the supplier and we've had no bread delivered this morning.' A worry-crease appeared on his brow, and Marnie felt an overwhelming urge to do whatever it took to make it go away.

'Well, I can rustle up some loaves. What do you need?'

Pat tutted and rolled her eyes. 'Now look what you've done, I'm sure Marnie's too busy to be bothering about bread. We'll be fine,' she said firmly.

'Actually I'm looking for reasons not to work,' Marnie said, grinning. 'And you know I love baking, it's really no trouble.' She glanced at her watch. 'I'll have a few loaves for you this afternoon, okay?'

Matt smiled, the worry-crease gone, and kissed her cheek. 'That would be a real help, thank you. Only if you have time though.'

Marnie smiled. 'Plenty of time.'

'Ooh, you are a little star,' Pat said, her face wreathed in smiles, despite her previous grumbling. 'So how's the cottage? Settling in now?'

'Oh yes,' Marnie said, thinking of Lauren's miserable expression as she left for the school bus that morning.

Matt cleared his throat. 'How, uh—Had any word from Ian?'

There was a hiss as Pat drew in breath, pursing her lips. She'd never hidden her disapproval of Marnie's choice of husband, and the awkwardness Marnie felt about this was one of the reasons she'd stayed away these last few years.

The mention of her ex's name sent a flurry of memories tumbling through Marnie's mind – the way his hair flopped over his eyes, the way he threw his head back when he laughed, the delight in his expression when he made her giggle uncontrollably. The voices he put on when he read Roald Dahl books aloud to her and Lauren, making them laugh until tears dripped down their cheeks. The look on his face when he was so obviously lying about where he'd been.

'Really, Matt,' Pat said, hobbling back to her chair and thumping down onto it. 'What did you have to bring that flibbertigibbet into it for?'

Matt shrugged, looking apologetically at Marnie. 'Well, you know, he is Lauren's dad and . . .'

'More's the pity.' Pat's head began to wobble with barely controlled fury.

'It's all right,' Marnie said, stroking Pat's arm to calm her as though she was an agitated dog. 'He's right, we can't just pretend Ian doesn't exist.' Much as part of her would like to. 'He's um—Well, he's planning on a bit of a career change, I think.'

Marnie held her breath, waiting for the inevitable explosion. Pat's head wobbled so hard Marnie feared it would fall off her shoulders. 'Well you could hardly call those bits of odd jobs he had a career in the first place, delivering pizzas or whatever when he wasn't too busy trying to be a pop star, but what hare-brained scheme is he up to now?'

Marnie glanced at Matt, who gave her a sympathetic look. She couldn't deny that Ian's track record with jobs was hardly impressive, but at least he'd always worked. He wasn't lazy and he would happily do any job to support her and Lauren, it just had to be something that fitted around his commitment to the band. He'd worked variously as a waiter, bartender, delivery driver, cleaner and lunchtime supervisor, among other things; Marnie had always admired his work ethic, truth be told, and Pat's criticism only made her want to defend Ian.

'He wants to train to be a yoga teacher. Abroad, I think.'

Pat snorted. 'What, an actual proper job? It'll never last. Abroad where?'

'Well . . . it's in Bali.' Marnie flinched in preparation for the outburst.

'Bali? Bali!' Pat turned to them both, her face as red as the cherries on the Bakewell tarts, with an expression of exasperated disbelief. She dinged the till open and began counting out the notes, slapping each one on the counter with unnecessary force. There weren't enough of them to keep her busy for long. 'Of all the stupid, selfish—Do you know, I'm not even surprised? That's the worst of it. Not even surprised.'

She shook her head, angry tears shimmering in her eyes. Matt walked over to her and gently rubbed her shoulder.

'Well, it's just in the planning stage right now, so perhaps he won't—' Marnie said.

She was so used now to biting her tongue about Ian in front of Lauren that she couldn't break the habit. But she'd had been equally as shocked when Ian announced his plans. Having found a younger, more exciting version of Marnie and ruined their marriage he had promptly dumped his new love interest and decided it was himself he needed to find after all. And apparently Bali was the place to do it.

'And what about your daughter?' Marnie had asked, in fury and disbelief. 'How can she expect to find you while you're busy finding yourself?' He had always been such a devoted father, doing the school run whenever he was around and making Lauren's packed lunches when she was small, leaving little notes with jokes in there. Marnie didn't understand how he could choose to be so far away from his daughter, even for a short time.

Ian had shoved his hands in his pockets, a pained expression in his eyes. 'I'll FaceTime. It won't be that long.'

Marnie thought that six months was actually quite long, especially for a thirteen-year-old.

He had looked up at her, desperate, dark hair falling into dark eyes. 'I just can't stay around here if we're not together.' His voice shook and he stopped for a moment, swallowing. 'I just wish—I know it's all my fault, but if you could bring yourself to forgive me, I'd stay in a heartbeat. Just say the word, and everything can be how it was before, I'll forget Bali right now.'

He had gazed at her with love and pain, hope and desperation. It was a look that had always melted her. She had shocked herself by holding firm. She couldn't forgive him for hurting her so badly; the deception, the betrayal.

She was broken from her reverie by Pat's ranting. 'It's too much, it really is. That poor girl! What a waste of space, I knew he was a fly in the ointment from the moment I clapped eyes on him, I said so at the time, didn't I say so?'

She glared round at Marnie and Matt. They nodded and murmured to calm her down, Marnie fighting the urge to leap to Ian's defence. Matt gingerly patted her shoulder. 'Don't upset yourself, love.'

Marnie wanted to stay, wanted to find something to say that might comfort Pat. But she had nothing to offer, having gone through the same raging and confusion herself and only come out the other side exhausted and unable to change the situation. And she had some baking to do.

She said her goodbyes and left. Matt smiled and nodded, but Pat was too busy laying out all of Ian's faults in great detail to respond. Marnie wasn't sure she even noticed.

She spent a happy few hours making the bread, getting her work done while she waited for it to prove, and soon the cottage was filled with the delicious smell of the baking dough. She took them back to the bakery, still warm and smelling so good that her mouth watered.

'Ah, perfect,' Matt said, taking them from her and tapping the bottom of one of the loaves, smiling and winking at her at the hollow sound it made. 'Beautifully baked.'

'Well, I learned from the expert,' Marnie said, giving him a wink.

'We'll have to put her on the payroll at this rate, what do you think Pat?'

Pat hurried over, taking the loaves and placing them behind the glass counter. 'Ooh lovely, just in time for the after-school crowd,' she said. 'Thank you, Marnie. But you know she's far too busy to keep helping us out!'

Marnie looked around the deserted shop, wondering if the 'after-school crowd' would ever appear. She thought about her equally empty inbox, and doubted whether she'd ever be too busy with work for anything. But she wasn't going to argue with Pat on either point. The school bus had just driven past, and Marnie didn't want Lauren to come back to an empty house, so she said her goodbyes and walked home, feeling good that she'd helped them out in some small way.

They arrived at the door together, Marnie flushed from hurrying, Lauren pale and quiet.

'Hi, darling. How was your day?' Marnie asked as she turned the key and let them in.

Lauren shrugged and dropped her bag and coat in a heap on the floor. Marnie bit her tongue. Priorities.

'Fancy a cuppa?' she asked brightly. 'I made biscuits, those ones you like with the chocolate and apricot.'

'Not in the mood,' Lauren said, but she followed Marnie into the kitchen, accepting the tea and absently taking a biscuit from the tray.

Marnie sat opposite her. 'Bad day?' she asked, sipping her own tea and reaching for a biscuit.

'It was okay.'

This was an improvement. Marnie had to stop herself from clapping. She nodded, and resisted the urge to press further. 'I saw that girl smiling at you at the bus stop, what's her name? She seems friendly.'

'Emma? Yeah. She's in my year.'

'Do you,' she almost said play, 'see her at breaks?'

She held her breath. This was the worst part of parenting, the part no one told you about, when you saw your child struggling and couldn't do a thing to help them. Lauren dunked her biscuit in her tea and shoved it in her mouth before it broke, chewing thoughtfully. She shrugged and said something that sounded like, 'Not really,' around the mouthful.

Marnie could see this was all she would get out of her daughter. She held herself back from asking more, or suggesting ways to approach the friendly looking Emma. Trying to force Lauren to be happy wouldn't work. Marnie clung onto the one positive as she chewed her biscuit – that Lauren had said her day was okay. Not exactly a ringing endorsement, but the most positive response from her about their new life so far.

Lauren jumped up from the table, jolting it and sending tea spilling from her cup as she ran to the window. 'What's that?'

'What?' Marnie joined her. 'It's not a rat, is it?' She knew about living in the country, and she had no problem with the wildlife found there. So long as it stayed outside and didn't invite itself into her home.

Lauren was shaking her head and running out of the door, returning a minute later cradling a fat, furry bundle. Rosie. Marnie sighed. She should have known.

'Oh that stupid dog,' she said, tickling her under the chin. 'She seems to think this is her second home.'

Lauren nuzzled her face into Rosie's fur. The little dog squirmed and wagged her tail so hard that her whole body swung from side to side. 'She's so cute,' Lauren said, her words muffled.

'She's so fat,' Marnie said, breaking off a piece of her biscuit and holding it out.

'Mum, no!' Lauren snatched Rosie away and gently placed her on the floor, where she happily snuffled her way around the room. 'It's bad for her.'

'Well it's bad for us too, but a little treat every now and then . . .'

Lauren was shaking her head vigorously. 'No, the chocolate, really bad for dogs. It'll make her sick.'

Marnie looked down at the happy little bundle of fur waddling round her kitchen and felt a pang of guilt. 'Oh.'

There was a knock on the door and it immediately swung open as Grumpy Andrew stepped in. 'Ah,' he said. 'I thought she'd be here.' Rosie ran over to him and pressed herself against his legs, as though they were now reunited after a great absence, and not in fact a gap of about two minutes. He bent down to ruffle her fur. 'Hello, girl.'

'Mum nearly fed her a biscuit with chocolate in,' Lauren said.

Andrew didn't look up. 'No worries, she's fine.'

'And apricots, are they bad for them too? You'd never believe her brother's a vet, I'll have to get Uncle David to give you some lessons.'

'What breed is she?' Marnie asked quickly, giving her daughter a please-shut-up-now glare. Not that she cared what this curmudgeon thought of her. But still.

'Thoroughbred mongrel,' he said, again without tearing his gaze away from the dog. 'Aren't you, girl?' He straightened up. 'No harm done, but no chocolate for her in future please.' He glanced at Lauren, who looked smug in response. 'She'll have a cuppa though.'

He took a bowl from the draining board and set it down on the floor, helped himself to the milk on the table and added it, then poured in tea from the pot. Rosie lapped it up, her little bottom wiggling as she wagged her tail.

'You don't mind, do you?' Andrew asked.

Marnie very much did mind. It was not hygienic for dogs to drink out of human bowls, and not polite to help yourself to someone's food without asking. He really was the most infuriating man, marching into her kitchen and helping himself to stuff as though he owned the place. She watched as Lauren sat next to Rosie, stroking her and patting her head as she drank, laughing as Rosie nuzzled her and dribbled tea down her school uniform.

'I'll get her a bowl of her own,' Marnie said.

Chapter Seven

December came, and it was as though it had brought some kind of Christmas fairy with it, sprinkling Babblebrook with twinkling lights and bright baubles. Tasteful, tinsel-free, white-lights-only Christmas had never arrived in the village, and Marnie was glad.

Lauren, she knew, would not approve. Long gone were the days when Marnie had been permitted to hang her daughter's homemade decorations on the tree, though she still kept them, of course. It didn't seem so long ago that they'd sat together at the table, Lauren's little tongue poking out as she concentrated on gluing glitter to every available surface of robin and star decorations.

The school bus swished past the window, and soon Lauren was tumbling through the door, shedding scarf, gloves, coat and bag and leaving them in a pile on the floor.

'I'm starving,' she said, rubbing her hands together and hopping up and down.

'Come and warm up by the fire,' Marnie said. 'I'll make you a hot chocolate.'

'Great, thanks Mum.' Lauren rose onto her toes to press her chilly face against Marnie's and kiss her cheek. 'And biscuits, loads of them.'

'Ah.' Marnie had been busy, a few pieces of work had arrived and she'd been rushing to meet deadlines, happy to have a little bit of money coming in just before Christmas. But there had been no shopping or baking done for a couple of days. 'Satsuma?' she asked.

The look on Lauren's face was answer enough.

'Tell you what, let's pop to the bakery and choose something nice.'

Still disgruntled, Lauren didn't speak as she piled her coat, scarf and gloves back on. Outside, a quick movement caught Marnie's eye; a squirrel on the birdfeeder, helping itself to her fat balls.

'Hey!' she shouted, waving her arms to shoo it away. 'That's not for you, on your bike, go on.' She clapped her hands and at last the cheeky creature scuttled away.

Lauren stood on the step, shaking her head. 'Squirrel on a bike, what are you on about,' she muttered, grinning and rolling her eyes. 'Embarrassing.'

'Soap in a sock.'

The voice came from the street, and Marnie spun around to see her grumpy neighbour getting out of his truck, presumably just back from work. His clothes were paint-spattered, and she wondered if he was a painter-decorator. He didn't seem the artistic type. She stared. What nonsense was this now? But he just nodded, as though what he'd said was perfectly normal, and continued up his path.

They gaped after him. 'All you old people are weird,' Lauren muttered, and walked ahead, the gate clanging and swinging back open as she walked through it.

Andrew turned on his doorstep, sighing loudly and glaring. 'Can you pair not do that with the bloody gate,' he said sharply.

Marnie felt hackles rise; she might get annoyed with Lauren at times, but no one – *no one* – else was permitted to criticise her daughter. Especially not this bad-tempered stranger. 'What's it to you? It's my bloody gate,' she snapped.

He strode over to her, leaning over the hedge, blue eyes sparking with fury. 'Rosie could get onto the road. Is that what you want?'

Her heart was racing as she glared at him, and she felt her cheeks flush. 'That's ridiculous. There's a hedge between the gardens.'

He leaned closer, so that she could see the flecks of grey in his eyes, and for a crazy moment she felt like he was going to kiss her. 'There are gaps,' he said. 'She can get through.'

'Well, I'd be surprised if she can, fat little thing,' Marnie said. She felt a stab of guilt at being mean about the sweet dog; it wasn't her fault her owner was so cantankerous.

Andrew was already walking back to his door. He threw his head back dramatically and groaned. 'Just close the bloody gate.'

Marnie walked off. 'Close your own bloody gate,' she shot back, realising her response was childish and made no sense. She was too incensed to care. Almost incensed enough to deliberately leave her gate open, but the adult in her won out and she closed it quietly, resenting her neighbour for every second it took.

The air was sharp and cold, the evening beginning to sink into a soft pink light that edged every hedgerow and field. She hurried after Lauren, who was waiting at the corner, and they walked quickly to the shops, stamping to keep warm.

'What took you so long?' Lauren grumbled.

'That man, he's just such a . . .' Words failed her. Or at least, words she could say in front of her daughter. 'Never mind.' She blew out a breath, letting all her frustration out. She wouldn't allow him to spoil precious time with her daughter, she thought, picturing again his face so close, those eyes blazing.

Pat and Matt had joined the rest of the village in entering the Christmas spirit as soon as December arrived. The bakery window glittered with twinkling lights and paper snowflakes that they'd no doubt made sitting in front of the fire one evening. Inside, the air was warm and filled with a delicious scent of gingerbread, chocolate and fruit cake. Marnie's mouth watered, and she felt her fury ebb away. This was definitely a good decision.

Pat's description of their festive bakes had not been an exaggeration; there were slices of Christmas cake with little sugar robins and snowmen sitting on smooth white icing, homemade mince pies topped with pastry stars and iced biscuits in the shape of Christmas trees, sugar canes and holly leaves, all sitting behind a counter draped with tinsel.

Their efforts didn't seem to have had the desired effect on custom, though. The shop was deserted and, though Pat smiled as she greeted them, her eyes looked worried.

This used to be a busy time, parents and children piling into the bakery on the way back from school, some driving to make a special trip. Today, Marnie and Lauren were the only customers. The sweetshop was heaving with rowdy children desperate for an after-school treat, but they all passed the bakery by. Marnie battled the urge to grab a few by the scruff and drag them in.

Despite the Christmas decorations the bakery looked a little shabby. If it was Marnie's she would paint it in pastel colours and add vintage wooden sideboards with pretty little cake stands to display the goods. Not Pat and Matt's style, perhaps. But she'd seen some cute wicker baskets on Etsy, they would look great with a few loaves and bakes in. She'd order some. Maybe some nice, bright bunting too, she thought, looking around at the fading paint on the walls.

'Everything looks delicious,' she said brightly.

Lauren was already bending over the counter. The biscuits were on a three-for-the-price-of-two offer and she picked out a star, snowman and Christmas tree, grabbing the bag from Pat and biting into the first one straight away.

She closed her eyes. 'Mmm, yum.'

Pat laughed, and handed Marnie the mince pie she'd picked out, which she ate with only a little more restraint than Lauren.

'On the house,' Pat said, just as Matt arrived from the back.

'No, I insist,' Marnie said. She doubted they could afford to be giving their goods away. 'Anyway, I'd better take some more. Our cupboards are bare, and I have a starving teenager to feed.'

She grinned and turned to Lauren, who was finishing up her second biscuit, oblivious. The bell dinged and Marnie saw the girl from the bus stop walk in.

There was a moment of awkwardness as the two girls eyed each shyly. Emma smiled, and then Lauren did too.

Marnie stood impotently, willing her daughter to walk over, or even just say hello to this sweet girl. Lauren glanced at her and she nodded encouragingly.

'Afternoon, Emma,' Pat said. 'Nice to see you.'

'Hi, Pat,' the girl replied. 'Dad's just coming, the Tesco order came without the bread so he said we'd get some here and I could choose a treat.'

Slowly, her expression both fearful and hopeful, Lauren stepped towards Emma, carrying the open bag containing her last biscuit. Just as she held it out, just as Emma glanced at the bag and then at Lauren, a man walked into the shop, smiling round at everyone and saying to Emma, 'Want your favourite?'

Marnie could have kicked him.

Emma immediately turned and followed him to the counter, though she did glance back and give Lauren a little smile as she did so.

Marnie watched as he bought a loaf of bread and a doughnut, chatting to Pat about the weather.

'Come on, Em,' he said. 'We need to get going. Quick, or I'll eat your doughnut.' He took it out of the bag, pretending to take a bite, and Emma squealed and ran after him, laughing.

They left the shop, Emma's giggles still ringing through the air as her dad playfully pretended to snatch the doughnut away from her, then finally handed it to her, throwing his arm around her shoulder and pulling her in for a brief, affectionate hug.

Marnie held her breath, watching Lauren watching this father and daughter together, an expression of pain pinching across her features.

There was a moment's silence in the bakery, as they all looked at Lauren. She turned to them, and Marnie knew immediately that this scrutiny in her moment of sadness would be too much for her. Lauren's face crumpled, and she ran from the shop.

'Oh,' Marnie said, dithering for a minute trying to grab all the biscuits and mince pies she'd bought.

'Go,' Matt said, waving his hand. 'Go after her, we'll bring these home and you can pick them up later.'

Marnie nodded her thanks and dashed out of the shop. Lauren had already disappeared. She hurried home, allowing herself to curse Ian and his selfishness out loud, even shaking her fists in her frustration, oblivious to the stares of passers-by.

The door was locked when she reached the cottage. Her fingers were clumsy with cold and it took a few attempts to get in.

Marnie knew immediately that Lauren wasn't there. But she ran through the rooms anyway, calling her name. There was no reply.

The house was empty.

Keep calm, Marnie told herself. It's Babblebrook, nothing bad can happen.

She checked the green and the cow field first, then walked up and down the village street for a while, peering into the gardens and warmly lit windows without attempting to hide her nosiness.

Marnie reached the end of the street, passing the church, the farm drive and the fields where sheep peered at her through a gate held together with bailer twine. She swore it hadn't been fixed since she'd last been here.

Rounding the corner, she tramped along Lowering Lane to the brook, its muddy banks hardened by frost. Even this time of year it was pretty, bubbling over rocks, reflecting the sunset. Her last hope had been that Lauren might have come here for a bit of peace, but the place was deserted.

Sighing, she turned away. Lauren was probably back at home now anyway, staring into her phone, oblivious to Marnie's fears. She hurried down the street. At any other time she would have stopped to admire the lights, twinkling through windows and lining eaves. Inside, she could see the shape of Christmas trees, and in gardens hedges were wrapped in lights, large baubles dangled from branches.

Marnie loved Christmas, and had always gone the extra mile to make it special for Lauren. Usually, walking through this festive wonderland would fill her with happiness. But today, all she cared about was finding her daughter.

Lauren wasn't at home. Marnie tried calling again. No answer. She checked her WhatsApp. Lauren had still not read her message, but a new one popped up from Pat just as she opened the app.

> Marnie,
> Andrew from next door to you has messaged us to say that Lauren is with him.
> Love, Pat cc

Relief flooded through Marnie, mingled with confusion and more than a little irritation. What the hell was her daughter doing with the grumpiest man in the village?

Marnie pocketed her phone and dragged on the boots she'd just kicked off. It pinged again.

> Sorry, that was supposed to be
> Xx

Another ping as she stepped out and hurried next door.

> Marnie,
> You really should get on the village WhatsApp group. It's very useful.
> Love, Pat xx

For heaven's sake. She shoved the gate open, making sure it was fully closed again, and marched up the path to Grumpy Andrew's, banging the heavy iron door knocker with more force than was entirely necessary.

'Is my daughter here?' she demanded, before the door was fully open.

'Yes,' he said, stepping back to let her in. 'She's just—'

'Why is she here?' All her worry about Lauren, not just this afternoon, but over the past months as the family broke up and then the two of them moved to Babblebrook, seemed to have erupted into a rage that verged on tears, and that was all directed at the man in front of her. It was unjustified, Marnie knew. But it was what she felt. And she was still angry about his rudeness earlier.

Andrew frowned and shrugged, leading her through a cosy living room. He still wore his wedding ring, she noticed as he pushed the door to the kitchen open. He must have loved his wife very much. She found herself regretting her sharpness.

Lauren was sitting on the floor cradling a blissful Rosie and patting the dog's round stomach.

'. . . bumped into each other,' Andrew was saying. 'Just as I was coming back from walking Rosie and she came in to pet her for a bit.' He began to sound irritated. 'I don't know, she's your kid, isn't she? You should know where she is, she looked cold and I was just—'

Marnie glared at him. How dare he question her parenting? He didn't know anything about her, or Lauren. She was about to tell him so, but Lauren looked up, smiling, and the relief at seeing her daughter happy silenced her.

All trace of Lauren's earlier distress was gone. Beside her sat a half-empty pack of custard creams and a mug half-full of tea 'Look, Mum,' she said, holding one of Rosie's paws up to her cheek. 'Look how little her paws are.'

Rosie gave a long-suffering sigh, but made no other objection.

'Well,' Andrew said. 'She's fine, see? You want a cuppa or something?' He was looking at her so intently that she felt self-conscious; what was wrong with him, staring like that?

'No.' Marnie could not keep the bite of irritation from her voice. If this was his attempt at an apology she was unimpressed.

'Suit yourself,' he muttered. He was still staring, his gaze focused on her mouth. She wiped it surreptitiously; probably covered in mince pie crumbs. Annoying, that he should catch her in such a state.

Somewhere, Marnie was aware that she was behaving badly, and somehow it only made her more cross. 'We have to go. Lauren, leave that poor dog alone and pick up your cup.'

Looking hurt, Lauren gave Rosie one last cuddle and placed her gently on the floor. 'Thank you,' she said quietly to Andrew, putting her cup and the biscuit packet on the table.

'Come back if you want,' he said a little gruffly. 'She's taken a shine to you.'

Lauren gave a small smile and nodded as Marnie propelled her back through the living room and outside. 'Make sure the gate's closed,' she called to Lauren as she trailed sulkily behind, satisfied to hear the click of it shutting.

'Sorry I was cross,' Marnie said as they took off their shoes.

'You were rude.'

'I was worried. Text me next time.'

Lauren nodded, and made towards the stairs. Marnie couldn't bear for her to disappear just yet, not with this hanging between them.

'Wait,' she said. Lauren paused, her expression sulky. 'I—Love, I'm sorry it's so hard for you here.'

She waited, heart beating a little faster, unsure if Lauren would react with tears or anger. The last thing she wanted was to make her daughter feel either. But she needed to let her know that she saw how upset she was, that was sorry for the hurt she felt.

Lauren ran to her, throwing her arms around her and burrowing into her like she used to as a small child. Marnie held her tight, as though this would protect her from every pain the world might hold. She felt her jumper dampen with her daughter's tears.

'I know the change is so hard,' she said, into the top of Lauren's head. 'And I know you miss your dad so—'

'I don't want to talk about Dad,' Lauren snapped, pulling away abruptly and thudding up the stairs to her room. Marnie tipped her head back, trying to stop her own tears from falling. It broke her heart to see Lauren suffer like this, to know that she missed Ian so much. And if Lauren wouldn't talk about it, Marnie didn't know how to comfort her.

Chapter Eight

That night, Marnie made the Christmas cake. She was late this year, but there was still time. She worked out all her frustrations beating the butter and sugar into a smooth, creamy mix, breathing in the scent of the dried fruit as she did so.

Her mind and body were completely occupied as she stirred the ingredients, feeling calmer with every stage until at last she poured the rich, spicy, mixture into the pan and put it in the oven. Sipping the leftover brandy as she tidied the kitchen, she found herself humming 'Good King Wenceslas'. She would let the cake sit for a couple of weeks now, lovingly feeding it brandy every now and then to keep it moist. Just as Matt had shown her when she was a girl.

Baking brought order to her life, she thought, as she wiped down the clear kitchen worktops. The ingredients would behave the same every time, transforming into something rewarding and delicious, so long as you followed the instructions. It was comforting. It was reliable. It calmed her every time. No matter how annoying her ex-husband was. Or her neighbour. There was something about that man that just irritated her; he annoyed her even when he was just giving tea and biscuits to her daughter. Never mind that nonsense earlier – it wasn't even his gate, for heaven's sake, what was he getting so het up about? And why did he stare so much, she thought, picturing again the intensity of those blue eyes. It was just rude. He really was the most annoying man.

There was a creak on the stairs, and Marnie looked up to find Lauren peering round the kitchen door. She wore navy fleece pyjamas with silver stars on and her face was pale, a little blotched around the eyes.

Marnie smiled. 'Hi, darling. Can I get you anything?'

Lauren pulled up a chair and sat at the kitchen table. She eyed Marnie's glass of brandy. 'I'll have what you're having.'

Marnie gave a sharp bark of a laugh. 'You will not! I was thinking more along the lines of milk and a biscuit.'

Lauren smiled. 'Spoilsport. But okay.'

Marnie brought two glasses and the bottle of milk while Lauren grabbed the biscuit tin, and they were soon happily dipping and crunching.

'Sorry I was grumpy. I am glad you had a nice time petting the dog.'

'Sorry I didn't tell you where I was.'

Marnie took a breath. 'I know things are—'

'Rosie's so cute isn't she?'

Marnie blinked. 'What? Uh, yes, she's quite a sweet little—'

'Jane got her, you know.' Lauren reached for another biscuit, broke it in half and jiggled it around in the milk until it was sufficiently soggy, then shoved it into her mouth.

'Jane?'

Lauren nodded, speaking around a mouthful. 'Yeah, she didn't even tell him she was getting a dog, just came home with this puppy and all the stuff, and he said he was all grumpy about it and he was like, a dog's the last thing we need, but she just laughed at him and then the next thing you know he's daft in love with Rosie and he was the one that got up in the night to take her for a pee and that kind of thing.'

Marnie watched as her daughter nonchalantly leaned back in her chair, twisting her hair and easing a band off her wrist to tie it into an impromptu bun. How had she managed to get the most morose man they'd ever met to talk about, presumably, his late wife? 'So he was telling you all about her?'

Lauren shrugged. 'The dog, yeah. He said that now he thinks maybe she knew.'

'Rosie?'

Lauren looked at her as though she was an idiot. 'Jane.' She refilled her glass. 'He thinks she maybe knew and she didn't want him to be alone. I mean, not knew exactly, but had a feeling. That he'd need someone else. You know?'

Marnie did not know. In fact, she felt as though she knew nothing, compared to this compassionate girl who had apparently managed to get Andrew to open up to her. Marnie thought back to her own painful attempts at conversation with him; perhaps her daughter could teach her a thing or two.

'So you had a good talk then?'

Lauren shrugged. 'Yeah. He's nice really, I don't know why you're so down on him.' She drained her glass, wiped her mouth and belched. 'Well. I'm off to bed.'

She dropped a kiss on the top of Marnie's head and sauntered to the stairs, yawning. And Marnie was left with the empty glasses and almost empty biscuit tin, wondering what on earth had just happened.

She tried to picture Andrew chatting so easily to her daughter about his late wife. Could this be the same man who'd lost his temper over nothing that morning? The man who, according to village gossip, had a vicious temper. She just couldn't imagine it. But he had, apparently, been kind to Lauren. She didn't know which version of him to believe in, now. She remembered, just for a moment, how he'd smiled when they'd been at the duck pond, remembered how her stomach had melted.

She abandoned the milk and went back to her brandy.

*

Lauren seemed a little brighter the next morning, eating a pile of toast and guzzling a couple of mugs of tea before she left for school. She wasn't exactly smiling as she headed off towards the bus stop, but she looked less miserable. And, as Marnie watched from behind the curtain, she was sure that Emma smiled at Lauren and gave her a little wave.

This was progress, Marnie decided. Painfully slow, perhaps, but a move in the right direction none the less. Her mood lifted so much that she actually felt inspired to tackle the document she needed to translate; just as soon as she'd brewed a nice cup of coffee. And refilled the birdfeeder. Bloody squirrel was hovering in the tree above, and she shook her fist at it.

'Not for you,' she yelled.

'All right, dear?' Anne Walker asked as she passed, frowning slightly at Marnie's raised fist.

'Squirrels. Keep stealing the bird food.'

'Oh ah—ha-ha.' Anne gave an awkward laugh, still frowning in confusion. 'Well, I'll see you later then.'

Marnie sighed as she returned to the kitchen and opened her laptop. Everyone who went into the sweetshop today would hear about her strange behaviour now. She took a sip of coffee. Delicious. She just needed a biscuit to go with it.

Someone hammered on the door as she rose to fetch the biscuit tin, and she glanced at the document with little regret as she made her way to answer. She'd paid for next-day delivery for the baskets, so it must be them.

Opening it she found David leaning against the porch, head thrown back in a dramatic fashion. 'Save me,' he said, grasping her arms so hard she thought he was about to shake her.

'What on earth's going on?'

'Please, help me, take me in.' He glanced over his shoulder as though he was being pursued by a hit man.

Marnie stepped aside and he ran in, slamming the door shut behind him and leaning against it.

She couldn't help laughing. 'What are you up to? Aren't you supposed to be at work?'

'Day off, long weekend, it's supposed to be a romantic getaway but Greg insisted on coming here for a run first and he tried to get me to join in!' He looked aghast, and Marnie couldn't blame him. 'So I told him you needed my support and you couldn't do without your little brother in this time of need, okay?'

He shed his coat and took off his shoes, wandering towards the kitchen. Marnie followed, laughing as she admired the mustard and navy striped socks he was wearing. Perhaps she'd ask him to knit her a pair for Christmas.

'What time of need?' she asked.

He shrugged. 'Don't know, doesn't matter, make something up.'

'I'm perfectly fine, thank you,' Marnie said. She hugged him, breathing in the smell of bacon that clung to his hair. 'But it is nice to see you.'

He grinned and eyed the almost-empty biscuit tin. 'You too. But where are your manners, aren't you going to offer me sustenance?'

'Help yourself. Thought you might be full after that cooked breakfast you've just had, that's all.'

He stopped mid-bite, frowning. 'Wait, how did you— You some kind of witch or something?'

She glanced at the egg stain on his jumper and tapped her nose. 'Ah, I have my ways.'

'You're a strange and wonderful woman.' He picked up her empty cafetiere and rinsed it, then began randomly opening cupboards.

'Just wonderful will do.' She grinned and opened the fridge, retrieved the bag of ground coffee and threw it at him, laughing as he scrabbled and almost dropped it. 'Butter fingers.'

'So how's life in Babblebrook treating you?' he asked, spooning coffee. 'Full of excitement?'

'Well. That bloke next door's an odd one, isn't he?'

David glanced over his shoulder at her, raised his eyebrows and turned to fill the kettle.

Marnie felt herself flush. 'What are you smirking at?'

'He on your mind, is he?'

'No, it's just—Lauren went over there yesterday to play with that dog of his and she said he was talking about . . . well, she said he was nice but you know, we've seen him around and he's just been weirdly rude, to be honest.' David leaned against the counter, arms folded and a stupid, smug smile on his face that made Marnie flush even deeper. And talk even more. 'And it's not just me, people seem to think he's a bit of an odd one, and I know he lost his wife and everything and I feel so bad for him of course, but apparently he's got a terrible temper and some stuff happened, I think, I'm not sure but . . .'

She trailed off. She was sweating, the heating must be on too high. She flapped at the neck of her jumper, trying to fan herself.

'Handsome, though, right?'

David was grinning. It made Marnie want to slap him. An image of Andrew's bright blue eyes and broad shoulders swam into her mind. That heart-melting smile.

'What? No I don't—I mean I haven't . . .'

David stepped over and put an arm round her. 'Poor heartbroken, handsome Andrew, cutting himself off from the world, just waiting for a little brunette who loves baking and talks like an old woman to bring him back to—' Marnie reached for the nearest weapon she could find, which turned out to be the biscuit tin lid, and batted him on the head with it. 'Hey!' he protested, laughing and rubbing the top of his head.

'Oh shut up,' Marnie said. 'Make your coffee before I call your lovely husband and tell him you're desperate to go on a run.'

That wiped the smile off his face. Marnie carefully steered the conversation away from her neighbour until at last Greg arrived, looking as fresh as a daisy after a 'quick three-miler', and took David off to begin their romantic weekend.

She finished her work, made a list of presents to buy Lauren for Christmas and cooked a risotto for dinner just in time for her daughter's return from school. They ate, chatted, tackled Lauren's physics homework together, and watched their favourite programme on TV, *All Creatures Great and Small*. And Marnie very deliberately did not think of her neighbour once.

When she went out to refill the bird food ready for the next morning, she saw him leaving his house with the dog, wearing headphones, on an evening walk presumably.

'Hello there,' she said brightly, trying to see the version of him that Lauren had evidently seen. And trying to stop the words 'heartbroken, handsome Andrew' ringing through her mind.

He turned to her with a look of surprise, grunted and continued trudging on his way.

He still seemed like Grumpy Andrew to her, despite everything her daughter had said.

Chapter Nine

Pat and Matt had made as much effort decorating their cottage as they had the bakery.

Twinkly, coloured lights lined the pretty little V-shaped porch. Inside, a tree stood in the corner, sparkling with fairy lights and dripping with the same decorations Marnie had seen as a child – hand-painted baubles, glass robins that clipped to branches. Underneath teetered a pile of ribbon-tied presents. Marnie hadn't even begun her shopping yet. Her chest felt tight at the thought; it wasn't like her at all, she'd usually bought everyone's gifts by the end of October.

A fire crackled in the grate and the room was filled with the scent of pine and the tang of woodsmoke. Marnie and Lauren settled on the sofa together, gratefully accepting tea and mince pies. Pat had messaged to invite them round just as Marnie had finished filling the birdfeeder – and attempting to be friendly to her neighbour – reminding her to come over and collect the biscuits and mince pies she'd bought from the bakery. After all the upset of the day before, Marnie had completely forgotten them.

They'd gone straight round. Lauren was already in her pyjamas, but that didn't matter. Pat and Matt's cottage already felt like home-from-home. They must get their own decorations up, Marnie thought, admiring the tinsel on the mantelpiece. Their own cottage felt much more welcoming than when they'd first moved to Babblebrook, but a touch of Christmas sparkle couldn't hurt.

She took the baskets and bunting round, explaining to Matt how they could display the bread in there and hang the bunting. 'I'll come and help you,' she said.

'Oh what a good idea,' he said. 'You are a marvel, we really should start paying you!'

Marnie laughed and kissed his cheek. 'It's nothing, just helping out a bit now and then.'

Pat hobbled in, grunting as she bent to admire the baskets and unfold the bunting. Marnie wasn't sure if it was her imagination, but she seemed to be leaning harder on her stick every day.

'Ooh lovely, Marnie. We can put this over the counter, maybe. Perfect now it's Christmas! And we've got a little Christmas something for you both here.'

She grinned, her cheeks pink, and reached over to the mantel, picking up two advent calendars that were propped there, one chocolate and one just pictures. As she leaned, she wobbled a little, grunting, and Marnie leaped to her feet.

'I'm all right, don't fuss,' Pat said crossly, but she still held tightly onto Marnie's arm as she guided her to a chair.

'I thought you were going to fall for a minute there.' Marnie strove to keep her voice light, but didn't quite manage it. Lauren looked worried too. Perhaps Pat was more frail than they'd realised. She pushed the thought away.

'Nonsense,' Pat said. 'What a load of codswallop, I was perfectly fine.'

'She's working too hard,' Matt said, as he passed the biscuit tin around. Marnie really shouldn't have any, she'd eaten her fill today, but she took one anyway. For the shock.

'Rubbish,' Pat said, pointing her stick at him. 'Don't start that again.'

Matt flopped down onto a chair, looking defeated. 'You're not getting any younger, love,' he said. 'Neither of us are. A rest might be nice, eh?'

Marnie tried not to take in what Matt was saying. They'd always been so busy, so full of energy, working long hours to run the bakery and loving it. She couldn't imagine them any other way. She wouldn't.

Pat obviously felt the same. She sucked her lips in and pointedly turned away from Matt, holding the advent calendars out to Lauren. 'Here you are, chick,' she said. 'Chocolate one's for you, of course.'

Marnie watched as Lauren's face lit up, and she rushed to give Pat and Matt a kiss. She might constantly remind Marnie that she was no longer a child, but you were never too old for chocolate.

Matt smiled and patted her shoulder as she thanked them. 'Well, we're a bit late giving them to you so you've got a few windows to open straight away,' he said. Lauren needed no more encouragement than this, prising the doors open and stuffing the chocolates into her mouth.

Marnie admired her own calendar, a glittery Victorian scene of children skating on a frozen pond. Pat and Matt had always bought advent calendars for Marnie and David when they were children. 'Oh, you really didn't need to,' she said, already searching for the first door.

She leaned over to show Pat as she opened it, revealing a robin sitting on a snow-covered branch. 'Ooh,' Pat said. 'How lovely.'

'Ah, *Erithacus rubecula*.' Marnie grinned at their blank faces. 'That's a robin to you lot. They're actually little bullies, you know, but I still love them.'

Pat rubbed her hands together and smiled. 'I'm so excited for Christmas, aren't you? You must get on the village WhatsApp, Marnie, we've got lots planned, there's the tree decorating and the bring and share meal and the carol singing and—'

Marnie smiled, listening to Pat list all the Christmas events with excitement, her cheeks growing rosier and her eyes brighter by the minute. This was the woman she had always known, full of enthusiasm. She refused to think of her as tired and unsteady on her feet.

*

Carol singing was the first village Christmas event. Marnie wasn't sure that Lauren would come but, though she did complain about being dragged away from FaceTiming her old school friends, she reluctantly agreed to join them in wrapping up in bobble hat, scarf and mittens and trooping out into the cold night air. Marnie saw her catch Emma's eye across the crowd, and the girls smiled at each other, grimacing in embarrassment.

The night was clear, with a bright moon lighting their way and stars sprinkling the sky. Marnie stamped her feet and blew out a plume of foggy breath.

'Lovely night, isn't it?' Pat said. 'Might even get a white Christmas this year.'

'Oh, I hope so,' Lauren said.

'We never get a white Christmas,' Marnie said. 'As long as it's not raining I won't complain.'

Pat pulled a face at Lauren and grinned. 'What a killjoy.'

The carol singing started at the other end of the village, and they began to walk down, gathering people who came out of houses to join them on the way. They walked slowly, taking up the rear, to accommodate Pat. Andrew, Marnie noticed, didn't join them and his cottage was in darkness. Not that she cared.

'Remember that year it snowed so heavily for our Christmas day walk?' Matt asked.

Marnie did. She'd been about nine, David about seven, and they had been based in Babblebrook that winter. They'd all gone round to Pat and Matt's for a delicious turkey dinner and then had a walk afterwards, Lily pulling them on a sledge for most of it. She could be such fun, when she was focused on them.

Marnie nodded. 'The drifts were so high, we were walking on top of the hedges.'

'That's right.' Matt nodded. 'We opened the front door on Christmas morning and the snow was up to our waists.'

'Your mum dug us out,' Pat said, puffing slightly with the effort of walking.

'Did she?' Marnie didn't know why she didn't remember. Her memories of Lily when they were children were all of her flightiness and the way she constantly moved them without warning; getting dragged from their beds to pack bags and leave Babblebrook without the chance to say goodbye as Lily drove them to a new town, talking all the while of the exciting job she'd found, the fun that life in a town with parks and cinemas and sports centres would offer them. But she always lost interest in the new-and-exciting job within a few months. And she never took them to the park or cinema or sports centre.

They were met at the end of the village street outside The Plough by a small group of people, who appeared to be led by a tall woman wearing a massive duffle coat and Doc Martens, and sporting a haircut that was chin length on one side and shaved to a buzz cut on the other. She clapped her hands together. 'Right,' she said, in a voice that boomed around the nearby cottages. 'All present and correct?'

She glanced around and they all nodded, as though she was a schoolteacher and they were her pupils. She beamed. 'Perfect. Let's make a start, I want to be get back here before Gillian closes up.'

Gillian, who was standing outside with a tray full of glasses of sherry, gave her a thumbs up.

Lauren was gazing at the woman with undisguised admiration, and Marnie felt herself responding in a similar way. She threw a questioning glance at Matt.

'Reverend Pauline,' he whispered. 'She replaced the bloke we had after—Well, never mind. She's a marvel, shaken us all up nicely. Don't get on the wrong side of her though!'

Marnie made a mental note. Although she felt anyone with sense would try to stay on the right side of this formidable woman.

It was only as they all began to sing 'Silent Night' that Marnie remembered how terrible her voice was. She was sure she saw Matt actually flinch, and Lauren definitely edged away from her. Anne Walker, who was standing just in front of them, turned around to throw her a sympathetic glance.

'Never mind, dear,' she whispered when the carol was done. 'We all have our gifts, this just isn't one of yours.' She smiled encouragingly, and Marnie flushed with humiliation, remembering Ian wincing when she had sung along as he was rehearsing. He'd chuckled and taken her in his arms as the others in the band had laughed at her. 'Not to worry, babe,' he'd said. 'Even you can't be good at everything!'

Mrs Walker glanced around at the gathered crowd of villagers and leaned in closer to Marnie as Reverend Pauline asked for suggestions for the next carol. 'I see your neighbour didn't come again this year. You know I'm not one to gossip, but perhaps it's just as well.' She shook her head and pursed her lips, a gleam of delight in her eyes as she began talking again. 'I wouldn't say that we don't want him here, of course. But,' she opened her eyes wide in an expression of shock,

'My goodness. Not good to have in a crowd, I can tell you that.'

She raised her eyebrows, gave a dramatic shudder and said no more, turning to join in with 'O Come All Ye Faithful'.

Marnie had no chance to ask for more information, and she supposed she shouldn't. It wasn't fair to talk about someone behind their back. But still, he was their neighbour, and it wasn't the first time Anne had warned that he was volatile. And while Lauren had apparently found him friendly, Marnie had seen precious little evidence of that so far. She would put nothing past Grumpy Andrew, and she desperately wanted to know what he'd done. Mouthing the rest of the words and looking forward to the inevitable sherry that Gillian would hand out when they'd finished, she was fleetingly grateful that he wasn't there to witness her humiliation, though.

Many sherries and many mouthed carols later, she, Lauren, Pat and Matt linked arms as they reached their own end of the village.

'It's so beautiful,' Pat said, slurring just a little, as she stopped to admire the decorated houses.

They all stood for a moment, looking around at the twinkling lights. Their own cottage was now tastefully decorated with white lights and, through the window, their tree glinted with silver. Lauren had insisted that their decorations were colour-free, and Marnie had been so happy that they were doing them together that she hadn't argued. The only house still to be decorated was the one next door. Of course. She supposed Andrew was too dour to celebrate.

'It was beautifully decorated when Jane was alive,' Pat said, a wistful tone to her voice.

'Oh, they loved Christmas didn't they?' Matt said. 'They had the whole village round for a party, do you remember?'

Pat chuckled. 'And Andrew dressed up as Father Christmas at the bring and share.'

Marnie couldn't imagine that. They all stared at the plain, dark house.

'We should Christmas bomb it,' she said. She only realised that she'd spoken aloud when the others turned to look at her. And they were all smiling.

Matt laughed. 'We can't.'

'He's working late. And I have his spare key. So we can,' Pat said.

Marnie wondered just how many sherries she'd drunk. 'Oh, I was just . . .'

'It might cheer him up,' Lauren said. 'Like a Christmas present.'

Matt rubbed his chin. 'He does need coaxing back to life. It's been three years.'

'Nearly four, it was February he lost her. Come on, Matt, come on, let's get the spare lights.' Pat was moving to her own house as quickly as she could. With that mischievous expression and her red bobble hat, she looked like a naughty elf. Matt followed her without question.

'We've got all that tacky stuff left,' Lauren said.

'Tacky stu—Those are my treasured decorations!' Marnie protested.

'Well, we can give him some tinsel at least. We're not going to use that.' Lauren curled her lip at the very idea.

She ran into the house to raid the spare decorations, just as Pat arrived with a spool of lights slung over her shoulder and Matt followed, carrying a large plastic reindeer.

Pat tutted. 'Don't just stand there gormless, Marnie, he could be home any minute. Go and get the step ladder, you know where it is.'

And before she knew what was happening Marnie found herself balanced none too steadily on the ladder, draping lights around Andrew's porch while Pat leaned on her stick and barked instructions. Like a slightly tipsy little sergeant major. This was the happiest Marnie had seen her since they arrived.

Inside, Lauren arranged tinsel over picture frames and mirrors, and ran around dangling the bright baubles she'd banished from their own house from door and cupboard handles.

Matt placed the reindeer on Andrew's lawn and fiddled with it until it lit up, red nose and all. 'Ha,' he said. 'There you go.'

He began to warble a little too loudly. 'Little donkey, little donkey . . .'

'It's a flipping reindeer,' Pat said.

Caught in the Christmas spirit – and still full of sherry – Marnie joined in, forgetting for a moment that she couldn't sing.

'Grumpy Andrew, Grumpy Andrew,' she sang, giggling at her own cleverness. 'Such a grouchy man.'

She laughed and almost tipped herself off the stepladder. Oops. The others weren't joining in, in fact they had suddenly gone silent, but Marnie was caught up in her little carol now. Leaning back to drape another layer of lights, she continued.

'Must he keep on, being so rude, he is just so . . .'

As she reached unsuccessfully for the high note a voice spoke behind her.

'Think you've got the words confused.'

Jumping, Marnie forgot she was on the ladder and tried to turn to see Andrew, standing with arms crossed, frowning at her. The ladder wobbled and she shrieked, almost falling off. Clearing her throat, she climbed down with as much dignity as she could muster. Which was very little.

'What on earth are you doing?' he demanded. He glared around at them all, his expression stony, jaw set, and in the light of the street lamp Marnie couldn't help but notice the chiselled lines of his face.

She swallowed. This was a mistake, a stupid mistake, and it was all her fault. Her failed attempts at forging some kind of friendly relationship with him had been difficult enough, and now she'd gone and made things far worse. This village was bringing out a side of her that she wasn't sure she liked; reckless and infantile. She was acting like her mother.

'Sorry,' she muttered, cheeks burning. 'It was just supposed to be a bit of—'

'We wanted to do something nice for you,' Pat said.

'Just . . . to help you remember. You used to love all this, and we want to help you get back to that a bit.' Matt placed a hand on Andrew's shoulder. 'Time to let yourself have a bit fun, eh?'

'It's our Christmas present to you,' Lauren said in a small voice.

Andrew glared round at them all, then sighed and rubbed a hand over his face. He nodded and turned back to the house, standing with hands on hips, looking at the lights. Everyone waited in silence.

'These aren't even straight,' he said, frowning. 'You've done a terrible job, are you drunk or something?'

He turned to look at Marnie. She straightened up, offended. 'Certainly not,' she slurred.

'Right.' One side of his mouth lifted in a half-smile. Marnie was sure she detected a twinkle in those blue eyes of his, and found herself smiling up at him.

Get a grip, she told herself.

Must be the sherry.

'You know I thought you were kind of straight-laced and boring,' he said quietly, so only she could hear, his lips almost brushing her cheek.

'Hey!' She tried to look dignified but she was having trouble standing still without wobbling.

'But I think you're actually a bit mad.'

'I am not!'

'I kind of like it.' Again, Marnie found herself breaking into a smile – a big, uncontrollable smile. She'd definitely had too much sherry. 'Right.' He looked up at the wonky lights straggled over his porch. 'I'll hold this.' He indicated the ladder. 'Get back up there, then. If a job's worth doing, it's worth doing properly, right?'

And Marnie found herself climbing back up, adjusting the lights into a more aesthetically pleasing arrangement, all the while very aware of Andrew's eyes on her. He hummed 'Little Donkey' as she worked.

'There we go,' he said. 'Much better.'

She tried to climb down as elegantly as possible; tricky when you had a belly full of booze and were suddenly very aware of the view the man holding the ladder would have of your backside edging towards him. She stumbled on the last step, flushing, and Andrew steadied her, his hand warm around her waist. Her skin prickled into goosebumps.

'All right, there?' he asked, voice soft. Did his eyes linger a little on her face? His hand linger a little at her waist? Was he flirting with her?

Surely not. They didn't even like each other.

So why had his touch sent electricity firing through her?

'That's great, Mum,' Lauren called, and Marnie realised she was still standing gazing up at Andrew. She eased herself away from him, clearing her throat and straightening her bobble hat.

'Oh, uh, thanks. Good yes. Right-oh.'

She looked at Lauren, still admiring the lights, and Pat and Mat, who stood holding hands and smirking at her with knowing expressions.

To complete her humiliation, as she finally stepped away from him she put her foot down a rabbit hole and lurched to the side, twisting her ankle and yelping as pain flared through her foot.

'Woah,' he said, taking her arm with a firm but gentle hand and steadying her, the only thing that stopped her from face-planting the ground in front of them all. 'You okay?' he asked softly, his gaze resting on her face.

She nodded and tried not to whimper, attempted a step and immediately cried out as pain shot up her leg.

'Okay,' he said, taking charge. 'Let's get you inside.'

'You all right, Mum?' Lauren asked, her voice threaded with concern.

'Yes, yes,' she said. 'Just clumsy.' She tried to laugh, but the truth was her ankle was throbbing. Of course she would fall over nothing and hurt herself in front of Andrew. And Lauren and Pat and Matt she added quickly, she didn't particularly care about what her grumpy neighbour thought of her, did she. How undignified, though.

'Don't worry, Lauren, it's probably just a little sprain,' Andrew said. He nodded towards Pat and Matt, who were hovering, Matt with a look of concern and Pat trying not to laugh. 'You two get in the warm, I'll make sure she's okay.'

All this time his arm was around Marnie's waist, warm and firm, and she was acutely aware of it. She had to stop herself leaning into him.

That sherry had really gone to her head.

Lauren led the way to their own cottage, with Marnie hobbling after, supported by Andrew. Through his jacket she could feel his firm chest as she leaned against him, and he smelled of soap and, faintly, wood smoke. When they were in he lowered her gently onto the sofa, pulling out the foot stool and propping her leg onto it.

'Thank you,' she said. 'I'm fine now, thanks for your help.' She smiled as he kneeled by her feet, desperate to reassure him that she needed no more from him. She'd made enough of a fool of herself already.

'Nonsense,' he said, standing and shrugging out of his jacket. Marnie couldn't help but notice the tightening of his shirt over his shoulders as he turned to hang his coat on the back of a chair. She tried to look away, but somehow couldn't bring herself to. 'What kind of a man would I be if I left you like this?' He smiled, that bolt of sunlight smile that had her stomach flipping again, and walked through to the kitchen.

Marnie sat in the living room, gazing happily at the lights twinkling on the tree, her beloved decorations glinting, and basking in the warmth from the embers in the log burner. She listened as Lauren, who had immediately gone to make tea, chatted easily with Andrew about which frozen veg would be most suitable to put on Marnie's injured ankle. Sprouts, carrots and broccoli were rejected in favour of sweetcorn.

They returned together, Andrew with the sweetcorn and Lauren with tea for them both.

'Here you are, milady,' he said, kneeling to remove her boot and peel back her sock. Marnie was relieved that she'd painted her toenails. A week or two ago, and they were looking more than a bit scrappy now, but it could be worse. Had definitely often been worse. Tentatively, she wriggled her toes as the chill from the sweetcorn spread over her skin, wincing a little.

'Thanks,' she said. 'I feel like an idiot.'

He shrugged, 'Could happen to anyone. Especially when they've had a bellyful of sherry.'

'Hey,' she said, leaning forward. 'I did not have a—'

But he just grinned and winked, and she was disarmed, feeling that stupid smile spread over her face again. She could think of nothing to say, and couldn't tear her eyes from his.

Only after several moments did she become aware of Lauren, standing at her side. 'Mum! What's wrong with you, did you bash your head as well as your foot?' She rolled her eyes. 'I've been standing here with your tea saying your name for like an *hour* and you're just sitting there staring into space.'

Marnie gave an awkward laugh and dragged her gaze away from what she realised she'd actually been staring into; Andrew's eyes. 'Oh dear, silly me, I must be in a daze,' she gabbled, trying to hide the blush that raced across her cheeks. 'Thank you, darling, that's perfect.' She took the tea and slurped it, her eyes watering as it scalded her throat.

Lauren was frowning at her. 'You're being weird.'

'Right, well,' Andrew said, standing and reaching for his jacket. 'I'll leave you to it. Keep that foot up for a bit.' He gave a fake stern look and she nodded.

Then he left, and Lauren went to her room, and Marnie found herself sitting alone, her ankle soothed by the chill that spread through it, trying not to think of the way Andrew's arm had felt around her waist, or of how embarrassed she was that she'd been caught singing a stupid song about him, then falling over nothing and hurting herself. She was all in a spin, and she didn't like it. She was flustered, and the more she thought about it the more irritated she felt.

That man was so very annoying.

Chapter Ten

'... wondering what your plans are for the cottage? Because Lauren and I are all settled and—' Marnie stared at the image of her mum, stuck now in an unfortunate expression, eyes half-closed and mouth open. She sighed. 'Oh, you've frozen.'

The screen flickered and glitched, the image changed jerkily and snatches of words could be heard. '... ing it ... the vill ...? ... and ... at doing?'

Marnie frowned. 'I can't hear you, Lily.' Their mother had always preferred them to call her by her name, even when they were little children. Calling her 'mum' would have cramped her style, Marnie supposed. 'You asking about Babblebrook? It's the same as ever.'

Not quite the truth, but there was no point worrying her about Pat's health or the state of the bakery. She was halfway round India, there was nothing she could do from there, and Marnie honestly didn't know how much Lily would care anyway. She'd never been fond of the village. The cottage was no more than an occasional base that she had little interest in otherwise.

'Lily?' Marnie said as her mum screwed up her face and leaned closer, then froze again. 'I need to ask you about what you're planning to do with the—' The signal gave out altogether and she found herself talking to a blank screen. She sighed. Maybe they'd have better luck next time.

Sometimes she thought she was better off when her mum was out of the country, anyway. She was an unreliable, unsettling presence, even in her sixties, changing plans at the last minute or forgetting that they'd arranged to meet. Lauren loved her, oblivious to the fact that she never remembered a birthday and had never offered to babysit in her life. She was exciting Gran, who sent postcards from all over the world, turned up randomly with exotic presents and encouraged her granddaughter to 'experience life', by which she meant bunk off school and try a bit of small-time shoplifting.

Marnie felt boring in comparison, working in a steady job, taking Lauren to gym club and piano lessons, cooking her meals and reading her bedtime stories. She'd always been the quiet one, the one in the background looking after the people that shone, providing stability for David when they were growing up, helping him wash his face and clean his teeth when Lily was too busy. She'd played the same part for Ian, she was his rock, on the sidelines earning a wage and cooking dinners and caring for Lauren while he went on tour with the band. She would make sure she provided that stability for her daughter, too.

Still, she sometimes envied Lily her laissez faire attitude to life; Marnie felt uncomfortable if she didn't have that week's meals planned, she couldn't imagine taking off to another country on a whim. And living in the cottage without knowing whether Lily planned to rent it out to someone else at any moment, or even sell it, was doing nothing for the state of her nerves.

Thinking of being prepared, she went back to her online shopping. Almost done, and it would arrive in plenty of time to be wrapped and ready for Christmas. She wished she could afford more, but she was waiting for a couple of clients to pay her invoices; she'd send another reminder tomorrow. At least the extra few pieces of work that had come in meant she could buy some presents and provide a decent spread. This year, she would invite Pat and Matt, perhaps David and Greg too.

She wondered what Andrew would do for Christmas, trying to steady the quickened beating of her heart at the memory of his hand on her waist, of the way he'd looked at her as he'd taken care of her ankle. Would he be alone? No, he must have family, or friends. Not that she'd seen evidence of any. He wouldn't need an invitation from her, anyway. Surely.

*

Saturday was the tree decorating, an event that involved the whole village. An eight-foot spruce had been bought and erected on the green, next to the old iron pump. Everyone gathered, even Lauren and Emma had managed to drag themselves out of bed at ten o'clock on a Saturday morning, despite the bitter wind whipping down the street. Marnie's ankle was recovering quickly, and she was able to join in, barely limping now

The Barretts, who lived in the nearest house, cheerfully provided an endless supply of tea, coffee and bacon butties to those in need. Which was everyone. Marnie attempted to introduce herself through mouthfuls of hers, but they knew who she was already; she should have learned by now that no new arrival in the village went unnoticed.

Together, laughing and shouting instructions, and occasionally breaking into Christmas songs, they wound lights around the tree and hedge, and hung baubles. There were some people that Marnie remembered from childhood – Gloria and Bob, who lived on the corner by the lane to the brook, and in whose house Marnie and David had spent many a happy hour when they were children; the farming family, the Woods, and the Walkers.

Barbara Wood didn't recognise her at first, but then she suddenly exclaimed, 'Oh yes, little David's sister! I remember you.' She shook her head, smiling. 'He loved to come and play with the cows, didn't he? He was always such a sweet, cheeky boy.'

Marnie nodded, wondering how long it was since she'd seen 'little David,' who now stood a good head taller than Barbara.

Others were more recent additions to the village and Marnie didn't recognise them, but all were friendly, asking about her work and how Lauren was settling in. A few took her aside and asked in hushed tones how Pat and Matt were, commenting on how good it was that she was here to support them.

She avoided Andrew, who stood at the edge of the crowd with Rosie. She'd grown even fatter, if that was possible, waddling along the street and lying down at his feet, panting. Once, when Alan Wood guffawed particularly loudly, she jumped up and cowered, trembling, behind Andrew's legs, but he bent to stroke her and she soon settled. When Marnie glanced his way again, she found her eye meeting his; he was looking at her across the crowd, and she felt caught in the hold of his gaze, unable to break away as a slow smile spread across his face, and she felt herself respond in the same way. At last, she looked away, her heart beating a little quicker as she recalled the touch of his hand on her waist and the way his gaze had lingered on her face. That wink. The memory gave her goosebumps.

She was mortified about her behaviour the other night, Christmas bombing his house and singing stupid carols and falling over for no reason. She didn't know what had come over her lately, and she wasn't sure she liked it. It was Pat and Matt's fault anyway, getting carried away like that. But Andrew had kept the decorations up, she noticed. So perhaps it hadn't been such a bad idea after all.

Pat's voice cut through her reverie, a wail that could be heard even over the wind and had her rushing over. 'Oh no! But what will we do? We can't miss it.'

'What's the matter?' Marnie asked.

'Barbara's just told us there's been a leak in the village hall, it's out of use for at least a month now, we'll never get the work done this close to Christmas,' Matt said.

'Oh dear,' Marnie said, confused as to why this was such a crisis.

'It's the bring and share next Saturday,' Pat explained, pulling her bobble hat down around her ears. 'And there's nowhere to do it now, and we have it every year, you remember, don't you?'

Marnie did remember. It had been that same winter when the snow was so heavy; the village hall had been decked out in tinsel and paperchains, everyone had brought a dish to share. She remembered a delicious stew and a table covered in cakes and pies and pastries. Her young eyes had widened at such a feast, and her young stomach had been filled to the point of almost bringing it all back up.

There had been a tree in the corner and someone dressed as Santa handing out presents to the children at the end of the night. She had been given pens, David a colouring book, and they'd shared them, spending a happy few days lying in front of the fire colouring in pictures of stockings and elves.

It was a fond memory, and she understood why the event meant so much to Pat. Marnie had never seen her this upset.

'Don't worry,' she said. 'We'll find a way.'

'Oh, but there's no time now,' Pat said.

Matt patted her shoulder. 'We could do it after Christmas? A winter celebration.'

Pat shook her head. 'I love you for trying, but don't be stupid, it just wouldn't be the same.'

'How about the bakery?' Marnie said, the words out of her mouth before she'd thought them through. But she would say anything to make that look on Pat's face go away. 'There's the kitchen for tea and coffee, and keeping the food warm, and we could squeeze everyone into the shop space, couldn't we?'

She looked around, warming to her idea.

'Great plan,' said a voice beside her. Andrew, she realised with a start. She hadn't noticed him come to stand with them. 'We can bring tables and chairs from the hall, and the bakery's already decorated, so that saves us a job.'

He glanced at Marnie as he mentioned the Christmas decorations, his eyes twinkling. When he smiled like that he looked like a different person. A warm, friendly, handsome kind of person. A gust of wind blew her hair over her face, catching in her mouth so that she coughed and shook her head. Andrew laughed, gently brushing her hair aside.

'You look lovely today,' he said softly.

Marnie's breath caught as his gentle touch gave her goosebumps. A pleasant, warm sensation grew in her stomach. Well, she had put some lippy on that morning and taken extra care with her eye makeup. She found herself smiling at him stupidly, as he smiled stupidly back.

The moment was broken as Andrew cleared his throat and dropped his hand. 'Well?' he asked, his voice falsely jovial as he turned to Pat and Matt. 'What do you think? Good idea? We'll use the bakery, yes?'

He marched off without waiting for an answer, leaving Marnie trying not to blush as Pat and Matt grinned and raised their eyebrows at her.

*

Somehow, Marnie ended up in charge, and she enjoyed it more than she'd expected. The bakery looked a bit brighter with the pretty bunting hanging over the counter and the baskets of various sizes lined with matching fabric filled with French sticks, rolls and Matt's homemade biscuits. She helped Andrew and some other volunteers to push the display units right back against the walls and put out the tables and chairs, draping them with festive tablecloths and glittery centrepieces as they listened to carols on the radio. David was working, he would join them later, but Greg lent a hand.

She'd seen him in his running gear, sprinting past in the cold early morning just as she was leaving the house, stopping to fill the birdfeeder. There was no sign of the squirrel lurking today, and as soon as she walked away there would be a little mob of sparrows, blue tits and robins descending, she knew. It hadn't taken long for the local bird population to discover there was a new food supply. Greg waved and smiled, looking far more cheerful than anyone who was just finishing up a morning run had any right to.

'Hey, Marnie,' he said, stopping and wiping his forehead. 'Lovely morning.'

'Are you mad?'

He laughed. 'Ah, nothing better than a run in a beautiful place like this. Good for the soul.'

Marnie thought that biscuits were better for her soul, but decided now wasn't the time to mention it. 'If you say so. You don't even look out of breath.'

'Just a short one today, only six miles.'

Marnie laughed, but it appeared that he wasn't joking.

'Anyway, just popping to Pat and Matt's for a shower,' he said, as though this was perfectly normal. And judging from the welcome he received when he knocked on their door it was. 'I'll be along to help out in a bit.'

'Thanks,' Marnie called, hurrying on. She stopped herself from suggesting that he had a lie down and eat a slice of cake instead. Apparently that wasn't Greg's style. And she needed all the help she could get.

She'd arranged for all the crockery and cutlery to be brought from the village hall and put a call out for wine glasses. Having satisfied herself that this was all under control, she spent the day cooking.

She made a hotpot that simmered away gently for hours, filling the bakery with the rich scent of lamb and vegetables, a sherry trifle topped with thick cream and strawberries, and set mulled wine to heat. Soon the aroma of cinnamon and cloves mingling with the wine and brandy had her mouth watering.

'Drinks for the workers?' she asked. 'Tea, coffee? Mulled wine?' Every head turned in her direction at this last offer, and she was soon ladling the warm liquid into glasses and doling them out.

Andrew dipped his nose into the glass and breathed in appreciatively. 'That's the stuff,' he said. 'Lovely.'

Marnie almost jumped. These were the first words she'd heard him speak all day; he had worked solidly and silently, and she'd tried not to notice his shirt stretched tight over the muscles in his back. But now he smiled, his eyes crinkling, and her heart gave an extra beat. Why did that keep happening? She cleared her throat.

'Matt's recipe,' she said.

'How's the ankle?' he asked.

'Oh that,' Marnie waved a hand, trying not to relive her humiliation at her clumsiness. 'Much better. Thanks to you looking after me so well.' She glanced at him, and found he was already looking into her eyes.

He shrugged, and a look of pain passed over his face. 'Well. I had a bit of practice.'

Marnie placed a hand on his arm. 'I'm sorry.'

He sighed and smiled sadly. 'Not your fault.' He cleared his throat. 'Glad you're better anyway. I have something for you, by the way.'

He reached into his pocket and brought out a little wooden keyring in the shape of a house, engraved with an image of what was unmistakably her cottage, with the little porch. Underneath was the word, 'home'.

Marnie turned it in her hand, admiring the delicacy of the work. 'It's beautiful, thank you. You made this?'

'Yeah, just a little . . . you know, to remind you that you're really home now. After all that moving around when you were a kid.' He met her eye. Marnie stared back. She couldn't believe he'd remembered what she'd told him about her childhood, and given her such a thoughtful gift. She felt tears begin to burn in her eyes.

'Oh that's so kind of you, I can't believe you did this.'

He shrugged and blushed behind the stubble, beginning to scowl a little. 'Not a big deal, only took a couple of minutes. And you know—We got off on the wrong foot, so . . .'

Marnie opened her mouth, but couldn't think what to say. It felt like a big deal to her. Andrew just nodded and scuffed his foot against the floor. She was relieved when Lauren arrived and Andrew turned away, allowing her heartbeat to steady.

Emma walked in immediately afterwards, and came over to them, smiling shyly at Lauren. 'My dad said you might need some help.'

'Ah,' Marnie said, pocketing the keyring. 'My little band of workers!'

Lauren rolled her eyes, pulling a face at Emma, who grinned in response. 'So embarrassing,' Lauren said.

'My mum and dad are the same,' Emma said.

'I know, right?' Lauren said, then turned back to Marnie with a sigh. 'What do you want us to do?'

Marnie had always thought she was quite a cool mum, but she supposed there was no such thing when you were thirteen. And anyway, if this was how Lauren was going to bond with Emma, then she'd happily put up with it.

'Come here,' she said. 'I'll show you how to fold the napkins into Christmas trees. Do you want a drink?'

Lauren eyed a glass of mulled wine on the table next to them.

'Tea or coffee,' Marnie said firmly.

'Tea?' Lauren pulled a face at Emma, and they both giggled.

'Fine,' Marnie said. 'Hot chocolate? That's my final offer.'

They both nodded enthusiastically. 'Thank you,' Emma said. 'Show us how to do the napkins first though, then we can get going.'

Lauren glared at her as Marnie led them to a table where a pile of paper napkins printed with a holly pattern sat. The folding wasn't hard, and the girls soon picked it up, chatting and giggling as they worked, showing off their finished napkins happily. Rosie waddled over and lay at their feet, and Lauren reached down to pat her absent-mindedly.

Marnie added whipped cream and marshmallows to the girls' hot chocolates, placing a little gingerbread snowman on each saucer. Seeing her daughter making a new friend, their heads bent together as they compared their handiwork, Marnie let out a breath she felt she'd been holding for months.

It seemed that Lauren was finally settling in Babblebrook. This was more than Marnie had dared to hope for. She must find a way to keep them here, she thought. Which meant she must pin Lily down about her plans for the cottage, then she would know for sure if Andrew was right, and she really was home at last. And then she must also find a way of earning a reliable wage. She didn't want to break into the small nest egg the sale of the house had given her, she might need that one day, and though she'd built up some regular clients with the translating work, it was hardly what you'd call a reliable income. Especially when some of them seemed determined not to pay.

She watched as Lauren bit into the gingerbread snowman, decapitating it, and both girls collapsed in a fit of giggles.

She couldn't let her daughter down now.

Chapter Eleven

The bakery was ready in the nick of time, with all the tables set and the counter cleared for everyone to place their offerings. Marnie took coats and guided people in, providing them with drinks. There were plenty of appreciative oohs and aahs at the transformation of the little place.

At last the guest of honour arrived, and Marnie eagerly helped Pat with her coat, watching as she gazed around the room. 'Oh,' she said, eyes and cheeks shining. 'It's beautiful. It's like a proper little café!'

Marnie saw it then, for a moment; the bakery transformed, with a fresh new sign and little gingham curtains at the window. She shook herself. 'What a shame Matt isn't well enough to be here, poor thing.'

'Oh, I know, he's so disappointed, but he's full of cold. Best not to share it around. I'll take him some leftovers.' Her gaze was already raking over the mouthwatering display of food.

'And what about the other—'

Pat waved a hand and hurried across to the table. 'Never mind that, all sorted. You've got enough to worry about.'

Marnie would've liked more information, but Pat was already loading her plate and chatting to Gloria, so she had no choice but to trust that all was in hand. Hopefully Matt would be rested enough to make an appearance later.

The evening couldn't have been more successful. Everyone ate and drank their fill, and there was plenty to choose from; David had made a cauliflower and chickpea curry, Gloria and Bob brought their homemade rice and peas, Matt had sent mince pies, Christmas biscuits and Christmas pudding and Andrew brought a Tesco's chocolate cake in the shape of a reindeer head that went down very well with the children. The little room was bright with fairy lights and bubbling with the sound of talk and laughter. Children skipped between tables, filling their fists with cakes and biscuits, huddling in corners away from their distracted parents to eat them.

The only person who didn't appear to be enjoying himself was Andrew; he stood at the edge of the room, talking to no one and eating nothing, hands in his jeans pockets as he glowered at the ground, studiously avoiding the eye of anyone nearby. The only time he smiled was when his phone buzzed, and he looked at it briefly.

Just as Marnie was wondering whether to approach him, he pulled at the neck of the soft, checked shirt he wore, glancing around with an expression of desperation, catching Marnie's eye. He gave a small nod, and she flushed, embarrassed that she'd been staring at him.

Turning away, she saw David hiding in the kitchen, grinning as he stuffed a mince pie into his mouth.

'How many of those have you had?' she asked as she went over to him, glad of the distraction.

He shrugged. 'Who counts at Christmas? Great spread, you've done an amazing job here.' He took a biscuit out of his pocket and shoved it into his mouth. 'Should be proud of yourself.'

Marnie smiled, looking around at the happy crowd of people. 'Oh, it was nothing really.'

David brushed his hands down his trousers, leaving a smear of crumbs on each leg. 'So, how's it going with Handsome Andrew?'

'Hush, stop that.' She batted him on the arm and glanced behind them, but no one was close enough to hear. 'And stop smirking like that, I told you, I don't even like the man.' She didn't know why she was blushing. And she really wished she could stop.

'Oh, that's a shame,' David said, still smirking. 'Because he's been looking at you all evening.'

'He has not!'

Marnie couldn't help but glance over to where Andrew stood, leaning against the wall near the door. He was indeed looking at her, and she found it impossible to tear her own gaze away as their eyes met, feeling for a moment as though there was no one in the room but the two of them, until at last he broke off, staring at the floor and kicking at a stray roast potato.

Clearing her throat, she glanced at David, who was grinning as he watched on. 'And you're looking particularly glam today,' he said. 'Any special reason you got dressed up?' He nudged her in the ribs and eyeballed Andrew pointedly.

Marnie's cheeks burned. 'Oh shut up,' she said. The truth was she had bought a new top and skirt, a flattering outfit that nipped her in at the waist nicely and looked pretty good with the knee-high boots she was wearing, she had to admit. But that was just because she wanted to look nice for the special occasion, that was all; no other reason, she thought, sneaking a glance at Andrew again over David's shoulder.

'What's going on here?' Greg stood in the doorway, frowning. 'What are you pair up to, hiding out together? Come on, David, Gloria seems to think I'm the one who knits, she keeps asking me about making little Santas for her Christmas tree. I haven't got a clue, help me.'

David caught Marnie's eye as Greg guided him out, pulling a face and grinning. He loved showing off his skills, however much he pretended otherwise.

Marnie went to check the counter, refilling plates and bowls where necessary. From the corner of her eye, she watched Lauren and Emma giggling together as they piled their plates with sweet treats. And she kept her back to the door, where Andrew stood, refusing to let herself look that way.

Then a raised voice whipped through the room, causing a sudden hush and a turning of shocked faces towards that corner.

Andrew stood, red-faced and scowling, with Gloria, who had her hand stretched out towards him. She was frozen, wide-eyed with shock. Marnie couldn't imagine that this woman, one of the kindest she knew, could have done anything to cause offence.

Andrew glanced around at the silent room, seeming to come to his senses. 'I'm sorry, Gloria. It's just that I'm not a face-stroking kind of person and I—I . . .'

He looked miserable, and Marnie didn't know whether to pity him or feel angry on Gloria's behalf.

Gloria laughed, and the tension in the room eased a little. 'Oh no, dear, I wouldn't dare. You've got a little . . .' She indicated her own cheek and Andrew wiped his, his hand coming away smeared with glitter. Perhaps he'd been a little too enthusiastic when he was making the table decorations earlier.

'I—I . . .' He glanced around, and even from where she stood, Marnie could see his chest heaving. He looked at Pat. 'Sorry. I—I just can't—Tell Matt I'm sorry.'

He grabbed Rosie, who was stoically enduring cuddles and pats from a group of rather too eager village children, and ran from the bakery.

Everyone stared. No one spoke. No one moved, except Pat, who followed him with a look of determination.

The room was immediately filled with the hubbub of voices again, as people bent heads together and discussed Andrew's shortcomings, now he'd gone. Marnie hurried after Pat, to make sure she was steady with her stick.

As she stepped outside the door she saw Andrew and Pat huddled together on the village street. She could hear only snatches of their conversation.

'. . . the point, without her,' Andrew was saying, and his voice throbbed with grief. '. . . not the same, and I knew I'd just spoil it for everyone, it's just like last time when—'

Pat laid a hand on his arm. '. . . want you to . . . time to start . . .'

Andrew tipped his head back. '. . . at home it's like she's still . . . kid myself that she's just working late, or walking by the brook, or out with her friends and she'll fall out of a taxi any moment, slurring that we're soulmates, you know, and I just . . . to stay in the cottage with Rosie and imagine her back to life.'

This was too much. She was being intrusive, eavesdropping on such a personal conversation. Such a painful one. She turned towards the bakery.

'What about Marnie?'

Pat's use of her name stilled her. She froze, listening harder than ever.

'Don't ruin it for her, she's worked so hard. Just, take a break and come back in a bit.'

Silence for a moment.

'You like her, don't you? Please do this for her.'

Marnie's heart beat so hard that she feared it would drown out his response. But she heard it, just.

'All right,' he said. 'Okay. I don't want to let her down.'

*

The rest of the evening passed in a blur.

Marnie had dived back into the bakery before Pat could find her eavesdropping, her mind reeling. She didn't understand what she'd heard, that Andrew would put himself out like this for *her*. He was obviously struggling, clearly it was all too much for him without his wife, especially at this time of year.

Anne Walker took her arm as soon as she stepped in, and started talking immediately. 'Well, I could've told you that was going to happen, we're lucky it wasn't worse really, I told you he had a temper, didn't I? Of course, you know about the year when he . . .'

Marnie shook herself out of Anne's grip. 'Excuse me,' she said her voice firm. 'I need to check the food.'

She had no intention of checking anything, in fact she'd somehow lost her appetite and the noise in the room was giving her a headache. She smiled at the people who spoke to her, nodded as they thanked her, watched as they ate every last scrap of food. She helped to clear the tables when everyone was done, and protested when she was shooed away to leave others to wash up.

But she felt as though she was only half present. Part of her still lingered in the cold street, listening to Andrew and Pat's conversation, trying to understand it.

Just as everything was tidied away, a loud, deep voice broke through the happy hum. 'Ho, ho, ho.'

They all turned to see a figure by the Christmas tree, dressed in red with his stomach clearly plumped out by a cushion. Relief washed over her; Matt had promised to play this part, and she'd been worried that he wasn't well enough. They couldn't have the bring and share without Santa, the children would have been so disappointed.

Marnie squinted. But surely that wasn't Matt. Surely she recognised those blue eyes peering over the fake beard . . .

Gratitude flooded through her. It was Andrew. He must have made a huge effort to come back here, and to put on this show of festive cheer.

And he'd done it for her.

The children were already lining up to receive their presents, hopping up and down excitedly and ripping the paper off as soon as they'd received their gift and thanked Santa. Pens and colouring books. Marnie smiled. Some things had not changed in Babblebrook over the years.

'And now,' Andrew-Santa boomed. 'One extra present, to thank the woman who made this happen. And what an amazing job she's done. Marnie.'

A shock bolted through Marnie at the sound of her name, and she felt her face redden. Embarrassed, she waved a hand and scuttled towards the kitchen. 'Oh, no,' she said. 'It's nothing, please, I hardly did a thing, it wasn't much work or . . . Just carry on without me.'

But everyone applauded and laughed, and some even began to chant her name. Grinning, David took her by the elbow and guided her to the front of the room as she blushed furiously and tried to smile through her embarrassment.

'Come on,' Andrew said gently. 'Can't hide away forever.'

Marnie disagreed; she'd done a pretty good job of it so far.

'Open it later,' he whispered as he handed her the present. Marnie thought she saw a little glint in his eye, but she was too busy hurrying back to her seat to think about it.

Chapter Twelve

The rest of the tidying up took place the next day, carried out by a band of volunteers that were still enthusiastic, if a little jaded. Pat and Matt came, but Marnie insisted they sit and watch. They both looked tired, and Matt was still a bit sniffly.

David and Greg were the next to arrive. Greg immediately set to work, folding tables and chairs and leaning them against the wall.

'I'll just make us all a nice cup of tea,' David said, having chatted to Pat and Matt for a good ten minutes.

'Bring through the mince pies,' Pat called, as he headed to the kitchen.

'But don't eat too many of them,' Greg added. Marnie noticed how he stared at them though, as he sipped his tea and watched the others eat, a look of yearning in his eyes.

Groups of villagers trickled in, helping to pack everything away, sweep the floor, wash up all the cups and plates. And wine glasses. Andrew brought his truck, and began to pack the tables and chairs into it, the muscles tensing under the soft material of his shirt.

Marnie tried not to watch him. He frowned as he worked, looking every bit the surly neighbour she'd first thought him to be. And he could be sharp, he could be rude. God knows, she'd seen that. But now, she wondered about the side of him that she'd occasionally seen; the flashes of warmth beneath that bad temper. She'd seen it in the way he cared for his little dog, and in the way he'd welcomed Lauren's interest in her. She'd seen it in his acceptance of their interference when they'd decorated his house, when he helped her with her ankle, and the keyring he'd made her. And in his emergency-Santa performance the day before, smiling at the children and crouching to talk quietly to the shy ones, when she knew that all the time his heart was breaking. There was something nurturing in his nature, hidden below that grouchy exterior. She wondered, for a moment, what it would feel like to be the one he was nurturing.

At one point, she saw him huddled in a corner with David, both crouched over Rosie. David spoke earnestly, and Andrew nodded, looking serious. David was probably telling him to put the little thing on a diet, Marnie thought.

Slowly, they stripped the bakery back down, removing the pretty tablecloths and napkins, packing away the crockery ready to go back to the village hall.

'Shall we leave the Christmas tree?' Marnie asked.

Matt looked around the front of the shop. It felt bare, and a little bleak, the faded paint and shabby counter more stark somehow, now the cheerful clutter of the previous night had been removed. He nodded. 'I think so, don't you, Pat?'

'Ooh yes, lovely,' she said, beaming. 'The more Christmas gubbins the better.'

It was as though she didn't see the shabbiness of the bakery at all, Marnie thought. As though she still saw it all as it had been a decade ago. From the corner of her eye she noticed Andrew running his thumb over the chipped counter, frowning.

'Right,' she said brightly. 'All done, I think.'

'Where's Lauren today?' Matt asked.

'I left her doing homework with Emma.' Marnie had been delighted that the girls had made this arrangement the day before, and had made no word of complaint that there seemed to be a lot of chat and giggling, and not much homework taking place.

'Such good girls,' Pat said. Marnie had to agree. 'Take some of those biscuits for them, will you?'

Marnie knew they would welcome any such treats. 'Are you sure?'

'You'd be doing us a favour,' Matt said. 'We'll never sell them all before Christmas.'

Pat whacked her stick into the side of his leg, so that he jumped and gave a yelp. 'Oops,' she said, smiling innocently. 'Slipped.'

'Come on,' Marnie said, helping Pat to her feet as everyone filed out. 'Let's get you out of here.'

Matt snorted, an unusually cynical sound from him. 'You'll be lucky, she'll stay here till she kicks the bucket if you give her the chance.'

Pat waved her stick again. 'If you start banging on about retiring again, I'll have your eye out with this, don't think I won't.'

Matt sighed and took her other arm as the three of them walked out of the shop. 'You're seventy-six, love, and I'm not far behind. Can't carry on forever.'

Pat's face set into a look of pure determination. 'Just watch me.'

Marnie settled them into their cosy front room. Dozens of cards were now pinned to the wooden beams, showing pictures of robins, glittery snow scenes and cute puppies and kittens in stockings, and the fire was still warm in the grate. They were soon on the sofa, and Marnie told herself that they were fine, they were fit for their age and surrounded by friends.

As she unlocked her front door, weighed down by a bag filled with biscuits, Andrew pulled up in his truck.

'Hey there, songbird,' he called. Marnie flushed. She'd rather forget that he caught her singing a daft version of a Christmas carol about him. Especially as her singing was so bad.

'Hey there, Santa,' she said.

He smiled. 'Good job, yesterday. You've got a flair for that, haven't you?'

Marnie shrugged, embarrassed. She'd never thought of herself as the kind of person who had a flair for anything. A squirrel scuttled across Andrew's lawn and scampered up the stand of his bird table. It seemed to be struggling, losing its grip, and eventually sliding slowly back to the ground with a startled expression. Marnie frowned. What was wrong with it?

'Opened your present yet?' Andrew asked, stepping down from the truck and walking up his garden path, straightening the giant reindeer on his way. He made no comment about the squirrel, now scrambling up a tree with apparently no problem whatsoever.

'Hmm?' She dragged her eyes away from the squirrel. 'Not yet.' She had been so exhausted after the bring and share that she'd dumped the present on the counter when she got home and forgotten all about it. 'Thank you for that, by the way, it really meant a lot that you did it. Being Father Christmas, I mean, not just the present . . . Meant a lot. To the children, I mean.' She cleared her throat and shifted from foot to foot, feeling herself begin to blush. She didn't know why. But she couldn't stop thinking about Andrew saying that he didn't want to let her down.

He nodded, giving that half-smile that made her stomach drop, and disappeared into his cottage.

Curious now, Marnie let herself in, barely acknowledging Emma and Lauren as they sat at the kitchen table, surrounded by empty cups and chocolate wrappers, putting down their phones and turning their attention to their schoolbooks rather hurriedly. She dumped the bag of biscuits between them, hardly aware of their murmurs of delight when they discovered the contents.

Marnie hurried over to where she'd left the present last night, ripping off the paper.

The gift was a soft toy donkey, wearing a Santa hat and with a little button on its backside that said, 'push here'.

Marnie did, and the toy played a tinny version of the tune to 'Little Donkey'. She laughed to herself, imagining Andrew grinning as he picked it out.

*

Emma stayed for tea, a comforting cottage pie that oozed through the mashed potato topping, and headed off afterwards. She and Lauren hugged and giggled on the doorstep, saying their goodbyes as though they were about to be parted for months, and not see each other at the bus stop the next morning. Marnie refrained from asking them to close the door. She would put up with a blast of cold air to see her daughter this happy.

'Remember when you were little?' Marnie asked, as Lauren helped her load the dishwasher. 'And we used to have girls' nights when Dad was out? Watch a film and paint your nails?'

Lauren smiled. 'And you let me stay up late.'

'And eat sweets. Shall we ... we could do that tonight? Find a film?'

Lauren wrinkled her nose. 'I'm not a kid anymore, Mum. And anyway, it's school tomorrow.' She took the dishwasher tablet Marnie passed her and shut the door. 'I'm going to FaceTime Dad,' she said.

Marnie sighed. This refrain of Lauren's was one she heard on almost-daily basis since her daughter became a teenager, and most of the time she found it funny. Jo, who had two older daughters, assured it was perfectly normal. But at times, like now, it felt like a rejection, and that stung. Sometimes she still saw flashes of the little girl Lauren had been. She'd learned to treasure each one.

She looked around the kitchen. It was tidy and calm. Unwrapping the Christmas cake, she breathed in its rich scent as she pricked it with a skewer. There was a scrabbling at the door, and she went to open it.

'Hello, Chubs,' she said. 'Escaped again?'

Rosie wagged her tail and sat by the fridge, gazing expectantly at Marnie. She took down the little bowl with bones painted on that she'd bought, and put a bit of ham into it. Rosie guzzled it happily.

'Greedy guts,' Marnie said.

She took the brandy bottle and gently poured a little into the holes she'd made in the cake. She ignored the tap at the door, knowing Andrew would walk in without waiting for invitation.

He chuckled. 'Caught you hitting the bottle, have I?'

'You can see very well I'm putting it in the cake,' she said, laughing.

Both of their gazes fell on the toy donkey, lying on the counter. Neither said anything, but Andrew smirked.

He took a deep sniff. 'Ah, no wonder Rosie likes it here so much. You like the way it smells, don't you, girl?'

Marnie put the cap back on the bottle and wrapped the cake again. She glanced at Andrew out of the corner of her eye. He looked dishevelled and tired, his eyes red-rimmed; she hadn't noticed that when they'd met at the front of the cottages, but perhaps she'd been too distracted by him telling her she had flair.

'You still recovering from all your work yesterday?' he asked, pulling out a chair and sitting at the table. Apparently he had no intention of leaving anytime soon.

Marnie sat opposite him, shrugging. 'Oh, I didn't do that much, really.'

'Well,' he said softly, clearing his throat. 'Like I said earlier, I thought you did a great job.'

'Thank you. And thanks again for, you know, coming and being Santa.'

'Ah.' He leaned back in his seat, tapping his fingers lightly on the table, stretching his leg out so that it brushed against Marnie's. The accidental touch jolted through her. 'You'd worked so hard, so . . .' He shrugged, smiled. 'Did you go to all this stuff when you were a kid? The bring and share and carol singing and all that?'

'I—What?' She was a little taken aback. 'I didn't realise you knew I'd lived here before.'

He nodded, reaching down to lift Rosie onto his knee. 'Yeah, you said when we went for a walk that time, about how you used to live here when you were a kid but your mum moved you around a lot.' He tickled Rosie under the chin. 'But Babblebrook felt like home.'

Marnie stared. He had said nothing when she spoke of all this, and she'd assumed he hadn't been listening. But he'd taken in every word, it seemed. She wasn't used to someone paying such attention to her. 'Oh well—Yes, when we were around. The bring and share was our favourite because of all the food and the presents. David ate so much he was sick, once.'

Andrew chuckled.

'It must have been tough, though,' he said.

'What?'

'All that moving around.' His blue eyes held her gaze, full of sympathy and genuine interest.

'Oh.' Marnie gathered the few crumbs that sat on the table, brushing them into a small pile, thinking of the keyring. No one else had ever acknowledged the effect all that moving around as a child had on her, and she was taken aback that this man, who had at times been the rudest she'd known, had listened to what she'd told him and apparently considered how it had made her feel. For once, she fought the urge to downplay it and deny the importance of her feelings. Perhaps if he thought she was worth considering then she should too.

'I suppose it was a bit, yes. Always trying to make new friends, you know? And then as soon as we did, she'd move us again. And none of those places felt like home, we were never there long enough to decorate our rooms or anything like that, and David's got no sense of direction you know, he used to get lost every time we went to a new school.'

He was smiling at her, something in his expression causing her to stumble in her train of thought. Something playful.

'What?'

'I bet you were cheeky.'

Marnie hiccupped a laugh, embarrassed. 'What? No, I wasn't!'

He grinned outright now, nodding as he spoke. 'Oh, yes you were. Weren't you? You pretend to be all serious and straightlaced, but I think you're secretly still that cheeky kid.'

'I . . .' Marnie flushed, laughing. That twinkle was back in his eye, unmistakable this time, and she didn't know how to respond. But she thought she might be enjoying it. He was off the mark, she thought, she'd always been the sensible one as a child. But a memory flashed through her mind of a time she'd been baking with Matt and had flicked icing onto his face as she'd giggled uncontrollably. How had she forgotten that?

Andrew raised his eyebrows. 'I bet Pat has photos.'

'Don't you dare!'

He laughed and loosened his hold on Rosie, who took the opportunity to scrabble onto the table and make a beeline for the crumb-pile Marnie had made.

'Hey, no you don't,' he said, scooping her up. Not before she'd slobbered over Marnie's table a little though. 'Sorry.'

'It's fine, I don't mind.' She was surprised to find this was actually true. She even felt a little giddy as she rose to fetch a cloth.

'It's nice to see her so relaxed here, though,' he said. 'She's a nervous thing, she gets panic attacks.'

Marnie stared. 'What?'

'She gets anxious, poor girl. That's why I'm going to let her—'

Marnie laughed. 'But she's a dog!'

Andrew looked affronted, stroking Rosie's head. She nuzzled his face. 'She still has feelings. Anyway, we've got a plan, haven't we, girl? I'm going to let her—'

Marnie's phone buzzed, and Matt's name came up. She frowned. He never called her.

'Sorry, it's Matt,' she said. 'I'd better take this.'

Andrew nodded.

'Hi, Matt,' she said. 'You okay?'

She heard him take a shuddering breath, and a chill crept over Marnie's skin.

'What is it?'

Andrew glanced up at her. She held his gaze.

Matt took a breath. 'It's Pat,' he said, his voice shaking. 'I need help.'

Chapter Thirteen

Marnie didn't even need to speak. Andrew took one look at her face and was by her side in a moment.

'It's all right,' he said, placing an arm around her shoulder and guiding her to the front door. 'Whatever it is, I'll help.'

Marnie managed to garble out a version of what had happened as she pulled her boots on with trembling hands. She was holding back tears, just. Matt had sounded so upset, so frail and afraid.

Andrew nodded, his face grim. 'I knew something like this was on the cards,' he muttered. 'Should've done something. Wait,' he said, as she opened the door. 'Where's Lauren?'

'In her room.'

She heard him run to the bottom of the stairs and call her, talking in a low, urgent tone. 'And please can you look after the dog?' he called.

Marnie heard Lauren's footsteps thud down the stairs as they left.

'They're in the bakery,' Marnie said.

Andrew nodded. 'Of course they are.'

Marnie didn't understand. It was Sunday night, and they were an elderly couple, however much Pat tried to deny it. Why weren't they at home with their feet up?

The door of the bakery was unlocked and they rushed in. It smelled sweetly of syrup and gingerbread. Immediately, Marnie heard Pat's irritated voice. She almost wept with relief.

'Oh hell's bells,' Pat said from her position on the floor when she saw them. 'What did you go and call them for? Such a flipping fuss.'

'Nice to see you too,' Marnie said, kneeling at her side.

Andrew went over to Matt, who had stood up to greet them. Marnie could see him trembling, and see the relief on his face at their arrival. 'Cup of tea?' Andrew said, clasping Matt's shoulder and then disappearing into the kitchen.

Marnie turned her attention back to Pat. She tried to shift and winced, pulling a face. Despite her brave attempts to hide her pain, she was pale and sweat gathered on her forehead. Marnie's stomach twisted. She took off her coat and folded it to make a pillow for Pat.

'Just rest for a minute,' she said. 'Have you called an ambulance?'

Matt nodded. 'Here soon, they said. Few more minutes is all.'

'Fuss and nonsense,' Pat said. But her voice was weak.

'What were you doing here on a Sunday night?' Marnie asked, working to keep the accusatory tone from her voice. Now was not the time.

'She insisted,' Matt said. 'Wanted us to bake a gingerbread house and get it decorated and in the window for tomorrow morning.'

That explained the delicious aroma. Marnie stopped herself protesting that this was not an emergency that required them to be working on a Sunday night, that she could have baked it for them.

'It'll look lovely in the window,' Pat said, her mouth sitting in a stubborn line, as though Marnie had spoken her thoughts aloud. 'Bring in a few more customers.'

Andrew returned with a mug of tea for Matt, who took a gulp. He was in shock, Marnie thought. Neither of them were in a good way. Matt was right, they worked too hard.

Andrew took his jumper off and laid it gently over Pat. She didn't protest. She must be feeling bad.

'There you go, milady,' he said, his voice light. 'All this just for a bit of attention, eh? You didn't have to go this far, we're happy to wait on you hand and foot anyway.'

'Be off with you,' Pat said. She was smiling though, and Marnie was grateful for this side of Andrew she was seeing more and more of. Before, she might have expected him to be grouchy and snappish under pressure, but she found herself unsurprised that he was a calm and reassuring presence right now.

A blue light flashed through the windows of the bakery as the ambulance pulled up. Matt made towards the door, putting his mug on the counter with a jerk so that tea slopped out.

The paramedics were calm and cheerful, talking gently to Matt about what had happened and to Pat about what would happen next.

'What a silly fuss,' she said. 'I'm fine really, just a stupid little trip and now everyone's acting as though I'm at death's door.'

They chuckled. 'No one's saying that at all. We just need to get you checked out.'

She winced and clenched her fists as they lifted her onto the stretcher, careful though they were. Marnie swallowed tears. She would be no help to anyone if she broke down.

'Oh,' Pat cried as they began to carry her to the ambulance, 'Oh no, no!'

Everyone froze, alarmed at her distress. She must be in such pain, Marnie thought.

'What about the bakery? What about tomorrow, Matt can't manage on his own and I—'

There was a crash as Matt swept his mug from the counter and it smashed against the floor. Startled, Marnie jumped. She'd never seen him angry.

'Oh, forget about the bakery for once,' he yelled. 'You're what's important, think on that, forget work for a minute! This bloody bakery will be the death of you.'

*

At the hospital, it was soon established that Pat had broken her hip and would need an operation.

Marnie was torn. She wanted to stay, but she didn't want to leave Lauren alone for too long. Matt was looking worn out, and she was worried about him as well as Pat.

'You get back home,' Andrew said. 'I'll stay for a bit, keep Matt company.'

'You sure?' she asked.

She glanced over at Matt, who was sitting by Pat's bed and holding her hand as she waited to go into surgery. She wanted to wave a magic wand and fix everything. She wanted it to be ten years ago, when they had still seemed invincible.

'There's nothing you can do here, and Lauren needs you,' Andrew said. 'I'll make sure Matt gets plenty of tea and biscuits, don't you worry.' He smiled, his eyes crinkling up.

'All right,' she said. 'Thank you.' She had a ridiculous urge to kiss him. 'Pop in and let me know how they are when you get back?'

After she'd said her goodbyes and turned to walk away she heard Matt's voice. 'Thanks for being here, Andrew. Can't be easy for you, we know that.'

There was a moment's pause, in which she was sure she heard Andrew take a shuddering breath, and she thought again of the conversation she'd heard him have with Pat. 'Ah. Anything for you, Matt.'

*

The cottage was quiet when she got home, the living room in darkness. This wasn't like Lauren, she thought, bending down to switch the tree lights on. That was better, at least.

'Lauren,' she called. 'You okay?'

The kitchen was empty too. She went upstairs, listening for the reassuring sound of YouTube or FaceTime from Lauren's phone. Nothing.

'All right, darling?' she called, tapping on her bedroom door. 'Can I come in?' She made herself wait for a reply.

'Uh-huh,' came the noncommittal reply.

Lauren sat up as she walked in, but Marnie had glimpsed her lying curled in a foetal position on the bed, cuddling Rosie like a teddy bear. Her eyes were watery and her nose was red.

Marnie sat on the edge of the bed, reaching out to stroke Rosie, who thumped her tail in response, but stayed firmly in Lauren's arms. 'You worried about Pat?' she asked.

Lauren shook her head and sniffed. 'I mean, I am, but it's not just that.'

Marnie paused. 'Okay. Well, Pat's broken her hip but don't worry, she's having an operation to fix it.'

Lauren pressed a hand over her mouth, and her eyes filled again. 'Oh, poor Pat, she'll hate that.'

'She was not best pleased, it's safe to say.' Marnie smiled, trying to appear reassuring. 'But she'll be fine.'

'And poor Matt too!'

'Also not best pleased. But Andrew's looking after him.'

'That's nice of him.'

'So what else is upsetting you?'

Lauren drew in a shaky breath, and wiped a tear that trickled down her cheek. 'I don't want to hurt your feelings.'

Marnie was taken aback. Lauren had dealt with so much, the split and then moving to Babblebrook, starting a new school, and she was still thinking about Marnie's feelings. 'Oh darling. I'm a grown up, you don't need to worry about that.'

Lauren brought Rosie in for an even tighter cuddle, and the dog grunted slightly. Marnie was worried for a second that the fat little pooch might actually pop, but she just wriggled until Lauren released her grip a bit. Lauren buried her face into her fur and muttered, 'I miss Dad.'

Relieved that Lauren was able to talk about this at last, and touched that it had been concern for her own feelings that had made Lauren reluctant to broach it, Marnie pulled her into a hug, careful not to squish Rosie any harder. There was only so much love a dog could take.

'Sorry,' Lauren muttered.

Marnie sat back, holding her daughter by the shoulders and dipping her head so that they made eye contact. 'Oh, darling, you never need to be sorry for that, and you never need to worry that it might upset me! I know you love your dad, and of course you miss him. He misses you too, you know. And he loves you. So much.'

Lauren buried her head into Marnie's shoulder, something she hadn't done for years. 'Then why is he leaving?' she wailed. 'How can he leave me if he loves me?'

Marnie bit her lip. She'd tortured herself with similar thoughts about Ian – he loved her and he loved Lauren, she knew that. Never doubted it, even now. But how he could hurt them both so much? She missed him too, and a part of her still felt that she should have forgiven him and worked on their marriage; seeing Lauren so upset pierced her with a fresh pang of guilt.

'He's . . . I think he's struggling a bit at the moment.'

Lauren snorted. '*He's* struggling!'

'We all are. I think—I think he's trying to make himself a better man.' Too late. 'And he'll FaceTime as much as he can when he's there.' She squeezed Lauren and smoothed her hair away from her damp face. 'And he'll come back to you an even better dad.'

Lauren nodded, sniffing. 'I hate him.'

'He loves you.'

'I know.'

They waited for a moment, petting Rosie who yawned and snuggled deeper into Lauren's arms. 'Well,' she said at last, giving Marnie a smile. 'A hot chocolate always helps when you're sad, doesn't it?'

Marnie laughed, ruffling her daughter's hair. And made her way downstairs.

Chapter Fourteen

Hot chocolates drunk and tears mopped up, Lauren at last settled to sleep. It was school the next day, and Marnie could see she was exhausted. It had been a long night. She even allowed Marnie to tuck her in.

'Snug as a bug in a rug,' Marnie whispered.

'Weirdo,' came the reply.

Marnie laughed. This was becoming their new routine, equivalent to the warm milk and stories from when Lauren was little.

Rosie snuggled down too, resting her head on the pillow next to Lauren's. Marnie was sure that wasn't hygienic, but they both looked so content, she couldn't bear to part them. And what harm could really come of it? Not so long ago, she would have insisted on moving Rosie, but now she just closed the door softly, and crept down the stairs.

The living room was cosy, with the fire flickering and the tree lights twinkling. It looked so much better since they'd decorated. Walking into it felt like walking into the embrace of an old friend, one you shared many memories with. Marnie's nerves still jangled a little, her thoughts immediately going to Pat and Matt, and then to her brave and caring daughter. She wished things were easier for them all. But she was glad to be here.

Picking up her phone, she checked her bank balance; one client still hadn't paid her, and was studiously ignoring every reminder she sent. She didn't know what else to do. She scrolled through her emails with waning hope of finding more offers of work. Well, she thought, this was always going to be a quiet time of year, everyone was winding down for the holidays, not planning work deadlines and targets. She tried her spam folder, just in case. Nothing, not even from one of her regular clients.

Marnie tried to stay calm, gazing at the pile of brightly wrapped presents sitting under the tree until her eyes blurred. She'd bought all the gifts, she'd ordered all the food. Christmas was paid for, at least, and she had savings to fall back on if she really needed to.

She closed her eyes and tried to will away the panic that was starting to boil in her belly. What if no more work came in? She'd have to break into her nest egg while she searched for another job. And what if Lily changed her mind about letting them stay in the cottage? Even if she could afford to move she didn't want to; Lauren had just settled and Marnie liked Babblebrook.

She breathed slowly, counting seconds, trying to calm her nerves.

Absently, she picked up a Christmas card that someone had delivered, turning it over and doodling on the back. Sometimes drawing calmed her. Her mind steadied as the images of hanging baskets and pots of flowers emerged, next to a few tables and chairs set on a pavement.

She added checked tablecloths, pots of tea and cups and saucers. And slices of cake, naturally.

She sighed, imagining the gentle sound of happy conversation and laughter, the warmth of the sun and the smell of freshly brewed coffee. Focused now, and calm, she reached for the envelope the card had come in, drawing more tables and chairs, a window with tieback curtains, fairy lights strung across the ceiling and a log burner in the corner. She had just started on shelves with books and plants when a noise made her stop.

The knock on the door was quiet, but it still made her jump. She knew it would be Andrew and stood to open it, automatically patting her hair down. He hadn't used the front door since that first day in Babblebrook, when he'd been so rude and she had been so dishevelled. At least she was dressed, this time.

'I didn't know if you'd still be awake,' he said, when she opened the door. 'But I saw the living room light on so . . .' He rubbed a hand over his eyes as he leaned his broad shoulder against the side of the porch.

'No of course, come in,' Marnie said, stepping aside. She managed to stop herself immediately demanding to know every detail of how Pat and Matt were, but only just.

'Lauren in bed?' he whispered, as they crept to the living room.

Marnie nodded. 'And Rosie's in with her, I'm afraid.'

A smile twitched at his lips briefly. 'How sweet, she'll love that.'

'Drink?' Marnie asked. 'Tea, hot chocolate or . . .'

They spoke at the same time. 'Something stronger.'

Marnie laughed. 'All I have is the Christmas cake brandy, I'm afraid.'

'I'll take it,' Andrew said, following her through to the kitchen. 'If the Christmas cake can spare it.' He smiled as she poured a slug into two glasses and pushed one towards him. He looked tired.

They sat at the table, both taking a sip of brandy. The taste was rich and strong, warming Marnie as she swallowed. At last, Andrew turned to the subject she was burning to ask about.

'Pat's having surgery tomorrow. They've made her comfortable, you know, and she's still herself.' His lips quirked into that little smile again.

'Oh yes, ruling the roost, I expect,' Marnie said wryly.

Andrew nodded, tapping his finger onto a biscuit crumb and idly weaving patterns with it on the surface of the table. He'd rolled up the sleeves of his shirt and Marnie found herself staring at the gentle flexing of his strong forearms, imagining tracing her finger over them. 'Of course, she was complaining that they wouldn't let her have a cup of coffee when I left.'

She dragged her gaze back to his face. 'Ha, well that's good, I suppose.'

'Yes,' he agreed. He frowned, and Marnie felt that she knew where his thoughts were, because hers were there too.

'I'm almost more worried about Matt,' she said.

Andrew took another sip of brandy and nodded. 'Me too. I've known him since we moved to the village, and they've always been so . . . I've never seen him like this. He was upset and, and angry, I suppose, and I suppose that's—'

'To be expected.'

'Yes.'

They were quiet for a moment, nothing but the occasional snap of the fire in the living room and the gentle creaking of an old house. Neither of them wanted to face this, Marnie thought. But Pat and Matt were their friends. They had to.

Andrew spoke just as she was taking a breath to broach the subject. She was happy to let him speak first. 'But this seems almost more than would be expected, you know?'

Marnie nodded. 'I think he's been upset for a while. At least for as long as we've been back, I just think I didn't really want to . . .'

'Face it, I know. Me too.'

'Is it too much for them, do you think? The bakery?'

Marnie found herself holding her breath waiting for the reply. She knew the answer. She still didn't want to hear it.

Andrew sighed, placing the glass down and resting his head in his hands. 'I think so. They're too stubborn for their own good too. I keep offering to fix it up a bit for them but they won't hear of it, Pat keeps saying Matt can do the work, but it's too much for him. Matt keeps saying they'll pay me the going rate when I know they're not making enough money for that, I mean there's never anyone in there. I go in most days,

I hardly see anyone, they all shop at Tesco instead. And I've heard people saying that it's just the same old stuff they sell, but I don't see what's wrong with that, and you can't expect Matt to try new recipes now. I think it's just getting on top of them.'

For a moment, Marnie found herself arguing internally. What did he know? She'd known Pat and Matt for years, much longer than Andrew had, she would know if they were struggling to cope.

And perhaps she would have known, had she been there.

She sighed. 'They're pig headed, the pair of them. But it's their pride and joy. It's beyond the pale, to think they'd give it up.'

He snorted a small laugh. 'Lauren's right, you do talk like you're ninety.'

Marnie flushed. 'I do not!'

'Don't be angry, it's kind of cute.'

'I am not angry.' She took an angry swallow of brandy, more than she intended, and it caught in her throat, so that she choked, spitting some onto the table. Great. Andrew was openly chuckling as she stood to get a dishcloth and wiped up the splattered liquid with more force than was necessary.

'You could do it,' he said suddenly.

'Do what?' She sat down with a thud and took her drink again, swirling what was left of the contents.

'Run the bakery.'

Marnie stopped with the glass suspended in mid-air and her mouth gaping. 'What? I couldn't.'

'You could, you know. You were brilliant at the bring and share, organising everything and getting it all ready and your food is always . . . It smells really good anyway, and Rosie likes it, so I think . . .'

Marnie laughed. 'Rosie likes it? Well I might as well set up a dog food factory then.'

'Come on,' he said softly. 'You're a good cook, that's all I meant.'

Marnie sighed. 'I just can't imagine it without them.' To her horror, her voice wobbled on the last word, and she felt tears burn her eyes.

Pat and Matt had always been the one thing she could rely on, right back from when she was a child; even when she'd been living away and married to Ian she'd been able to call them for advice or just a catch up. They were always full of energy and enthusiasm. She couldn't bear for that to change.

'I know,' he said, reaching out to place his hand over hers. His palm was warm and rough. 'Me too. They're like family. They were so good to me when I lost Jane.'

Marnie looked at him, at the wedding ring he still wore. 'I'm so sorry,' she said.

He shrugged. 'Thanks. It was shit, it still is shit a lot of days. But it's not your fault.'

Marnie waited, not sure what to say.

'And I lost it,' he said. He was staring into his glass now, addressing the remains of his brandy by all appearances. 'I was vile, I was just so angry with everyone, even with her, you know? I was . . . I was horrible to be around. Horrible.'

He shook his head.

'Swear to God, I wouldn't have made it through if it wasn't for Pat and Matt. They just, they just let me rage and break stuff—I was mean, *properly* mean to people. To everyone. And they just held me up, you know?'

He looked at her, tears trembling in his eyes now too.

'They—they fed me, they brought food and made me eat when I just wanted to die really. They tidied my house and made me shower.' He hiccupped a laugh. 'Seriously. I was a mess. I was disgusting. And they just, they listened and they were just there. All the way through. Even when everyone else stepped back, and I don't blame them, I was awful, but they were the only ones that . . . well. And now this, and I—I don't know how to help them.'

She turned the hand he still held, so that she could grip his fingers. He returned the pressure, rubbing his thumb over hers. His touch felt good, it felt right, in a way that nothing had for a long time. She wanted to stay this way all night.

'You've already helped them,' she said. 'And me.'

He looked up. 'You?'

'Yes. It would have been awful if I'd been alone when I got that call, if I'd had to . . .' Once again her voice betrayed her, and she was forced to stop.

'Well,' he said softly. 'You weren't alone.'

She held his gaze. Nothing but the snapping fire, the blue of his eyes and the touch of his hand in hers. And a feeling inside her, warm and a little frightening.

Must be the brandy.

She pulled her hand from his just as he cleared his throat and dropped his gaze. They spoke over each other.

'Well, it's time I . . .'

'It's getting late.'

They stood, Andrew's chair scraping across the floor tiles, the noise jarring through Marnie.

'Thanks for the . . .' He indicated the brandy bottle.

'Thank you for your help.'

They stood either side of the table. He nodded. Marnie smiled. Her cheeks were growing warm and she prayed he didn't notice. For heaven's sake. She wasn't a teenager, she needed to pull herself together.

She was exhausted by the events of the day, thrown off kilter by the shock. That was all.

She followed Andrew through the living room and out to the front door, smiling and waving as he walked away.

Only when she'd locked up did she remember Rosie, still snuggled with Lauren upstairs.

Chapter Fifteen

The smell of bacon frying drifted through the house, and Marnie soon heard signs of life coming from Lauren's room in response.

She had decided that they all needed a cooked breakfast to set them up for the day, after the events of the previous evening. Sausages sizzled in the pan and butter spat as the eggs and mushrooms fried.

Above, she heard Lauren's bed creak as she rose, the swish of drawers as she pulled them open.

Rosie was less patient. Soon her little footsteps cascaded down the stairs and she made an appearance in the kitchen, all happy-waggy tail and huge feed-me-please eyes.

'Yes all right, don't worry, Chubs,' Marnie said as she poured tea from the pot and a good helping of milk into Rosie's bowl. 'I've put an extra sausage in for you.'

She watched Rosie waddle over to the bowl and happily slurp up her morning cuppa. 'Although I feel like you should be on muesli or something instead, really. What do you think to that, eh? Bit of doggy muesli? Fancy that?'

Rosie ignored her, but Lauren's voice came from the doorway. 'Are you actually talking to the dog about muesli?' She giggled. 'You're mad, Mum.'

Lauren was dressed and ready for school, her hair tied back with a thick strand left on each side to artfully frame her face. She was pale, her eyes pinched and tired. 'What's this?' she asked, holding the envelope that Marnie had been doodling on the night before. 'This yours?' She peered at the paper. 'It looks great, Mum, is it a café?'

It was all Marnie could do to stop herself snatching the paper off Lauren. 'Oh, it's nothing, I was just—I don't know. Daydreaming, I suppose. Come and eat.'

Lauren put the paper on the side as she moved to the table, and Marnie slid it into her pocket. 'You're not giving me muesli, are you?' Lauren grumbled.

'As if I'd dare. Rosie is a bit fat, though, isn't she?' Marnie said, dishing up the food and putting an extra rasher of bacon on Lauren's plate, then sidling over to Rosie's bowl while Lauren's back was turned and dropping a sausage in.

Lauren sat on a chair and began squirting ketchup onto her food. She laughed. 'Maybe you should stop feeding her sausages then,' she said, without turning around.

*

Rosie had no lead and, though Marnie was almost sure she wouldn't run away, the thought of losing Andrew's precious pet was more than she could bear. She tied a length of tinsel through her collar, and led her out of the back door. Appropriately festive.

Rosie gave one last, hopeful look at her now-empty bowl before allowing herself to be led through the gate into Andrew's back garden.

Marnie walked as fast as the dog's little legs would allow. She wanted to get this over quickly, then go straight to the hospital. But she had to admit she was looking forward to seeing him; everything that had happened with Pat the night before had been awful, but it had somehow all been okay because he was there with her.

Andrew's garden was neat, a lawn edged with tidy flower beds. His hedge, like her own, backed onto a field where cows munched slowly. In the corner was a shed, and Marnie thought she heard a noise coming from it. She pushed the door open, and realised immediately that the sound was caused not by Andrew, but by a blackbird that flapped around in a panic. There was a broken window at the side, and it had presumably come in through that and got trapped. She held the door open and the bird flew out. It seemed out of character for Andrew to leave a broken window unfixed, but the whole shed looked like it was a time capsule, untouched for years.

Marnie should have gone to find Andrew, but she found herself mesmerised. As Rosie lay on the floor, grunting, Marnie stepped in, gazing round at the walls where dusty tools hung neatly, cobwebs stretched between them, breathing in the scent of sawdust and damp.

She wandered round the little workshop, carefully lifting a bowl that rested on the workbench, leaving a mark in the grime where it had sat, running her hand over the smooth surface of a set of shelves that stood in a corner.

*

The most impressive piece by far was a rocking chair, made from gleaming dark wood. On the seat lay an embroidered cushion, stitched with images of wildflowers. Marnie sat, resting her hands on the smooth arms, leaning her head back and gently rocking.

'What the hell are you doing?'

She jumped up, startled by the sharpness of Andrew's voice. He stood in the doorway, face pale and jaw clenched. The top button on his shirt was open, and she had to drag her gaze from the glimpse of his broad chest. She cleared her throat. Her mouth was suddenly dry.

'Oh, I—I brought Rosie home. She dressed up for the occasion.' Her attempt at light-heartedness didn't work; he didn't even glance at Rosie. 'These are really beautiful,' she said.

'Get out.' His face was white, voice shaking. 'Now.'

Marnie hurried to the door. She wasn't sure exactly why the shed was out of bounds, but she had a good idea. 'I . . . I'm sorry.'

He said nothing, simply stood, chest heaving a little as he breathed fast. Marnie could see the battle inside him, his desire to shout or sob, to throw something. She saw his struggle to hold it in.

At last, he nodded, standing aside so she could pass. And Marnie left.

*

She cursed herself as she drove to the hospital. Why had she not realised why the shed was left untouched, and who the chair must have belonged to? Last night they'd talked like friends, he'd opened up and there had even been a moment when she'd felt . . . what? Her mind drifted back to the warmth of his hand on hers. She dared not let herself think about it. It didn't matter now, anyway. She'd ruined everything, lumbering round his workshop like a clumsy elephant, and he would be back to the distant, grumpy man she'd first met.

Well. It was a shame, but she had more important things to worry about now.

Pat was conscious but groggy when Marnie arrived.

'What's up with you?' she asked, squinting at Marnie's hair. 'Look like you've been dragged . . . you know.' Her voice trailed off, and she closed her eyes again.

Marnie smiled at Matt as he rose to hug her. 'Sorry,' he said. 'It's the anaesthetic, she doesn't know what she's saying.'

'Stuff and nonsense,' Pat said, without opening her eyes. 'Looks a mess.'

Marnie and Matt shared an exasperated look. Marnie sat on the chair the other side of the bed to Matt, surreptitiously patting her hair down and trying to remember whether she'd brushed it that morning. With all the upset over Andrew, she thought as she tugged at a tangle, she might have forgotten.

'How's she doing?' she asked, keeping her voice low so as not to disturb Pat.

Matt smiled, but the crease in his forehead didn't shift. 'Oh, not too bad. The surgery went well, they said, they seem pretty pleased so . . . We'll get there.'

For an awful moment, Marnie thought he was going to cry. He sagged in his chair, rubbing a hand over his tired eyes. Marnie had never seen him look so small.

It was her turn now to be strong, to offer comfort just as they had always done for her. She put on a brave face.

'She's stubborn, she'll be up on her feet in no time, skipping around the pl—'

'I'm not a flipping kangaroo.'

Pat still didn't open her eyes, but it took more than major surgery to stop her making her opinion known. Despite herself, Marnie smiled. Pat looked tiny, just a pale little face and the shape of her body hidden by the blankets. But she was still herself.

Just as Marnie and Matt shared a grin, Pat became agitated. Her eyes flew open and she scrabbled at the sheets, trying to lift herself up.

'Wait,' she said. 'Wait, wait, who's . . .'

Marnie and Matt had both risen to their feet, trying to soothe her.

'What is it, love?' Matt asked.

'Why are you here?' she asked, her voice wavering. 'Who's—Who's running the shop?'

Matt stilled as he bent over her, his expression freezing over. Marnie thought for a moment that there would be another outburst, or that he would storm off.

'I'm doing it,' she said, before she had the chance to think what that entailed. 'That's why I'm here. To get the keys.'

'Oh.' Pat sank down, closing her eyes again, her face relaxing.

Matt straightened up and closed his eyes. Marnie worried that he might be about to faint, but he simply sighed and reached into his pocket. He opened his eyes as he handed the keys to her, clasping her hand in his. She felt the slight tremble there.

'Thank you,' he said.

Marnie smiled brightly. 'No problem.'

Oh God. What had she done?

Chapter Sixteen

The day was grey and cold, the bakery itself not much better, and Marnie shivered as she let herself in. She flicked on the Christmas lights, and the little sparks of colour scattering across the floor, walls and window brought some small joy, at least. She cleared up Matt's broken mug and the drying pool of spilled tea. The air still held the sweet, spicy scent of gingerbread, and Marnie found the pieces that Pat and Matt had baked last night ready to make the gingerbread house.

Here was something she could do.

Trying to feel optimistic, she turned the sign on the door to 'Open' and added the last of the mince pies and biscuits Matt had baked to the display counter. This wasn't like her, she would never usually take on a task like this without planning every eventuality first, but what else could she do? Pat and Matt needed her. Andrew's words after the bring and share drifted into her mind – 'you've got a flair for this kind of thing' – and she fizzed a little with pride. She wished harder than ever that she hadn't been so stupid that morning, going into the shed and upsetting him.

Sighing, she played the message blinking on the landline, from a confused delivery man who obviously knew

Pat and Matt well enough to be concerned that the shop wasn't open when he'd arrived that morning. Marnie returned the call, relaying the events of the previous night once again. She'd told this sad tale so many times now, to Lauren and to David, and now to this stranger, that it was beginning to feel unreal. She promised to pass on the good wishes of the local bakery that supplied bread to Pat and Matt. The sound of the receiver clicking into place seemed to echo round the shop. She doubted the bread would be missed, she had hardly seen a customer in the bakery since she'd moved back to Babblebrook.

Switching on the little radio that Matt kept in the kitchen, Marnie turned her hand to what she loved to do as Christmas carols drifted through the air. Here was something productive, at least. Something that would fill her mind and busy her hands.

She put aside the sheets of gingerbread that had gone soft and misshapen after being left out – she would break them up as a treat for the birds. She began again, heating the butter, syrup and dark sugar, mixing it with the flour and ginger, and beating until the sweet scent rose and her mouth watered. The bakery had two large ovens, but she only needed one for her task today.

Marnie didn't need a template. She'd been making these for years, and she had a good eye and steady hand. She rolled the mixture and slowly, expertly, cut pieces for each of the walls and for the roof, enough to make three. One to be the bakery, one the post office and the third the sweet shop. She cut holes for windows and added boiled sweets to make the glass.

She hummed along to 'Good King Wenceslas' as she tidied, allowing herself to think of nothing but the next step, of how the finished houses would look. She would make some more. She would make the village, with the school and church, the pub and train station.

Her mind was so full of these images, of how she would ice snow onto the roofs and how she would add little lights inside so that the windows glowed, that she completely forgot she was in charge of the shop. Only when a jokey voice called, 'Service' did she come to her senses.

Hastily untying her apron and patting down her hair, she hurried to the front.

'David.'

'Thought you'd abandoned the place,' he said. He smiled, but there was a strain to his light tone.

Marnie reached across the counter and hugged him. He held on for a second or two longer than usual.

'I've just been on the phone to Matt,' he said, joining her behind the counter and sitting on the chair there. He helped himself to a biscuit.

Marnie nodded. 'How was he?'

David chewed and swallowed. He shrugged. 'Tired more than anything, I think.' He reached for a Christmas cake slice and bit into it morosely, beheading the icing snowman as he did. Marnie winced. 'Said Pat's back on form, though.'

Marnie gave a half-laugh. 'Takes more than a tumble to keep her quiet.'

'Hmm,' David said, swallowing the last of the cake, his gaze immediately returning to the counter. It was a sound of agreement, but she heard the doubt in it. She'd heard the lie in her own words, too.

'Shouldn't you be at work?' she asked, hearing herself return to the role of bossy big sister from their childhood. There was something comforting in it.

'Cancelled everything for today,' he said. 'Thought you might need some help.'

He reached for an iced bun. Marnie raised her eyebrows. 'Help demolishing the stock?'

David frowned. 'It's the shock,' he said.

There was a pause filled only with the sound of munching, and the faint strains of 'We Three Kings' coming from the kitchen. They were both, Marnie knew, remembering this place in happier times.

'It's not just this you know,' David said. 'They've been tired for a while. Greg was saying just the other week that Matt was talking to him about how he's going to volunteer at Riding for the Disabled when they retire, and how Pat could go back to race meets.'

Marnie laughed. 'Oh typical! Everyone else is planning to garden and join the WI. Still though, I bet he didn't say it in earshot of Pat.'

David shrugged and turned towards the kitchen. 'God, what are you making? Smells good.'

He started walking to the back, following his nose like the child in that Bisto advert all those years ago. Marnie scrambled after him.

'Oh no you don't,' she said, hurrying past him and blocking his way to the oven. 'This is the gingerbread street, not to be eaten, even by greedy brothers!'

'Gingerbread street?' he asked, laughing. 'Anyone else would be happy just doing a house, but you do a whole street. Once you get into something you just have to go big, don't you? Remember that summer we were in Babblebrook and you got into birdwatching and you were—You were—' He bent over, laughing so hard that he could hardly speak. 'You were all kitted out in the gear Matt bought for you, like a little twitcher, and you used to hide in the fields with your binoculars and keep notes in a book and—'

Marnie flushed. She still had that notebook, filled with neat lists of birds that she wanted to see, with the ones she'd spotted ticked off in red pen. Perhaps adding a golden winged warbler to her wish list had been a tad ambitious, but still, she remembered the little spark of satisfaction that came with ticking off every new species.

'It wasn't that bad,' she said. 'Just a bit of birdwatching.'

'You were thirteen!' David was howling with laughter now. 'Such a little weirdo.' His voice was affectionate, but Marnie felt like walloping him even so.

She drew herself up. 'I think birdwatching's an interesting hobby, actually. You should know that, you're a bloody vet.' She still liked the idea of twitching, if she was honest, and it had crossed her mind more than once that the move to Babblebrook might afford her the chance to sit in a little hut, quietly admiring the local birdlife.

David sighed and wiped his eyes, patting her arm. 'I'm just teasing,' he said. 'And I am not greedy.'

Still irritated, Marnie batted him out of the way and pulled the gingerbread sheets from the oven. They were perfectly golden, and smelled delicious. Carefully, so they wouldn't break, she placed them on the side.

'Ooh,' David said, his eyes widening as he licked his lips.

'No, no, no,' Marnie said, shooing him out of the kitchen. 'And you *are* greedy. Perhaps you should join Greg with his training?'

David pulled a face. 'Ugh, no thanks. Then I'd end up in hospital too! You won't tell him I ate all those cakes, though, will you?'

Marnie laughed. 'Don't worry, I'll keep quiet.'

'Thanks. So?' He nudged her and gave her a meaningful look.

Marnie understood what he was asking, but chose to pretend otherwise. 'What?'

'How are,' grinning, he made quote marks in the air, 'neighbourly relations?'

Marnie snorted. 'Not great, he bit my head off this morning.' She flushed, more at her own insensitivity at what she'd done than at Andrew's reaction.

'Ah.' David sucked in a breath. 'You know, he's just not been the same since Jane died. He has these outbursts, let's say. You're lucky he's being as civil as he is, there was a proper upset with the tenants before you, that's why they left in such a hurry.'

'I heard something about that. What did he do?' Marnie was annoyed, but as much with herself as with Andrew, though she wouldn't admit that right now. Secretly, she understood his rudeness that morning. And she still couldn't quite imagine him doing anything scary enough to drive someone from their home.

David shrugged. 'Don't know. Heard it from Lily, so not a very coherent story.' He nudged her again. 'Shame he's got such a temper though, isn't it? I mean, he is gorgeous.'

Marnie flushed. 'I can't say I've noticed.'

He poked her in the ribs. 'Oh yes you have.'

Irritated now, and her cheeks burning, Marnie slapped his hand away. 'I have not! I told you, I don't even like the man, you know Anne Walker warned me about him, she told me to stay away. No wonder no one in the village likes him, now I see why. You never know what mood he's going to be in, and people keep saying he's got a temper, and now I think they're right, I don't think he's good for Lauren to be around, I'll have to put a stop to her visiting the—'

It was only when David kicked her on the shin that she took a breath, and realised that he'd turned to stare at the door. Looking past him, she saw Andrew standing there, his face pale.

Shamed, she met his gaze, expecting to see anger in his eyes. But there was only a deep hurt.

He turned and walked away. Marnie sighed and covered her face with her hands. She could have bitten her tongue off.

The worst thing was, she hadn't meant a word of it.

*

Marnie worked all day, baking sheet after sheet of gingerbread, cutting them into shapes ready to build a confectionary version of Babblebrook. Or, the highlights, at least.

She mixed icing and stuck the walls together, adding icicles dangling from every roof. She built each house around a bowl to keep it steady and left them to firm up overnight. This was the only thing she could do to soothe her agitated mind; she kept picturing Pat, so small and pale in her hospital bed. She kept going over and over what Andrew had heard her saying about him. Stupid nonsense, all of it, she'd just been venting because she was embarrassed about her own behaviour, truth be told. He was already angry with her over the shed, and she thought she understood why, she should have realised straight away what it meant to him. And now she'd made things even worse. But the process of baking, the sure knowledge that at the end she would have created something delicious and beautiful, calmed her. She forced herself to focus.

When it was time to close the shop she was exhausted, but satisfied. She'd only had one customer all day and that was her own daughter, so it hardly counted. A group of parents and their children had gathered outside the post office, obviously on the way back from the school pick up. Through the window, Marnie heard them laughing and chatting as the children pressed their faces up against the bakery to see the little Christmas tree. They stayed for some time, and Marnie was tempted to go out and offer them a cuppa. But if the bakery was going to survive, she would need to think of a way to tempt them through the doors instead.

*

The more Marnie worked, the more she thought about the gingerbread village, and how she would display it in the window. All the next day she decorated the little buildings, icing the names on the shops and making a sign for the station, piping coloured lights onto everything and fashioning miniature robins out of icing. She imagined it all sitting in the window, a little Christmassy version of Babblebrook, resting on cotton-wool snow and lit up to twinkle away in the window. And she had an idea of how to bring more people into the bakery.

She made more sheets of gingerbread, forming them into houses and leaving them to firm up. One for each cottage in Babblebrook.

Her work was rarely disturbed by a customer. Anne Walker popped in for some mince pies, though she seemed much more interested in chatting about how Pat was than in her purchases.

She clicked her tongue and shook her head. 'Terrible thing, poor Pat. Mind you, something like this has been on the cards for a while. Thank goodness you're here to help out.'

Marnie sighed. 'Did you think they were struggling?'

'Well . . . I don't know about struggling, exactly, but I think they—Well, Matt at least, he'd like a break. They've lived and breathed it for so many years, you know? And Pat will just keep pushing herself, even after she broke her collar bone back in—'

Marnie leaped up. 'She what?'

'Oh. They didn't tell you.'

Marnie shook her head. Her throat was too full to speak.

'I don't want to talk out of turn,' Anne said, leaning conspiratorially over the counter and lowering her voice, 'but she fell off her bike at one of the races.'

Marnie sank down into the chair behind the counter, resting her head in her hands. 'I should have been here, I haven't been around enough. I knew she'd fallen off the bike but no one mentioned a broken collar bone.'

Mrs Walker patted her arm. 'Oh, it's all right, dear, you're here now. How would they manage without you to mind the shop?'

Marnie glanced around the empty room. 'Not much to mind, is there?'

Mrs Walker made a pretence of opening her paper bag and inspecting the mince pies. 'Well,' she said at last. 'Everyone goes to the supermarkets now, don't they? Don't even need to go, you can have it all delivered in one fell swoop. No one needs to come out specially for a loaf of bread, these days.'

'You're busy though.'

'Oh, well.' She smiled. 'Sweets and comics, just up the road from the primary school and right by the school bus stop? No child can resist us!'

She patted Marnie's cheek. 'Don't worry, it'll all come good, you see if it won't.'

Marnie couldn't see how. 'I know,' she said. 'Thank you, Mrs Walker.'

She laughed. 'Oh, my dear, call me Anne. You're not eleven now!'

Lizzie Lee

Marnie's phone buzzed as she waved goodbye, and she snatched it up, hoping it might be a text from Andrew. She hadn't seen him all day, and had picked up her phone more than once to message him, but her courage had failed her each time. But it was an email, from her most regular translation work client. Saying that they no longer needed her services.

Chapter Seventeen

'Do you have a wheelbarrow?'

Marnie's heart beat fast as she waited for Andrew's response, smiling brightly and willing herself to apologise for her thoughtlessness with the shed, and the stupid things she'd said about him. But he avoided her eye, scowling, and she lacked the courage. She stamped her feet and pulled her coat tight. Perhaps this was a mistake.

She'd been afraid to call on him. She knew he'd still be angry, and she was embarrassed about how she'd behaved. But she needed to keep busy to stop herself dwelling on the uncertainty of their living situation and her now fairly dire financial prospects. And this was part of her plan to bring people into the bakery, so she'd braced herself, and asked anyway.

He glanced behind her at the street, lit by a bright, starry night. 'What?'

'I have some deliveries to make, I need a wheelbarrow and we don't have one and I don't want to bother Matt.'

He snorted. 'Deliveries? What are you, Santa?'

He still refused to meet her eye. Apologise, Marnie thought. Tell him you're sorry, that you didn't mean what you said. She opened her mouth.

'Sort of,' she said.

*

It was Lauren's idea to decorate it, and she giggled as she wound tinsel around the handles and taped the lights that usually framed her bedroom mirror around the edge.

'Ta-da!' she said, waving her arms at the finished wheelbarrow. She'd laid a red fleece blanket inside, so nothing would get damaged or dirtied.

Andrew nodded and gave her a half-smile. Lauren had been so excited to show him her handiwork, and he had stayed, though Marnie could see he was desperate to leave. Plucking up courage at last, she blurted an apology.

'I'm sorry about earlier, I was just being . . .'

His frown deepened to a scowl, and then his phone buzzed and he took it out of his pocket, ignoring her. The surly expression lifted from his face for a moment as he read the notification, then he turned to go back into his cottage. Marnie's stomach twisted with an envy she didn't expect; she didn't know who was on the other end of the phone, making him smile, but she had an absurd rush of jealousy that they could make him happy while she only seemed able to upset and annoy him.

'Oh but—You could come with us, if you like?' she said. Her voice sounded tight with desperation, and she knew he'd refuse; he wasn't exactly sociable, she couldn't imagine him wanting to visit the whole village at the best of times. Never mind with a woman he'd caught bad-mouthing him.

He shook his head, barely able to look at her.

'All right, well, take one, though.' She smiled as she held out the gingerbread house. He glanced at it, but his expression didn't change.

'She's done one for everyone,' Lauren said, and Marnie thought she heard a note of pride in her daughter's voice.

'Fine,' Andrew said, taking the house and turning his back.

Lauren pulled a face. 'What's his problem?'

'Oh it's my fault, I . . . never mind.' Marnie smiled and lifted the handles of the wheelbarrow.

She wasn't going to let this spoil her plans for the bakery; yes, she'd made a mistake with the chair but it wasn't deliberate. She had been upset about that, embarrassed that she'd done it and shaken that he'd reacted so badly, and that's why she'd said all those silly things about him. She wished she hadn't. Although there was some truth in it, wasn't there? She had been warned about his temper. But she felt guilty, all the same, and stupid for ruining things between them just as they'd been getting to know each other. But she had other things to think about now. She wasn't going to give it another moment's thought, she decided, as she went over every detail of what had happened in her mind again and again.

Matt was their first stop. He was not long back from visiting Pat, and the cottage held neither its usual warmth of the fire nor the aroma of his baking when he opened the door. He looked tired, but he brightened when he saw them.

'What's all this?'

'Early Christmas present,' Marnie said, as Lauren carefully picked a gingerbread house and held it out to him. 'You can decorate it yourself, and then keep it if you like or bring it to put in the bakery window.'

Matt took the house, holding it gently, his gaze falling to the pile of others in the wheelbarrow. He laughed. 'You've never done one for the whole village?'

'You know Mum,' Lauren said. 'Always goes a bit over the top.'

Marnie cleared her throat. 'How's Pat?'

'Oh, fine, you know. Back home tomorrow, she'll be better for that.' He lifted the house a little. 'She'll be thrilled to bits with this.'

'Wait till you see what else Mum's got planned for the window,' Lauren said.

'Ah, spoilers!' Marnie kissed Matt's cheek. 'We'd better be on our way.'

'Thank you,' he said. 'For everything.'

They walked the whole village, and were greeted with delight everywhere, and promises to decorate and bring the houses back. This was going better than Marnie had dared hope. There was only one person who hadn't been thrilled by her idea, but she blinked that thought away.

The last house on their list stood on the corner by the lane to the brook. Marnie had happy memories of visiting Gloria and Bob when she was a child, eating the chicken patties Gloria made and building LEGO towns with David. They had seemed old then, but these days Gloria's once-dark curly hair was completely grey.

She smiled when she saw them, wrapping her arms around Marnie, and holding Lauren by the shoulders. Her nails were painted in a rainbow of colours.

'Oh, my goodness, look how you've grown,' she said, a trace of her Jamaican accent still present. 'You were just a toddler the last time I saw you. Well, I've seen you around the village of course, but not properly.' She turned to holler over her shoulder. 'Bob, come see who—'

But Bob was already standing behind her, dressed in shirt and a navy tie with brightly coloured planets printed on, though he must be retired by now.

They cooed over the gingerbread house and promised to add it to the bakery window. Gloria invited them in for tea and fried biscuits. Marnie looked around the little house, happy memories washing over her; it had hardly changed at all. The same shiny Christmas decorations dangled across the ceiling, the same cotton chairbacks embroidered with brightly coloured macaws hung over the sofa. The place was immaculate. Gloria even dusted inside the phone box that stood outside their house once a week.

Finally, warm with good food and good cheer, they made their way home, the empty wheelbarrow swaying a little. Lauren yawned loudly, her breath clouding in the frosty air.

'You go in, love,' Marnie said. 'I'll de-Christmas this and I'll be there soon.'

Lauren nodded and headed into the cottage, letting out a stream of warm air as she stood in the doorway untying her boots. Marnie bit her tongue, and began unwrapping tinsel. She took the wheelbarrow round to Andrew's back garden, leaving it next to the shed he'd brought it out of. She dared not set foot in there again. The kitchen window was lit, and she was tempted for a moment to knock on the back door, to apologise and make things right between them. Imagining that everything would thaw between them, they'd sit in his neat kitchen with Rosie pottering at their feet, having a drink and a chat like before.

But she just turned and walked away.

Chapter Eighteen

Marnie worked all day, baking her special festive recipes for the event later.

She finally stopped for a cup of tea at half-three, watching the after-school group through the window. The adults stamped their feet and tucked their hands under their armpits while the children ran about, squealing. A few of them pressed against the window, hands cupping faces, to stare at the Christmas tree again. Marnie smiled and waved.

On impulse, she strode to the door and flung it open. 'You all look so cold and I've just boiled the kettle, who wants a cuppa on the house?' She caught the eye of a little girl with a tangled dark bob. 'Or hot chocolate?'

The children piled in, faces pink from running around, immediately stripping off their coats, followed by the parents. Marnie handed out mugs of tea, luckily there were cups left from the bring and share, and milky hot chocolate for the children, and they all propped themselves up against the walls and chatted.

'Are these all homemade?' one of the dads asked, eyeing up the display of cakes and biscuits.

Marnie nodded. 'They buy the bread in now, but everything else, yes.'

They began to gather around, picking out treats, and commenting on how much better they looked than shop-bought biscuits. Marnie hastily bagged them up and rang up the cost. This was more custom than she'd had all week.

Feeling a tug on her jeans, Marnie looked down. The little girl with the brown bob was staring up at her. There was a smear of ketchup in the corner of her mouth. 'My mummy's tired, she's been working all day, she needs a sit down when she has a cup of tea,' she said. 'You should have chairs.'

'Amy,' her mum scolded. 'Stop bossing Marnie around, please.'

Marnie laughed. 'It's fine.' She bent so she was level with the girl's serious eyes. 'You know, that's not a bad idea. But for now, if your mummy says it's all right, you could have a chocolate decoration from my Christmas tree, if you like?'

There were three other children in the shop, and they all immediately clustered around Marnie, gazing at her with huge eyes. She laughed. 'Well I hope there's enough—Let's look, shall we?'

Chocolates found, unwrapped and eaten in minutes, the parents handed their empty cups to Marnie and gathered up their bags of biscuits and cakes. Amy even gave a lick of hers to her baby brother, sitting gurgling in his buggy.

'You know, your Amy's not wrong,' one of the women said. 'It's the only thing missing in Babblebrook, isn't it?

Somewhere to get together. Other than The Plough, but it's a bit early for that!'

They all laughed, and someone muttered, 'Oh, I don't know.'

'Not wrong, but still bossy.' The woman tousled her daughter's hair fondly. 'What time's the window display, Marnie? We can't wait.'

'Six-thirty,' Marnie said, thinking of all the work she still had to do and wishing she'd arranged it for an hour later. At least it kept her mind off worrying about how she was going to pay her bills next month, though. Not to mention how she was going to fix things with Andrew.

'Lovely, see you there.'

'We stuck sweeties to our house,' Amy said. 'And Mummy wouldn't let me eat any.'

Her mum smiled. 'Yes, I'm a tyrant. Well, it should be fun, everyone's coming, I think.'

Her friend rolled her eyes. 'Not quite everyone, hopefully, we don't want that nasty bas—' She glanced at her son, who had turned to look at her with a curious expression. 'That rude man here, do we? That bloke next door to you, Marnie.'

Amy's mum grinned. 'Oh, I don't know – brightens the place up a bit, doesn't he?'

Her friend giggled, slapping her arm lightly. 'Julia! You're a happily married woman.'

'Well, I know,' Julia said, wheeling the buggy through the door that Marnie held open for her. 'But I'm not blind, am I?'

Laughing, they waved their goodbyes, and Marnie hurried back to her icing, glad that she hadn't been expected to respond to their comments about Andrew. Something had twisted in her when they'd talked about him that way, she'd felt almost annoyed. Almost possessive. Ridiculous. Luckily, she had far too much to do to dwell on what they'd said, she thought, banishing the image of Andrew's crooked smile from her mind. For once, she was glad that she knew there would be no more customers that day.

*

She was ready just in time – the icing on the sign of the station was still wet as she placed it in the window, gently setting it in the cotton wool snow behind the toy train track she'd borrowed from Gloria and Bob. It had belonged to their children, now grown up, and was still used when the grandchildren came to visit, so Marnie had promised to have it safely returned for Christmas Day.

There wasn't room to map out the whole of Babblebrook, but she'd made a small, snow-covered version of the green with a cardboard oak, a tin-foil duck pond and a model of the pump – a last minute addition created by Lauren from Plasticine. On either side Marnie placed the gingerbread versions of the shops, school, pub, church and station. Hopefully there was enough room left for the houses people would bring.

The train puffed quietly round the track, and a little toy Santa sat on top of the school roof. She'd placed the last LED tea light in and had just switched on the

Christmas lights that edged the display when she heard a squeal from outside. Looking up, she saw Amy with her nose pressed to the window, her eyes shining. Behind her stood Julia, carrying a gingerbread house that had every surface covered with Jelly Tots.

Marnie opened up the door, and a stream of people poured in, chatting and gazing in admiration at her work, unbuttoning coats and reaching for the glasses of mulled wine she had lined up on the counter. Gloria and Bob, she saw, carried their exquisitely decorated house, complete with an iced biscuit in the shape of a phone box to go in front. Both Bob's tie and Gloria's navy-painted nails were decorated with a pattern of snowflakes.

A group of children queued up to place their houses in the window, and Marnie helped them find the right spot to gently put them down, smiling at the bright blobs, trickles of icing, and huge quantity of sweets. A few were missing, leaving an indented patch of icing, and more than one child was surreptitiously chewing as they walked away.

One little boy found he couldn't part with his house after all, screaming and sobbing, clutching it to his chest as his harassed mum and dad tried to prise it from his fingers. Marnie caught the mum's eye, smiling and waving. 'It's fine, don't worry,' she said. 'They're a gift really, to do whatever he likes with.'

The woman gave a watery, grateful smile and reached for a glass of wine.

At last Marnie heard Andrew's truck pull up outside. She watched as he and Lauren carefully lifted Pat out and sat her in the wheelchair Matt was holding.

Marnie went out to meet them. Pat's face lit up when she caught sight of the window, and she clapped her hands together, demanding that Matt wheel her over to have a proper look.

'Oh,' she cried. 'Look at the train, look! And the shops. And the church. Oh and there's Father Christmas!'

She gave a low, throaty chuckle and clasped Marnie's hand as she approached. 'Oh, it's wonderful. Just wonderful! I'll have to topple over more often.'

She laughed and looked around as though expecting them to join in. There was a shocked silence for a moment.

'Please don't,' Andrew said. 'I don't think my back could take it, heaving you in and out of cars like this.'

They laughed, and Pat batted him on the arm. 'That's enough cheek from you,' she said, as if he were a teenager and not a middle-aged man.

Andrew caught Marnie's eye and nodded towards the display. 'Looks good,' he said gruffly.

'Thank you.' If this was the beginning of things between them thawing, she was glad of it. He hadn't brought his own house to be a part of the village, but he had brought Pat, and she could only be grateful for that.

'Now stop this gassing and get me inside, I want to say hello to everyone.' Pat waved as though she was the queen as Matt pushed her in, and a small group crowded round her, offering drinks and snacks, asking what she thought of the display. Marnie noticed the mum who had complained about Andrew earlier frown as she saw him come in, and turn to whisper something to her husband. Apparently oblivious, he went to pick out a loaf of bread and some mince pies.

'Oh, it's marvellous isn't, what a wonderful job Marnie's done.' Pat beamed around and grasped Marnie's hand. 'You're quite a star, we should get this in the paper, it looks so good. Bob, what do you think? Eh Bob? Front page of *The Blast*?'

Marnie looked around in confusion. 'The what?'

'*The Babblebrook Blast*,' Gloria said. 'Bob's been running it for years now, all the local news and events, and he's done so well, haven't you, love? It goes out to all the local villages.'

Bob smiled, shrugging. 'Well it's just a pamphlet really but yes, we've got quite a reach now and I'm sure all our readers would love this, Marnie. Perhaps I could come in and interview you next week? Take some photos?'

Marnie looked at her twinkling little window display, and at the bakery full of people who were busily eyeing up the goods. She had wanted no more than to bring in a few customers, to remind the villagers that the bakery existed. Interviews and pictures in the paper, however small, were more than she'd bargained for, and she couldn't believe anyone would be interested in her small efforts. But somehow she found herself nodding.

*

At last everyone began to drift away. Children were wrapped back up in hats and coats and strapped into buggies, or lolled sleepily on a parent's shoulder as they were carried back home. Marnie was hugged and kissed, thanked and congratulated. Soon, only she and Lauren, Pat and Matt, and Andrew were left.

She found herself alone in the kitchen with Andrew for a moment as they cleared glasses. Quickly, before her courage could desert her, she garbled an apology.

'I'm really sorry. About the shed and the chair, and that silly stuff I said, I was just . . . it was stupid of me.'

'Oh.' He waved a hand, rocked back on his heels. 'No. I was being sensitive.'

'Well. You have a right to be.'

He rubbed his fingers across his eyes. 'No, I—Have a problem, sometimes I get so . . . and I can't get it under control. Sorry. You know, I'm really not this difficult.' He sighed. 'Or, I didn't used to be.'

Marnie nodded.

'I just—It used to be a sort of hobby, you see, the carpentry, but since she's gone I haven't been able to face it, not until that little keyring for you.' He shook his head. 'All the things I made for our life together, Jane's and mine. The chair was the last thing I made her. The birthday before she was diagnosed, she was already ill, really, but we didn't know how badly. Thought she was just a bit run down, you know? She—she worked too hard, she loved those students, and we just thought . . .' His voice wavered and he stopped, swallowed. Marnie found a lump rising in her own throat. 'God, I wish I'd taken more notice, I wish I'd sent her to the doctor straight away, then she might still be—'

Someone watching from the street sniggered, and she turned her attention to the group loitering there. The eyes that looked on her gleamed with curiosity, as though they stared at a strange exhibit at the zoo. The whole village would be talking about this today. She flushed and swallowed, still fighting tears. She'd humiliated herself, and Lauren too, acting on a mad impulse. This wasn't a sensible way to behave, making a show of herself, it wasn't like her. She was usually so measured. This was like Lily.

Just as she was about to rush into the house and hide away there for as long as possible, there was a sound of chuckling that grew until it became a guffaw. Andrew. He was shaking with laughter, tears streaming down his face.

And Marnie felt her own lips twitch into a smile, the threat of tears falling away.

'Oh God,' he said, straightening up and wiping his eyes, words still broken by chuckles. 'That's the best laugh I've had in years. What the hell are you doing, you crazy woman?'

Marnie grinned, and indicated the birdfeeder, where the squirrel was still helping itself. 'Bloody thing keeps pinching the bird food, and it uses that branch to get across, so I thought . . .'

He barked another laugh. 'So you thought you'd lop it off with an axe while you're in your PJs at eight in the morning?'

'Pretty much.'

'Ah God,' he sighed, still chuckling. 'You know, you seem so serious sometimes and I think it's maybe because you looked after David when you were kids, and you moved around so much.'

She gaped at him. He really had listened to everything she'd told him.

He grinned, leaning on the bird table and watching her with a twinkle in his eye. 'That's not the real you though, is it? You had to grow up too soon. But there's a big, naughty kid in you, you know.'

His laughter was infectious, and suddenly the absurdity of it hit her; but in a way that didn't feel as though she'd committed a disastrous faux pas. In a way that felt okay. Because he just found it funny. And somehow endearing, apparently. The real her, even the parts she tried so hard to keep hidden, the playful childlike parts that she was so ashamed of; perhaps it wasn't so bad to let those out every now and then after all. She laughed until she also had tears in her eyes, all the fear and tension she'd felt dissolving. Remembering the onlookers, she glanced towards the street, but the crowd had disappeared.

'Oh don't worry about that lot.' He waved an arm towards the street. 'They'll find something else to gossip about soon enough. Tomorrow's chip paper, and all that.' He smiled, and Marnie found she really wasn't worried about what the villagers thought after all. 'The squirrels are a pain,' he said. 'It's a constant battle. Didn't you try the soap in a sock?'

She stared at him in confusion. He indicated an old sock hanging from a branch over his bird table, and she vaguely remembered him shouting something about it at her once. Things were beginning to make sense. Sort of.

'Oh, *that's* what you were hollering about. What, they don't like the smell of the soap or something? Does it work?'

He shrugged. 'Not really. I'm trying oil on the stand at the moment.'

Marnie remembered the squirrel slipping down the birdfeeder. 'Ah.'

They stood, smiling at each other, and Marnie was suddenly very aware of the bright blue of his eyes, warm with laughter, and the lopsided quirk of his smile. She was staring. Was she staring? She willed herself to look away. Couldn't bring herself to. He cleared his throat, examining something invisible at his feet.

They stood, either side of the small hedge that separated their front gardens, as silence grew between them. A stupid, smiling, schoolgirl-with-a-crush silence.

'Um, I'd better get on with . . .'

'Yep, yes, time to be heading – remember, soap in a sock.'

She nodded, and they parted, quickly and awkwardly. And Marnie was still smiling.

*

The bakery in order at last after the event the night before, Marnie threw some crumbs out for the birds, watching as a little blue tit hopped down and pecked at them. She put the kettle on and flipped the sign on the door from closed to open.

'Oh,' she said, finding a small group gathered around the window display. They began to pour through the door as soon as she stepped aside. 'I wasn't expecting . . .'

'Oh lovely, we didn't know if you were open today,' Julia said as she stepped in.

'Not that anyone could blame you for having a day off after yesterday,' her friend said.

'Absolutely! And the window looks so lovely and Christmassy with all the houses in, you've done a great job.' Julia put the brake on her baby's buggy and smiled, stamping her feet and blowing onto her mittened hands. 'Freezing out there.'

'I've just put the kettle on if anyone wants—'

A chorus of grateful acceptances drowned her out, and she went to take the tea bag out of her mug and make a pot instead while they all picked out the cakes and biscuits they wanted. She was relieved that no one had mentioned her antics that morning. So far, anyway.

Marnie turned up the radio so that they had a background of carols as they leaned against the walls and drank tea, chatting and eating the cakes they'd just bought, telling stories of the outrageous requests children had made of Santa over the years. Marnie sighed. She was tired, but she had a strange sense of contentment that she hadn't felt for a long time. Fleetingly, an image of gingham curtains flashed once again through her mind.

The day continued with a steady stream of customers drifting through the doors, stopping first to coo over the window display. There was another little glut after school as pink-nosed children clutching glitter-covered cardboard Christmas trees chose iced biscuits, and their parents once again accepted a cuppa.

By closing time, the counter was almost bare. Marnie thought such a busy day would have left her exhausted, but the company and activity were invigorating. She had to admit that she missed the company of going into the office, and this was certainly more satisfying than sitting alone at her kitchen table translating boring documents, finishing the day with her mind drained and her body twitchy. She hummed along to 'Away in a Manger' as she tidied up and switched all the lights off. She would have to come in early to bake some new stock.

Her phone pinged just as she was locking up:

Marnie,
    Thank you for the beautiful window and for looking after the bakery.
    Please come round on your way back for a cup of tea. Matt has made special biscuits as a thank you.
    Love, Pat xx

Marnie smiled, bagging up the last few mince pies to take with her. They were probably not up to Matt's standards, but still. Her phone pinged again:

Marnie,
Please bring Lauren too.
Thank you.
Love, Pat xx

As it turned out, Lauren was all too happy to take a break from her homework and eat biscuits in Pat and Matt's cosy living room. They huddled round the fire, as coloured lights twinkled in the tree, breathing in the scent of freshly baked gingerbread.

Marnie was pleased to see that Pat looked her usual self, her cheeks plump and pink, her eyes bright behind her glasses. She hobbled to her feet, leaning on a walker to stand and kiss their cheeks.

'Don't get up,' Marnie said.

'Oh, stop fussing.' Pat lowered herself back down gingerly. 'They said I have to keep moving.'

Marnie glanced at Matt. He raised an eyebrow and shook his head a little. 'You can't tell her.'

'Ignore them,' Pat said to Lauren. 'Talking codswallop. You go and get that tub of Celebrations from under the tree, let's break into it shall we?'

Lauren didn't need telling twice, bringing the tub and taking it straight to Pat.

'Choose your favourites, chick,' Pat said. 'Leave those two out of it. We might let them have the Bounties, eh?'

She chuckled, and Lauren sat on the floor at her feet. They dug in, grabbing and unwrapping sweets by the handful, Lauren shovelling them into her mouth one after the other until her cheeks bulged.

Marnie laughed. 'You look like a hamster.'

'Don't care.' Lauren's voice was so muffled by sweets that she laughed, a chocolate-stained sliver of dribble slipping down her chin.

'You should be ashamed of yourself, Pat,' Matt said, smiling. 'You're a bad influence.'

'Oh be off with you,' Pat said, unwrapping a mini Mars bar and popping it into her mouth. 'Now, Marnie, tell us all what you were doing hacking off bits of your tree this morning.' She grinned.

'Oh—' Marnie felt herself flush. 'I was just – it was the squirrels that . . . I didn't know you saw.'

'The whole village is talking about it, Anne Walker told everyone who went into the shop.'

Marnie groaned. 'They're all going to think I'm mad.'

Matt patted her shoulder. 'I think they were mostly just shocked to hear Andrew laughing – hasn't happened for years, it's the talk of the village!'

'Well, yes,' Pat said. 'That and what the crazy new woman was doing chopping up trees in her pyjamas at breakfast time.'

Marnie hid her face in her hands.

Matt tutted at Pat and turned to Marnie, holding out a paper bag of iced biscuits in the shape of robins. 'Never mind that. We wanted to thank you for looking after the bakery while Pat was in hospital, we're so grateful, and you've done a wonderful job – that window display. Beautiful.'

Marnie took the biscuits, smiling. Glad to change the subject. 'Oh robins, my favourites! But it's no bother. I've enjoyed it, actually.'

Matt caught Pat's eye, and Marnie was sure she gave a little shake of her head. He cleared his throat. 'Well, I'm very happy to hear that because we were wondering— uh, I mean, I wanted to ask how you'd feel about . . .'

Pat stopped chewing, fixing Matt with a stern stare that he studiously kept his face turned away from. Marnie placed her cup carefully on the coffee table.

'It's too much for us,' Matt blurted. 'How do you feel about taking over?'

'Oh . . .' Marnie found herself surprisingly unsurprised. A part of her had been expecting this.

'Oh really!' Pat smacked the lid back onto the Celebrations. 'What nonsense, Matt. The bakery's done with, let's face it, it's dead in the water. There's no future in it. And we're not going to saddle Marnie with that.'

For a moment no one spoke. Pat's words hung in the air, the only sounds the spitting of the fire and Lauren's surreptitious slurping. Pat glared at Matt, her head wobbling a little and tears trembling in her eyes. She was too stubborn to let them fall, Marnie knew.

Marnie's heart broke to see Pat like this. They all knew what the bakery meant to her, and what a wrench it must be to give it up, let alone accept that it had no future at all. Marnie had to take a minute to swallow down her own sorrow before she could speak.

'Well,' she said at last. 'I keep thinking about this crazy idea that just might—'

She was interrupted by a burst of frantic knocking on the door, so loud that she leaped up and yanked it open before Matt had even got to his feet.

Andrew stood on the step, his face white.

'Thank God you're here,' he said. 'I need your brother. It's Rosie.'

Chapter Twenty

They all huddled around the little dog as she lay in a basket on a pile of blankets in a corner of Andrew's living room. He knelt by her, forehead creased with worry, and she didn't take her eyes off him.

They had all insisted on coming, Pat leaning on her walker and instructing Lauren to bring the Celebrations tub. 'It might be a long night,' she said. 'We need to keep our blood sugar up.'

Rosie climbed out of the basket, panting and digging at the rug before climbing back in and heaving herself down with a grunt.

'All right, girl,' Andrew said, stroking her head.

There was a knock at the door, and David and Greg stepped through without waiting to be let in. 'Cavalry's here,' David called.

He walked into the living room, pulling off a striped knitted bobble hat and his coat and leaving them in a pile on the floor. He shook his head at the sight of them all crowded round the dog. 'Good grief, move back can't you? Give the poor thing some space.'

Obediently, Marnie, Matt and Lauren shuffled away.

'Told you,' Pat said, from where she sat on the sofa. She had done nothing of the sort, but no one argued.

'Right,' David said, kneeling to examine Rosie and smiling reassuringly at Andrew. 'Let's get these pups out, shall we?'

'Did you know she was pregnant?' Marnie asked Andrew in a whisper.

He turned to look at her with an expression of disbelief. He didn't bother to reply.

'Of course you did.' Marnie blushed. 'Sorry.'

Pat waved the chocolate tub towards her, grinning. 'Here, have a sweet. It'll stop you talking.'

Marnie glared at her. And helped herself to a Twix.

*

Pat was right, it was a long night. Marnie made endless cups of tea, and the chocolates quickly became depleted. Matt sent Lauren to bring the tin of gingerbread biscuits he'd baked, and she handed them round. They all grabbed one, apart from Greg, who shook his head but his gaze kept drifting to the open tin as everyone else dunked and crunched.

'I don't know how you do this day after day,' he said, looking with admiration at David as he bent over the little dog. 'So stressful.'

David smiled and reached out to pat Greg's knee. 'Not usually this exciting, to be fair. It's mostly vaccinations and worm tablets. Anyway, she's doing fine. Aren't you, Rosie?'

The little dog rolled her eyes to give him a baleful look as she strained, as if she were thinking, easy for you to say. Marnie sympathised.

Greg pulled a face and wiped his forehead, his gaze straying to the biscuit tin again. 'Too much for me. Give me a nice, boring spreadsheet any day.'

Lauren grabbed Marnie's arm. 'Look,' she whispered, her eyes grown round and large. 'Look, I can – see something. I can see a tail!'

'Oh—breech, is that . . . ?'

David was already shaking his head. 'Perfectly normal, nothing to worry about.'

Slowly the pup emerged, born in a little sac that Rosie licked away immediately. Marnie found her cooing turning into a small groan of surprise. This was not the cute, fluffy, large-eyed creature she had been imagining, but a tiny, rat-like thing with a naked tail and closed eyes.

'Mum,' Lauren said, frowning. 'Don't be rude, it's cute.'

'I know, sorry.' Marnie glanced at Andrew, but he was too focused on Rosie and the pup to notice her. 'It's just they're a bit . . .'

'That's just what they look like when they're first born,' Lauren said. 'They'll grow all fat and fluffy soon.'

Marnie nodded, feeling chastened that she had to be schooled by her own daughter. When had she grown so clever?

'More tea, anyone?' she asked, and was relieved when they all nodded.

*

Finally, at almost midnight, Rosie gave birth to her fourth, and last, pup. She'd been calm throughout, occasionally butting her head into Andrew's hand for a stroke.

The last pup lay in its sac, and they all waited in silence for Rosie to start licking it free. But she simply let her head flop down, eyes closed, as she panted quietly.

'Come on, girl,' Andrew said softly, encouraging her with a gentle nudge. 'You're almost done, come on.'

The other pups crawled blindly, bleating a little, as this one lay silent and still. Marnie found herself holding her breath.

'She's tired, poor love,' Pat whispered.

David was frowning. Not a good sign. 'Just another few seconds and then if she—'

'Oh I can't stand it, do something, David, for pity's sake.' Greg was whispering – none of them wanted to tire Rosie or frighten the puppies – but there was an unmistakable urgency to his voice. He rose and paced up and down, running a hand through his hair.

'All right, let's help you out Rosie,' David said, reaching over to break the bag the puppy lay in. He used the edge of the blanket to wipe its nose clean.

Still the puppy lay unmoving.

Lauren moved closer to Marnie, and stood biting her nails as Marnie put an arm round her and held tight.

'Don't worry,' Marnie whispered. 'David knows what he's doing.' She spoke as much to comfort herself as her daughter.

David didn't respond, but he still frowned. He picked the little creature up and held it with its face down, opening its mouth so that fluid dribbled out. Still, it showed no sign of life. Marnie could feel Lauren's breathing coming quick and jagged. She forced herself to remain calm.

David began to rub the puppy's body with the blanket. Still, no sound, no movement from the tiny figure.

Marnie glanced at Andrew just as he looked her way. She saw the concern in his eyes, and knew hers mirrored it. An urge to walk over and take him in her arms swept through her, and she felt her body lean towards him. But an attempt at a reassuring smile was all she could offer. Even then, she found herself able only to twitch her mouth slightly. Still, he seemed to understand, giving her a small nod before turning his attention back to the puppy.

David rubbed the puppy harder, and Marnie feared that he would hurt the poor little thing. No one moved. No one spoke. Marnie felt Lauren trembling, now.

At last, the puppy kicked its tiny limbs out and gave a thin whimper.

Every held-breath was released, and a murmur of relief and quiet laughter rippled around the room. Lauren threw her arms around Marnie. Over her daughter's shoulder, she found her eye meeting Andrew's again. A smile exploded across his face, and she felt herself respond in the same way.

'Well,' David said, smiling round at them all. 'That was a—Oh dear.'

They followed his gaze to see Greg perched on the edge of the sofa next to Pat, empty biscuit tin clutched on his lap, and crumbs sticking to his lips.

David laughed. 'I don't believe it, Mr Health and Fitness has pigged the lot!'

Marnie saw the warmth in his gaze as he looked at his husband, saw how his face softened at the sight of him. For a moment she felt a stab of an unexpected and unwanted emotion.

She was glad for her brother, but she couldn't help wishing she could also find such happiness. She didn't think she'd ever loved like that. Her marriage to Ian had been a whirlwind of heady romance that had suddenly soured when he betrayed her; what David and Greg had felt unbreakable.

Under all their amused stares, Greg flushed. 'It wasn't me, it was Pat, I was just . . .' His shoulders slumped, as Pat turned to stare at him, her mouth wide as she protested. 'It was too stressful,' he said. 'I couldn't help myself.'

David grinned. 'How many did you eat?'

Greg hung his head. 'Seven.'

Matt eased the tin from Greg's grip with a kindly smile.

'Right,' David said. 'Let's leave this man and his new family, shall we?'

Slowly, they began to make their way out. David and Greg helped Pat as she shuffled on her walker, her face pale but her eyes bright. 'What a night,' she said. 'Thank you for letting us be part of it, Andrew.'

Marnie guided Lauren out. This was far too late for a school night but she couldn't have dragged her away before all the pups were safely delivered. Lauren crept over to the basket and gazed down at the little, wriggling things as they nuzzled into their mum.

'Well done, Rosie,' she whispered, stroking the little dog's head. Rosie thumped her tail in response.

'Come back and see them whenever you like,' Andrew said.

Lauren turned wide, grateful eyes to him. 'Really?'

Marnie laughed, and eased Lauren towards the door. 'Come on, let's leave Andrew in peace.'

At the doorway he caught her arm and pulled her a little closer, so that she could feel warmth radiating from him. She breathed in his scent of soap. 'Thank you for being here, tonight,' he said.

Marnie hesitated, taken aback. She was standing so close to him it was hard to concentrate. 'Oh, I—Well, I didn't really do anything.'

'You did.' He grinned. 'You made a lot of tea.'

She laughed. 'Well, we aim to please.'

What a stupid thing to say.

Her embarrassment was not helped by Lauren giggling and saying, 'So weird. No one in this century talks like that, Mum.'

But Andrew caught her eye, giving that lopsided smile that made his eyes crease, and Marnie had a sense, as she'd had that morning, that he saw her in all her quirks and vulnerabilities, all those parts of herself that she'd tried to hide all these years in fear of being judged for them, and that he liked her despite them. Or even because of them. She scuttled off before she could embarrass herself any further.

Lizzie Lee

It was only later, as she brushed her teeth and half-heartedly scrubbed at her makeup, that she realised they had never finished the conversation about the bakery. And she felt only relief that circumstances had stopped her opening her big mouth – what had she been thinking? Making a pretty window display was one thing but what on earth had possessed her to begin blurting out her silly dreams of turning the bakery into a café, she didn't know. She'd never done that kind of job before, she wouldn't know where to begin. She was lucky they'd been interrupted by the drama of Rosie and the puppies.

But still, the image of gingham curtains swam through her mind as she crawled into bed and closed her eyes. The envelope with her café doodle still sat on the bedside table; somehow she couldn't bring herself to part with it.

Chapter Twenty-One

The bakery soon returned to its usual emptiness, though a new habit had developed with a few people dropping in on the way back from the school pick up. The parents tried out Marnie's fresh bakes and drank her tea while the children crowded around the window display, shrieking with delight whenever the toy train passed them on its circular journey.

Marnie wasn't going to keep the bakery afloat by selling the odd mince pie and giving away free drinks, though. She had hoped the display might keep people coming in, but she needed to do more. She needed to reach further afield than Babblebrook. Picking up her phone, she called Bob and arranged for him to come and take a photo the next day. She dreaded being the centre of attention, and fervently hoped that Bob wouldn't want to put her picture in the paper, but perhaps *The Babblebrook Blast* would work some magic.

She wondered how she would keep the children entertained after Christmas, when the display had been taken down and the train returned to Gloria and Bob. A box of toys, perhaps, or children's books. Or a new display, something wintry and sparkly to make up for the disappearance of Christmas trees and lights.

She shook herself and tried to focus on the tidying up so she could go home. Silly daydreams, nothing more. She must stop letting this crazy fantasy of hers run riot. What was making her think she could pull off something like this? Ian's voice rang through her mind, and she remembered him laughing affectionately as she placed all the tins in the cupboard with their labels facing outwards. 'What would happen if I went round after you and turned them all the other way?' he'd said. 'You know, just for fun.' He'd winked at her and then, seeing her expression of horror at the very idea, laughed and taken her in his arms. 'Don't worry, babe. I'll never let that happen. You can keep your world as safe and ordered as you like.'

He wasn't wrong; she liked order and predictability. Running a café would be very far from her comfort zone. A few of her friends had paid her to bake birthday cakes for their children when Lauren was little, but that was hardly the same thing. No, after Christmas she wouldn't be here. She would be back to translating, trying to drum up some more business and provide a bit of security for Lauren and herself. She was just helping out in the bakery while Pat and Matt needed her to, and she mustn't let silly pipe dreams distract her from her real responsibilities.

Her stomach shrank at the thought, and she almost lost her appetite for the salted-caramel mince pie she was eating. A new recipe. It was important to try out the wares. She demolished it in two bites and smacked her lips. Delicious. Just a shame there weren't more customers to discover it.

The idea of spending a grey January sitting alone in her kitchen trying not to feel guilty about putting the heating on just for herself did not appeal. And so far, no work had come in anyway. Plus, she'd lost her most regular client. The prospect of seeing in the new year destitute was even less appealing. She needed to focus on how she was going to pay her bills if she couldn't drum up some more work, and where on earth they were going to live if Lily didn't let them stay in the cottage, instead of filling her head with dreams about running a café.

Marnie sighed as she locked up, pushing these fears away. She distracted herself by admiring the window; she left the lights on and the train running. The little gingerbread Babblebrook really did look like some kind of magical winter wonderland. For a moment Marnie found herself wishing that the real village was such a carefree place, where Pat and Matt still ran a busy, prosperous bakery and she and Lauren could picnic by the brook in the summer, safe in the knowledge that they could live there as long as they wanted to.

Get a grip, she told herself, marching home down the frosty street. Lauren was not at home, but Marnie had a good idea where she would be; the same place she'd been every night this week.

'Andrew's going to think you've moved in with him,' she said, as Lauren pulled the door open and immediately turned away to go back to the puppies.

'Look how cute they are,' Lauren said. She knelt by the basket, gazing at the pups and gently stroking Rosie's head. The little dog didn't respond. She didn't even have the energy to wag her tail. Poor thing must be exhausted.

'This is the small one,' Lauren said, pointing to one of the squirming creatures. 'You know, that last one to be born? She's littler than the others but look, she doesn't take any sh—nonsense.'

Lauren threw a guilty glance at Marnie, who frowned slightly in response. It wasn't so long ago that 'bother' was the worst word her daughter knew.

Marnie watched the tiny pup scramble over one of its siblings to reach Rosie and suckle. Its difficult start didn't appear to have affected its appetite; Marnie admired that.

'Where's Andrew?'

Lauren didn't respond, completely focused on the dogs.

Now familiar with Andrew's pristine kitchen, Marnie made three cups of tea. She took her own and Lauren's through to the living room.

'Should I make one for Rosie, do you think? I don't know if she's allowed tea while she's nursing.'

Lauren shrugged, barely taking her eyes off the pups.

'I'll ask Andrew, I'm taking his tea anyway. Where is he?'

'In the shed.'

'The shed?' Marnie remembered the cobwebs that had covered the tools in there, and his assertion that he couldn't face carpentry after losing Jane.

'Yeah—Oh, but you can't talk to him.'

Marnie paused. 'What?'

Lauren dragged her attention away from the dogs momentarily. 'Yeah, he said to tell you that you can't go in there.'

Marnie flushed. She supposed she deserved that. 'I won't sit on the chair again, if that's what it's about,' she muttered.

But Lauren had stopped listening again, bending to coo over the puppies.

Marnie flopped into a chair, slurping her tea so quickly that she scalded her mouth. She was a little disgruntled. Surely they were past this now; they'd moved on, or at least, Marnie had thought so. Yes, she'd made a mistake going into the shed before, but she didn't need to be told to keep out now. It was a good sign, though, that he was working in there again. If that's what he was doing. It must be, she supposed.

She grimaced as she swallowed down the last dregs of tea, still piping hot, her mind buzzing.

Well, she would just have to assume that Andrew simply didn't want to be disturbed and it was nothing personal. Perhaps it was better she didn't see him anyway; she'd been feeling a little discombobulated whenever she was around him lately. It was an uncomfortable sensation and she wasn't sure she liked it. She took her mug back into the kitchen, setting it on the counter. It was about time she got the dinner on, she thought, suddenly keen to get out of Andrew's cottage.

'Lauren,' she called. 'We're leaving.'

Lauren frowned at her as she marched back into the living room. 'But I haven't had my tea. And what about the puppies?'

'They'll be fine, Andrew's only in the shed. Come on, I'll make us some nice stodgy pasta and you can try my new recipe for chocolate and orange cupcakes.'

Lauren needed no more persuading than this.

*

The house was quiet, and Marnie could just make out the sound of Lauren FaceTiming her dad, talking and laughing quietly. She'd taken a plate of cupcakes up to her room. Apparently taste testing involved eating at least four. Marnie decided to take that as a sign of approval.

Now she was alone, Marnie was plagued by guilt. Perhaps they shouldn't have left the puppies unsupervised. She'd been in such a hurry to leave that she'd dismissed Lauren's warning that they shouldn't be left alone, but now she was worried that something might have happened.

She'd just pop round quickly, to reassure herself, she thought as she put on her coat. It would only take a minute. She would hardly see Andrew at all.

She stopped at the mirror by the door and brushed her hair until the soft curls gleamed, and swiped on a bit of lipstick. Not for any reason; just nice to feel her best.

He smiled when he opened the door and stood back, waving her in.

'I'm just having a sherry and a mince pie,' he said. 'Want to join me?'

'Well, I'm just here to—' Marnie stopped, gaping at him. 'I'm sorry, you're what?'

'Sherry,' he said, enunciating clearly as though she was stupid. 'Mince pie. Want?'

Marnie stepped in and struggled out of her boots. 'Well, I'm just popping round . . .'

He poured her a glass of Bristol Cream and waved a Tupperware tub of the bakery's mince pies at her. 'Help yourself.'

'I'm not stopping,' Marnie said, taking a sip of sherry and choosing a mince pie.

'Okay.' He sat in an armchair, stockinged feet stretched out towards the fire, gazing at the pups, who all seemed to be fine. Music was playing, and he tapped his feet to the sound of a woman singing about a nice dress and sunsets.

Marnie threw her coat over the back of a chair and sat down, picking up a cushion and holding it on her lap. 'I really just came to—wait, you drink sweet sherry?'

He glanced at her, looking a little defensive. 'Only at Christmas. And sometimes on Sundays. Why?'

'No, it's just . . . not what I expected.'

'Ah.' He stood up and poked at the fire, and Marnie tried not to stare at the stretch of his back under his shirt. He added another log, and settled back down with a wry smile. 'Thought I was a pint and scratchings kind of man, did you?'

'No.' Yes. 'Is this—You listen to Taylor Swift?'

He shifted in the chair. 'Sometimes. What? It's catchy.'

'Okay then.'

Marnie took another sip, another bite, and silently counted the puppies; four. All present and correct as they wriggled blindly over their prostrate mother. They'd grown a little fluffier, but still looked more like rats than dogs.

'I just wanted to check—'

'Did you come round, earlier, by the way? I saw the tea and I thought maybe you had.'

Marnie shifted in her chair. 'Lauren said you were busy, so I didn't stay, and I won't bother you now, I just came to check that . . .'

He gave her that quirked-lip, creased-eyes smile that made her stomach drop. 'You're not bothering me,' he said softly.

Marnie gulped her sherry, almost choking, and took another bite of mince pie, spilling icing sugar down herself. Her face felt hot and she crossed and then uncrossed her legs. Somehow she'd forgotten how to sit normally. She hadn't felt this awkward since she was a teenager. 'How are the puppies doing?' she asked, desperate to talk about something neutral.

'Fine, I think. David's going to pop round again at some point.'

'Rosie doesn't seem her usual self.'

'I think she's just tired.'

Marnie looked at the dog as she lay on her side, ignoring the bleating of the pups. She'd thought Rosie would be a more involved mother than this. But Andrew was probably right. He knew her a lot better than Marnie did.

They sat in silence for a while, watching the basket of dogs contentedly, listening to the snapping of the fire. Andrew's phone buzzed and he picked it up, his expression softening as he read whatever message he'd been sent. Something twisted in Marnie's stomach. She cleared her throat and studied the cushion she held, noticing now that it was beautifully embroidered with images of birds. This must be his wife's work; she was clearly very talented.

'Someone's a twitcher,' she said, immediately wishing she hadn't, in case the bird lover had been Jane.

But Andrew smiled and raised his hand. 'Guilty as charged.'

Marnie admired the delicacy and detail of the work, looking closely at the carefully stitched wrens, swallows and magpies. And there, in the corner, a breed she hadn't expected to see.

'Wait, that's a—'

They spoke at the same time. 'Golden winged warbler.'

Marnie smiled. 'Beautiful. Did you hear about that one that was spotted in Kent that time?'

Andrew took a sip of sherry and leaned forward in his chair, eyes alight. 'Hear about it? I saw it.'

Marnie almost dropped her glass. 'No! I'm so jealous, I always wish I could've seen it. But you couldn't, you must've only been . . .'

'A kid, yeah. My dad took me, it was something we used to do together, you know.'

'How lovely. I spent a good few summers hiding in fields here when I was young, Matt got me all the gear and I had a little notebook that I wrote everything I saw down in.'

'Oh, me too! Dad and I used to spend whole days that way.'

Marnie grinned, imagining him as a boy. 'I can't believe you actually saw the golden winged warbler! What was it like?'

He smiled and shook his head, and Marnie could tell that he was reliving the experience. 'Oh, wonderful. Those little flashes of yellow, it was just a beauty. I used to talk about it all the time, that's why she put it on the cushion.'

He stopped, and gave her a small, sad smile before staring into the flames. Marnie was very aware, suddenly, of the cushion in her hands. Gently, she placed it on the chair next to her. As though it was made of glass.

'It's beautiful,' she said.

Andrew nodded and cleared his throat. She thought she saw him quickly wipe his eyes. 'You're doing well with the bakery,' he said, his voice a little shaky. And Marnie followed his lead with the change of subject.

'Oh, not really. Had a little rush after the display, you know, but back to the usual now. But thank you,' she added as an afterthought.

He raised an eyebrow. 'Not so good with the compliments, are you?'

Marnie flushed. She wasn't used to compliments, truth be told, she'd never been the one people noticed;

it was always vivacious Lily or cheeky David or charismatic Ian. 'What? I—I'm fine with compliments, thank you very . . .'

'Bit on the defensive side, too. If you don't mind me saying.'

Marnie very much did mind. The comment was unfair, but there was no way to say so without proving his point. She downed her sherry, and he refilled her glass.

'I did have an idea about the bakery,' she said, immediately wishing she hadn't. She was so desperate to move the subject away from the painful one of his wife that she was gabbling.

'Oh yes?'

'Thinking of turning it into a café.' For heaven's sake, Marnie. Stop talking. Why was she even mentioning this mad pipe dream of hers?

Andrew shifted in his chair to fully face her. 'That's a great idea.'

Marnie smiled. 'You think?' She'd never voiced her plan before, hadn't even fully admitted to herself that this was what she wanted.

'Great, yes. We need that in the village, somewhere people can get together.'

'That's what I was thinking, because after school some of the parents come in with their children and they need somewhere to stop for a chat and have a bite, I thought I'd have a children's area with toys and . . .'

'And you could do breakfasts, people could have a fry up or pick up a bacon butty on the way to work.'

'Perhaps. I was thinking more along the lines of cakes and . . .'

'Marnie's Caf!'

Marnie was indignant. 'It will not be Marnie's Caf!' The image of a greasy spoon with dirty lino and sticky tables flooded her mind. 'Ugh, no. It'll be The Village Café, and it'll have little tablecloths and teapots and gingham curtains and flowers on the tables.'

He pulled a face. 'Sounds a bit genteel for Babblebrook.'

'Babblebrook *is* genteel,' she said, trying not to picture the Woods' farm.

'Well,' he said, his voice gentle now. 'Marnie's Caf or,' he put on a fake posh voice, 'The Village Café, I'm sure you'll do a great job.'

'Oh.' Marnie shuffled her feet, twisted her glass. 'I don't know, it's just a silly idea, I've never really . . .'

'Ah.' He held up a finger, smiling. 'See, can't take a compliment. Just accept it. You'd be good at it.'

'Oh, well. We'll see.' It was the best she could manage. Perhaps there was some truth to what he said after all. Annoyingly.

But she didn't feel annoyed. She felt warm, and confident.

It was uncomfortable. She preferred it when he was being prickly, she knew how to handle that.

Once again Andrew's phone buzzed, and Marnie caught a glimpse of the notification – apparently someone called Lorraine was sending him what appeared to be a line of emojis. Her stomach knotted. Including hearts. She cleared her throat, placed her glass down a little too heavily so that it thumped against the surface of the coffee table. 'Well I—oops, uh I'd better go. Lauren, you know . . .' Oh God, Lauren! She hadn't even told her where she was going.

He saw her to the front door. She stopped to stroke Rosie's head on her way out. The dog didn't stir.

'Thanks for popping round,' he said.

They stood for a moment, and she felt almost dizzy, standing so close to him with those blue eyes looking at her so intently. She had to resist a sudden urge to lean against the soft cloth of his shirt. 'It was lovely to see you,' he said gently. 'And you know, if you want company next time you're birdwatching . . .' He gave her that lopsided smile. 'If you follow the brook up to the river there's a place you can see a kingfisher sometimes, I could show you.'

'Oh, ah yes, lovely. Good idea.' She couldn't get her words out. It was as though she'd forgotten how to speak. 'Th—thanks for having me.' Marnie blushed. What was she, fourteen?

Her cheeks were burning when she arrived at her own door, even though the night air was so cold. She called up the stairs to Lauren and got no answer. She was still talking to her dad. She hadn't even noticed that Marnie had gone.

Chapter Twenty-Two

It wasn't often that Marnie allowed herself a lie in. Sunday mornings were her only chance, when the bakery was closed and Lauren didn't need to be cajoled out of the door to school.

Christmas was just around the corner, but the presents were bought, mostly wrapped, and the food had been ordered. Everyone had accepted her invitation for Christmas dinner. She felt no guilt as she peeked over the duvet at the clock, saw it said eight-thirty, and burrowed back down. She would give herself the luxury of another half an hour.

The knocking started just as she was beginning to drift back to sleep and feeling a little smug, thinking of all those poor harassed people dashing round crowded town centres doing last-minute shopping. Her eyes sprang open and she lurched upwards.

Who could be calling on her now? It must be an emergency. No one in their right mind would knock on the door at this time on a Sunday morning.

She grabbed her dressing gown and pulled it on as she ran down the stairs, yanking the front door open and blinking in the cold, bright light.

'No one in their right mind would knock on the door at this time on a Sunday morning,' she said, glowering at Andrew who stood grinning at her. 'Unless it was an emergency.'

'It is an emergency,' he said cheerfully. 'I need to go Christmas shopping.'

If she hadn't been so flabbergasted she'd have closed the door in his face.

'And I need someone to keep an eye on Rosie and the pups, so I thought maybe you or Lauren could help me out? Please?'

Marnie had planned to spend her Sunday baking, reading and putting her feet up by the fire in her own cosy cottage. But, as Andrew looked down at her, his blue eyes twinkling, she couldn't resist him. She nodded. 'Of course.'

A smile burst across his face, and Marnie cursed herself as her stomach turned in response. 'Great, thanks. I owe you one. I'll just give you time to, uh—' His gaze focused on the bird's nest of her bed head, and he raised his eyebrows. 'Clean up.'

She dragged a brush through her hair. That man had a knack for catching her unawares. And seeing her at her worst, she thought, trying to massage the pillow-crease out of her cheek. Not that she cared.

There were no signs of life from Lauren's room. Marnie knocked quietly. No response. Despite the very clear instructions her daughter had given, she entered anyway, picking her way across the debris scattered over the carpet. Luckily it was too dark to see what lurked there.

'Darling?'

The lump of bedding didn't move.

'Squidge?'

The duvet was thrown back and Lauren's angry, dishevelled head rose up. 'Don't call me that.'

'Okay, sorry.' Marnie supressed a smile. 'I'm going round to sit with the puppies, do you want to come?'

Lauren crashed back down and pulled the covers over her face. Her reply was muffled but the meaning was clear. She declined the invitation.

Armed with her book and plenty of homemade biscuits, Marnie knocked on Andrew's door. As she waited, she watched a particularly fat squirrel climb up the stand of his bird table, reaching a slinky that was attached to it, and then immediately sliding to the ground with a disgruntled expression as the slinky unravelled under its weight. She laughed. Perhaps he'd finally got the better of those cheeky creatures.

A tantalising smell of fresh coffee drifted out as he opened the door. 'Oh great, you're here,' he said. 'You look . . . nice.' His eyes were focused on the pillow-crease.

Marnie cleared her throat and turned away. 'Anything I need to do with them?' she asked, walking through to where the puppies wriggled in their basket.

He shrugged. 'Not really, just keep an eye out. Rosie didn't eat much of her breakfast, if you could encourage her that would be good.'

'Oh that's not like her.' Marnie gazed down at the little dog, lying with her eyes closed.

Andrew frowned and bent to stroke her. She thumped her tail once. 'I know, and she needs to eat to keep her milk coming. I think she's just really tired. Aren't you, girl?'

The puppies were a small, sprawling mass, the littlest one the noisiest of all, climbing over the pile of her siblings until she reached the top, grunting as she made herself comfortable, and promptly falling asleep, now she'd woken all the others up.

Andrew laughed. 'Quite a personality that one, eh girl?' he said, stroking Rosie. 'But that's not the one we're keeping is it? We have other plans for her. We'll choose a nice, quiet one to keep you company, eh?'

'Oh, you're keeping one?' Marnie hadn't thought about what would happen to the pups once they were old enough to leave their mum.

'Always the plan. Bit of company, you know, to help with her nerves. It's working already. Isn't it?' He ran his finger over her head. She didn't stir.

He stood and reached for his phone, laughing quietly as he read a message, then pocketed it and grabbed his jacket and keys. He smiled at Marnie, and she found she was frowning, thinking of the emoji message she'd seen on his phone the night before. She hastily changed her expression.

'Won't be long,' he said. 'Coffee in the pot for you.'

Marnie glanced around. Andrew had already lit the fire and the room was cosy enough. He still had no Christmas tree but the decorations they'd put up hung where they'd left them. The brown leather chairs were made more inviting by the cushions scattered over them, all embroidered with wildflowers, except for the one with the birds.

She followed the smell of coffee to the kitchen, and poured herself a cup, taking a sip. It was rich and delicious, humming through her and gently waking her up. Andrew's immaculate kitchen calmed her; the orderliness was soothing. She took her coffee and went back to the pups.

Marnie knelt by the basket. She was preparing to open her book and dig into the biscuit tin, settling down to a quiet morning of relaxing and glancing at the pups every so often, but something troubled her. They were noisier than they had been before, she thought, all crying at the same time.

Well, they were a bit older now. Perhaps that was just what happened.

Marnie placed her coffee on the table and bent to look more closely. An unpleasant smell rose from the basket that she was sure hadn't been there before. The puppies were energetic enough, crawling onto Rosie and trying to latch on, but they seemed to be having trouble feeding. Not one of them settled and fed; they all, after a short time, cried and wriggled and tried to suckle somewhere else.

Marnie bit her lip. They were bigger now, they needed more food. Perhaps Rosie was just taking a while to catch up to their growing demands. Perhaps this was a normal stage. She would have more milk coming in soon.

That would be tricky if she wasn't eating, though.

'Rosie,' she called. 'Here, Rosie, come on, girl. Breakfast!'

In the past Rosie had always jumped up at the sound of her name, wagging her tail and looking hopefully at her bowl. Nothing, today. She didn't stir.

Marnie tickled her under the chin. 'Come on, girl. Up you get.'

Nothing.

She brought the bowl of food through, picking out the little biscuits one by one and holding them under Rosie's nose. All she needed to do was open her mouth. But she just turned away.

This couldn't be right. She was feeding four puppies, surely she should be hungry.

Marnie raided Andrew's fridge and found some bacon. This was bound to work, she thought as it sizzled in the pan and the mouth-watering smell rose up. No one could resist bacon, especially not greedy little dogs.

She hurried through to the pups. 'Here you go,' she said, waving a rasher under Rosie's nose. 'This'll do the trick. Come on, just a little nibble.'

Rosie sniffed and lifted her head, and for a moment Marnie was filled with hope. She hadn't been so invested in another person's appetite since Lauren was a baby. But Rosie dropped her head again without giving the bacon so much as a lick. The smallest pup, the one Lauren said had been born last, shuffled over and lifted its tiny head, sniffing at the air.

'Not for you, greedy,' Marnie said, stroking it gently with her finger. It was soft and warm. 'Oh, Rosie. What are we going to do with you? Hopefully your dad will be back soon.'

She glanced at her phone. He'd been gone twenty minutes. Probably hadn't even parked yet. Surely she was worrying over nothing.

'All right. How about a nice cuppa, eh? That'll do the trick.'

She made tea and poured it into Rosie's bowl, good and milky, just how she liked it. She considered eating some of the bacon while the kettle boiled, but didn't fancy it. She really was worried. It took something serious to spoil Marnie's appetite.

Rosie couldn't be tempted by the tea. She refused the bacon again, refused the dog biscuits again. The pups grew louder, and hungrier.

Marnie began to pace round the little living room. She called Andrew. No answer. She called David. His phone was off. She left messages for them both, attempting to stay calm for Andrew, failing to do so for David.

She tried again to tempt Rosie to eat or drink, without success. She watched the puppies, who at least still seemed to have enough energy to move around and protest at their lack of nourishment. How long could they last, without food? She had no idea.

She tried calling again. No answer from either.

Her coffee grew cold and the biscuit tin was left unopened. Bacon fat congealed in the pan left in Andrew's tidy kitchen. Marnie could think of nothing but Rosie, and the puppies.

For a brief moment she found herself longing for Ian. He'd been so decisive in moments like this. He always made the world feel safe in scary moments, he never worried about anything. She reached for her phone. He would know what to do.

For heaven's sake. He knew no more about dogs than she did; less, probably.

She needed to trust herself. She didn't know much about dogs, but she knew Rosie and this wasn't right. She would call Andrew and David once more. If no one picked up, she would call the vets.

Still nothing from Andrew. She left another message, trying not to sound desperate.

This time, David picked up.

'Hey, what's up?'

'Where the hell have you been? Your phone was off.'

'Wow, okay snarky, Greg and I are just out at—'

'Sorry to snap but I'm dog sitting the puppies and something's not right.'

'What? What's happening?'

David was all business now. Marnie was in awe of her little brother as he asked with calm authority for details. Until the puppies were born, she'd never seen him at work, and she still struggled to imagine him in such a serious role.

'Sounds like Rosie has an infection. You need to get her to the vet.'

'Andrew should be home soon, so . . .'

'It can't wait, this could get serious for her. You need to go now.'

Marnie swallowed, glancing at Rosie. It would be terrible if anything happened to her. 'What about the puppies? Can't you come over?'

'I would, but Greg and I are out, we're miles away, it'll take too long.'

'Okay. I'll get Lauren to sit with the puppies and I'll take Rosie in.'

'I'll call and tell them you're coming. Let me know how she gets on?'

Marnie was not reassured by the edge of concern in his voice.

She called Lauren, who had mercifully emerged from her bed and was coherent enough to immediately dash round.

'Don't worry, Mum,' she said, her own face pinched with concern. 'I'll look after the babies, you take Rosie.'

Marnie wrapped Rosie in a blanket Lauren had brought. The little dog didn't protest. She barely moved, and she lay silently as Marnie drove to the emergency vets, trying to find a happy medium between the need to go carefully so as not to disturb Rosie, and her sense of urgency. She prayed, as she drove down the icy country roads, that they could make Rosie better.

Chapter Twenty-Three

Forewarned by David, the vet had run out when Marnie arrived, white-faced, and taken Rosie from her. The poor dog made no sound, no movement, and Marnie was gripped by a sudden fear that she was already lost to them.

She'd waited too long. She should have come here straight away.

She paced the small waiting room with its plastic chairs and drab ropes of tinsel, clasping and unclasping her hands. Trying to keep her voice calm, she left Andrew another message saying where they were. The last thing he needed was to feel he had to comfort her.

Marnie sat. She read the posters on the wall that gave details of what foods were poisonous to dogs without taking in a word. She picked up a leaflet on how to keep rabbits and stared at it blankly. She watched as people arrived with cats in crates and dogs on leads, and sat patiently waiting. She paced. She checked her phone. Nothing.

At last the same vet that had taken Rosie from her appeared and walked towards her. Marnie's heart crashed. The woman wore a serious expression, but looked less worried than when she'd taken Rosie.

Marnie opened her mouth to ask the question that consumed her, but her throat was too dry to allow her to speak. Just as she managed to squeak out the words, Andrew burst in, letting the door hit the wall with a crash. He had a sickly pallor, and Marnie could see the fear in his eyes.

'I'm afraid Rosie has metritis,' the vet said.

'Is that—What is that?' Andrew said. His voice shook. Without thinking, Marnie took his hand. He held on.

'It's an inflammation of the uterus, it can happen after—'

'Is it serious?' Andrew spoke sharply. He sounded angry, but Marnie knew it was fear that he felt.

The vet sighed, frowning. 'It can be. It looks like you've caught it quite early, so I'm hopeful, but we need to do more tests. She needs to be kept here for a while for treatment and . . .'

Andrew's breath caught and Marnie felt a tremor run through him. She squeezed his hand.

'But what about the puppies?' she asked. 'They need her.'

'They'll have to be hand reared, can you do that?'

'Yes,' Andrew said. 'Yes, we can do that.'

'It's a lot of work, it'll be round the clock.'

'It'll be fine,' Marnie said. 'We'll manage.'

'Right, well. We'll get everything you need,' the vet replied.

'Can I see her?' Andrew asked.

The vet looked sympathetic, but shook her head. 'I'm sorry. She needs a lot of care right now.'

Andrew nodded. He turned to Marnie with a blank, shattered expression. She guided him to a chair, collected the equipment for the puppies and listened intently to the instructions, then led him outside.

The cold, fresh air was a welcome relief after the disinfectant-scented stuffiness of the vets. Marnie glanced around the car park. Andrew's truck was parked a little skew-whiff, but he was more or less in the white lines. It could be left like that for now.

'Come on,' she said. 'I'll drive you home.'

'But I've got my . . .'

Marnie was firm. 'You're in no fit state. We'll collect it another time.'

She guided him to the passenger's side and helped him in. He said nothing, and he was so pale that she worried he might faint. She had to stop herself reaching over and fastening his seatbelt.

*

They wasted no time preparing the milk and feeding the pups. Lauren helped, weighing each one and making careful notes. She used the names she'd given them; Spot, Smudge, Sam and Holly, the little brown one that had been born last. The greediest of them all, it turned out, happily drinking her milk in half the time it took the others.

'She's got some catching up to do,' Lauren said, cradling the tiny creature and gently kissing the top of her head.

Their work done for now, Lauren returned home to catch up on schoolwork, Marnie made tea and brought some to Andrew. His hand shook so much that she had to take the mug back off him and put it on the coffee table.

He dropped his head forward and covered his face with his hands. 'It's my fault.'

Marnie kept her voice soft. 'It's really not.'

'No, you don't understand. It's happened again, I missed the signs and I didn't – why do I always manage to let everyone down? I was—I was shopping for God's sake, and she was here and so poorly and I didn't even notice. Why didn't I just call David when she didn't eat? I thought she was just—'

'How could you know? It's not your fault, Andrew.'

'If only I'd noticed, I could've called them earlier and then she'd be fine, she wouldn't be scared and sick, away from home and away from her pups. I just can't stand to think of it.'

Marnie knelt in front of him, placing her hands on his knees. 'Hey, she'll be okay. You'll see, she'll be back in a day or two, eating you out of house and home and begging for a bowl full of tea.'

He snorted a small laugh. There were tears in his eyes. It was cruel, after all he'd suffered, that he was burdened with this too.

He gazed at her with a stricken expression, his voice little more than a whisper when he spoke. 'What if she doesn't make it?'

'She will.' Marnie kept her voice firm, kept out all the fear and doubt she herself was feeling.

'Thanks to you.' He took her hands in his. 'Because you were here, because you noticed and you did something about it.' He rubbed her hands with his thumbs.

'Oh, I . . . no, it was just that I happened to be here.'

'No. You saved the day, Marnie.'
'Really, anyone would—'
'No. Thank God you were here.'
She lifted her gaze to meet his, his blue eyes both intense and sincere.
'Thank God for you,' he said.
He stroked her hands. His eyes were locked on hers. She could barely breathe.
'You know you're . . .' His gaze moved over her face and he brushed her hair from her cheek, his gentle touch lingering there. Marnie's heart pounded. Everything in her yearned to press her lips against his, and she could feel him lean towards her.
Renewed bleating from the puppies, loud and insistent, brought her to her senses. Quickly she removed her hands from Andrew's knees and went to inspect the basket. Two of the pups were tangled in a blanket, little Holly stranded on her back and waving her legs furiously.
Marnie chuckled, lifting them free and righting them. Her hands trembled a little and her heart still crashed. Forcing herself to focus on the pups, she rearranged the blanket into a more comfortable position; it was important that, without their mum to warm them, they were kept snug.
'Right,' she said brightly. 'More tea?'
He hadn't drunk the last cup, and it wasn't even cold yet, but that didn't matter. She needed an excuse to hurry to a different room, carefully avoiding his eye. She'd almost made a fool of herself, there.

Chapter Twenty-Four

Christmas was nearly upon them, just days away, and it was the last day of term. The usual crowd of school-run parents and children had been rather noisy – the children excited and the parents frazzled. Marnie had offered free hot chocolates all round, and more than one parent bemoaned the fact that it was too early for a mulled wine. Marnie was glad to have this slightly rowdy crowd to keep her busy; in quiet moments she found herself thinking of the look on Andrew's face as he'd stroked her hair, and giving herself a shiver as she imagined what it would be like to kiss him.

Little Amy had run in before her mum had even reached the door, waving a glitter-covered card at Marnie.

'Oh,' Marnie had said, smiling. 'What's this?'

Julia struggled in, dragging the buggy, and Marnie rushed to hold the door open for her. 'They made Christmas cards at school and she decided to give hers to you.'

'Oh!' Marnie was genuinely touched, crouching so that she was face to face with the little girl. There was a blob of what looked like baked bean juice in the corner of her mouth and she smelled of bubble bath and cold air. 'That's really for me?'

Amy nodded, unusually shy.

'Yes,' Julia said, smiling, pulling off a bobble hat and patting down the auburn curls that sprang up around her head. 'She's chosen you even over Granny Joan, who spoils her rotten, so you're honoured.'

Marnie took the card, admiring the glittery cardboard Christmas stocking glued rather wonkily to the front, and opening it to read the large, shaky writing. 'To Marnie, love from Amy. Ah, thank you. I'll put it on the counter. I think that deserves a treat, don't you?'

She glanced at Julia, who nodded her consent as she unstrapped the crying baby from the buggy.

'What would you like?'

Marnie lifted the little girl onto her hip so that she could gaze at the goodies behind the counter. Her eyes grew round and she poked her tongue between her lips in concentration as she made her decision.

She chose a chocolate snowball, demolishing it in two very messy, happy bites. Marnie smiled, trying not to feel guilty at the thought that she wasn't helping Pat and Matt much by giving away their profits. Still, Julia was one of their best customers now. And it was Christmas, after all.

When everyone had gone, she was about to lock up; no one ever came in after the school-run parents and she wanted to get back home. But just as she was about to turn the sign from open to closed, she saw another group of parents and children tumbling out of cars and heading towards the bakery. They stopped at the window, cooing and pointing, taking photos, and then piled through the door.

'Oh it's just as lovely as we thought it would be!' said a woman with a boy in school uniform wearing a Paw Patrol bobble hat. 'Better in fact, don't you think, Alex?' The little boy nodded.

'Oh . . . thank you,' Marnie managed to stammer. She stared around at the group of people crowding into the shop, picking out her new festive bakes and chatting excitedly about the display.

'Are you selling them?' the woman asked.

'I'm sorry, selling what?'

'The gingerbread houses to decorate. My in-laws read about it in *The Blast*, and then I saw pictures of it on Instagram and Alex was so taken with the display we thought we'd have a little trip to come and see it on the last day of school. I said we'd buy one of your gingerbread houses to decorate and we'll do it over the holiday.'

'Oh good idea!' a man with a girl of about eight who was picking out iced biscuits said. 'We'll take a couple.' He looked around. 'You are selling them, aren't you?'

'Oh—uh, yes,' Marnie said. Her mind was reeling and her heart beating a little quickly with the excitement of seeing the bakery full of customers who had driven specially to come and see her display, and at the thought of people posting about it on Instagram. It was more gratifying and less embarrassing than she'd thought. 'Yes, definitely. But we, uh, we've sold out.' A look of disappointment settled on the children's faces. 'But I'll have more. Tomorrow! I'll have more tomorrow so come back then.'

She smiled and they all smiled too, and nodded and agreed that they would come back the next day. In the meantime they bought plenty of biscuits, salted caramel mince pies and Christmas cake slices before eventually leaving.

Marnie flipped the sign to closed and tied her apron back on, turning up the radio and mixing a great quantity of gingerbread. She hummed as she worked, planning the signs she would put in the window advertising her 'Decorate your own' gingerbread houses, and making a mental note to set up an Instagram account for the bakery.

It was dark when she'd finally finished, the gingerbread cut and propped up around bowls to dry. She was late, and she would have to come in early the next day to finish them off, but she consoled herself that Lauren was probably too distracted to notice.

She hurried out, leaving on the lights and little toy train. The gingerbread Babblebrook still gave her a wave of happiness every time she looked at it, and she marvelled now at what a success it had been. Fired up, she couldn't stop herself planning a new display for January. Perhaps with accompanying 'Ice your own' snowflake biscuits.

She went straight round to Andrew's. It was no surprise to find Lauren still there, placing the pups on the scales one after another, carefully noting down each one's weight in her book.

'They've all got heavier,' she said, with a huge smile. 'Especially you,' she crooned, holding the little bundle that was Holly to her face. 'Haven't you? Yes, because you're so greedy.'

The puppy seemed perfectly content to lie in Lauren's arms as she played with its ears and tickled its tummy.

'Tea?' Andrew asked, heaving himself up from the sofa. He looked exhausted, and rumpled. He was up every few hours through the night feeding the puppies.

'I'll do it,' Marnie said.

'No. You've done so much already, I think you should let someone look after you for once.'

He walked to the kitchen, running a hand over his eyes. Marnie followed.

'Any news on Rosie?'

His face lit up and he nodded as he ran water into the kettle and flicked it on. 'Yes, David called earlier, she can come home in a day or two.'

'Oh how wonderful!'

Forgetting herself for a moment, Marnie threw her arms around his neck, stepping close so that she was pressed against him, and she felt his arms circle her waist, pulling her in. He smelled of soap and wood shavings. His heart beat fast against hers and he gazed down at her, those blue eyes locked on hers.

She should move. She should step away.

Her heart raced, and all the many reasons that she should stop this disappeared; she could think of nothing but the warmth of his arms and the intensity of his gaze. And how much she wanted to kiss him, how good it felt to be this close to him. Slowly, she reached up, pressing her lips to his, and he kissed her back, softly at first, and then passionately, clasping her to him tightly, and heat spread through her. She was lost in the moment, knowing only that she wanted this. She wanted him.

And then, nothing.

He stopped, pulled away. Gently pushed her so that her hands fell from his neck, and she was standing at arm's length, staring at him in confusion.

'Marnie, I—I can't.'

She didn't understand what was happening. The moment had felt so right, there had been such a strong connection between them. And she was sure he'd felt it too.

'This isn't what you want,' he said.

'Don't tell me what I want,' she said softly. 'I know my own mind, I know how I feel about you.'

He was shaking his head. 'Not with this. Not with . . . with me.'

'But—'

'I need you to leave.'

Marnie felt her eyes fill with tears of humiliation and she forced herself to bite them down. 'But we—I thought you . . .'

He turned his back to her, leaning his arms on the counter, the muscles in his back tensing through his shirt.

'Just go,' he said.

And so she did. Burning with embarrassment, forcing back the hot, angry tears that had gathered in her eyes, she hurried through the living room, past Lauren and the dogs, grabbed her coat and left.

Lauren ran after her. 'Hey, Mum, you okay?' she called. 'What's up, are you . . .'

Lizzie Lee

She stopped, staring just as Marnie did at the car parked outside their cottage, at the man climbing out of it, pushing away the hair that flopped over his eyes and giving them both a cheeky grin.

'Oh my God, oh my God,' she cried, her hands pressed to her mouth. 'Dad!'

Chapter Twenty-Five

Marnie's head was spinning.

She watched as Lauren threw her arms around Ian, and he hugged her so tightly her feet lifted off the ground.

He was here. Why was he here?

He set Lauren back down and looked past her at Marnie.

'Hey,' he said, his voice soft, walking up to her and flicking his hair out of his eyes. His gaze travelled her face and he smiled in his relaxed, confident way.

'You look great,' he said, kissing her cheek, and he felt so warm and familiar, and humiliation still burned through her, and for a moment she leaned in to his embrace, resting her head against his shoulder. When she pulled away he gazed at her with a look of concern, gently pushing the hair from her face. 'You okay?'

She nodded, speechless, her mind spinning with the events of the last few minutes. As if in a dream, she followed as Lauren led Ian into the cottage, chatting enthusiastically to him about their life in Babblebrook. Marnie made tea, brought out mince pies, sat quietly as Ian nodded and laughed at Lauren's stories. As he caught her eye, time and again, giving her that charming smile, as though he couldn't tear his gaze away from her. All the while she was in turmoil, trying to make sense of what had happened with Andrew, and what was now happening with Ian.

'This is the best Christmas present ever!' Lauren said. 'You can have my bed if you like and I'll sleep on the sofa for a bit.'

Marnie almost fell off her chair. Lauren loved her bed almost as much as she loved her phone, and her room was out of bounds to anyone but Emma. She'd made it clear to Marnie that a teenager's bedroom was their private safe haven, and not to be invaded by family members. Marnie had respected that. Apparently Ian wasn't required to. And now, it seemed, he was staying with them. Well, he was Lauren's dad, she could hardly kick him out four days before Christmas. Even if she wanted to. The cottage only had two bedrooms though, and if someone was going to end up on the sofa, it wasn't going to be her.

'And there's plenty of food for you to stay for Christmas, Mum's bought enough to feed the whole village, haven't you, Mum?' Lauren chattered. 'And she's invited Uncles David and Greg so you'll get to see them, and Pat and Matt are coming of course and—Oh, Dad! You must come round and see the puppies next door they're so cute and we're having to feed them because—'

Marnie almost spat her tea out. 'No!'

Lauren stopped talking, and turned to look at her in confusion. 'Why not?'

Marnie stared at her, her mouth opening and closing, her mind filled with the smell of soap and wood shavings, her skin prickling with the sensation of being in Andrew's arms. Her cheeks burning with the rejection she'd just endured.

'Well, it's . . . it's not a good idea, they're still so tiny, it's not good to crowd them.' She flushed, waiting to see what their response would be.

Ian nodded, seemingly unbothered. Lauren frowned, but moved on to telling her dad about the school project she and Emma had been working on.

And Marnie sat back, her body in this room but her mind still next door, reliving over and over the kiss that had awakened a fire in her she had thought would never be rekindled. Then the sting of humiliation as Andrew pushed her away and told her to leave. Her stomach plummeted.

And now, Ian was here, with that easy ability of his to make everything better.

Damn it, and still as handsome as ever.

*

At last, Lauren remembered that she'd been invited to Emma's to have dinner. She gathered her things and gave Ian another hug. He saw her to the door, glancing over the hedge into Andrew's garden as he did so.

He frowned, doing a double-take. 'Why has the next door neighbour got a slinky on the stand of his bird table?' he asked.

'Squirrels,' Marnie said.

Ian turned a questioning look to Lauren, and she shook her head as she left. 'Don't bother, Dad. They're both as mad as each other.'

Julia was passing with the baby in the buggy, the wheels squeaking as she pushed. Ian waved. 'Hey,' he said. 'Sounds like you've got a mouse trapped in there!'

Julia laughed. 'Oh yes, they're a bit—'

Marnie watched as Ian sauntered over, smiling and chatting, pulling faces to make the baby laugh and bending to fiddle with the wheels of the buggy. He'd always been this way, talking to strangers, charming anyone that met him.

'WD40,' he said. 'Got some in the car, hold on.' He smiled at her as he jogged over and scrabbled in the boot, returning with the can.

'There you go,' he said, oiling the wheels. 'Try that now.'

Julia pushed the now-quiet buggy up and down, laughing. 'Thank you, I've been meaning to do that for weeks.' She glanced at Marnie. 'Useful kind of a person to have around!'

Marnie nodded, and Ian turned to smile at her briefly.

'No trouble.' He wiped his hand down his shirt and then held it out for her to shake. 'Ian, by the way.'

'Julia. Nice to meet you. And thanks again.'

He waved and turned back to the cottage. Julia caught Marnie's eye, glancing at Ian and pretending to fan herself, then grinning as she gave her a thumbs up. Despite herself, Marnie laughed, filled with a familiar warmth that this man everyone loved had chosen her.

'What?' he asked, glancing from her to Julia, who quickly turned and trotted off.

Marnie shrugged, trying not to smile as he put the oil in the cupboard under the stairs and followed her into the kitchen.

'Nice woman,' he said, wiping his hands down his shirt again, and then pulling a face as he noticed the stain.

'It's all right,' Marnie said, holding out her hand. 'Give it to me, I'll fix it for you.'

He gave her a sheepish grin and began unbuttoning. 'How did I ever think I'd manage without you?'

Marnie didn't answer. She was too busy trying and failing to drag her gaze from Ian's toned torso. 'Um—Uh, bicarbonate of soda, that's what we need.' She busied herself in the cupboard. 'Now, where did I—Ah there we go. The answer to all stains and stinkies.' She laughed, and felt the edge of hysteria to it.

He went to fetch another top from his car as she blotted the stain with kitchen paper and then sprinkled it with the bicarbonate of soda. 'There,' she said. 'It'll be good as new by the time I've finished with it.'

He took the paper off her and threw it in the bin, then helped her as she started to load the dishwasher. There was something comforting about the familiarity of doing this mundane job together.

'Still looking after me,' he said.

'Oh, it's no—'

'Marnie. I know you're wondering why I'm here.'

Quite the understatement. Marnie rinsed a plate, waiting for him to continue.

He reached for her hand as she put the plate in the rack, gently stopping her from finding more work to do.

The warmth of his touch familiar, welcome even, after her humiliation earlier.

'I'm sorry,' he said, his voice so low she could barely hear him. 'I'm sorry, I shouldn't have come without . . . I think I was afraid that if I asked, you'd tell me to get lost.' He smiled, rueful. 'And you'd have every right, of course.'

She sighed, easing her hand from his, unwrapping the Christmas cake and reaching for the bottle of brandy. She needed to keep busy.

Ian shoved his hands in his pockets. 'I just—I miss you so much, you and Lauren.' His voice shook and he stopped, cleared his throat. Marnie tried not to feel sorry for him. It was his fault he was in this position. 'And it's Christmas, and I, look, I know I'm to blame, my God, I was such an idiot.'

Marnie dripped brandy onto the cake. She didn't disagree.

'And if I could go back, I'd never, never treat you like that, I'd be the best—' He sighed, ran his hands through his hair. They were shaking. 'But I can't, I know. It's just—It's so hard.' His voice dropped to a whisper. 'Without you.'

Marnie met his eye. He was looking at her with genuine remorse.

It would be so easy to fall into his arms. To go back to the good times, and there had been so many of those. To be a family again. She felt like she'd lost herself recently; she was behaving oddly, being childish and reckless, and now throwing herself at a man who clearly wasn't interested. She'd been so upset when she ran from Andrew's, fighting tears, and when she'd seen Ian standing there out of the blue, he'd felt like the answer to everything for a moment. He'd always had an ability to make light of whatever was troubling her, to make her feel like everything would be all right. And she had many troubles right now. She was struggling to remember the pain he'd caused.

'What about Bali?' she asked.

He sighed, shrugged. 'It's in the plan. But only if— if things can't be worked out, if there's even a chance, even the smallest . . . that you might forgive me. I'll stay.' He looked at her with raw desperation. His voice was a whisper when he spoke. 'You know that, that stupid—' He swallowed. 'Affair, it's over, been over for . . . it was nothing. Nothing. I promise.'

Yes. Marnie knew it was over. He'd broken it off as soon as Marnie had found out. But it was already too late. Suddenly she was finding it a little easier to remember how much he'd hurt her.

'You must . . . aren't you finding it hard too?' he asked, gazing at her with those dark eyes. 'Being on your own, starting all over again? You always were a little worrywart, and this is – this is a lot.'

Marnie thought about her dwindling bank balance and her empty inbox. She thought of her seemingly fruitless battle to bring customers into the bakery, of the upheaval Lauren had suffered moving schools, of the threat of Lily taking their home away at a moment's notice.

Lizzie Lee

Sighing, she took a swig from the brandy bottle. Her hand shook a little.

Ian watched her swallow, his eyes widening. Then he laughed and winked. 'Seems like I got here just in time,' he said.

Chapter Twenty-Six

The next morning, Marnie was exhausted, her eyes smarting and her head fuzzy. And not just because Ian's snoring could be heard all through the cottage – an aspect of married life she certainly had not missed – but because her mind had been too active to let her sleep.

She was in the middle of brushing her teeth when the knock on the door came. Quickly rinsing, she hurried downstairs; ever since Pat's fall she feared the worst when someone called unexpectedly. Neither Lauren nor Ian, curled into a ball under the spare duvet on the sofa, stirred at the interruption.

As soon as she opened the door and saw Andrew standing there, leaning against the porch, looking down at her with those blue eyes, that quirk of a smile, she felt as though she'd known it would be him all along. And yet her heart still gave an extra beat at the sight of him, her cheeks still burned at the memory of how he'd rejected her.

She drew herself up. 'Yes?'

'Look, I just want to say I'm sorry about yesterday, I was—It was . . .'

'Just a misunderstanding,' she said, readying herself to close the door on him. She didn't particularly wish to relive yesterday's humiliation.

He stepped forward a little. 'Marnie wait, I—It's not what you think, it's not that I don't want . . . it wouldn't be good, is all. For you. I'm not—There are things I've done, things you don't know about me.'

She stared at him. His expression was pained and desperate. Ashamed. What on earth could he have done that was so terrible?

'But it's not, not you, it's not that I don't—' He reached out, brushed her cheek gently with his thumb, and despite her efforts to feel nothing, his touch sent a shiver through her. 'Believe me, I think you're . . .'

He froze, staring behind her. She turned to see Ian, standing yawning and running a hand through his hair. 'Got any coffee, babe? I'll make us a pot.'

He was in his boxers. And she couldn't help but notice that he hadn't exactly let himself go; he must have been working out.

She cleared her throat, dragging her gaze away. 'Uh, it's in the . . . well, Ian this is . . .'

She turned to introduce him to Andrew. But Andrew had gone.

*

Thankfully she was too busy to dwell on what had happened, arriving at the bakery early to finish the gingerbread houses. She worked on autopilot, having made dozens of these over the years; her mind was anything but clear right now.

She felt dizzy, as though she'd been spun around and around. Still smarting from Andrew's rejection, she was none the wiser after his visit that morning. Even more confused, if anything. She had no idea what he was talking about, and being faced with the classic 'It's not you, it's me' line had done nothing for her confidence. If he was trying to let her down gently, he'd failed.

And now Ian was here. And she couldn't even begin to process that. There were no mysteries in his past. His love had been like a drug, a heady whirlwind of excitement and disbelief that this gorgeous man who could have any woman had chosen boring, sensible Marnie. But they had completed each other, in a way, his stardom sprinkling a little sparkle over her and her steadiness grounding him, her unwavering belief that he was special making him feel good about himself even as the success he dreamed of drifted away, his relaxed attitude to everything reassuring her when her fretful nature got too much. They were a team.

Then he had hurt her, so badly that she could still barely breathe when she thought about it, shattering the stable world she thought they'd built together, and she had left, unable to live with that uncertainty after he'd lied to her.

But that didn't mean she no longer loved him. There was something about being with Ian that was irresistible, and she could feel herself wanting to be drawn back into that world of being loved by him, chosen by him.

He had been what made her special, made her interesting; without that, she was just a middle-aged mum who couldn't take a trip to the shops without planning out every eventuality. Life was carefree with Ian around.

She was as starstruck now as she'd been when she first met him. She just hadn't been able to forgive him.

She sighed and shook her head, trying to chase these thoughts away. Trying to focus on packaging up the gingerbread houses for her new-found customers. They were ready just in time for opening, and she already had a queue outside the door as she turned the sign. Despite her reeling mind, her stomach fizzed with excitement. She had made this happen.

The new customers were delighted with their purchases, and had told their friends about the bakery. More visitors from the local villages arrived throughout the morning, admiring the display and buying her gingerbread houses to decorate.

Marnie's new bakes were proving to be popular too, even people from Babblebrook had started coming in for her salted caramel mince pies and gingerbread cupcakes. More than one person commented on how nice it was to have something fresh and different in the bakery now.

When at last the shop quietened down, and she was able to sit behind the counter with a much-needed cuppa before she started baking some new stock, her mind immediately began to spin again. She couldn't deny that having Ian here felt right. No one knew her like he did; they'd been together since they were not much more than children, they'd raised Lauren together. They had planned to grow old together. And a piece of Marnie split apart at the idea that they wouldn't.

And Lauren still missed her dad, of course; Marnie couldn't turn away from the misery she'd suffered without him, and her joy when he'd arrived out of the blue. A part of her had always doubted that she'd done the right thing in leaving Ian, and tearing their family apart. She'd never stopped loving him, and she was sure he felt the same way about her; perhaps she should have forgiven him, if only for Lauren's sake.

But she was settled in Babblebrook now, and so was Lauren. At last. For as long as they might be able to live there. However long that may be, depending on Lily's plans.

Once again, an image of gingham curtains and pretty tablecloths drifted through Marnie's mind, and she imagined the school run crowd drinking coffee, eating cake and chatting as the children entertained themselves in the special play area. She remembered Andrew's enthusiasm for her idea, his belief in it. A crazy part of her really felt she could pull this off, this dream that wouldn't leave her alone, that kept her awake at night planning menus. Her heart skipped at the thought. And only partly through fear.

She yawned and debated eating another mince pie. Cliff Richard crooned on the radio, and she swayed in time to the music, relieved to be able to enjoy it without Lauren groaning and complaining. She had dug out the ancient bird book that Matt had given her all those years ago, and now flicked through the pages, admiring the pictures and breathing in its musty smell. Anything to distract herself. She was filled with memories of hiding in Babblebrook's fields as a child, identifying the different breeds she spotted and ticking them off in her notebook, and later of Lauren sitting on her knee, her little fingers tracing beaks and wings as Marnie told her about the birds in the book.

The bell on the door dinged and she roused herself, expecting to see a customer, but it was Pat and Matt who came in.

'Just popped in to say hello,' Matt said, smiling amiably.

Pat said nothing, moving determinedly towards Marnie with a grim expression, making good speed with her walker now. And Marnie knew immediately why they were here, and what they had come to talk about.

'Oh no, not Cliff bloody Richard,' Pat grumbled, as Marnie slid off the chair and helped her to sit down.

'Leave him out of it, I like it,' Marnie protested, smiling. 'And I don't suppose he's the one you came here to talk about.'

'Well, what is *he* doing here? That gormless lump.'

Matt caught her eye, grimacing a little. No doubt he'd heard this tirade a few times since last night. They must have seen Ian arriving; nothing got past Pat when she was peeking through her curtains.

'I'll put the kettle on,' he said, looking grateful for the chance to leave them to it. Marnie guessed the drinks wouldn't make a speedy appearance.

'Well, it's not fair is it? Turning up like that, just when you've got all settled,' Pat continued. 'And what about poor Lauren? I mean, it's not like he's going to stick around is it? She'll just get used to him being here and then he'll be off again with some new hare-brained plan or some new flibbertigibbet.'

Marnie regretted now the phone conversation with Pat when she'd vented about Ian, having just discovered his betrayal. She still felt the urge to defend him. 'Well, he does love Lauren you know, maybe he'll . . .' Pat threw her a sharp look, and she hastily changed tack. 'What can I do? He's her dad, I can't just send him packing.'

'That's exactly what you should do, if you want my opinion.'

'She didn't ask your opinion,' Matt called from the kitchen.

'Oh be off with you,' Pat said crossly. 'Just make the flipping tea.'

Matt came through with three cups on a tray that he placed on the counter. 'Try not to get yourself worked up, love,' he said gently.

'Well, it's really—'

'Actually, I'm glad you're here, just the two of you,' Marnie interrupted, taking the opportunity to change the subject and broach another. What the hell. Her dreams weren't going to come true if they stayed inside her head. 'There's something I want to talk to you about.'

A glance passed between them and Matt rested his hand on Pat's shoulder.

'It's about the bakery.' The words rushed out of Marnie's mouth in a tumble, and she was glad to get them out before her confidence deserted her and she started listening to that voice in her head that was asking how on earth she thought she could do this. But she had to do something; it was clear that her translating work wasn't going to support them, and clear that Pat and Matt were ready to let the bakery go at last.

Pat puffed out a breath and shook and her head. 'I knew this was going to happen, this is your fault Matt. Marnie, I really don't want you to burden yourself with—'

'I want to turn it into a café,' Marnie said. She spoke loudly, her voice ringing with an enthusiasm that surprised her.

Pat and Matt stared. Matt opened his mouth then closed it again.

'What? But . . .' Even Pat appeared to be speechless. Marnie tried to remember if this had ever happened before. Not to her knowledge.

'I've thought it through,' she said. 'It's not just a whim, I really think there's a demand for it. I've got a little bit of a nest egg from the house sale so I could invest in it. And already there's a group that come in after the school pick up and I make them all a cuppa and they stay to chat. And I thought I'd have a little corner with small tables and chairs and toys and books for the children.' She rushed over to the designated area, waving her arms around. 'See, here. And I could do activities sometimes where they ice biscuits or whatever, and I think there's a demand for breakfasts, and people are coming from other villages now so . . .'

Pat and Matt were laughing, Matt holding up his hands in mock surrender. 'Sounds like a great plan to me,' he said. 'What about you, Pat?'

Pat smiled and clasped her hands together. 'Marvellous. Just marvellous! And I can sit here and talk to whoever comes in.'

'Well that's a win-win, getting you out from under my feet,' Matt said, grinning, and she gave him a playful poke.

'So, how's it going to work? Tell us all about it,' Pat said, her eyes shining and cheeks turning pink.

Marnie couldn't help grinning back at them, lifted by their enthusiasm. 'Well, it'll have to be refurbished of course, and then I'm thinking of doing a grand opening so that . . .'

The bell dinged, and Marnie faltered in her enthusiastic descriptions as Ian walked in. He strolled over to her, smiling, as though she was the only person there. She felt herself smile back in response.

'Hey,' he said, voice soft.

She opened her mouth to speak, but at that point Ian clocked Pat's most unsubtle eyerolling. He faltered, glancing towards Pat and Matt.

He gave them his best hundred-watt smile. 'So this is the social hub of the village, is it? What's the gossip?'

'Marnie's just been telling us about her plans to turn the bakery into a café,' Pat said.

Ian laughed, then, catching sight of her expression, quickly stopped. 'Oh, you're serious?'

'Absolutely,' she said, sounding more sure than she felt.

'What?' Pat asked sharply. 'We think it's a wonderful idea.'

He nodded, but his expression was doubtful. 'Oh uh, yeah. Of course, yes, I just thought – you're normally so cautious, and it sounds a bit, I don't know, reckless I guess, but I'm sure . . .' He trailed off, then nodded, and Marnie could see he was trying to arrange his features to look convinced. 'No, of course. I'm sure it's a—great, yeah.'

Marnie registered Ian's doubt, and it landed in some deep part of her that felt he was right, that she was mad to even consider it, that this was a crazy risk to take. He knew her better than anyone, her skills and her faults. Who was she trying to kid?

Pat was talking angrily and at an increasing volume, spelling out for Ian in no uncertain terms just how capable Marnie was, and just how confident they were in her ability to succeed at whatever she turned her hand to. And Marnie loved her for it. And she would have told her so, except now all the risks involved, all the possible ways to fail, were running through her head.

Matt glanced at Marnie, and she tried to smile at him, but realised she was too busy biting her fingernails to manage it.

'Well,' he said, in a calm but firm tone. 'We should be heading home. Ian, could you give us a hand please? Pat still struggles with this walker a bit, and it's icy out there.'

Pat stopped mid-sentence, glaring at Matt and turning a furious shade of beetroot. 'But, wh—I certainly don't need any help, from him of all—'

'Yes,' Matt said. 'Today we do. Come along, Ian. Let's leave Marnie in peace.' He gave Pat a meaningful look that even she decided not to argue with.

'Of course,' Ian said. 'See you later.' His eyes locked on Marnie's, as though there was no one else in the room, and he smiled as though he couldn't help it. And Marnie found herself smiling back. She couldn't help it.

Chapter Twenty-Seven

A few hours later, Matt came back.

'Everything okay?' Marnie asked. It wasn't usual to see him alone.

He smiled. 'Yes, yes. Pat's on her third cuppa, I think she's finally calming down a bit.' He twinkled a mischievous look at her.

'She's never been a fan of Ian's.'

'No, well.' He took her by the shoulders. 'But she's a big fan of yours. We both are, and we have every faith in you.'

Marnie trailed over to the counter, offering the chair to Matt and, when he shook his head, flopping down on it herself, resting her elbow on the glass and her chin in her hand. 'I don't know,' she said. 'Maybe I'm in cloud cuckoo land.'

'Nonsense,' he said, waving a hand around, indicating all the new bakes, many depleted by that morning's rush, the decorations and the gingerbread Babblebrook in the window. 'Look what you've achieved here! You've given this your all, and with fresh new ideas. We haven't been this busy for years. You've even got people driving in from other villages, I hear.'

Marnie looked around; the bakery twinkled with coloured lights, it was immaculately clean and tidy and the till was satisfyingly full after the rush that morning. She had a flash of memory of Andrew, leaning forward in his chair, face lit with enthusiasm as he told her she would make a success of the bakery. But she had only just met Andrew, he didn't really know her. And then she saw Ian's face, full of doubt.

'Well, I have gone at it hell for leather,' she conceded. She sighed. 'But a café's a different matter, isn't it? And Ian obviously thinks—'

'Oh bugger Ian,' Matt said, with unusual vehemence.

Marnie laughed. 'Well, I was married to the man. He knows me best, after all.'

'There are different ways to know a person, aren't there? Sometimes we only know one version of them, perhaps an old version, the one we first knew. Or even,' he was looking at her meaningfully, 'the one we want them to be.'

Marnie stood and hugged him. 'How did I manage without you all these years?'

'Ah.' He smiled. 'You're perfectly capable on your own. But I will take a cake as my reward!' His eager eyes travelled the display, and eventually he picked out a chocolate and candy cane cupcake. 'See, I'd never have thought of this.' He took a bite. 'And it's delicious.'

His words about only knowing one version of a person were ringing through Marnie's head. 'Andrew said something odd to me. About how there are things I don't know about him? And I've heard rumours but no one's ever really told me . . .'

Matt stopped mid-chew, carefully avoiding her eye.

'Matt?'

He sighed and swallowed. 'Well, yes. He's . . . he's been through a rough time.'

'I know.'

'And he, it was years ago now, but yes, he—lost his temper, shall we say. Quite badly and not in a good— well, it was Christmas and everyone was there, the children, and he just—it was frightening for the kids, and upsetting for the parents and, well for everyone, and some people just thought that it wasn't forgivable, even in the circumstances. So, yes.' He sighed again. 'There are some in the village that are wary of him, I suppose.'

Marnie opened her mouth to ask for more details, but Matt waved his hand. 'Anyway, that was all a few years ago, now. Ancient history.' He smiled.

'And what about the neighbours, though? The ones before us? Anne Walker said that he threatened them or something.'

Matt rolled his eyes. 'Anne Walker is not the most reliable source of information.'

Marnie had to concede that. 'Well, yes, I suppose. But there must be something in it?'

'Well, there was a bit of an upset. They were not the best neighbours, Pat and I can confirm that, loud parties late at night, and we did explain to them about how the walls between the cottages are only one brick thick and you can hear everything but they just didn't . . . anyway. That was about Rosie.'

'Rosie?'

Matt nodded. 'Yes, that time was particularly bad. It was bonfire night, and they had a party, so loud, but then they started setting of fireworks in the back garden. Poor Rosie was terrified, apparently, he was up all night with her and then he went over on his way to work the next morning. Seething. Started yelling, really let them have it and then, they had this silly little gnome on the doorstep and he smashed it against the wall.'

Marnie sucked in a breath. 'Oh no.'

'Hmm, yes. But the worst of it was, it wasn't even the neighbours that had opened the door, it was this little old lady, and he really let her have it with both barrels. Scared her a bit. Visiting relative, apparently.'

Marnie could imagine just how terrifying that must have been for her. 'Oh dear.'

'Yes. Not his finest hour, but you could say they brought it on themselves. And as I say, he's been through a lot.' He sighed and shook his head. 'Like I said. Ancient history. Don't—Don't judge him by that. None of us know how we'd be if the worst happened. Do we?' He smiled, and she nodded. 'Now, I'd better take some of these excellent bakes of yours for Pat, I think. What do you think she'd like?'

There was so much more Marnie needed to know. She understood why he'd flown off the handle with the neighbours, but Matt had told her hardly anything of what had actually happened that Christmas, of what terrible thing Andrew had actually done. She already knew people were upset with him. But she knew when a conversation was over, and she knew Matt wouldn't be budged when he'd made up his mind. She helped him pick out a bag of treats to take, and kissed his cheek as he left.

A smell of garlic and onion frying gently greeted her as she let herself in; Ian was cooking his signature bolognaise.

'Hey,' he said. 'Thought I'd take care of dinner, you've had a busy day.'

'Oh.' She was a little taken aback. There had been many days like this when they were married, days when he was sweet and made her feel special. When they had fun together. Before those final few bitter months when everything had soured. That's what had made his betrayal such a shock; she'd thought they were happy. 'Thanks.'

'Here.' He poured a glass of wine and gave it to her. 'Sit down. Tell me about your day while I make our spingetti.' He laughed, and Marnie smiled at the shared memory of Lauren's first attempts to say the word spaghetti. She could almost imagine herself back in that life, little Lauren running around as she and Ian cooked, ready to share a meal as a family. Everything she'd ever wanted.

Gratefully, she sank into a chair and took a sip of the wine. She hadn't realised how tired she was. She told him about the success of her window display, and how it had drawn in customers from further afield; of the new bakes that had brought back customers in Babblebrook and of the crowd of parents and children that came in after the school run.

She took a breath. 'So that's why, you see, I think the café idea can work,' she said tentatively. 'People are coming in for a cuppa and a chat anyway, so why not make it official?' She laughed, but the sound was hollow, even to herself.

Ian had his back to her, stirring the tomato sauce. He said nothing.

'You don't think I can do it, do you?'

'Oh, babe.' He put the spoon down and came to sit opposite her, reaching across the table and staring into her eyes, his expression earnest. 'I think you're such a smart woman, you know that, clever at so many things – like languages, I wish had your knack for that, and baking, all the amazing things you make, I mean if it was just that side of it I'd be cheering you on, but this, it's . . .' He sighed, sat back and brushed a hand through his hair. He looked at her affectionately. 'It's just—It feels kind of risky, and you're always so careful. You know? You're so sensible.' He grinned. 'You're always the grown-up, Marnie. I'm kind of surprised you're talking about doing something this impulsive. Doesn't feel like you, that's all.'

He cleared his throat, his expression serious now. 'And I just—I never imagined you stuck somewhere like this, where nothing happens, maybe that's why you're thinking of doing something so rash. And it can't be easy, in the back end of nowhere, living in your mum's cottage – and I bet she's not exactly a reliable landlord. Trying to manage on your own. I know you worry about stuff like that.'

Marnie's stomach tightened as she thought once again of the possibility of Lily wanting the house back.

Ian's voice was soft. 'I just, I want you to know that you don't have to do all this. You—You're not tied to all this. If it's not what you want.' He paused, staring deeply into her eyes. There was no sound but the bubbling of the pasta. 'We could go back to the city. Start again, be a team again. We're so good together, and it's not the same without you, the best gig in the world means nothing if I don't have you to come home to afterwards, the band means nothing, it's all just . . . you—You're my home, babe. We can have that again, God, I'd give anything to have that again, I'll do anything, I'll be the best husband, the best dad, I just—' His voice shuddered to a stop and he pressed his lips together, hung his head and wiped his eyes. 'If—Only if it's what you want, though.'

He squeezed her hands. His were trembling a little. Marnie was burning with sadness, it hurt her to see him like this, and she so longed to reach over and kiss him, to make everything right and believe all that he promised. He looked at her with fear and hope, but she could do nothing. She couldn't bring herself to comfort him, couldn't let herself trust him again. He smiled sadly, like he understood, then went back to his sauce that was now filling the room with the rich, tantalising aroma of beef, garlic and tomato.

Marnie simply sat, trying to take in all he'd said. Imagining the life he spoke of. And she felt the temptation to sink into that, to turn away from all the fears and responsibilities of her new life, to let him make everything seem light and breezy, like he always had.

'But this café thing?' he said. 'I don't know. Sounds a bit like something Lily would do, that's all.'

Chapter Twenty-Eight

Marnie closed the bakery early. Business had finally quietened down now it was so close to Christmas, and even Andrew still hadn't been in, which saved her the humiliation of reliving his rejection, at least. She'd seen him walking Rosie, oblivious to her presence, headphones on and bopping his shoulders in a dad-dance as he sang something that included the lyrics 'Bad, bad boy' loud enough for her to hear from a few feet away. More Taylor Swift, she presumed. She had laughed, despite herself, and felt a pang of something she tried desperately to ignore.

Walking home, she thought of all the jobs that waited there for her. She still had the cake to ice, some presents left to wrap and the finishing touches for quite a bit of the food. There was a nativity service at the church on Christmas Eve and Marnie had 'volunteered' (or, in actual fact, been roped in by Pat) to help with decorations.

She met Matt walking up his garden path just as she reached her own. He was dressed in jodhpurs and jacket, and carrying his riding helmet.

Marnie smiled. 'You look well.'

His eyes were bright and his cheeks flushed. She hadn't seen him this relaxed since she'd been back in Babblebrook.

'Alan let me take their new mare out, she's a beauty.' He laughed. 'Spirited, but you know I like a horse with a bit of personality. Had a good long ride across the fields, did us both the world of good.' He leaned over the hedge and pecked her cheek, and she could smell fresh air on his cold skin. 'You know we can't thank you enough. Without you taking over the bakery I'd never have had time to do this. And you've done such a wonderful job!'

He grinned, and she smiled as they parted ways, allowing herself to feel a sense of achievement; she had actually helped Pat and Matt, she was making a difference to their lives. Perhaps now was the time to be brave, after all.

The feeling didn't last. As she stepped into the cottage, all her worries crowded in. There was plenty that she should be doing, there was dinner to cook for a start. And yet she could concentrate on none of it; she started wrapping presents in her bedroom, went to fetch Sellotape from the drawer downstairs and, forgetting what she'd come down for, began to half-heartedly make a list of drinks she thought she should buy, and then began chopping an onion.

Her life was in turmoil; she had no regular source of income, no real security in her home. Perhaps Ian was right; it was too risky to be thinking of starting up a new business venture right now. The freelancing wasn't exactly a roaring success, was it? She couldn't seem to get enough clients to make it viable, and she couldn't even get all of those she had to pay. And that was much simpler than running a bakery, surely.

Ian's presence in their lives had brought a sense of stability at least. They'd quickly fallen into a familiar pattern, and she had to admit that she was enjoying his company. He strummed his guitar by the log burner in the evenings and entertained them with hilarious stories of disasters the band had encountered over the years. They'd heard all these many times before, but he was so good at telling them that they never failed to be entertaining. Marnie felt herself relax, remembering Julia's admiring glance at Ian and basking once again in the reflected glory of her charming, popular husband. It was like old times; the really old times, before everything had been tainted. The good old times. She was caught in a memory of the times she'd lain in bed with him, entwined in a post-sex embrace, laughing and laughing until her stomach ached and she thought she'd never stop, as he joked and told outrageous stories. Her lips twitched at the memory even as grief for those past times twisted in her; no one had ever made her laugh the way Ian did.

Marnie shook her head, trying to clear her mind. She was in a spin. She abandoned the onions and for the hundredth time considered icing the cake, then decided to have a hot chocolate first. She needed to keep her energy levels up. There were footsteps on the stairs as she reached into the cupboard, and she marvelled once again at her daughter's ability to hear the rustle of a chocolate wrapper from any distance. But it was Ian who poked his head around the kitchen door.

'Oh,' she said. 'I thought you were Lauren.'

'No, just me.' He smiled and flicked his hair out of his eyes. He was so handsome. Marnie's stomach flipped, even after all these years. 'Sorry to disappoint,' he said.

'Not at all. It's just that I'm making hot chocolate and usually when she hears me start she's down here like a flash, it's uncanny, her ability to . . .' She was gabbling. And she couldn't stop.

'Well.' Ian's voice was playful. 'I'm afraid you'll have to make do with me for now.'

He stepped towards her. Marnie was clutching the chocolate so tightly against her chest that she felt it begin to soften. Gently, he took it from her and placed it on the counter, then stroked the hair from her face. She hadn't brushed it since that morning. She must look a state.

'You're so beautiful.'

It was all Marnie could do not to snort.

'I mean it.' He looked deep into her eyes. 'Every bit as beautiful now as you were the day we met.'

He leaned in. Marnie didn't move away. And as their kiss grew more passionate she felt the years fall away; she was young again, she was a girl, watching Ian playing with his band and thinking he was the most gorgeous man she'd ever seen.

Something had come over her that night, the night they met; she had danced as never before, right at the front of the crowd, the music beating through her body, lost in the swooping of Ian's voice as he sang, gazing up at the sheer beauty of him. She was filled with longing as he caught her eye and seemed to be singing just to her, she was filled with excitement as he found her afterwards and walked her home, kissing her on the doorstep until Lily had banged on the bedroom window, and he'd grinned and walked away. She had been dazzled by him from the very beginning, and before long her adoration had dazzled him, her steadfast faith in his talent keeping him going in the face of failure. He would always be a star to her, no matter what.

His mouth was hungry against hers. He was the man she married, handsome in his suit, leaving their guests howling with laughter with his speech and singing a love song just for her. He was Lauren's father, his face full of wonder as he held her, tears dripping down his cheeks.

His hand slipped under her blouse and Marnie snaked her arms around his neck. He moaned quietly. This was right. It felt right. She wanted this, she wanted her old life with Ian. He'd learned his lesson, and they could be a family again, she didn't need to keep struggling on her own. They breathed fast, their kisses urgent, and for now there was nothing but this.

Except there was.

Marnie pulled away. 'Lauren,' she gasped, straightening her hair and glancing furtively over Ian's shoulder, fully expecting to see her daughter standing there staring at them with horror. 'We can't, what if . . .?'

Ian was not so easily dissuaded. He laughed lightly and nuzzled her neck. 'Don't worry,' he said. 'She's out.'

Marnie frowned. 'Out?'

'Yes,' he murmured. 'So it's fine, we're alone, there's no one to—'

'Out where?' She pushed him away. She'd assumed Lauren was holed up in her room with her headphones on. 'It's nearly time for dinner, she always lets me know if she's going to miss it.'

Ian shrugged and pulled her in close again. 'I'm not sure, I saw her bedroom was empty that's all.'

Marnie wriggled out from his grasp. 'But she's never late, she always lets me know.'

He laughed. 'She's a teenager, Marnie. I'm sure she's fine. Come here.' He slipped his arm around her waist and tried to kiss her, but she ducked away.

'Stop that, Ian, the moment's clearly gone,' she snapped.

His mouth drooped a little. 'You're overreacting.'

Marnie shook herself, feeling the world settle into place around her. The here and now. She was no longer a girl in a dream-induced passion. She was an adult with responsibilities.

'I expect you're right,' she said. 'But I'll just message her.'

She tried calling first, but Lauren's phone went straight to voicemail. 'Hi, darling,' she said, straining to keep her voice light. 'It's Mum.' Lauren would know that, of course, and always laughed at Marnie when she said this. 'Just wondering when you'll be home. Give me a call.'

Next she sent a WhatsApp message. One tick, and Lauren had not been active on there for a couple of hours.

'You know you always do this,' Ian said as he bent to rake out the log burner. 'You overreact. She's a teenager, she's fine. Give her some space.'

Marnie stared at her phone. Still just one grey tick.

Ian was right. Lauren was growing up, no doubt she'd far rather be with her friends than her boring old mum. She'd probably just forgotten the time. This was

Babblebrook, after all. In all seriousness, what could possibly have happened?

She glanced out of the window at the dark evening.

'I'll just call Emma's dad,' she said, and Ian shook his head.

*

Lauren had been at Emma's but she'd left a couple of hours ago. Emma's dad was reassuring; she must have stopped in at someone else's house. Babblebrook was a friendly little place. And very safe.

Marnie agreed and finished the call. She tapped out a WhatsApp message to Pat with shaking hands. The reply came immediately; they hadn't seen Lauren all day. But she was bound to be at Emma's, or another friend's house. This was Babblebrook, after all.

'She's not at Emma's,' she said.

Ian frowned, then shrugged. 'She'll just be exploring. Nothing could've happened to her here! She's fine, babe. She's probably petting the cows, she loves them, you know that.'

Of course Marnie knew that. But it was dark and cold. And Lauren was never late for dinner.

Glancing out of the window, she saw her own worried face reflected back at her, and beyond that, dimly, splashes of light on the path reflecting from the fairy lights on the porch.

There was only one more place to try. Marnie put on her coat.

Chapter Twenty-Nine

'My dinner's ready,' Andrew said, before the door was even fully open. He was scowling, but when he looked at her face his expression softened a little.

'Oh sorry,' she said. 'I won't keep you anyway, I was just wondering if Lauren was here?'

He shook his head.

'Visiting the puppies?' she asked, as though he might have somehow overlooked her presence and now realise that she was in fact in his living room after all.

'No,' he said. 'Tried Emma's?'

She nodded, trying to bite her nails through her mittens. 'She left there two hours ago.'

Andrew looked past Marnie into the dark night, and she turned to follow his gaze. Frost crusted the ground and spiked the hedge, fog crept across the fields.

'And she hasn't been home since?'

Marnie shook her head, fighting tears.

'Shit,' he said, shrugging into a soft, brown duffle coat and tying on leather boots. He reached for a torch. 'Come on.'

'What's happening?' she asked.

He stepped out, taking her by the arm gently. 'Well we'd better go and look for her, hadn't we? And get Pat to put a message in that bloody village WhatsApp that she loves so much, in case Lauren's drinking cocoa with Gloria and Bob or something while we're trekking round in Arctic conditions looking for her.'

'I know I'm being silly,' Marnie said, her voice wobbling, as they trudged down the road.

'No, you're not. This isn't like her, is it?'

She shook her head.

Marnie huddled into her coat. It was freezing. And her daughter was out here, somewhere.

'Is there anywhere she likes to go?' Andrew asked. 'The brook, the churchyard, something like that?'

Marnie shrugged, shivering. 'Not really, she—she likes the cows, but I think it's too late for . . . She's usually either at Emma's or in her bedroom looking at her phone.'

Andrew glanced at her and frowned. He grabbed the beanie off his own head and placed it on hers, gently tucking in the curls that fell around her face. 'Not to worry,' he said softly. 'We'll find her.'

There was no sign of Lauren by the cow field or on the green. The pond was frozen over, the ducks huddled in an unhappy-looking heap at the side. They shouted, but it was clear that no one was there.

As they continued up the street people began to trickle out of their houses to join the search. Pat's message was taking effect. The fog was so thick she could barely make out the ghostly shapes of her neighbours.

'Thank you,' Marnie said every time someone joined them. 'I'm sure she's fine. I'm just being silly.'

She wasn't to be found in the churchyard, the grounds of the school or The Plough.

Andrew took Marnie aside. 'Why don't you go with Emma and Phil to search the brook and the station?' he said, keeping his voice gentle. 'I'll go with Matt and Gloria, we'll start checking the fields on the other side of the green.'

She nodded, then clutched his arm just as he was about to leave. 'Thank you for doing this. Perhaps I'm overreacting, but—'

He placed his hand over hers. 'You're her mum, you know her better than anyone. And you're worried. That's enough for me.'

Chapter Thirty

Marnie veered between fear and fury as she walked down Lowering Lane with Phil and a tearful Emma.

Mostly fear at this point, if she was honest. She couldn't stop picturing Lauren lying frozen in the dark somewhere, her lips blue and her skin cold to the touch. Or hit by a car and left injured and helpless. Or kidnapped. Or abducted by aliens.

Her imagination was running away with her.

They swung their torches side to side and called. Nothing.

Emma checked the phone box, a ludicrous thought really, but they were desperate now. Nothing. Marnie called again, checked her WhatsApp again.

Nothing.

She knew in her heart that something was wrong. Lauren wouldn't stay out this late, missing dinner and not replying to messages and calls. Not without telling her. Marnie swallowed and batted her eyes with her mittens. They would find her. They had to. And everyone had come out to help.

Well. Not quite everyone.

She'd messaged Ian when her phone picked up a signal momentarily to tell him that people from the village were helping to look for his daughter. He'd read it but not replied.

He had never been good at losing face, she remembered now, the arguments they'd had with him insisting black was white rather than admit he was wrong. And he'd been so adamant that Lauren was fine.

'You're worrying too much,' he'd said, laughing affectionately as she hastily buttoned her coat. 'You always do this, you catastrophise everything. Relax. Just let your daughter hang out with her mates without you turning up and embarrassing her.'

'*Our* daughter,' Marnie had said as she stepped out of the door. 'And she's not with her mates.'

His dismissal stung, but Marnie was too concerned about Lauren to think about Ian now. Ahead of her Phil put his arm round Emma.

'Don't worry, love,' he said. 'She'll turn up. Probably warming her toes by someone's fire and just forgot to message her mum.'

Emma nodded bravely. 'I know,' she said, her voice shaking.

They'd reached the brook, ghostly branches of skeletal trees stretching through the mist from the far bank and the water thick with frost.

'Lauren,' they called, though without much hope. 'Lauren, where are you?'

Nothing.

Marnie stamped her feet and wiped her dripping nose, pulling Andrew's beanie further down over her ears. How long would it take for someone to freeze in this weather? She couldn't remember if Lauren's coat was still hanging under the stairs or if she'd taken it with her. She must have taken it. She wouldn't go anywhere without a coat in this. Surely.

Phil swung the beam of his torch across the water and around the trees. A little pair of bright eyes reflected the light briefly on the other side of the water, then whatever creature they belonged to darted into the undergrowth with a rustle.

'I don't think she's here,' he said. He smiled at Marnie in what she supposed was meant to be a reassuring manner, but she saw the concern in his eyes. 'Let's try the station.'

She nodded, and they hurried back down the path, still calling Lauren's name.

Desperation rose in Marnie, a flailing panic that she could barely keep under control. She longed to hold Lauren in her arms, safe and sound. Longed to see her roll her eyes or hear her laugh at something Marnie had said. Longed to see her sleeping with her palm under her cheek and her hair in a mess across the pillow.

Marnie stopped and closed her eyes. She pressed her hands to her face, as though that would help her keep these feelings inside. As though that would stop her sobbing and screaming that she needed her daughter and she needed her now.

She prayed in a whisper, promising everything and anything if only Lauren could be safely returned to her.

A gentle touch on her shoulder brought her back to her senses. Phil patted her and ducked his head a little to catch her eye. 'Come on,' he said softly. 'Let's keep going. We'll find her any minute, I'm sure.'

Marnie nodded. She appreciated his kindness even if she struggled to believe his attempts to reassure her. 'Yes,' she said. 'Of course. Thank you.'

They'd reached the station, usually such a cheery place with green-painted wooden panels and an old-fashioned ticket booth. But empty and dark, wreathed in fog and without even the Christmas decorations lit up, it was eerie and depressing. A shiver bolted down Marnie's spine.

Emma ran to the window and pressed her face against the frosty glass. Marnie held her breath, trying to hold on to hope.

Footsteps reverberated around the village street.

'Marnie,' a voice called, ricocheting off the buildings. 'Marnie.'

She spun around, almost losing her footing, heart crashing in her chest.

A figure emerged from the mist, striding towards them from the fields behind Ivy Cottage. Andrew. And he was carrying something in his arms.

Chapter Thirty-One

Marnie was running towards them before she'd even fully registered that the bundle Andrew carried was her daughter. 'Lauren!' she cried as she reached them. 'Thank you, Andrew, thank you, thank you.'

Lauren turned towards her and held a trembling hand out. 'Mum,' she said, and began to sob.

'It's all right,' Marnie said, giving her an awkward hug as she lay in Andrew's arms. 'It's all right, you're safe now.'

'She's freezing,' Andrew said quietly. 'Best get her home.'

Marnie nodded and thanked Gloria, Phil and Emma a little shakily as they all crowded around. She held Lauren's hand as Andrew carried her back.

'She was in the field,' Matt panted as he hurried to keep up with them. 'Fell and twisted her ankle, she said, couldn't get up. Been lying there for hours, poor thing.' He shook his head. 'Couldn't get in touch with you. No signal on her phone.'

'Well, we've got you now, Squidge,' Marnie said, squeezing Lauren's hand. She felt a sob shudder through her. 'Thank you, Matt, thank you for finding her. Thank you, Andrew.'

'Just glad to help,' Matt said.

Andrew nodded. She guessed all his breath was saved for carrying Lauren.

Marnie hurried up the path when they reached the cottage and pushed the door open. 'Living room, I think,' she said. 'Fire should be lit.'

Andrew grunted as he stepped through the doorway.

'Found the wanderer at last?' Ian called from the living room. 'Where was she? In the Plough?'

He chuckled, but his face fell as they all stepped through, and he leaped to his feet, running a hand through his hair. 'My God,' he said. 'I—I thought . . .'

Andrew placed Lauren in the chair nearest the log burner and Marnie ran to fetch her duvet and wrap it around her. She was shivering, and tears still slipped down her cheeks. But she was home, and not seriously hurt.

'I'd better go and tell Pat the good news,' Matt said. He pinched Lauren's cheek gently. 'Take care, young lady.'

'I'll head off too,' Andrew said gruffly. 'Leave you be.' He rubbed his shoulder and winced.

Marnie thanked them again, and so did Lauren. Ian hovered in a corner, biting his lower lip.

'God, I'm sorry. I thought she was just—I'm sorry. I—I lit the fire,' he said, once it was just the three of them.

Marnie didn't reply. She needed to look after her daughter right now.

She was able to ease off Lauren's boots. Her left ankle was swollen and already showing signs of bruising, and

Lauren whimpered when Marnie touched it, despite that she was as gentle as she could be.

'I'm sorry, Mum,' Lauren said. The colour was coming back to her cheeks now, but her lips were swollen and cracked with cold and her eyes puffy from crying.

Marnie tucked the duvet tighter around her. 'It's all right, you're safe now, that's all that matters.' She stopped herself from asking what on earth Lauren was doing out in the far field in the dark on her own. Now wasn't the time.

'I wanted to get you some holly,' Lauren said, and for a second Marnie wondered if she'd voiced her question after all. 'We saw it the other day in the field and I said to Emma that you'd love some for Christmas decorations so I thought I'd get you some on the way back from hers this afternoon.'

'Oh, Lauren,' Ian said. 'You poor thing.'

'I'd got my pocketknife thing and I was going to get you some but it was really foggy and then I tripped and it really hurt.' Her voice went high and shaky, and she sounded for all the world like she had done when she was six. Marnie swallowed back tears. 'And my phone had no signal and I tried shouting but no one came and then I thought I was going to get eaten by a fox or something. It was really scary, Mum.'

She began to cry again, and Marnie leaned over to hug her through the bulk of the duvet. 'It must've been horrible.'

Lauren winced and Marnie gingerly drew the covers back to look again at her ankle, which was still growing in size despite the pack of frozen peas she'd made Ian get out of the freezer. Her best petits pois, melting to a mush.

'I think we need a trip to A&E.'

'I'll drive,' Ian said.

*

The long hours at the hospital gave Marnie time to respond to all the messages people from the village had sent, asking about Lauren, and for Lauren to admire the nurse dealing with them, who had a striking resemblance to Timothée Chalamet.

At last they made it home, with Lauren X-rayed and her sprained-but-not-broken ankle wrapped in a bandage. Exhausted, Marnie almost stepped on the pile of gifts that had been left on the step: homemade biscuits in a tin she recognised as belonging to Pat and Matt, a bar of chocolate with a Post-it on saying it was from Emma, a small blue teddy bear with a ribbon around its neck and a label saying 'From Amy' in wobbly letters, and a pack of Tesco's own custard creams that she suspected were from Andrew.

Once again, Marnie found herself swallowing down tears. It had been a long night. And without their friends in Babblebrook, she didn't dare think of what might have happened. This village really was a special place.

When at last she fell into bed, bone-tired, she couldn't sleep. Her mind immediately played image after image; Lauren crying and holding out her hand, her face white and tear-stained, the way she smiled shyly at the nurse as he joked with her, the pile of gifts waiting on their doorstep.

She turned over, the old bed creaking under her weight, and pressed her face into the pillow that smelled of her own face cream.

Lauren was fine. She had been hurt but she was okay, nothing more than a bruise or two. That was the main thing. Thank God Marnie had trusted herself. She'd known something had happened to her daughter. She sent up a silent prayer of thanks and tried to remember what she'd promised in return – something to do with not eating all the mince pies, although that hardly seemed fair compensation given the circumstances.

From the living room, the sound of Ian's snoring reached her. He was clearly not lying awake in turmoil.

Marnie closed her eyes, breathed slowly, relaxed her shoulders and tried to sleep.

Immediately, she felt herself to be in Ian's arms again, his lips at her throat and his hand working its way under her clothes. And then she remembered his condescending expression and then his look of shame when he saw his injured daughter, and she thought of how he'd dismissed her instinct about Lauren.

And then she saw Andrew, stepping out of the mist, carrying her daughter to safety.

Chapter Thirty-Two

The gifts kept coming.

Overwhelmed by the turmoil of the day before, Marnie couldn't sleep, waking early and creeping around her room so she didn't disturb Lauren, trying to hide the bags under her eyes with concealer. She almost stabbed herself in the eye with her mascara wand as someone banged on the door, making her jump. She hurried down the stairs, hoping the noise wouldn't wake her exhausted daughter.

She ran past Ian in the living room, who was no more than an oblivious lump, and yanked the door open, gasping at the rush of freezing air and glowering at Andrew for disturbing her once again. At least she was presentable for once.

Except it wasn't Andrew. Marnie hastily adjusted her expression when she realised that it was Gloria and Bob standing on her doorstep, clutching a beautiful bouquet made of ferns, pine cones and holly. Gloria's gaze travelled Marnie's tired appearance, and Bob, who was immaculately dressed as ever in a suit and a tie with little pink pigs on, smiled sympathetically.

'Sorry,' Gloria said. 'We won't keep you, we just wanted to drop these off for Lauren, after what happened yesterday.'

Marnie glanced up to where Lauren was presumably still sleeping soundly in the bedroom above. No sign of life came from there.

'We heard she was looking for holly for you, so we thought . . .' Bob indicated the bouquet.

'Oh.' Marnie pressed a hand to her mouth, and felt tears welling. 'That's so kind, thank you. She'll be thrilled, but I'm afraid she's still asleep.'

Gloria waved a hand, her nails painted pale pink. 'Of course.'

'Can I—Would you like a cup of tea?'

They turned her offer down, saying that they wouldn't disturb her further. She suspected this wasn't the last visit they would receive today. And she was not wrong.

Marnie barely had time to find a vase for the flowers before someone else was knocking on the door. She kicked Ian on the way past, hissing, 'Visitors. Shift yourself.' He squinted at her blearily from under the duvet, but the knocker banged again and she didn't have time to check he'd understood.

Anne Walker was the first visitor, bringing a sweetie-bouquet of all Lauren's favourites. She accepted the offer of tea and a mince pie, and Marnie was relieved partly because it meant that she could also have tea and a mince pie, and partly to see that Ian had finally vacated the sofa.

Just as Anne stood to leave the knocker went again, and Marnie opened it to find Alan Wood waiting there, clutching a soft toy calf and shuffling awkwardly. He tugged his trousers a little higher and tightened the belt that held them in place, clearing his throat.

'Don't want to disturb,' he said. 'But Barbara and me, well we heard about what happened to your lass and we were so sorry, and you know she's always asking about the cows so we thought we'd get her a little . . . She's too old for it probably, but we wanted to—'

A squeal came from behind Marnie, and she turned to see Lauren standing behind her, still in her fluffy onesie and resting against the chair as she held her injured foot off the floor. 'I love it!' she said. 'Oh thank you, it's adorbs.'

She took the calf from Alan's outstretched hand and pressed it against her face. His cheeks coloured.

'Tea?' Marnie asked. 'Mince pie?'

Alan nodded and bent to remove his mud-caked wellies.

Marnie smelled aftershave, and turned to see Ian, dressed and smiling, appear in the doorway. 'Let me help you, darling,' he said, glancing quickly at Alan before walking to Lauren and putting his arm around her to help her hop through to the living room.

'You sit yourself down here,' Marnie heard him say. 'And I'll light the fire for you.'

The cottage slowly filled with well-wishers through the day. When Emma arrived, Ian brought both girls a plate of the biscuits Marnie had made. When Julia brought Amy and little George to deliver a homemade card drawn on the back of a cereal packet and a box of chocolates, and to ask if Amy could please have the little blue teddy back because she had missed him in the night and had decided that perhaps a loan was better after all, he warned Amy to stay clear of Lauren's sore foot.

Lauren rolled her eyes. 'Stop fussing, Dad, she's fine,' she said holding her arms out for Amy to come in for a hug. The little girl did so gingerly, taking care to be gentle.

Julia smiled sympathetically as she tried to keep hold of a wriggling baby George. 'It must have been awful for you.'

Lauren squeezed Amy and reached for the bear that sat on the coffee table with a pile of other gifts. 'Thank you for lending me Blue Bear,' she said solemnly. 'He kept me safe last night, but he really missed you.'

Ian nodded. 'Thank you, Julia,' he said. 'Yes, it's been very hard. Nothing worse than thinking something's happened to your kid, is there?' He blew out a breath and ran a hand through his hair, catching Julia's eye and smiling. 'Sorry, I'm going on.' He touched her arm briefly and laughed. 'You're just very easy to talk to!' Julia smiled at the compliment, looking pleased, and Marnie knew what it felt like, to be the centre of Ian's attention. How special he made people feel.

She bit her tongue. Here spoke the man who had dismissed her, who had stayed inside while half the village went out in the cold and dark to search for his daughter, who had no concern at all until he was faced with the evidence of Lauren's injury with his own eyes.

'I'll make more tea,' she said. She needed to be away from him. She was starting to remember how he did this, performing to impress people. And it always worked. It had worked on her for years.

She knew Ian loved Lauren, of course he did. He'd been genuinely shaken when he saw that she was hurt,

Marnie could see that. He'd driven them to A&E, he'd lit the fire to keep her warm.

But the fact was, he had not believed her when she needed him to. He hadn't respected her instincts.

Someone was banging on the door again before the kettle had even boiled. On the third set of knocks Marnie sighed and went to open it, trying not to glare at Ian on the way past.

'Took you long enough,' Pat grumbled when Marnie opened the door. 'It's freezing out here.'

'Sorry,' Marnie said. 'We've got quite a crowd here.'

'Not to worry,' Matt said, patting her arm as they both bustled in, shedding coats and dumping them on the back of a chair.

'Now where's that girl?' Pat asked, marching through to the living room. 'I've brought her my spare walking stick.'

Marnie followed, watching as Lauren laughed and took the stick, waving it playfully at her dad. Ian was in the middle of telling Julia how he'd barely slept a wink with the worry of it all when Pat caught his eye and silenced him with one look. He couldn't pull the wool over everyone's eyes, Marnie thought, with a little spark of satisfaction.

*

By the end of the day they were out of Marnie's homemade mince pies and almost out of tea bags. Lauren was half-buried in a pile of chocolates, sweets, magazines, biscuits and soft toys, and Marnie was inundated with offers of all kinds of help, from food shopping to providing meals to taxi-services. None of which she needed, and all of which she was grateful for.

At last she sank down in a chair, sipping on yet another cuppa and breaking into the pack of custard creams that had been left on the step.

'What a day,' she said.

Lauren nodded, chewing on a chocolate and absently stroking the ears of the calf toy. 'Feels like the whole village came to visit.'

Marnie nodded, and bit into her biscuit.

Not quite the whole village, she thought.

Chapter Thirty-Three

Christmas Eve-eve, and there was so much to do. After all the hubbub of yesterday, she was behind on her jobs list.

Lauren poked her head around the door, leaning on the walking stick that Pat had lent her, now decorated with tinsel. Marnie was startled to see her bright-eyed and fully dressed, not the dopey, bed-headed teen in a onesie she was expecting.

'Just heading out,' Lauren said.

'I—What? But I'm making hot chocolate.' Marnie's confusion at this turn of events left her incoherent, apparently.

'Oh that's nice. None for me though, I can't be late.' Lauren grabbed a couple of the custard creams and shoved one into her mouth whole as she walked to the cupboard and took out her coat.

'You're turning down a hot chocolate? Must have something nice planned then.' Marnie smiled. She was so glad that Lauren had made such a good friend in Emma, they were practically inseparable, and the two no doubt had something fun planned for the day. She held herself back from asking Lauren to message when she arrived and when she was leaving. The accident was a one-off.

She couldn't let it make her afraid to let her daughter leave the house.

'Yep, I'm looking after the puppies.'

Marnie froze halfway through breaking the chocolate into chunks. 'The—Next door?'

Lauren rolled her eyes. 'Well yeah, Mum, what other puppies do you think I'm talking about?'

'Oh.' Marnie tried to laugh but it came out as an unconvincing grunt. 'Of course, yes. Sorry. So is—is Andrew shopping again, or . . .?'

She had a flashback to that day, suddenly, to the panic she'd felt when Rosie was so ill. Thank God she and the pups had come through.

Lauren tugged on one of her boots and an old slipper of Ian's over her bandaged foot. She opened the front door, letting cold air pour in as she turned to answer. Marnie bit her lip. The poor kid was trying to balance on one leg while holding a walking stick. Now was not the time to complain about her leaving the door open.

'Nah,' Lauren said, through the last mouthful of biscuit. 'He's meeting someone and he was complaining that he had to drive all the way into Waterfield to get to the nearest café, and then it's a Costa and he doesn't like chains. I think he'll definitely be a customer for you when you open your Babblebrook café, Mum!'

She grinned and stepped out, closing the door at last.

Marnie's mind was reeling. Absently, she ate the piece of chocolate she'd broken off, and took the pan off the heat. Upstairs, a toilet flushed, and she soon heard Ian humming as he made his way down the stairs.

'Hey,' he said, gazing at her warmly and flicking his hair out of his eyes. He was wearing Marnie's dressing gown and, by all appearances, not much else. 'Oh, are you making one of your famous hot chocolates? Could I have a chilli one?'

He fiddled with the radio, changing the channel from the Christmas one Marnie had chosen to one playing the indie music he liked, and settled himself at the kitchen table, gazing up at her with a confident, affectionate smile.

But all Marnie could see was the patronising expression he'd had as he dismissed her instincts about their child. The same one he'd worn when doubting her plans for the café.

'That's a Cath Kidston, you know,' she said.

He frowned in confusion. 'What?'

'The dressing gown. I treated myself to it last year, I'd wanted one for ages.'

He smiled. 'Ah, babe. I know things have been tough on you lately. But don't worry. Once we've got everything settled it'll be more—We'll be able to treat you to nice things again.'

Marnie looked at him, those gorgeous dark eyes that gazed so deeply into her, that lit up with the mischievous humour that had her and Lauren helpless with laughter. It would be so easy, wouldn't it, to go back with him, to take Lauren back to her old life and leave all their worries in Babblebrook. 'What do you mean?'

He ran a hand through his hair, sitting back in the chair. 'Well, it's hard for anyone being on their own, starting again. And especially for you, you know what you're like, you little worrier. Have to have everything under control, nice and predictable. Don't feel bad about it, it's just who you are. I know you, Marnie.' His voice was gentle, now. He was still as handsome as the day she met him. And still as patronising. 'Better than anyone. We were meant for each other, you and me, you're my rock, the wind beneath my wings.' He flashed a charming smile, aware no doubt that she found that song corny. 'I just can't be me without you there, sorting everything out, making our lives run smoothly.'

She stared at him. Suddenly her old life felt less appealing; that role of running everything, supporting him, always the cheerleader. 'You can't be you?'

He frowned. 'Yes, I—Did that come out wrong? I mean I—I need you, Marnie, I need you there to—'

'There in the background. Cooking your meals and washing your clothes and organising your travel for the latest tour.'

He spread his hands. 'No, I—What have I said?'

'Nice, boring, predictable Marnie, that's who you think I am, the girl who made you feel good about yourself even when your dreams didn't come true. But there are different ways of knowing someone, aren't there?' she said. 'Maybe you just know an old version of me. Or even the version you want me to be. That girl that adores you unquestioningly, that will do anything to support you. But things have changed, Ian.' She thought of all she'd achieved in Babblebrook, how she'd helped Pat and Matt, how she'd saved the bakery. The plans she had. There were people here that believed in her. 'I've changed. I'm not going to be that Marnie anymore, I'm done with working in the background to make everyone else's lives easier. Time I lived my own.'

She glared at him, watched the dawning of understanding in his eyes, the falling open of his mouth.

Her gaze fell on Andrew's beanie, still lying on the side after he put it on her the other night. The man who had listened to her and taken her concerns seriously. The man who had cheered her on when she told him about her plans. She swallowed, shook herself. Heaved herself off the side she'd been leaning on.

'Take that dressing gown off. And—' She wrinkled her nose. 'Wash it. I'm going out.'

He nodded, still gaping. 'Out where?'

'Waterfield.'

Marnie dashed upstairs and changed into a wrap dress that she knew accentuated the curves she was blessed with and zipped her knee-high boots on, then dabbed on a bit of her favourite lipstick. Smiling at herself in the mirror, she gave a little twirl and winked at her reflection; looking pretty good, though she said so herself. She ran down the stairs, grabbed her coat and handbag, and made for the front door.

*

Her dramatic exit was delayed somewhat by the need to scrape the car. Once again she cursed her diminutive stature as she leaned on tiptoe and stretched as far as she could to reach the middle of the windscreen; there was still a stubborn strip of ice in the centre that she couldn't reach.

How much easier life would have been if she were tall, she thought, not for the first time. And willowy. Willowy would have been good. Eventually she gave up, having cleared enough screen for her to see through, and plonked her short, plump self into the driver's seat.

Once she got out of Babblebrook the roads were gritted at least, so the drive was smooth after that. This was a route she'd travelled often as a child, when Lily had taken them to the supermarket or sometimes to a park or café, if she was feeling enthusiastic. Marnie drove on autopilot; not much had changed.

She parked at the Morrisons, silently promising to buy something on the way back in return for the free parking, and headed towards Costa. The little town looked so pretty, with Christmas lights strung above the cobbled streets and wound around the trees that lined the pavements. Every shop window was warm and inviting, sparkling with decorations. Children in bobble hats pressed their noses against the glass to gaze at the treasures inside, no doubt still making lists for Santa, and a choir stood in an archway, singing carols and smiling as shoppers dropped coins into their charity buckets. The scent of roasting chestnuts from the vendor on the corner drifted through the chilly air.

It was a wonderland. It was beautiful and festive, and at any other time Marnie would have happily stopped to gaze around and drink in all the Christmassy loveliness. But today, she barely noticed any of this. She marched along the street, making her way purposefully to Costa.

She didn't hesitate when she reached it, but swung the door open and strode in, searching for Andrew. Only as she stood breathing in the aroma of sweet coffee, her eyes at last resting on the two figures at the table in the far corner, did it occur to her that she had no plan at all of what she wanted to say. And only as Andrew looked up, an expression of confusion passing across his face as he saw her and his mouth hanging open as he was about to bite into a gingerbread robin, did she glance at his companion.

A woman. A young woman, leaning across the table towards Andrew, shaking out her long, glossy dark hair and laughing as she spoke to him.

Marnie flushed, frozen in the doorway. What a fool she'd been. An old, short, plump fool.

Chapter Thirty-Four

A relaxing bubble bath and a hot meal later, Marnie's nerves were beginning to settle.

Ian had said nothing of their earlier conversation over dinner. In fact, he'd said almost nothing at all. But there was a load of washing in the machine that included her dressing gown. She decided to take that as a good sign.

She should stick up for herself more often.

Marnie had made gingerbread cupcakes for the café, and there were a few left that had to be rehomed. What a terrible shame, she thought, as she placed the tin containing the last three on the table. Lauren grabbed one, kissed Marnie on the head and disappeared up to her room. Ian took his and sat opposite her at the kitchen table.

'Thanks,' he said.

Marnie's mouth was too full to reply. The recipe was rich and sweet, with treacle, dark sugar and golden syrup, and a pinch of mixed spice. Not to mention the ginger-flavoured butter icing. Perfect for this time of year.

Ian cleared his throat and shifted in his seat. Marnie reluctantly dragged her focus from the cake to her ex-husband; he clearly had something to say.

'I, uh—I think I owe you an apology.'

Marnie almost dropped her cake.

Ian sat back in his chair, groaning and pushing a hand through his hair. 'I think I was—I mean, you deserved . . . Oh God, this is hard.'

'Well you haven't had much practice. Keep going, it'll get easier.'

'Ha ha. Yeah, all right.' He gave a lopsided grin and took a deep breath. 'I'm sorry, I should've listened to you about Lauren. You're her mum, you know when something isn't right. I should've trusted you.'

This was more than Marnie was expecting; she'd never heard Ian admit that he was wrong, much less that she had been right. The shock caused her to gasp in a breath, and a piece of cake lodged itself in the back of her throat. Choking and spluttering, she felt her face redden and her eyes begin to stream. How very attractive.

'Oh, Christ,' Ian said, leaping up to give her a glass of water and thumping on her back so hard she thought her lungs might pop out through her ribcage.

'Thanks,' she croaked, waving a hand to ask him to stop.

'Okay?' he asked, peering at her with a concerned expression.

Marnie gulped the water and nodded, surreptitiously wiping her running nose as he sat back down.

'Look, I—That really shook me up, you know, seeing our little girl like that.' His voice cracked and he stopped, swallowing.

'I know,' Marnie said.

He wiped his eyes. 'And after what you said before I've been doing some – doing a lot of thinking, and I've realised that I don't want to move away.'

Marnie kept her voice as gentle as she could. 'I'm not going back with you, Ian.'

'No, no I—I know that. Now.' He gave her a wry look. 'It's just I can't go to Bali, it was a stupid—I need to be closer to Lauren. I can't leave her like that, even just for six months.'

Marnie had to stop herself from leaping up and shouting Hallelujah. Instead she tried to look wise and nodded sagely.

'So I'm going to stick around here. Not on your sofa!' He held his palms up and gave a shaky laugh. Again Marnie had to stop herself from jumping up and punching the air. 'Maybe what you said earlier is right, maybe I'm trying to hold onto an old version of you, you know?' His voice shook a little and he stopped, took a breath. There were tears in his eyes when he looked at her, but he smiled. 'I just wish I could go back and—All those years we were together, our little family, so precious, and I went and messed it all up, thinking I wanted something better or more exciting or . . .'

'Younger,' Marnie said drily.

He flashed her a look, but didn't argue. 'But it's too late. I messed up, I missed my chance with you.' He took a long, shaky breath. 'Lauren's what matters, now. So, I had a look today, and there's a small flat in Waterfield that I think I can afford, and a yoga teaching course not too far away, so—'

'Waterfield? But what about the band?'

'Oh well, the band—' He shrugged. 'We'll work it out. Maybe it's time I focused on other things, anyway.'

There was a squeal from the doorway, and Lauren came racing through, throwing herself into Ian's arms.

'Oh, Dad,' she said, and Marnie could see she was fighting tears. 'That's great news, I would've missed you so much. Best Christmas present ever!'

Ian pulled her to him in a hug and grinned. 'Where did you come from?' he asked.

Lauren rolled her eyes. 'I was sitting on the stairs, of course, I'm not going to miss out on one of your Big Discussions.'

'Oh, you were earwigging were you?' Marnie said, smiling. She yawned, heaving herself up from the chair. 'Well, I think this has all been too much for me. Time I went up the wooden hill to Bedfordshire.'

They both turned to stare at her.

'My God, *Mum*,' Lauren said, giggling, and then she and Ian spoke together. 'You sound like you're ninety.'

Chapter Thirty-Five

Marnie remembered the Babblebrook nativity services of her childhood – sweet, slightly boring traditional affairs where adults read meaningful Bible extracts and children were expected to stand in a silent tableau, no matter how itchy the tinsel on their angel costume might be. Things were going to be a little different under the guidance of Reverend Pauline, she suspected.

'Gloria,' she barked as she marched down the aisle carrying a pile of tinsel. 'Get down from that ladder at once, I'm not having—Carefully! Thank you, yes, I can't have bones broken in the Lord's house. Especially the day before his birthday.'

Marnie helped Gloria down from the ladder, secretly relieved that there was someone present that Gloria wouldn't argue with. All her own protests and offers to climb up instead had been dismissed with a wave of the hand and a glare. But no one argued with Reverend Pauline.

She dumped the tinsel pile in Marnie's arms with a beam that no one could resist. 'Could you just—I don't know, spread it around? Let's have a bit of sparkle shall we? Thanks.' She glanced around the busy church. 'Now,

I need someone young and spry to—Oh no, Lauren, not you with your war wounds, what about . . . Emma, would you mind? Pop up that ladder and attach the star. Great, thanks so much. And Lauren can you hold the – yes, perfect, thank you.'

Marnie watched as her daughter smiled and nodded and did as she was asked with all the docility of a newborn lamb. She'd been worried that Lauren would be upset that she and Ian had finally accepted they had no future as a couple, but Lauren had just rolled her eyes. 'I already knew that, Mum, you're divorced! I know I thought I wanted everything to back to how it was, but things are okay now you're friends again. I just didn't want Dad to leave the country, that's all.' And once again Marnie had been taken aback by the wisdom and maturity of her daughter. She and Ian had done one thing right, at least.

Dazed, she dumped the pile of tinsel on the pulpit and hurried away before anyone caught her. Her heart wasn't in this. She'd hardly slept, her treacherous mind going over and over the conversation with Ian, and lingering on the image of Andrew with the dark-haired woman who, in Marnie's imagination, was both tall and willowy.

Neither of them were here, which was a relief. She sighed and shook herself, turning to help Matt place the bouquets he'd made at the end of each pew. A festive mix of holly, fir, pinecones and berries, they were truly beautiful.

'These are stunning,' she said. 'They must have taken you ages.'

He smiled, colouring a little and looking pleased. 'Oh, well. It was a pleasure.'

'You have a real gift. Another talent to add to the list of baking and horse-whispering! I never knew.'

'Ah, there's more to most of us than meets the eye,' he said, handing her another bouquet to place by the pulpit, and frowning at the ungainly tinsel pile sitting there. 'Seen much of Andrew, recently?'

Marnie almost dropped the flowers. 'I—Not really. Why do you ask?'

Matt smiled, taking the bouquet out of her hands and carefully placing it at the side of the pulpit. He shrugged. 'Oh, no reason,' he said, his tone carefully matter of fact. 'I had a feeling you two might have hit it off, that's all.'

He watched her intently. Marnie tried to hide the heat rising in her cheeks by bending to fiddle with the flowers. She snorted. 'Not exactly.'

'Well, that's a shame,' he said mildly.

'Right.' Reverend Pauline's voice boomed across the busy church, and she clapped her hands in a redundant bid to get everyone's attention. 'I think it's time for a break don't you? Time for a cuppa, or perhaps over to The Plough for a quick—Argh!' Her eyes had fallen on the tinsel pile, and she shrieked, charging down the aisle to rectify the situation. 'Never mind, love,' she said, patting Marnie kindly on the arm. 'Not everyone has a gift for aesthetics.' She artfully laid the tinsel along windowsills. 'We're all grateful that God gave you the talent to make the best mince pies around. That'll have to be enough.'

Marnie was beyond caring. She sighed and began to follow the reverend out, but Matt caught her gently by the arm.

'He's a good man, you know. Andrew.'

Marnie could do nothing but nod.

*

The afternoon passed in a flurry of activity. Ian, having lit the fire and tidied the kitchen, took himself off for a walk. Marnie concentrated on the jobs she still needed to do, grateful for the edge of panic that kept her mind off her neighbour, and the woman he'd been drinking coffee with. The last few presents were wrapped, the finishing touches made to the food. Almost ready for the big day. Just one last job to do, one that she and Lauren had always shared.

Marnie knocked on the bedroom door, and waited patiently.

'What?' came a none too friendly response.

Marnie pushed the door open and peeked round to see Lauren on her bed, phone in hand and headphones pulled aside. 'Want to help me decorate the cake, Squidge?'

She could have bitten her tongue off.

Lauren rolled her eyes and groaned. 'God, Mum. Don't call me that.'

'Sorry.' Marnie started to back away. Perhaps it was time to accept that Lauren was growing up. These little things they'd always done together couldn't go on forever.

Lauren pulled her headphones off and swung her legs over the side of the bed. 'Can we have hot chocolate while we do it?'

Marnie smiled. 'Don't we always?'

Hot chocolate made and Christmas songs on the radio, they settled at the kitchen table. Marnie spread the marzipan and icing over the cake while Lauren picked through the contents of the ancient Roses tin they kept the decorations in. Little snowmen, Santa and his sleigh, reindeer, Christmas trees. Robins that stood taller than everything else.

They were not tasteful. But each one brought a happy memory of Lauren grasping it in her chubby little fingers and deciding with great care, tongue poking out of her mouth, where it should be placed.

She was less careful today, giggling as she put Santa upside down and balanced a snowman on the robin's head.

Marnie gasped in mock horror. 'Such disrespect for Jesus's birthday cake!'

Lauren grinned. 'It's his birthday, he'll be taking a day off, I don't think he'll care about how I decorate the cake.'

Marnie ruffled her hair and kissed her cheek. Lauren grabbed her round the waist for a hug. And Marnie began to feel that this Christmas was going to be a good one after all.

'Urgh, no,' Lauren grumbled, as 'Mistletoe and Wine' came on the radio. 'Not . . .'

'Cliff sodding Richard!' said a voice from the door, and they both turned to stare.

Marnie blinked, unable to believe her eyes. Surely she was hallucinating. Must be the stress. Surely it wasn't . . . not now.

The woman in the doorway grinned, pulling off a brightly coloured Peruvian hat and unwinding an enormously long hand-knitted striped scarf, then opening her arms out.

'Gran!' Lauren shrieked, hopping across the kitchen and into her embrace.

Chapter Thirty-Six

Marnie struggled to keep the frost from her tone. 'Hello, Mother.' She knew her mum hated to be called anything but her name by her children, but she couldn't help showing her disapproval this way.

Lily snorted. 'Mother?' She pulled a face and winked at Lauren. 'Sounds like I'm in trouble.'

Marnie thought it was reasonable to be 'in trouble' if you turned up on someone's doorstep on Christmas Eve afternoon without warning.

Lily and Lauren embraced again in another tight hug. 'I've missed you, Gran, you should've said you were coming.'

'Oh, where's the fun in that? Last minute decision. Decided I couldn't be away from my little Lauren for Christmas!'

Marnie almost snorted, thinking of all the Christmases of her childhood where the day had barely been acknowledged, or they were in yet another dump of a flat in yet another town where they knew no one. There had been many Christmases that had passed without her sending them so much as a card, never mind making an appearance.

Lily was squeezing Lauren and exclaiming about how much she had grown, then shrieking about her injured ankle. 'What happened to you? Honestly, Marnie, can't you keep her safe even in Babblebrook?'

Marnie flushed with rage and bit her tongue. She had done a damn sight more to protect Lauren over the years than Lily had ever done for her.

Lauren looked from Lily to Marnie and back again, shaking her head. 'It wasn't Mum's fault, I just tripped in the field. It was Mum that organised the search party that found me.'

Not strictly true, but Lauren was so full of pride, and Marnie so full of gratitude that her daughter had defended her that she didn't argue.

Lily placed her arm around Lauren's shoulder, leading her from the room, whispering to her about presents that she'd brought back from her travels. 'Put the kettle on, love, won't you?' she called over her shoulder. 'I'm gasping.'

Honestly, Marnie thought as she slammed the kettle onto the base a little too hard, it was a wonder she and David had turned out sane at all.

She made a pot of tea, piling it onto a tray with the mugs, milk and a tin of freshly baked mince pies. She bit her lip, wondering what her mum's plans were. Did she intend to move in with them, now she was back? Or even kick them out? Right now, Marnie wasn't sure which was the worse option. But at least with Lily here in the flesh she might get the chance to have a conversation about her plans without technological failures interrupting. Then she would at least know what the future held for herself and Lauren.

'Mum!' Lauren squealed from the living room. 'Come and see what Gran's bought me.'

Marnie gritted her teeth, painted a smile onto her face, and walked through, placing the tray on the coffee table. Perhaps now wasn't the time to broach the subject of the cottage. Lily was sitting on the floor, cross-legged and wearing striped knitted socks that had toes in, grinning up at Lauren who was wrapping a beautiful piece of cloth around herself.

'It's a Jaipuri Razai,' Lily said. Then, catching the blank expression on Marnie's face and rolling her eyes, 'That's a quilt, to you.'

'It's beautiful,' Marnie said, admiring the pale pink repeated block-print design on one side and the leaf pattern on the other side.

'Feel it, Mum,' Lauren said, holding a corner out to her.

The cotton was soft, and much lighter than she'd imagined. 'Oh, it's gorgeous—you'll be snug as a bug in a rug wrapped up in that.'

'You know, there's a huge market selling these in Jaipur, that's where I bought it, I knew you'd love this one.'

'I do,' Lauren said, wrapping the quilt around her shoulders and flopping into a chair, her injured foot propped up on a stool, brushing her cheek with a corner of the soft cotton.

'They're all handmade, the printing, the stitching, everything.'

'It's lovely,' Marnie said, smiling as she watched her daughter curl up in the quilt like a baby with a blanket.

'Well, don't get jealous, I brought something for you too,' Lily said, frantically digging around in one of the bags she'd left scattered all over the room.

'I'm not—'

Marnie's protest was cut off as her mum unwound a scarf to reveal a little bowl and held it out to her. 'Here,' she said.

'Oh.' Marnie was speechless. The bowl was beautiful, painted in a striking bright blue with a repeating pattern of flowers and petals around the side and a yellow flower on the bottom. 'Oh, it's beautiful – thank you.'

Lily shrugged. 'Blue pottery of Jaipur, another traditional craft, they use a cobalt dye, that's why it's so bright.'

Marnie turned the bowl and ran her hand over its smooth edge. 'It's really lovely.'

'Well, I thought you'd like it. Might brighten the place up.' She glanced around the room. 'I see you've decorated. Nice and fresh but it's a bit dull isn't it?'

'I told her to choose a different colour,' Lauren said.

'Any colour would be nice, not this boring old—Anyway.' Lily indicated the bowl. 'You can eat your mince pie out of it.' She tutted a little and shook her head. 'Always so traditional, Marnie. I suppose we're having turkey tomorrow, too?'

*

When the time for the nativity service came they wrapped up in coats, hats and scarves and stepped out into the frosty evening, Marnie stopping to refill the birdfeeder on the way. The sky was dark and clear, sprinkled with bright stars, and every hedge was hung with twinkle lights. Over on the green, she could see the Christmas tree with its coloured lights. Babblebrook couldn't have looked more beautiful.

'My God, this place hasn't changed a bit,' Lily grumbled. She blew onto her hands, encased in a pair of mittens borrowed from Marnie, and shoved them under her armpits. 'And I'd forgotten how bloody cold it is in England.'

'It is December, Mother.'

'And stop calling me that. Makes me feel old.'

Marnie had always marvelled that Lily allowed Lauren to call her Gran; she'd never once complained that made her feel old. Testament to just how fond she was of her granddaughter.

Lauren raised her face to the sky. 'I think it's going to snow,' she said.

Ian smiled. 'I think you might be right.'

Marnie put an arm around her daughter's shoulders. 'That would be lovely.' But she didn't believe it. She couldn't remember the last time there had been a white Christmas.

'I bloody hope not,' Lily said. 'Give me sunshine anytime over winter.'

Marnie wondered again why her mum had decided to return from her trip to sunny India without letting them know. She had to bite her tongue to stop herself suggesting that she could have stayed there. Ian had been far more pleased to see her than Marnie had, greeting her with a big hug. They'd always hit it off, kindred spirits who had bonded by gently – and sometimes not so gently – teasing Marnie about being a stick in the mud.

'You get younger every time I see you!' Ian had said, and Lily had laughed and batted him on the arm. 'Tell me all about your trip.' And he'd listened for a good hour, commenting and asking questions, saying he dreamed of travelling to India one day. And Marnie had, as ever, tried not to be envious of the ease of their relationship.

Pat and Matt had gone ahead; Pat was walking well now but she was still slow and refused to hold everyone up. Marnie suspected she also wanted to bag the best seat. David and Greg arrived, David in a coat that had a button missing, a striped knitted scarf and matching bobble hat, Greg as suave as ever in a fitted coat and leather gloves.

'Wait, what—Lily!' David shouted, running over to envelop her in a massive hug.

'Oh, hello love,' she said matter-of-factly, as though she'd seen him last week.

'What—I didn't know you were coming,' he said. He caught Marnie's eye.

'No one knew.' She tried to keep the trace of bitterness from her voice.

Lily extricated herself from David's embrace and pulled at the threads where his button was missing, giving him an accusatory stare. 'You look a mess.'

'Well, it's only Babblebrook,' David said, looking a little hurt. He and Marnie exchanged a glance. Not exactly the warm family reunion they might hope for, but exactly what they would expect from Lily.

'Now you,' she said, pushing past David to Greg and pulling him into a hug. 'You look gorgeous, as ever. Shame your sense of style hasn't rubbed off on my son.'

She laughed. No one else did.

Marnie was grateful for David and Greg's company as they walked down the street, and not only because of Lily's unexpected arrival – she'd heard Andrew's gate click as they passed it and was very aware of his footsteps behind theirs. This way, she could pretend she didn't know he was there. Like a schoolgirl with a crush.

David stopped walking, turned and waved. 'Oh, Andrew,' he called. 'Walk with us?'

Marnie stared furiously at the ground as they waited for Andrew to catch up, cursing her brother and his stupid friendly nature under her breath.

'What?' Greg asked.

Marnie was startled. 'Uh—What?'

'I thought you said something.'

'Me? No, no. Must've been wind. The wind! Not— not my wind, I mean, I don't have wind . . .'

Greg frowned. The evening was perfectly still, with not a hint of a breeze. Marnie was glad of the darkness to hide her burning cheeks.

'Andrew,' Lily called, pecking him on the cheek and shoving her hat back a bit so she could peer up at him properly. She wagged a finger. 'I hear you were very rude to my tenants, not very nice, but I'll let you off.' She cupped his face, her expression serious for a moment. 'How are you doing, now?'

Andrew was carrying what looked like a wooden box, Marnie couldn't really make it out in the darkness, and he shifted it to the other hand, shrugging. She looked up to find him gazing at her. 'Oh,' he said, his eyes still locked on hers. 'Okay, thanks. Better.'

Lily nodded and patted his cheek, and the spell was broken. They all walked on. She joined Lauren and Ian, regaling them with stories of her adventures, while David chatted easily to Andrew about Rosie and the puppies. They were all doing well apparently, the pups beginning to move around more now their eyes were properly open. Marnie listened silently, trying to keep her gaze ahead at all times and ignore the sense that Andrew was glancing at her regularly as he spoke.

'You've done a great job with them,' David said. 'I bet Rosie was excited to see you when you picked her up from the vet's.'

Andrew chuckled. 'She went crazy, she was running all round and, and she peed all over the floor.'

'Happens all the time,' David said.

'Honestly, I was so happy to see her I was just glad I didn't do the same thing.'

David laughed. 'That happens less often! Seriously, she's lucky to have you, not all pets are so fortunate. Some people just don't pay the proper attention, you know?'

Andrew didn't reply, and Marnie sensed a sudden shifting in his mood, but David didn't appear to notice. He continued to tell stories of his work involving cute animals and funny mishaps, chuckling at his own tales.

At last they reached the church, joining the cheerful group gathered around the iron gate. Reverend Pauline strode down the path in her cassock, although her Doc Martens still peeked out underneath. She flung the gate open and beamed.

'Oh wonderful, you're all here! Come in, come in.'

They all followed her down the path to the church, beautifully lit up in the dark night. Children wearing costumes ran ahead, shouting in excitement – Marnie recognised Amy dressed as Mary, with a blue scarf over her hair. There was a boy who was presumably Joseph with a tea towel wrapped around his head, and also, inexplicably, a unicorn, a spider with legs made from newspaper-stuffed tights pinned to a black jumper, and a crocodile.

Somehow, Pat and Matt had already settled themselves in the church. They sat right at the front. Best seats in the house, of course. Pat grinned and waved at them as they all squeezed into a pew, looking more than a little smug, until her eye fell on Lily. She nudged Matt in the ribs, pointing and talking animatedly, and they both waved. Poor Pat would be burning to know all about Lily's sudden arrival, Marnie knew, but she would have to wait now until the service was over.

Andrew walked up the aisle to where a baby doll lay in a cardboard box. He took it out and placed it in what he'd been carrying, and Marnie saw now that it was a manger, beautifully made with legs that crossed and wooden slats that were lovingly varnished.

Reverend Pauline took the cardboard box off him and threw it behind the lectern. She placed a hand on his shoulder and spoke softly. Marnie saw him nod, and slope into a pew, as those around stared and whispered and nudged each other.

She felt she'd just witnessed something significant, but couldn't quite fathom what.

The service began with a reading by Pauline. So far, so traditional. Followed by Anne Walker singing a solo of 'All I Want for Christmas is You', accompanied by Bob on the organ, and then a small boy reading out his favourite Christmas cracker jokes. So far, so Babblebrook. Lauren stared with wide-eyed amazement, Ian smirked, Lily beamed and David and Greg watched and smiled as though they were witnessing the most beautiful, moving service possible.

Marnie refused to look at Andrew to gauge his reaction.

All this culminated in the nativity scene, narrated by a unicorn and with gifts presented by a wise man, a spider and a crocodile. Mary dropped the baby and laughed as it bounced down the steps, Joseph hurrying to retrieve it and place it in the gleaming new manger. The angel farted and one of the sheep picked her nose throughout.

Soft chuckles of delight drifted around the church, and Marnie was sure she heard Andrew's voice in among them.

'This is hilarious,' Lily said in a stage whisper that could no doubt be heard by the whole congregation.

Reverend Pauline watched all with a benevolent smile. And somehow the uniquely chaotic service was indeed the most perfect and fitting Christmas celebration for the people of Babblebrook, everyone accepted and celebrated for who they were, and whatever they wished to contribute. Marnie was forced to swallow the lump in her throat.

The children bowed, everyone applauded, and Pauline once again stood at the centre.

'Well,' she said. 'I think we can all agree that was marvellous. Well done, children.' She smiled around at them. 'You can collect your presents from under the tree on the way out, but first we're going to sing my favourite Christmas carol, the Cliff Richard classic, "Mistletoe and Wine".'

Beside Marnie, Lauren let out a loud groan, then clapped her hand over her mouth. She and Emma fell into a fit of giggles, and Marnie found herself in danger of joining in, when there was a sudden bang, and they were all plunged into darkness.

Somewhere further along the pew, she heard Ian scream.

Chapter Thirty-Seven

There was a scratch and a hiss, a little flare at the front, and soon a pool of light as Reverend Pauline lit the candles at the altar.

'Aha,' she said. 'I knew these would come in useful one day.'

There were murmurs among the congregation as lights began to flicker into being, people finding their phones or reaching for torches. The faces that were lit up wore worried expressions.

'All right, let's not panic,' Pauline said firmly. 'Just a power cut, I'm sure it'll be sorted soon. Let's wrap up here. Everyone okay to get home? Grab your neighbour by the arm and take it steady! And a happy Christmas to you all.' She stood with her arms crossed, tapping the toe of her Doc Marten and surveying them all with a growing impatience.

There were shuffles and grumbles as people bent to retrieve bags and struggled back into coat sleeves in the gloom.

Ian leaned over Emma to pat Lauren on the knee. 'It's all right, love, don't you worry, everything's going to be okay.'

Lauren stared at him with an expression of disbelief. 'God, Dad, I know, I'm not six.' She rolled her eyes and she and Emma stifled giggles.

Marnie gathered her things and looked to the front of the church, where Pat and Matt were sitting. She wished she could be as carefree as her daughter. She felt a little shaken, not by the sudden darkness, but by the timing. It was Christmas Eve. And power cuts in Babblebrook could last for days, as she remembered from her childhood.

It had seemed like fun then, opening the door of the wood burner and toasting bread on the flames, and going to bed by candlelight. The adult Marnie was less enamoured with the prospect of cooking Christmas dinner for eight without any power.

She squeezed Lauren's hand. 'I'll meet you at the door,' she said. 'I just want to—'

Lauren nodded, so busy chatting to Emma that she barely noticed Marnie speaking. Marnie stood and inched into the aisle, working her way gently to the front of the church, moving against the crowds that were heading towards the door. She thought she heard footsteps following her, but it was hard to tell in all the commotion.

Pat and Matt were still sitting in their pew when she reached them. She knelt down in front of them, and Pat grasped her hands.

'Oh, Marnie,' she said. 'What are we going to do?'

Matt placed his hand on top of Pat's, squeezing gently. 'It's just a power cut, love,' he said. 'We'll manage.'

'But it's Christmas Eve!' Pat wailed. 'You know how long a power cut can last for us out in the sticks, we'll be eating cheese sandwiches by candlelight for Christmas dinner at this rate!'

Marnie felt someone kneel beside her. Smelled soap and wood shavings. He chuckled. 'Well, it wouldn't be so bad, would it? As long as you're with the right people.'

Did she imagine it, or did he briefly glance her way as he said this? She pictured again the woman he'd been sitting with in the coffee shop, with her flowing dark hair. Was that who he was thinking of?

'Exactly,' Marnie said, dragging her thoughts back to Pat. 'And you don't need to heat up the sherry, do you?'

Pat laughed. 'There's always a silver lining, I suppose.'

'All right, you big old lush, let's get you home,' Andrew said, standing up and heaving Pat to her feet.

She slapped him lightly on the arm. 'So rude.'

Matt grinned at Marnie as he stood up, crooking his elbow for her to thread her arm through. They walked together like that down the aisle, following slowly behind Pat and Andrew, ignoring Reverend Pauline as she sighed behind them and muttered, 'At last.'

Matt nodded to the pair walking in front of them and looked at Marnie pointedly.

'What?' she asked, though she knew full well his meaning.

'Good man,' Matt whispered.

Marnie sighed. 'I don't know. I think perhaps you're the last good one.'

He patted her hand as it rested on his arm and laughed. 'I think Pat would disagree.'

'What's that?' Pat turned round so quickly she almost fell over, and Andrew was forced to steady her. 'Taking my name in vain?'

'Nothing for you to worry about,' Matt said, smiling.

'Come along, come along,' Reverend Pauline called, flapping her arms behind them as though she were shooing a gaggle of unwanted geese from her church. 'I'm sure you all have homes to go to.' And then, quietly, 'And some of us want to see if The Plough's still open.'

Marnie found Lauren waiting at the door.

'Where's your dad?' she asked. 'And David and Greg?'

Lauren didn't even turn to her as she spoke, but continued to stare out at the dark night.

'Look, Mum,' she said, a dreamy note to her voice. 'It's snowing.'

Marnie turned to see that Lauren was right. Beautiful, soft flakes were falling slowly, beginning to settle on the hedgerows and gravestones in the churchyard. Otherwise, there was total darkness; not a street lamp lit, not a flicker at a window. Just black night and white snow.

Marnie gasped. There was something truly magical about it.

She squeezed Lauren's hand. 'Just like you said. It's as if you made it happen.'

Lauren laughed. 'I know I am brilliant, but I'm not that clever, Mum.'

Marnie looked at her cheerful, resilient, witty, caring daughter. 'Ah, I don't know,' she said. 'I wouldn't put it past you.'

'What are you talking about?' Lauren grinned, putting her arm through Marnie's as they stepped out into the snowy night and resting her head against Marnie's shoulder. 'Such a weirdo.'

All the slow walk home, Pat fretted about what they would do if the power wasn't back on for Christmas Day. Marnie, walking ahead with Lauren, found herself smiling at Andrew's attempts to cheer her, talking about sherry by candlelight and a grand feast of bread and butter with tins of beans heated on the fire. Of walks in the snow followed by mince pies and present opening.

It all sounded quite romantic to Marnie, but Pat wasn't sold. As they neared their little row of cottages, she huffed and removed her arm from Andrew's. 'Yes, yes, it's nice to be with the people you love and all that, but I still want my flipping turkey.'

Marnie felt a suppressed laugh shudder through Lauren, and had to bite her own lip. Although she had some sympathy with Pat's point of view. There was no gas in the village. No one would be cooking their Christmas dinner in Babblebrook, unless the power came back on. 'Well, you never know, it might be back on tomorrow, with a bit of . . . wait, what's this?'

From her window, a soft glow fell onto the pavement, the snowflakes that were beginning to settle there sparkling in the gentle light. Every other window on the street was dark.

Marnie looked at Lauren. Lauren shrugged. Together, they all shuffled into Marnie's cottage.

The dining room was in darkness, but through the doorway to the living room a soft light lapped.

'Ah, here they are,' Ian said as they all squeezed through into the little room.

Marnie stopped, gazing at the room in wonder. The Christmas tree was now adorned with two beautifully handknitted scarves wound around it, one pale pink and one light grey. They looked so soft and cosy; David's work, no doubt. He and Greg sat on the sofa, and Lily was cross-legged on the floor. A fire flared in the wood burner, and on every surface candles flickered, the light glinting off the baubles on the tree and the glitter on the Christmas cards that Marnie had pinned to the beams.

'It's beautiful,' she said.

'We wanted to make it welcoming for you,' David said. 'You're always looking after everyone else, it's your turn now.'

Ian shoved his hands in his pockets, flicked his hair out of his eyes and grinned in that way that used to make Marnie's stomach flip. Vaguely, somewhere inside herself, she registered that it had no effect on her tonight.

'Sort of a little thank you,' he said. 'For all you've done. There's hot chocolate.' He gestured to a pan sitting on the top of the wood burner and, now he mentioned it, Marnie detected a delicious, sweet aroma mixed in with the pine and woodsmoke. 'Not as good as yours, of course,' Ian said. 'But still.'

'That's great, Dad,' Lauren said, dumping her coat on the back of a chair and limping to the kitchen. 'I'll get cups, who wants one?'

Everyone called through that they did. All except one.

Andrew cleared his throat. 'I need to get back to the dogs.' He nodded awkwardly around at them all, his gaze snagging on Ian for an extra second. Ian smirked. Andrew glowered. 'Happy Christmas, then,' he grunted, a little ungraciously. And he was gone.

There was some hurried shuffling and rearranging as David and Greg vacated the sofa for Pat and Matt, Lily brought chairs in from the dining room and Lauren poured the hot chocolates and handed them round.

Marnie found herself settled on a cushion on the floor next to Lauren, sipping a hot chocolate that wasn't bad, although not as good as her own, and laughing along to the stories she'd heard Pat and Matt, Lily, and David and Greg tell again and again over the years.

The one about how Matt had overbalanced taking the turkey out of the oven one year and ended up sitting in a pile of presents, succeeding in keeping the turkey off the floor, at least. Too much Christmas cheer was the verdict, though Matt strenuously denied it. The one about how Pat had decided to go for an early morning ride on Christmas Day and promptly skidded on a patch of ice, so she and Matt had spent their Christmas in A&E, having her dislocated shoulder popped back in. The one about how when Lauren was little, having opened all her presents, she stuck her head up Pat and Matt's chimney and shouted, 'Thank you, Santa!', and emerged covered in soot.

Marnie listened, and laughed, and joined in with the reminiscing. Sipping hot chocolate by candlelight, surrounded by people she had known and loved for years. In many ways, it was the perfect Christmas Eve.

And yet. Somehow, her thoughts were filled with Andrew. Of the way his eyes creased when he smiled, and his ability to cheer Pat up in any situation, and the way his thumb had brushed her cheek when he had tucked her hair into the hat he'd put on her. Of how it felt to kiss him.

And of how he had laughed with the woman he'd been drinking coffee with.

Chapter Thirty-Eight

Marnie was jerked out of sleep, woken by a cacophony of banging and shouting.

She had no idea what time it was, her phone had run out of battery, but the house was in pitch darkness. Staggering, still sleep-drunk, she squeezed past Lily on the air-bed, spreadeagled and snoring contentedly, grabbed her dressing gown and optimistically flicked the light switch on the way out of the bedroom.

Nothing. This Christmas was going to be a little different.

The banging continued, and Marnie ran down the stairs as quietly as she could, past the sleeping figure of Ian in the living room – apparently it took more than the end of the world to rouse him – and fumbled her way through to the front door.

Yanking the door open, she blinked at whoever had dragged her from sleep at this ungodly hour, blinded by the bright wrapping of snow that covered every surface. 'What the hell is going on?' she snapped.

Andrew leaned against the frame of her little porch, his eyes crinkling as he smiled down at her. Marnie's stomach flipped. For heaven's sake, she scolded herself.

'What are you doing?' she demanded, irritation with herself somehow now aimed at him. 'It's Christmas bloody morning.'

'Come with me,' he said, and before she could protest, began marching off down the street.

Marnie groaned and patted down her bed head. How did he keep doing this to her? And what did he expect? That she'd just trot down the street after him in her dressing gown and slippers?

And yet that was exactly what she did.

She tried to fume at him, but the sun was rising, throwing a beautiful pink light across the sky and brightening the untouched sheet of snow that lay at her feet and covered every roof and hedgerow. Perhaps it wasn't the worst start to Christmas Day, after all.

Her breath clouded as she puffed along, trying to catch Andrew up. He marched purposefully to the end of the street and turned the corner to where the little row of shops stood. Marnie ran the last few steps, clutching her dressing gown to her and struggling a little as her slippers sank into the snow.

As she came round the corner, Andrew turned to her and grinned. 'I decided to have a walk earlier, and this is what I found. Look,' he said.

Marnie glanced up and down the street. Nothing of significance. No one around. Just the post office, bakery and sweetshop. Empty, because their owners were tucked up in bed, where any sensible person would be at this time on Christmas morning. A little wren hopped under a hedge. Surely he couldn't have got her out of bed for that?

'Not the bird?' she asked.

He laughed. 'Of course not.' He looked to where she did. 'Ah, I do love a wren, though.'

'Oh, me too. Troglodytidae. Such a cute shape and—'

'Show off.' He grinned. 'But yes, so little and round. Quite common of course, but shy so you don't see them that often.'

'I know.'

He looked at her then, his expression softening. 'Yes, of course you do.'

Marnie found herself smiling back at him, as her eyes watered in the cold and the snow seeping through her slippers reached her feet. She shook herself out of this stupor. 'Well, what am I here for, then?' she asked, exasperation making her speak sharply.

'What, you said you liked walking. Don't you want a nice Christmas morning walk?' He laughed. She raised an eyebrow at him. Infuriating man. She couldn't imagine what the dark-haired woman saw in him, she thought, as she stared distractedly at the stubble that lined his lips.

'Look,' he said again, gesturing to the shops.

And Marnie did. She looked at the lit-up Christmas tree in the post office, and the bright light in the shape of a lollipop on the sweetshop sign. She looked at her own display in the bakery window, twinkle lights still shimmering and the train she had forgotten to return to Gloria and Bob still chuffing round the track.

'Oh,' she said, breathing out a long plume of breath and staring at the bright lights. 'I see.'

Andrew grinned. 'You thinking what I'm thinking?'

Marnie bit her lip. 'It's a lot of people.'

'You can do it,' he said.

She turned to him. 'You really believe that, don't you?'

He shrugged. 'I know it. I've seen it.' His face split into a grin, that smile that made her stomach drop. 'Bit of a star really, aren't you?'

And Marnie, who had never thought of herself as a star, who had lived her life in the shadows of those around her, felt that she shone as she beamed up at him.

Ian and Lauren were up and about when they arrived back at the cottage, Lauren yawning and staring at her phone, Ian raking out and resetting the log burner.

'Hey,' he said. He looked up and smiled, although his expression soured when he saw Andrew standing with her. He cleared his throat and threw some wood into the log burner and slammed the door shut. 'Early morning walk?' he asked, his voice a little strained.

'Something like that,' Marnie said. 'We have a plan.'

'What kind of plan?' he asked, striking a match and setting it to the newspaper that lay under the kindling.

Andrew threw an arm around Marnie's shoulder and pulled her in for a quick hug. 'A plan to save Christmas,' he said.

'Well if anyone can do it, you can,' Ian said.

Marnie smiled. 'Thanks.'

Andrew removed his arm from her shoulder.

Lauren looked up, frowning as her eye fell on Marnie's soggy slippers, now leaking a puddle of melted snow all over the floor.

'I think you should open my present first, Mum,' she said.

They told Pat and Matt about The Plan next. Matt was already fully dressed in a shirt and tie, Pat still in dressing gown and slippers.

'Ooh,' she said, grasping Marnie's hands and turning a little pink in the cheeks. 'How marvellous, what a lovely idea.'

Matt looked a little doubtful. 'It's a lot of work, Marnie.'

'Don't worry,' Andrew said. 'She'll have plenty of helpers.'

'Of course she will,' Pat said. And then, waving Matt away as though he were an annoying insect. 'You old fusspot.'

He laughed. 'All right, then. And I shall be one of them. Now, we've got the kettle on the camping stove – cuppa, anyone?'

Marnie hugged him. She had a long day ahead, and the thought of starting without a cup of tea was too much.

Tea gratefully received, and Pat finally dressed in her Christmas best – a navy skirt with white spots, a red jumper with a reindeer on and red ankle boots – they all trooped back round next door, where Ian had the fire roaring in the log burner, Lily was huddled in front of it, blinking into the flames, and Lauren had apparently not moved a muscle.

She looked up as they came in, actually getting to her feet to give Pat and Matt a hug and wish them a merry Christmas. 'I've messaged Uncles David and Greg and the village WhatsApp,' she said, turning to Marnie. 'Only half the people have seen it though.'

'Well they've mostly got no data in the village and anyway half of their phones are probably dead. How is yours still going?' Marnie asked.

Lauren looked at her as though she was an imbecile. 'It's not ancient.' Then, conceding a little, 'The battery is on twenty per cent, though.'

'I could go and tell everyone?' Ian suggested.

Lauren beamed. 'I'll come with you, Dad. And I'll see if Emma wants to help too. Just let me get dressed.'

She disappeared and came back quicker than expected, having simply pulled her coat, hat and boots over her pyjamas. Well, no one would care in Babblebrook. Especially on Christmas morning. Especially when she was delivering news that Christmas was rescued.

On her way out, she ducked under the tree and emerged with a soft, bulky present that she pressed into Marnie's hands. 'Open this now, Mum.'

Marnie did. Inside, she found a beautiful pair of cosy boot-slippers. She laughed. 'Perfect! As if you knew I'd ruin my old ones this morning.' She gave Lauren a hug.

'Happy Christmas, Mum.'

'Happy Christmas, Squidge.'

Just this once, she was allowed the endearment, though Lauren did roll her eyes as she and Ian made their way out into the snow.

'Right,' Marnie said, clapping her hands together and looking round at her little band of helpers. 'Let's get this show on the road.'

*

The bakery was soon warm, with the heating and the cookers flicked on the minute Marnie set foot through the door. It looked just as festive and welcoming as ever, with the tree and lights and gingerbread Babblebrook all still in place, and Marnie was filled with relief that this one street with the little row of shops still had power. Andrew had gone down to the village hall and filled his truck with tables and chairs, just as he had once before, the muscles in his arms working as he set them out. Pat and Matt were soon busy laying out pretty cloths and napkins while Lily laid the tables. She glanced around, frowning a little, and Marnie knew she was taking in the dilapidated state of the bakery, so changed since she'd last been there.

It wasn't long before Lauren and Ian arrived, bringing half the village. Most were laden down with offerings of food – turkeys, potatoes, mountains of sprouts. But most were sorely in need of a cup of tea before anything else, having had no power for so long, and Marnie put Ian to work to meet this need.

Little Amy ran around the bakery wearing a fluffy onesie with penguins on it, banging a toy drum, while baby George sat in his buggy, surveying the chaos around him with an air of nonchalance.

'God, sorry,' Julia groaned, pressing a hand to her forehead. 'We couldn't prise it out of her hands. I don't know what possessed Santa to choose such a thing!' She glared at her husband, who busied himself checking the baby's perfectly dry nappy.

Marnie laughed. 'Don't worry, it's cute. And this was never going to be a calm event, was it?'

Julia grasped her arm with an enthusiasm that bordered on desperation. 'Thank you for doing this, I don't know what we'd have done otherwise. We were supposed to be going to my mum's, but the roads are impossible.'

'It's okay,' Marnie said, guiding her to where Ian stood with a huge metal teapot and a row of cups. 'It'll be fun.' She was beginning to sweat under her Christmas jumper and her heart was pounding as she tried to calculate the number of guests, the number of turkeys and the size of the ovens.

Just as the panic really began to hit, David and Greg arrived. They were expecting to eat at Marnie's anyway so hadn't brought any food, but were both laden down with boxes filled with bottles of booze. Marnie raised an eyebrow as she glanced at it all.

'You knew we were planning on staying at yours, right?' David asked.

'The more the merrier.' She was feeding the whole village, a couple of extra people camping the night hardly made much difference at this point. Once, she would have panicked about sleeping arrangements and bathroom queues, but now she felt it would all just work itself out somehow. 'Open that sherry, will you?' she asked.

She beat a hasty retreat into the kitchen, away from the cheerful chaos of chatter and children squealing, to make a list of which turkey needed to go in the oven when. She opened the door to put the first one in, a blast of hot air pouring into the kitchen, and almost dropped it when she heard a voice just behind her.

'Right, Chef. Tell me what to do.' She squeaked, and he laughed, steadying her elbow. 'Careful, there!'

Turkey safely in the oven, she turned to see Andrew wearing a striped apron and a grin that wouldn't look amiss on the face of a cheeky schoolboy.

'You're helping me?' She tried to keep the doubt out of her voice, but obviously failed. She couldn't help smiling though, the prospect of the day brighter now she knew she was going to be spending it with him by her side.

'Hey, I'm actually quite a good cook, you know! When I have a reason.' A momentary expression of sorrow passed over his face, but he soon smiled again. 'And it's not just me. There's a whole band of helpers – look.'

He turned to show her the crowd of people standing in the kitchen doorway, all eager and bright-eyed. Matt, Gloria and Bob, Lauren and Emma, and Reverend Pauline. Marnie felt a little overcome, not only by their generosity, but also by the challenge of getting this wayward crew to work together. Lauren and Emma were already giggling and whispering.

'Girls,' Pauline boomed. 'Settle down and listen to Marnie now – we're here to work not shirk.'

Immediately, they stood to attention. Marnie hid a smile. Perhaps this would go well after all.

Lizzie Lee

Marnie turned to Andrew, ready with her first set of instructions, but he was staring past her.

'Ah,' he said, his face breaking into a huge a smile. 'Lorraine! You made it – great.'

He hurried off, the crowd at the door parting as he made his way through to a tall, dark-haired woman standing just behind them. Lorraine. The woman who had sent him those emoji messages. The woman from the café.

Chapter Thirty-Nine

The tantalising smell of roasting turkey was already filling the air. Marnie had par-boiled the potatoes, Matt was preparing the veg, and Lauren and Emma chatted happily as they made their way through a constantly replenishing pile of washing up.

From the shop came the sound of happy voices and laughter. Occasionally a child's wail interrupted the cheer, but never for long – there were plenty of willing hands to offer a cuddle or distract with a game. Lily sat cross-legged on the floor with a circle of open-mouthed children around her, telling a story involving dragons and fierce princesses, waving her hands and using different voices for all the characters. Marnie had a memory, then, of her doing this when she and David were small, sitting with them on their bedroom floor under a makeshift tent filled with cushions and fairy lights, weaving tales of magic and mystery that had kept them spellbound. How had she forgotten?

In the kitchen, the radio was playing, just loud enough to be heard over the noise from the other room. Reverend Pauline screamed when Cliff Richard came on, turning up the volume and insisting they all stop talking and sing along. She grabbed Matt by the waist and waltzed him around the tiny space.

'I think I'm supposed to lead,' he said, laughing as they bumped into the kitchen counter.

'Nonsense,' Pauline replied, grinning. 'This is the twenty-first century, Matt, a woman can lead a dance if she wants to.'

He smiled, managing to free himself as the song ended, and went back to peeling sprouts. 'I'm not going to argue with that.'

'You know, when I heard the power was back on I thought The Plough might be up and running, but . . .' Reverend Pauline shook her head, her expression wistful.

'Sadly not, other end of the village,' Matt said. 'Power's out there, just like it is for all of us. Gillian did bring a good supply of food for us though.'

'Yes.' Reverend Pauline dried her hands on a tea towel. 'And who needs The Plough when we have Marnie, eh? This is all just wonderful.'

Marnie smiled. She chatted, she laughed, she calculated when each turkey needed basting, she even sang along to Cliff.

Everything was under control. And yet, all she could think of was Andrew, and the dark-haired woman.

As surreptitiously as she could, she peered over the heads of those around her and into the busy room next door. Every so often she glimpsed them, standing in a corner talking and laughing, helping to lay the tables, playing peekaboo with baby George when he became grizzly. At one point Andrew had Amy's toy drum around his neck so that it lay just below his chin and was marching around the room, tapping it with the little wooden drumsticks, as children shrieked with laughter and ran after him.

All these afforded only a sighting of the back of the woman's head or the sound of laughter. At last, peeking through once again as she transferred the potatoes into the trays to be roasted, Marnie caught a good look at her.

Marnie dropped the saucepan with a clatter. Luckily the potatoes were no longer in it.

Everyone in the kitchen jumped. Lauren laughed. 'You okay, Mum? Been at the sherry already?'

Marnie shook herself. 'Oh,' she said. 'Ha, oops. Butter fingers, eh?'

She laughed, but the sound was thin. The woman was young, and beautiful, smiling and playing with a group of children. Marnie needed a breath of fresh air.

'Do you know,' Marnie said, her voice brittle with a false brightness. 'I think I need to step—'

She staggered towards the back door, almost barrelling Gloria over in her haste, and at last ran out into the snow-covered yard, breathing in great gulps of cold, fresh air and trying to stop her head spinning.

Even from outside she could hear Lauren and Emma giggling. And she was sure there was another mention of sherry.

Marnie gave herself a minute or two to just stand there, admiring the little robin sitting on the fence and the bird footprints dotted across the snow. Later, she would bring some leftovers out to feed them. The poor little things wouldn't be finding any worms in this weather.

Absently, Marnie rolled a ball of snow around the back yard, until it grew big enough to reach her knees.

She didn't know why she felt so discombobulated. She hadn't come to Babblebrook looking for love; it had been the furthest thing from her mind. And yet, she couldn't stop thinking about Andrew, and of how she had felt when they kissed.

Marnie shook herself. There was no way she could compete with the youth and beauty of the woman with him, who was every bit as willowy as Marnie had feared. Andrew's voice rang through her mind, telling her there were things she didn't know about him. She thought of Anne Walker's warnings about his temper; perhaps there was something in it after all. Perhaps she was better off without him.

That was not what her new life was about anyway, she told herself determinedly. This was a fresh start, for her and Lauren. Time to step out from behind Ian and Lily, even David. Time for Marnie to stand in the light. And the café would be the start of that.

She settled the snowball in the centre of the yard and then began another, leaving a clear path now as she rolled.

So how had she let herself get sideswiped by these feelings? How could she have let herself succumb to these teenage butterflies every time she saw her crabby, secretly soft-hearted neighbour? She frowned. And she'd almost fallen back into Ian's arms, letting herself forget all he'd put her through.

She balanced the small snowball on top of the larger one, looking around for a couple of stones to use as eyes.

Well. This was the wakeup call she needed. The best Christmas present she could have had. Now was the time to focus; she had a teenager who needed her, and a business to get up and running. And an ex-husband to gently persuade to bugger off. She didn't have time to be mooning over her handsome neighbour.

She stood back, hands on hips, surveying her handiwork. Not her best, if she were honest, the head was a little lopsided. Lauren usually helped, that was why.

The sound of footsteps behind made her spin around. Gloria stood in the doorway.

'Mind if I join you?'

Marnie smiled. 'Not at all.'

Gloria stepped out, hugging her cardigan to her. Today her nails were painted a bright festive red, to match the Santas on Bob's tie, perhaps. Her eyes fell on the half-finished snowman, and she laughed.

'Are you playing in the snow by yourself, crazy lady?'

Marnie grinned. 'Got to enjoy yourself at Christmas, right? But I'm just about to come back.'

Gloria waved her hand. 'You've done more than enough. And I don't mean just today, although this is especially lovely, but I mean what you've done for Pat and Matt, and well, the whole village really, breathing life into the bakery again, and now I hear you're going to turn it into a café.'

Marnie had forgotten how quickly news spread in Babblebrook.

Gloria was beaming. 'I think it's wonderful, just what the village needs.'

A thought occurred to Marnie, and she took the older woman's hands, that wore a light dusting of flour. 'Oh Gloria, the trainset! I forgot all about it, but I'll get it back to you as soon as this is all done.'

Gloria laughed, a sound full of joy and mischief. 'Oh nonsense – it's perfect that it's here, and so are we all. The family couldn't make it anyway, they're snowed in.'

'Oh no, what a shame, I'm sorry.'

Gloria shrugged. 'We'll see them soon. And family comes in all sorts, doesn't it? Turns out we're with ours today, after all.' She placed an arm around Marnie's shoulder and squeezed. 'And I hope you know what a precious part of the Babblebrook family you are.'

Marnie was overcome, unable to respond for a moment. This, she realised now, was what she had searched for her whole life; this sense of belonging, this stability. This is what she'd found here. She needed nothing else.

'Now,' Gloria said briskly, clapping her hands together and eyeing the snowman once more. 'Let's head inside, shall we? I'm sure we can rustle up a spare carrot and borrow Bob's scarf and hat for that monstrosity.'

Chapter Forty

The bakery windows were misted up, the tables laden with turkey, potatoes, veg and nut roast for the vegetarians. Jugs of gravy steamed, crackers were pulled, glasses filled and refilled.

'You've really outdone yourself with all this,' David said, raising his glass of wine to her so enthusiastically that it was in danger of sloshing out onto the tablecloth. 'I'm proud.'

'You're drunk,' Marnie said, laughing.

He nodded. 'That too.'

It could have been the food, sitting warm in her belly, or her own wine, but as Marnie looked around at the cheerful villagers all squashed together on the tables at her impromptu café, she did feel a sense of accomplishment.

Without this, many would have been stuck in cold, dark homes, unable to meet up with family as they had planned to. Instead, everyone had company. Everyone was having fun. And the food, she admitted to herself, had been delicious.

'David,' Lily yelled across the table, although she was so close that he would have heard if she'd whispered. 'I want to give you your present.'

'Thanks.' David burped, earning a frown from Greg, and placed his glass down with care. 'Sorry I didn't get you anything. You know, because no one knew you were coming.' He caught Marnie's eye and grinned.

Oblivious, Lily bent to scrabble in her bag, emerging with three glass jars in her hand. 'I got these for you, I know you like to cook.'

David took them, rolling the glass in his hand as he stared at the brightly coloured contents.

'Kashmiri chilli powder,' Lily bawled. 'Fenugreek seeds and cinnamon quills.'

'That's great,' David said, looking pleasantly surprised. 'Really. I love them.'

Lily nodded and turned to Greg, who sat next to her. 'I didn't get anything for you, love.'

'Oh, that's okay, I wouldn't expect—'

Lily leaned in conspiratorially. 'Didn't know if you were still together.'

Greg glanced at David. 'But – you came to our wedding, we're married.'

Lily shrugged and pointed at Marnie. 'So was she.'

Marnie sighed. 'Thanks for that, Mother.'

'Ooh,' Lily said, taking a slug of wine. 'In trouble again.'

Marnie glanced at David, indicating the spices. 'Boxing Day curry's on you, then.'

David smiled. 'Got yourself a deal.'

There was a small crash and a squeal from across the room. Turning to look, Marnie saw Reverend Pauline lurching to her feet and quickly retrieving her fallen glass from the table.

'Of course,' she said, trying to catch David's eye, but he was reaching for Greg's hand across the table and oblivious to anyone else in the room right now.

The street was dark, lit only by the bright moonlight, and snow still drifted to the ground. They hunkered down into their thick coats – Lily had borrowed one of Pat's – and their breath fogged in the cold air. Nothing but the sound of the snow crunching under their feet. For all Lily had said she wanted to know about Marnie, she was showing little interest now. Marnie sighed. She was missing time with her friends and family for this.

'It's nice to have you back,' she said, eventually. What the hell. It was Christmas, after all.

Lily glanced at her and smiled. 'That's sweet of you to say, love. I suppose it's probably been a bit of a surprise.'

Marnie had to stop herself snorting. Bit of an understatement.

'I did try to say,' Lily said, stopping to stare at the row of cottages, still in darkness. The power hadn't been restored, then. 'I know you like things to be planned in advance. But the bloody signal kept cutting out, didn't it, so I wasn't sure if you got the message?' She looked hopefully at Marnie.

Marnie shrugged. Lily could have found a way to text or email, but Marnie knew she'd consider her one attempt at communication enough. Even if it had clearly failed. 'Doesn't matter,' she said. 'I'm finding it's okay to just go with the flow these days. You're here now.' They both stared up at the blank face of the family cottage, the Christmas lights hanging dully around the porch.

Marnie took a breath, and tried to keep her voice neutral. 'Are you back for good?'

Lily snapped her head round to stare at Marnie, before letting out a sharp bark of a laugh. 'Me? Settle in Babblebrook? I'm not dead yet!' She threw her head back and roared with laughter then, catching the expression on Marnie's face, put an arm round her. 'Oh come on, darling. Look, I can see why you like it here, it's very you, it's the Cotswolds, it's – quaint. But let's face it, I'm not a village type of person, never have been.'

Marnie thought back to the long list of towns they had lived in so briefly, so many that she couldn't remember them all. No. Lily was not a village person. They walked on.

She took a breath. There was no point delaying the conversation she so badly needed to have with Lily any longer, Christmas or not. 'And the cottage?' she asked. 'You can see we've done some work on it and Lauren and I are all settled so I really need to know what you're planning.'

Lily looked at her blankly.

'Are you planning to rent it out, Mother?' She hadn't the reserves of patience to beat about the bush now. 'To someone else, I mean. Because if you are we need to know and we need to know when you're planning that because we'll have to find somewhere else and I just don't know . . .'

Lily stepped forward, placing her hands on Marnie's arms, her expression soft. 'Oh, Marnie, I'm sorry. No, of course I'm not planning on renting to someone else while you and Lauren want to live in it.'

'No harm done,' she assured everyone, brandishing her unbroken glass. 'Lucky I'm drinking white, eh?' She hiccupped and smiled around at them all. Everyone looked on indulgently. No one was judging anyone, today. Even Greg simply caught David's eye, shaking his head and smiling.

'Anyway,' Pauline continued. 'I'd like you all to join in me – in a toast, and I think you all know to whom it's to.'

Everyone turned to look at Marnie, their faces full of warmth. She felt herself blush.

'To Marnie,' Pauline said, and everyone joined her. 'Our saviour of Christmas.'

Marnie laughed, standing up for a moment to take a playful bow. 'It's a pleasure,' she said.

Beside her, Lauren raised her glass of cola and leaned her head on Marnie's shoulder. 'To Mum.'

Ian, sitting on the other side of Lauren, raised his glass to her. 'You've done an amazing job.' He smiled and shook his hair out of his eyes.

Marnie reached over and took his hand. 'Thank you.' He squeezed her fingers and nodded. On the other side of the table, she thought she saw Andrew frown, but they were soon all distracted by Alan Wood belching loudly, blushing and saying, 'Beg pardon,' as everyone fell about laughing.

And, in amongst all the chaos, Marnie felt calm, and contented. Surrounded by those she loved. Looking forward to a new beginning here, with these people. This Christmas, which had promised to be the worst for some time, had turned out to be the best. Glancing out through the steamed-up windows, past the twinkly lights and the little train chugging round the gingerbread Babblebrook, she saw that it had begun to snow again. Soft, gentle flakes, twirling through the air. Everything was perfect.

It continued to be so. Soon every table was laden with Christmas puddings, trifles, mince pies, and Christmas cakes. Carols were sung. Friends and relatives were toasted, those present and those absent.

Eventually, people began to clear tables and bundle sleepy children into thick coats. Marnie was thanked numerous times, and though she insisted, correctly, that it had been a joint effort, something settled inside her; a sense of achievement, a feeling of confidence. If she could pull this off at the last minute, she could make a success of the café. So what if she didn't have every little detail planned out? She wouldn't doubt herself again.

'Hey, Marnie, hey. Marnie!' Lily leaned over the table, clicking her fingers in Marnie's face so that she was forced to jerk her head back to avoid being poked in the eye.

She was instantly irritated. 'Yes, what? I heard you the first time, you don't need to click at me.'

Lily lowered her hand and looked chastened. 'Sorry,' she said, voice quieter now. 'I just thought – shall we go for a walk? Just you and me? We haven't had the chance to have a proper catch up and I'd like to do that. I want to find out what's going on with you.'

Marnie stared. She couldn't remember Lily ever showing interest in her life.

Marnie laughed, and brushed the snow from Lily's hair. 'Well, there's nothing wrong with a bit of fun too, is there?'

Perhaps, after all, having the odd moment when she behaved like Lily wasn't such a bad thing, she thought.

Chapter Forty-One

She was allowed nowhere near the kitchen. Reverend Pauline was busy organising people into working parties to deal with the clearing and washing up, allocating jobs by waving her glass of brandy. Marnie began to wonder if she had actually missed her calling, and whether a career in the military might not have suited her better.

Pat and Matt walked over to her, in their coats and still wearing paper crowns. Marnie stood to embrace them, feeling slightly less steady on her feet than she was expecting.

'Oh, you did a wonderful job!' Pat said, her hat slipping down over her eyes. She pushed it up and smiled, a mischievous glint in her eye. 'Now, come with us. Present time!'

'Oh but I think I should stay and help tidy . . .'

'Nonsense,' Pat said firmly. 'Your mum will do it. Won't you?' She gave Lily a hard stare.

'Oh,' Lily flustered. 'I was just going to go and . . . but yes, yes of course I will. You get off.' She gave Marnie a smile that was almost convincing.

'You've done enough,' Matt said. He leaned in to Marnie and lowered his voice, glancing towards the kitchen. 'And I think we can safely say it's under control.'

Marnie was silent for a moment, trying to take in Lily's words.

'So you—We can stay?'

'Of course you can stay. For as long as you want. I might not be a perfect mother but I'm not a monster, what kind of person kicks their daughter and granddaughter out on the streets? I'm still your mum.' She smiled. 'And I do admire you, you know.'

Marnie stopped in her tracks, gaping. Her head was swimming with the sudden rush of relief that they were staying in Babblebrook, she was already on the verge of tears, and now this. What was it about her staid, boring existence that her glamorous, exciting mother could possibly find to admire?

Lily laughed. 'Don't look so shocked. You're such a good mum, Marnie, that girl is really lucky to have you. Look, I was young when I had you and I thought that adventure would be good for—' She stopped, sighed, looked around. 'Well, perhaps I just wanted it for myself. I know it was hard for you.' She clasped Marnie's arms and took a deep breath. 'I'm sorry.'

Marnie blinked back tears. This was a new experience, any attempt to discuss their wayward childhood had previously resulted in Lily brushing aside any complaints and insisting that it had been a blast for them all. She hugged her, breathing in the sandalwood scent she always wore. 'It wasn't all bad, you know. We did have fun.'

Lily grinned as they walked on, past the green with its frozen duck pond. 'We did, didn't we? Remember when we threw eggs over that bully of a teacher's car? And when we rescued that scrappy kitten from under a hedge and you carried it around in a rucksack?'

Marnie laughed, picturing all these memories. 'It really was fun,' she said, in surprise.

'But you, though. You're responsible, you're building a life here and you've got plans. And you're always there for Lauren, you put her first, you take care of her and you show a proper interest in her life. She's lucky. And I'm very proud of you.'

Marnie tried to take in the words. It wasn't the wine. It wasn't Christmas joy making her imagine things. Lily had really said she was proud of her, just for being herself.

'Oh, Mum,' she said, aware that her voice was wobbling a little. 'That's really—That's the best present that anyone could've—'

Before she could finish, Lily bent to scoop a handful of snow, balled it and threw it into Marnie's face, laughing uproariously.

Marnie froze, the shock of the cold snow blasting through her, stealing her breath and snatching her skin into goosebumps. She sighed, wiping her face clean.

'Come on,' she said. 'Let's go back and help with the tidy up.'

'Boo,' Lily called after her as she began to trudge back. 'Spoilsport, you always—'

But her words were cut short by Marnie making her own snowball and catching Lily right on the top of the head with it.

'Hey!' Lily shouted, trying to sound indignant but falling into laughter. 'You're supposed to be the sensible one.'

She followed his gaze to where Pauline stood in the doorway. 'Come along, Alan,' she chided. 'Wipe it properly, don't just show it the tea towel—Yes, that's more like it.'

Marnie allowed herself to be guided towards the door. 'Coming?' she asked Lauren. But seeing her daughter sitting with Emma, laughing at something on their phones, she already knew the answer. Lauren shook her head. 'In a bit.'

Just as Marnie was congratulating herself that she had managed to avoid seeing, and for the most part even thinking about, Andrew for the past few hours, he appeared right in front of them. There was no sign of the young woman he'd been with.

'Leaving already?' he asked.

'We want to give Marnie her Christmas present,' Pat said. 'She's worked hard enough.'

Marnie felt Andrew look at her, and couldn't resist meeting his blue eyes. He held her gaze.

'Yes, she has,' he said softly.

She cleared her throat and busied herself buttoning up her coat again. A harder task than usual, after those few glasses of wine with dinner.

'I'll come with you,' Andrew said. 'I have a present for you too.'

Marnie looked up sharply, just in time to see Pat and Matt catch Andrew's eye, and smile knowingly. Or was she imagining it? That last glass of wine was one too many, clearly.

She hadn't been expecting a gift from Andrew, and now she felt bad that she didn't have one for him. Perhaps there was something she could quickly wrap up? A spare bottle of wine, or box of biscuits? A bottle of sweet sherry? She had to stifle a giggle at the memory of him sipping sherry and listening to Taylor Swift.

All such concerns drifted from her mind as soon as she stepped outside. The moon shone bright through a puddle of cloud, and snow still drifted down, coating the street and hedges with a fresh, new layer and covering the footprints she and Lily had made just a little while before. As they turned the corner, it seemed that they stepped into a winter wonderland; every roof and porch of the pretty little cottages that lined the street was layered in snow and, even better, coloured lights twinkled through the white.

'Power's back, then,' Matt said.

'Can't have been on long,' Andrew said. 'I popped home a couple of hours ago and it was dead then.'

'Ooh, good.' Pat clapped her mittened hands together. 'We can have a nice cuppa and a mince pie to finish the day off, then.'

Their footsteps crunched underfoot, leaving a fresh trail behind them, leading to Pat and Matt's door. Inside, embers still glowed in the grate, and the tree lights were on, casting a rainbow gleam over everything in the room. Matt switched on the lamps and Andrew bent to build up the fire, while Pat rummaged among the presents under the tree. She leaned on her stick with one hand, but Marnie was still worried that she'd topple over. No one wanted to end Christmas Day in A&E. Again.

Thankfully, Pat straightened up with only a slight wobble, clutching a brightly wrapped parcel tied with a red ribbon. She handed it to Marnie, hardly able to suppress her excitement.

'Open it, then,' she said, before Marnie had even laid her hands on it. 'Matt, she's going to open it. Andrew, leave that now, watch her open it.'

Marnie laughed. She hadn't seen Pat this excited since she won the classic bikes race at Mallory Park a few years ago.

The parcel was soft and bulky. Carefully, she untied the ribbon and picked at the Sellotape.

Pat gave a sharp sigh. 'Oh for goodness' sake. Hurry up, will you? Rip it!'

'Okay, okay.' Marnie grinned, and tore the paper free to reveal a thick, folded bulk of cloth. She looked at Pat in confusion. Pat looked back, obviously bursting with excitement.

'Open it out,' Pat said, practically bouncing up and down in her eagerness.

Marnie did. There were four pieces of fabric altogether and as soon as she unfolded the first one, she knew what she was looking at; curtains. Red gingham curtains, with matching tiebacks.

Tears prickled Marnie's eyes and she had to swallow firmly before she could speak. 'Oh they're perfect! Just what I imagined. But, how did you know?'

'Lauren. Said you've been banging on about the curtains you want for the café, so Matt measured up and

I made them. To get you started.' Pat smiled, her eyes twinkling. 'Are they what you wanted?'

'They're perfect—I can just imagine it now! Thank you.' She folded Pat in hug. 'And thank you, Matt, for the measuring. You're both amazing!'

Matt clasped Marnie's hand. 'Just what you deserve. Lovely to have you back. We'll get all the paperwork signed and sorted after Christmas.'

'I can't imagine being anywhere else, now. Thank you so much. I won't let you down.' Marnie blinked away happy tears, thanking her lucky stars once again that she had ended up in this place, with these people. 'Shall I put the kettle on?' she asked brightly. 'Get you that cuppa?'

Pat and Matt both looked at Andrew, who was wiping soot from his hands onto his jeans. 'Nope. Time for my present, now. Come on.'

He walked out, apparently assuming Marnie would follow. She had a churlish urge to stay behind, but she was too full of Christmas cheer of every kind to act on it.

Andrew led her past his front gate and down the little path at the side of his cottage that led to the back garden.

'Wait – where are we going?' Marnie asked.

'You'll see,' Andrew said. He didn't even turn to glance at her.

He led the way through his beautiful garden, now covered with pristine snow, and to the shed, opening the door, leaning in to switch on the light, and waving her in.

'Here,' he said.

Marnie glanced around, remembering the sad, abandoned atmosphere of the place when she'd been there before, a dusty, untouched memorial to days gone past. Now, every surface was gleaming and tidy, the window was fixed, and there was a smell of fresh wood shavings. On the workbench lay a huge parcel, wrapped in cloth.

His eyes met hers, and for a moment she felt giddy. Must be the wine. 'Open it,' he said. 'Happy Christmas.'

The parcel was bulky, and heavy as she eased the fabric that was wrapped around it off. She couldn't begin to imagine what it could be.

At last the cloth came free, and revealed a carved wooden sign, painted the same red as the gingham curtains. It read: 'The Village Café'.

Marnie pressed her hands to her face. 'Oh, Andrew, it's beautiful. I can't believe you did this.'

'Well, you know, I was going to make one that said "Marnie's Caf", but apparently that's not—'

Before she could stop herself, she reached up and kissed him, and he responded, his lips tender against hers. Then, gently, he pushed her away. 'Marnie, I—'

She took a breath. Steeled herself to accept that this would never be; he'd rejected her when she tried to kiss him before, and now he'd moved on. She would just have to come to terms with that. 'I'm sorry . . . It's good that you've found someone new,' she said.

'—need to . . . wait, what?'

Marnie's palms began to sweat. He was staring at her, confused. 'The—the young woman that you met in Costa and brought to . . .'

Andrew frowned, his lips twitching, and then began to laugh.

'You really are an idiot,' he said.

'I am not!'

He took her hands. 'She's my niece,' he said, so gently that Marnie could barely hear. 'My sister's daughter, Lorraine, just moved to the area for a new job and she couldn't get home because of the snow, but she managed to make it here.'

Marnie's mind tumbled over his words. 'She's your niece?'

'Yes. And you are an idiot.' He grinned.

She had never had someone insult her so affectionately. It was confusing.

'You know, there's really nothing happening with me and Ian,' she blurted.

His eyes filled with doubt. 'Really? Because today it looked like you were—'

She shook her head, smiling. 'No. We've just—We're going to be friends, that's all, he's moving to Waterfield so he can stay close to Lauren, but that's—'

A smile spread slowly over Andrew's face. 'Well that's good news. That's really—'

She stepped forward, closing the distance between them, and placed her hand on his arm. Gazed up into his blue eyes. Heart pounding, mouth dry.

His expression changed, his eyes filling with doubt. He shook his head, staring down at the floor. 'But I really can't,' he said in a whisper. 'Marnie, I'm just not . . . I can't do this.'

Her breath caught in her chest. They stood so close she could feel the heat of his body. 'Why not?'

He looked at her, his eyes dark with pain. 'I'm not— You don't want to be with me.'

Oh, but she did. This man that made her laugh, that even in his grief was always kind to Pat and Matt. The man who had opened his bruised heart to Lauren, who would do anything for a fat little mongrel and her puppies, who could make something beautiful from a plank of wood, who understood the delight in catching a rare glimpse of a wild bird. She really did.

'Don't I get to decide that?'

He was shaking his head before she'd finished speaking, leaning with his back against the workbench. His voice was thick when he spoke, as though he fought tears. 'You don't know, though. You don't understand who I really am.'

'Look, I know you lost your temper, that's not—'

He hiccupped a small laugh that had no humour in it. 'They still haven't told you?' He met her gaze, his eyes alight with shame. She shook her head. 'I disgraced myself. Badly. A few years back, the first Christmas after . . . after—'

He ran a hand over his eyes. 'I was at the grave. It was—It was dark and cold, but I just needed to be with her.' He sighed and raised his head, staring above. 'All I wanted was to have her back. I just wanted to listen to her talk about her day, or to sit with her in the evening, or hold her hand as we walked Rosie. Even to see her grumpy little face when I brought her coffee first thing in the morning.' His lips rose into a brief smile.

'I just couldn't believe she was gone, really gone.' He shook his head. 'And then I heard people laughing, and I just couldn't—I didn't know how anyone could be happy, I didn't think anyone deserved to be happy, and I was just so, so furious.'

Marnie took his hands in hers. Tears stung her eyes.

'I didn't even know it was Christmas. I—I just saw all these people in the church, smiling, you know, so happy and I just, just couldn't believe it, I was so angry. I couldn't believe they were celebrating when she was gone. And I, oh God, I started yelling and I . . . I tore down the Christmas tree and yanked the tinsel and the lights down, I smashed up the manger, I was so . . . and then I, it was like I woke up, and I saw all these little kids staring at me, and they were all crying.'

Tears welled in Marnie's eyes as she imagined his pain and disbelief.

'And the poor vicar we had at the time, such a sweet man, he just cowered at the front and it was Matt, of course, who rescued me, just took me by the arm and guided me out. No judgement. But for everyone else – persona non grata. And completely deserved.'

Marnie thought of the beautiful new manger he'd made. A peace offering. Everything fell into place. All she wanted was to hold him.

'But you were grieving,' she said, her voice soft.

He was shaking his head. 'No, but—It's not just that, you don't understand. I can't—I'm not good for people to be around, I—I don't notice, I don't act.'

Marnie tried to follow his words. She couldn't.

'I can't look after you, Marnie.'

She took a step closer, wondering what it would feel like to be with someone who wanted to take care of her, even some of the time, instead of always being the one to care for others. 'I don't need you to.'

Still he didn't meet her eye. 'No, but—No one really knows what I did.' His voice was a whisper. 'It was my fault Jane died.'

Surely, this couldn't be true. She felt his hands tremble as she held them.

'She'd been tired for weeks, she'd lost her appetite. Not like her at all, that should have been a red flag if ever there was one. And all I did was book a holiday, I didn't take care of her, I didn't notice. If only I'd made her go to a doctor then, she might still be . . .' His voice shook. 'And then Rosie the same, I did it again, she almost died and I didn't notice, I didn't take care of her and . . . it's like David said today, some people can't look after their pets properly, and that's me, Marnie, I can't look after people.'

'But David wasn't talking about you! He didn't mean you, you take such good care of Rosie.'

He was shaking his head. 'But I didn't see Jane was ill, I let her down.' He stopped, his voice choked. 'And Rosie the same, I let her down, and what if it happens again?'

She breathed in his scent of soap and wood shavings. 'That wasn't your fault. None of it was your fault.' She took his face in her hands, gently. 'A terrible thing happened to you. But you didn't make it happen, Andrew, there was nothing you could do.'

'But I should have—'

She held his gaze. 'It wasn't your fault.'

'But what if I let you down too? What if I just can't take care of the people I—'

She could hardly speak. 'The people you . . .?'

He was silent for a moment, his gaze travelling her face. And then, slowly, he leaned in until their lips met, and he kissed her, full of hunger, his arms around her waist, turning her and pressing her against the workbench.

Marnie pulled him to her, heat searing through her veins. Lost in the moment. This was everything she wanted. He was everything she wanted.

*

By the time Marnie tore herself away from him and went back to Pat and Matt's Lauren was there, eating Celebrations by the fistful in front of the fire. Andrew, when he had finally let her leave, with one last kiss and a sweet, special smile, had promised he would be along in a moment. There was something he needed to do.

'You were ages, Mum, where've you been?' Lauren asked, a bubble of chocolate-coloured saliva gathering in the corner of her mouth. There was a strong chance she would throw up before bedtime.

Marnie hastily patted down her hair, quickly pulling out a piece of sawdust she found there, and glanced at Pat and Matt. They sat on the sofa with a glass of sherry and a mince pie each, exchanging a knowing glance and trying, not very hard, to suppress knowing smiles. 'Oh, I—Andrew had something to show me. I mean, there was a—He had a present for me.'

Her cheeks burned. She was sure she heard Pat titter.

'It was lovely, actually, he's made a sign for the café. It's beautiful, hand carved and painted red, and he made it himself, you know. He's a very talented man.' Her blush deepened, and she willed herself to stop talking.

Lauren frowned and gave her a suspicious look. 'Okay. You're being odd.'

Marnie laughed, a high-pitched, slightly panic-stricken screech that would do nothing to assure Lauren of her sanity. 'Well, I'm your mum, you're supposed to think I'm odd.' She looked at Pat and Matt desperately. 'Right?'

Pat smirked. Matt nodded, a look of growing sympathy in his kindly face. 'I'd say that's about right.'

Lauren looked unconvinced. 'Yeah but this is beyond even—Oh my God.'

She cut off halfway through speaking as the door opened behind Marnie, briefly letting in a blast of cold air. Andrew stepped in, carrying a soft bundle with a big silky blue ribbon around it.

He stepped over to Lauren and held the bundle out. 'Happy Christmas.'

It was a puppy, the little one that had been the last to be born. Holly. Wriggling in Andrew's arms and trying to chew the ribbon around her neck.

Lauren gasped and pressed her hands to her mouth, her eyes filling.

Gently, Lauren took the pup and cradled it, burying her face against its soft fur. 'Really?' she asked Andrew. 'She's—She's really mine?'

Pat and Matt watched, smiling and holding hands.

Andrew nodded. 'Yes. Not yet though, she needs to stay with Rosie for a bit longer, but as soon as she's ready she can come to you. If your mum says it's okay.' He glanced quickly at Marnie, a little apologetically. A bit late to be asking, she could hardly refuse now Lauren was cuddling and kissing the little thing. Luckily, she had no intention of refusing.

'Of course.'

'Oh, thank you, thank you.' Lauren hobbled to kiss Andrew on the cheek and then give Marnie an awkward, one-armed hug, so that she didn't squash the dog. 'I love her.'

Andrew blushed and shrugged. 'You deserve it, you've helped so much. I've made her a bed too, I'll show you later.'

They all watched as Lauren placed Holly on the floor, and the little pup rolled over to have her stomach stroked. Marnie looked at the expression of pure happiness on her daughter's face, and thought once again how well the move to Babblebrook was turning out. It was a perfect end to a perfect Christmas.

Quietly, Andrew sidled over to her and gently touched her hand. And Marnie cared nothing for the smug expressions on Pat and Matt's faces.

'Oh my God,' Lauren said, tearing her attention away from the dog for a moment. 'What are you all smiling like that for? Such weirdos.'

Epilogue

Everything was ready.

The Christmas window display had been replaced with gingerbread trees that Marnie had lovingly baked and iced liberally to represent snow. Snowflake biscuits and cakes in the shape of snowmen finished it all off. And the weather obliged, complementing her wintry display by remaining crisp, bright and snowy.

They'd worked tirelessly to prepare for the opening. Marnie had sourced tables and chairs, and a play area for the children, which Lauren and Emma set up. They'd repainted, Andrew had stripped and rebuilt the interior of the bakery so that the counter was freshly made, Pat had made tablecloths to match the curtains, and Matt advised her on what equipment she might need for the kitchen. She'd set up an Instagram account that already had many followers.

At last, a vase of chrysanthemums sat on every table, the books and toys were set out invitingly, every twinkly light dangled perfectly in the window and across the ceiling. Above the door hung the beautiful sign Andrew had made.

Already, the café smelled of coffee and baking. Marnie had made a huge batch of biscuits and cakes, and had learned how to operate the machine that made every type of coffee imaginable. The menu offered a tempting selection of her signature hot chocolates.

Now all she needed were the customers.

Andrew stood behind her and slipped his arms around her waist, resting his chin on her shoulder. 'Don't worry,' he said. 'It'll be packed. Everyone's talking about it, you've got your own hashtag on Instagram and remember Bob put it in the Upcoming Events in *The Blast*.'

She twisted in his arms to reach up and kiss him. 'I hope so. Otherwise we'll be eating biscuits and cakes every meal for the next few weeks.'

Andrew shrugged. 'Not a problem.'

'And I'll be out of a job.'

'Won't happen,' he said. 'It'll be brilliant. You'll see.'

Marnie checked the window display for the hundredth time, trying to calm her jitters. She could only hope he was right.

*

Six o'clock came, time for the grand opening, and everything was ready. Lauren, Andrew, Pat and Matt stood at Marnie's side, and she could feel them all brimming with excitement. Her own enthusiasm was edged with a little terror. What if no one came? What if Ian had been right, and this was a mistake? She scuttled to hide in the kitchen, busying herself with tasks that were already done, trying to avoid looking outside in case no one was waiting, and gave herself a stern talking to.

Of course she could do this. She had saved Christmas, after all. She was no longer that shy woman hiding behind Lily or Ian, she had made her dream of a café come true; it looked perfect and the food smelled delicious. And she had made it all happen.

She was ready to step into the limelight. And she was excited to do it.

'Come on, Mum,' Lauren said, gently taking an already clean and dry plate from her. 'It's time. Let's open the door.'

Pat clapped her hands. 'I'm so excited.'

Together, they ushered Marnie through to the café. It looked beautiful, with everything spick and span, and lit by pretty lamps. They waited at the counter, letting her go to the door alone.

She threw open the door to her own café, on its opening night, anticipation and fear charging through her. She was met with a cheer, and she soon saw the large group of people waiting, filled with familiar faces.

Everyone greeted her as they walked in. She was kissed on the cheek by Gloria and Bob, who brought little puppy Sam, one of Rosie's babies, now busy biting his lead. Reverend Pauline shook her hand enthusiastically, and Amy enveloped her in a waist-high bear hug. Jo, who had come to visit specially, squeezed her and said how proud she was. Soon, every seat was filled and already the books and toys in the children's corner were gripped in chubby hands. Every eye turned to her.

Marnie gazed around at this group of people who had come to support her.

Lauren, sitting with Emma and her family, beaming with what looked suspiciously like pride, while Holly and Spot, who had been given to Emma, slept in a heap at their feet. Pat, in her leathers now she was back to full health and biking again, though more sedately than before, or at least so she claimed, sat with Matt; both pink faced and smiling. Gloria and Bob, Reverend Pauline, little Amy and her family, Mr and Mrs Walker. Greg, who was nibbling on a wholewheat muffin, and David, who had already piled an iced bun and a cinnamon swirl onto his plate. Ian, sitting with them and Jo, chatting happily, perhaps about the new job and flat he had found in Waterfield. Andrew, gazing at her with a look of blatant adoration.

Her family and friends.

Marnie took a deep breath, the kind you take before diving into clear, fresh water. 'Hello, everyone,' she said. 'Welcome to The Village Café.'

Acknowledgements

I've always been a fan of romantic fiction, especially cosy Christmas books, and so it's no surprise that I emailed my agent, the lovely Lucy Morris, out of the blue one day to say that I wanted to write 'one of those Christmas books with a sparkly cover'. I will be forever grateful that her response was one of enthusiastic encouragement, and a promise to read the finished manuscript while drinking hot chocolate. For this, and for unerring support, wisdom and general brilliance, thank you! Thank you also to Rosie Pierce for her insightful feedback on and generous support for this book.

Huge thanks to Stephanie Carey for her excellent editorial notes, and the whole team at Embla for their support. I'm still pinching myself that my little Christmas book has made it out into the world!

I will always be grateful to the Pub Club (sorry for the terrible name!) – Cheryl, Deb, Den, Kitty, Pete E, Pete H, Ray and Sarah. An unbelievably talented bunch, I would not be here without you.

Thank you to Richard Beard, Rena Brannon and Ian Marchant for the wonderful experience of the National Academy of Writing. To Lorraine Blencoe, Sofie Baekdal

Brauner, Susan Haniford and Kate Mascarenhas – brilliant writers and precious friends. Thank you to Liv, for so many years of friendship, a shared love of books and being so supportive when I confessed to this writing hobby all those years ago. Thank you to Amanda for friendship over the years, and for medical advice for this book.

I am so lucky to have grown up in a small village, not unlike Babblebrook, a warm and friendly community. Thank you to my crazy, funny, loving family – may we have many more chaotic Christmases to come! This book has been written with our grandparents in mind, their love for their family, and their love of Christmas, happy memories that I treasure.

Lots of love to my smart, brave, kind children, Zoë and Ed. I am in awe of you.

Thank you to Pete, the most talented writer I know, and the most generous supporter anyone could wish for. Can't believe my luck.

And finally, to anyone reading this book, thank you so much! I hope you enjoy meeting Marnie, Andrew and the quirky inhabitants of Babblebrook as you read. Hot chocolate optional. Happy Christmas!

About the Author

Lizzie grew up in a small village where cows gazed over hedgerows into back gardens, everyone helped to decorate the village Christmas tree and took part in the nativity service. It was only a matter of time before this background, combined with Lizzie's love of cosy romance, led to the creation of Babblebrook and its quirky, loveable inhabitants. She also writes historical fiction under the name Elizabeth Lee. Follow her on Instagram @lizzieleewriter

About Embla Books

Embla Books is a digital-first publisher of standout commercial adult fiction. Passionate about storytelling, the team at Embla believe our lives are built on stories – and publish books that will make you 'laugh, love, look over your shoulder and lose sleep'. Launched by Bonnier Books UK in 2021, the imprint is named after the first woman from the creation myth in Norse mythology. Embla was carved by the gods from a tree trunk found on the seashore; an image of the kind of creative work and crafting that writers do, and a symbol of how stories shape our lives.

Find out about some of our other books and stay in touch:

X, Facebook, Instagram: @emblabooks
Newsletter: https://bit.ly/emblanewsletter